PA____ W9-DAG-727
LIBRARY SYSTEM

3650 Summit Boulevard
West Palm Beach, FL 33406

Dear Rosie

Meghan Boehman & Rachael Briner

Additional writing and coloring by Tom Pickwood

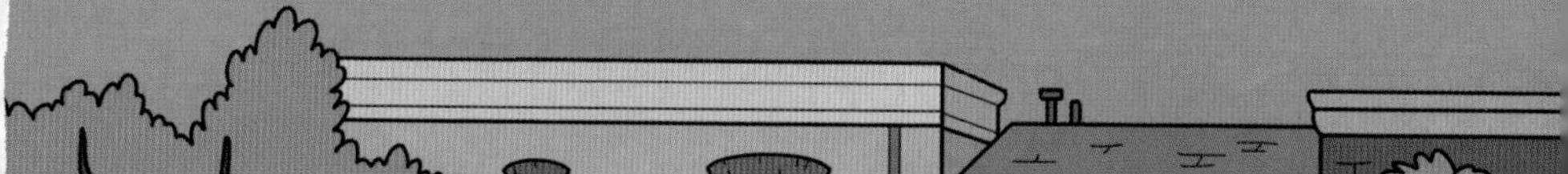
119
LAUNDROMAT
OPEN

ALFRED A. KNOPF NEW YORK

THIS IS A BORZOI BOOK PUBLISHED BY ALFRED A. KNOPF

Copyright © 2023 by Meghan Boehman and Rachael Briner

All rights reserved. Published simultaneously in hardcover and paperback in the United States by Alfred A. Knopf, an imprint of Random House Children's Books, a division of Penguin Random House LLC, New York.

Knopf, Borzoi Books, and the colophon are registered trademarks and RH Graphic with the book design is a trademark of Penguin Random House LLC.

Visit us on the Web! rhcbooks.com

Educators and librarians, for a variety of teaching tools, visit us at RHTeachersLibrarians.com

Library of Congress Cataloging-in-Publication Data
Names: Boehman, Meghan, author, illustrator. | Briner, Rachael, author, illustrator.
Title: Dear rosie / Meghan Boehman, Rachael Briner.
Description: First edition. | New York: Alfred A. Knopf, 2023. | Audience: Ages 8–12. |
Summary: A group of animal friends navigates a new school year together as they grieve the loss of their friend, Rosie.
Identifiers: LCCN 2022023297 (print) | LCCN 2022023298 (ebook) |
ISBN 978-0-593-57186-6 (hardcover) | ISBN 978-0-593-57185-9 (trade paperback) |
ISBN 978-0-593-57187-3 (ebook)
Subjects: CYAC: Graphic novels. | Grief—Fiction. | Animals—Fiction. | Schools—Fiction. | Friendship—Fiction. | LCGFT: Graphic novels.
Classification: LCC PZ7.7.B6235 De 2023 (print) | LCC PZ7.7.B6235 (ebook) | DDC 741.5/973—dc23

The text of this book is set in 10-point DearRosie.
The illustrations were created using Photoshop.
Additional writing and coloring by Tom Pickwood
Photographs on pages 202 and 203 courtesy of Meghan Boehman
Book design by Juliet Goodman

MANUFACTURED IN CHINA
10 9 8 7 6 5 4 3 2 1
First Edition

Random House Children's Books supports the First Amendment and celebrates the right to read. Penguin Random House LLC supports copyright. Copyright fuels creativity, encourages diverse voices, promotes free speech, and creates a vibrant culture. Thank you for buying an authorized edition of this book and for complying with copyright laws by not reproducing, scanning, or distributing any part in any form without permission. You are supporting writers and allowing Penguin Random House to publish books for every reader.

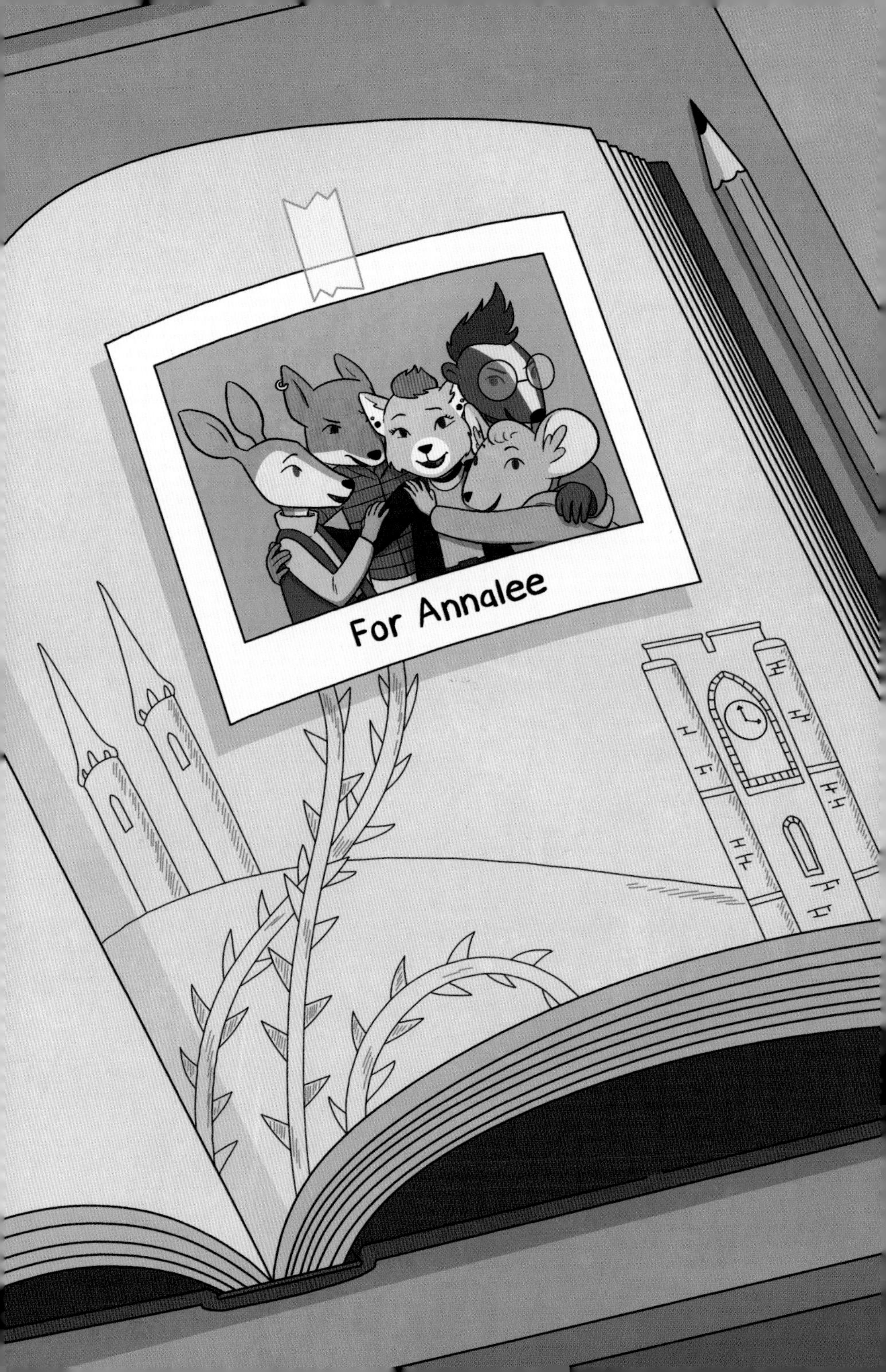
For Annalee

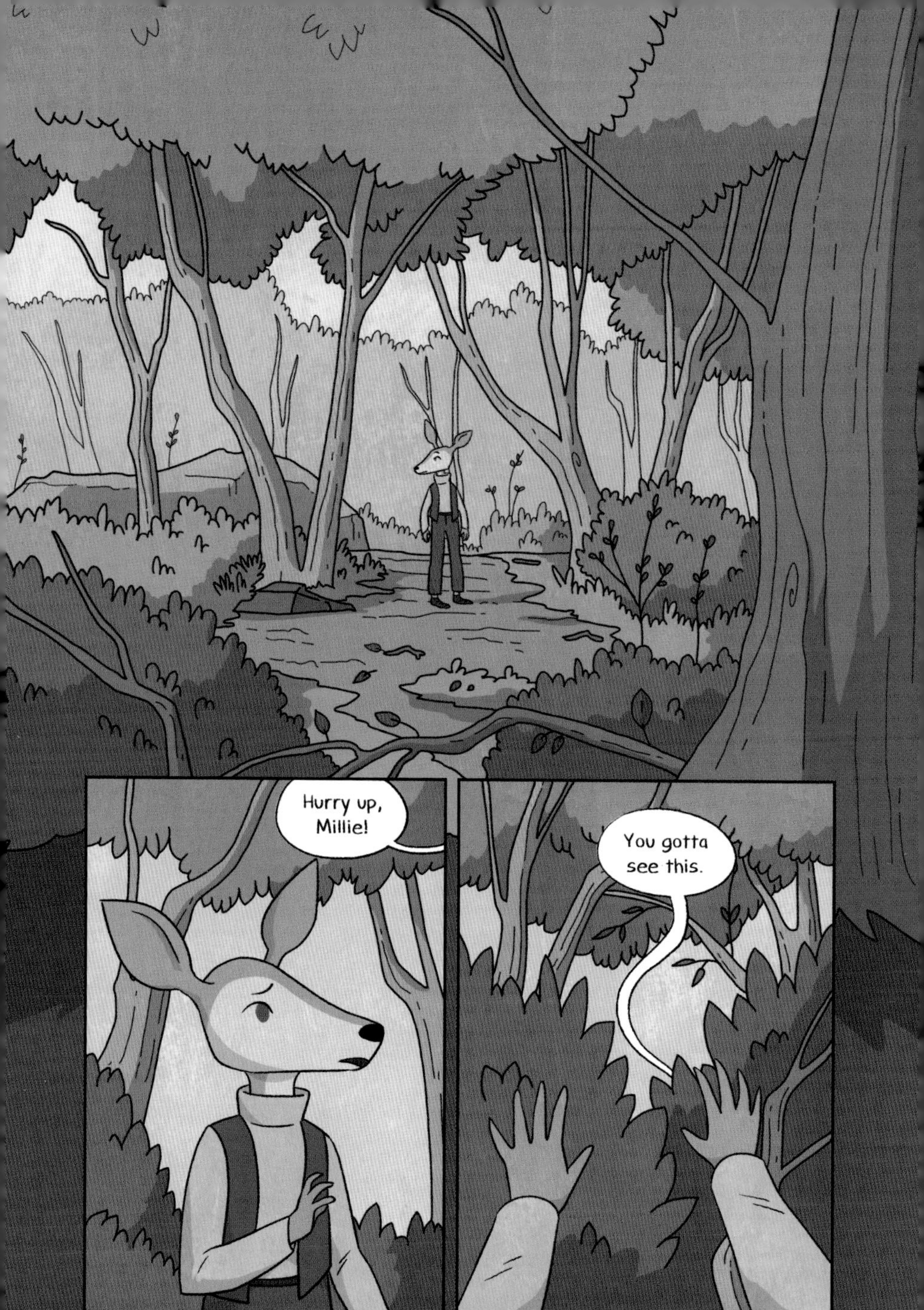
Hurry up, Millie!
You gotta see this.

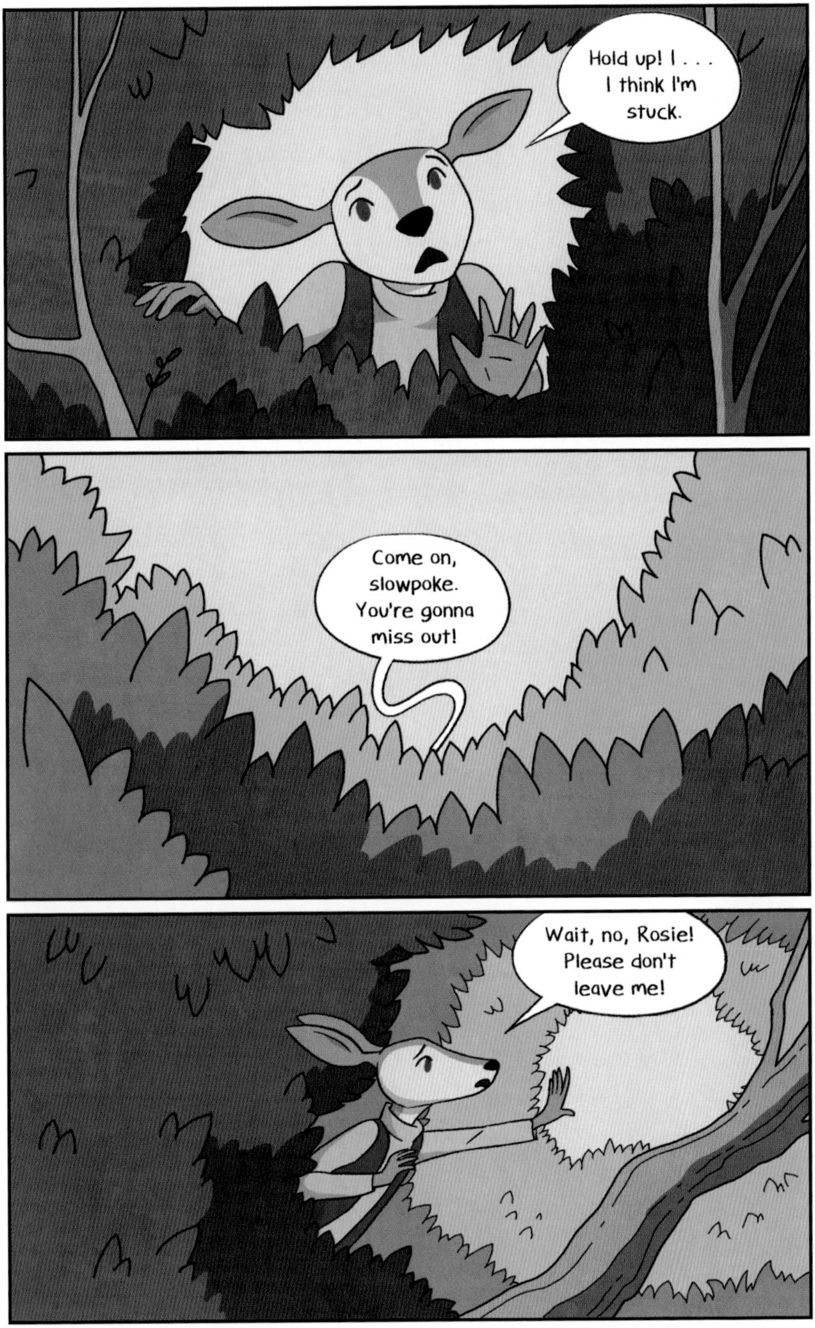
Hold up! I . . . I think I'm stuck.
Come on, slowpoke. You're gonna miss out!
Wait, no, Rosie! Please don't leave me!

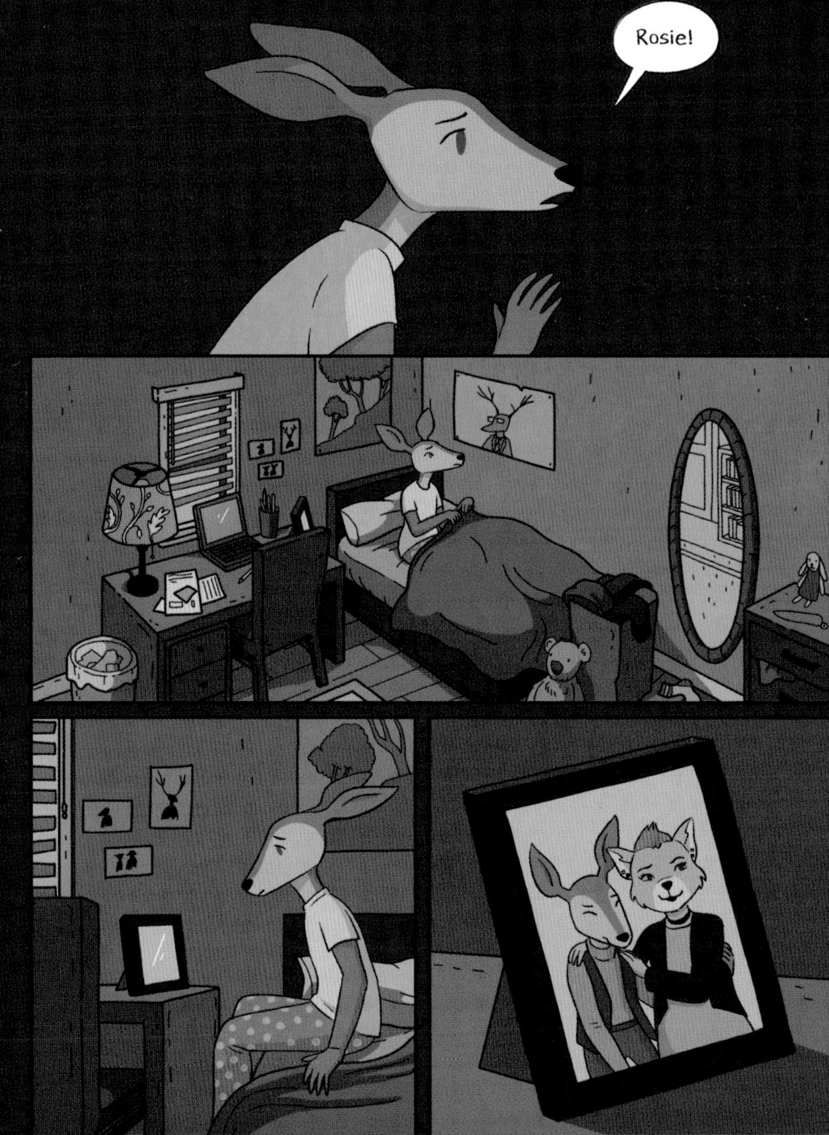
Rosie!

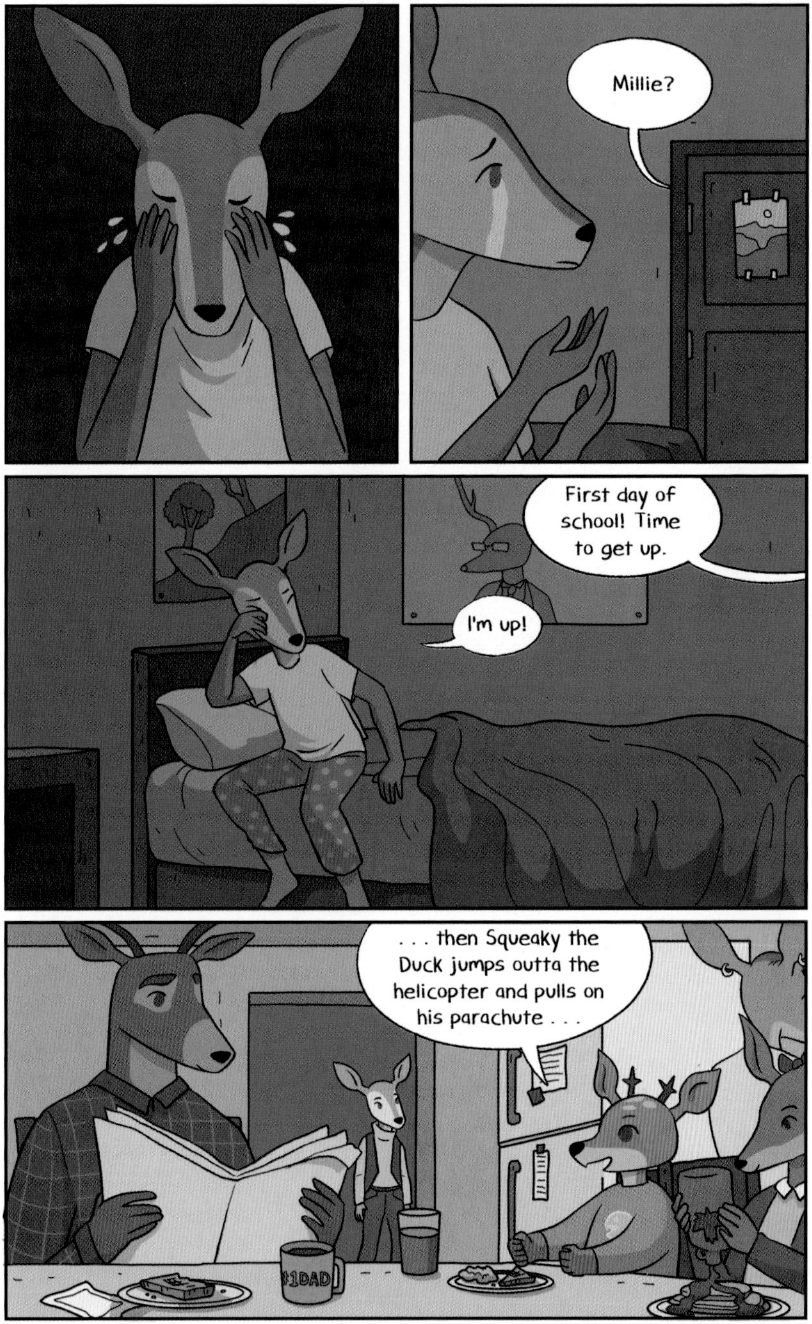
Millie?
First day of school! Time to get up.
I'm up!
. . . then Squeaky the Duck jumps outta the helicopter and pulls on his parachute . . .
#1DAD

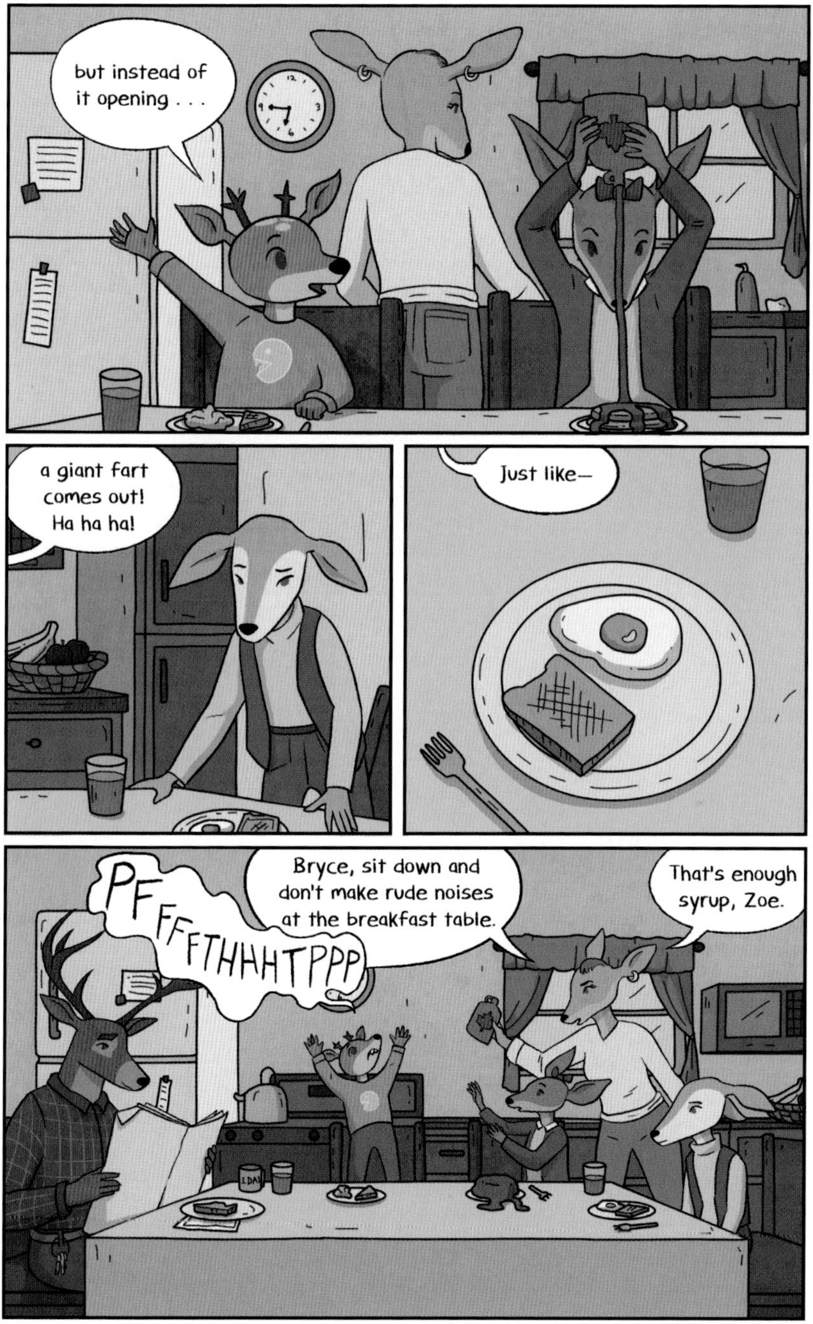
but instead of it opening . . .
a giant fart comes out! Ha ha ha!
Just like—
PFFFFTHHHTPPP
Bryce, sit down and don't make rude noises at the breakfast table.
That's enough syrup, Zoe.

Millie, eat your breakfast.

I'm not hungry. I have to catch the bus anyway.

You need to eat something.

At least take this. I'm sorry this summer was so hard, but it's a brand-new school year. Let's make it a new beginning for you girls too, okay?

Okay.

Don't forget you have to watch the laundromat after school!

I know!

Morning, Mr. DeAlba.

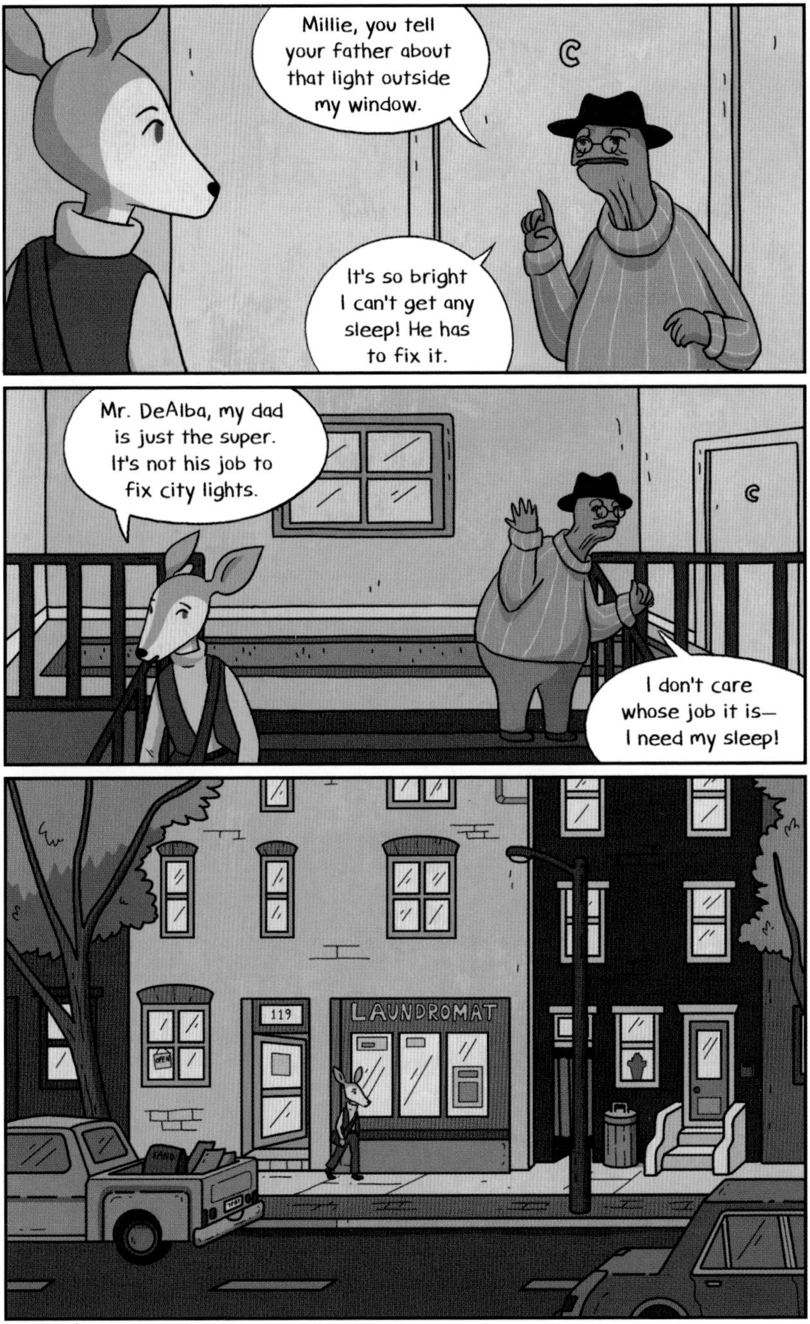
Millie, you tell your father about that light outside my window.
It's so bright I can't get any sleep! He has to fix it.
Mr. DeAlba, my dad is just the super. It's not his job to fix city lights.
I don't care whose job it is— I need my sleep!
119
LAUNDROMAT

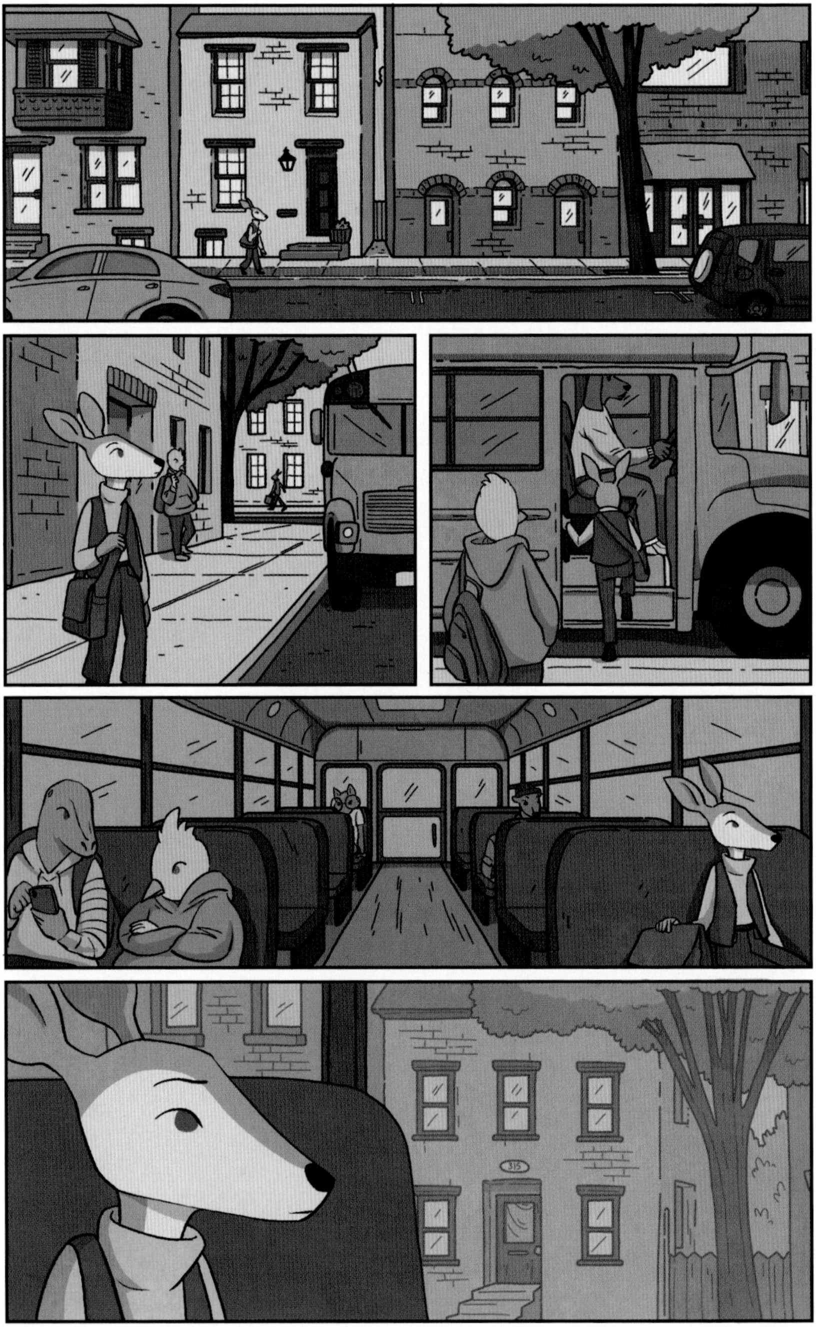
315

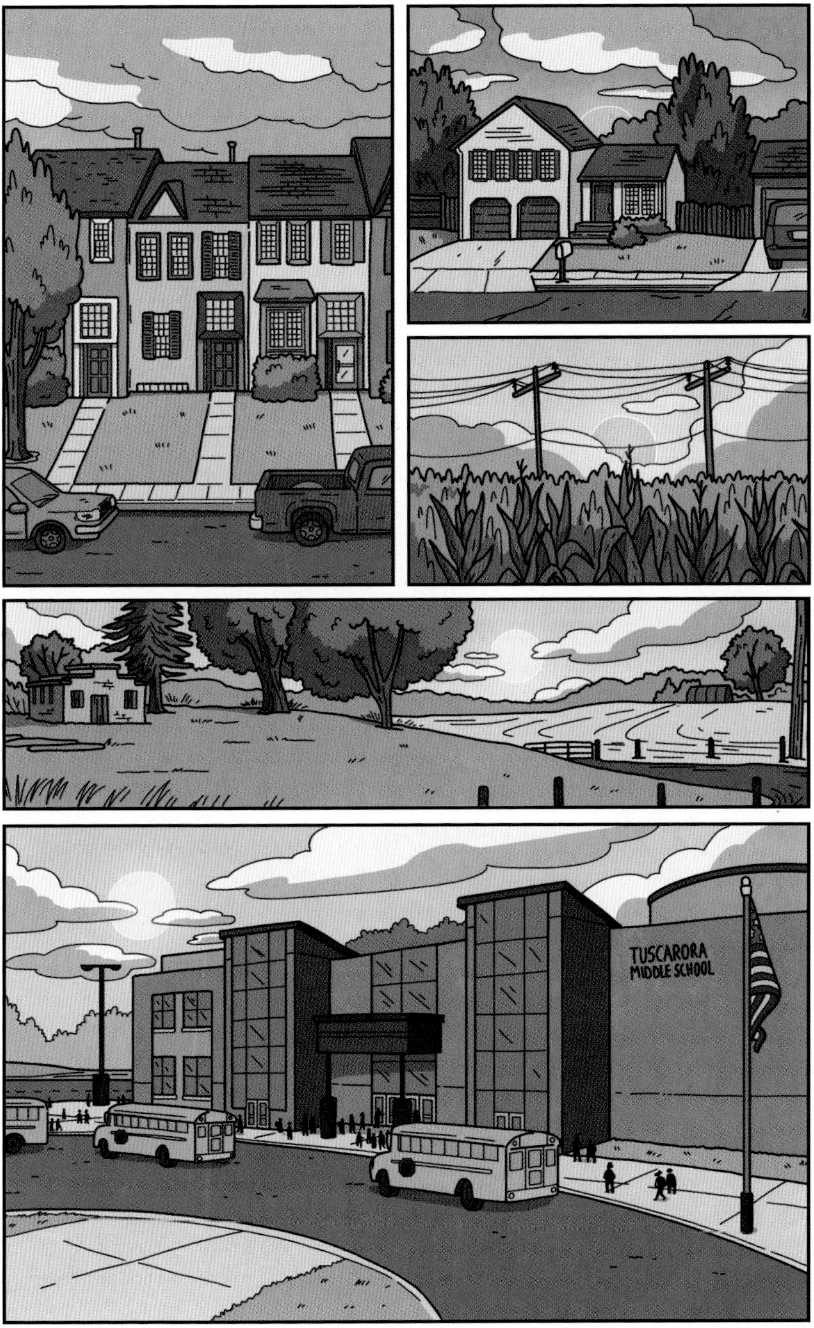
TUSCARORA
MIDDLE SCHOOL

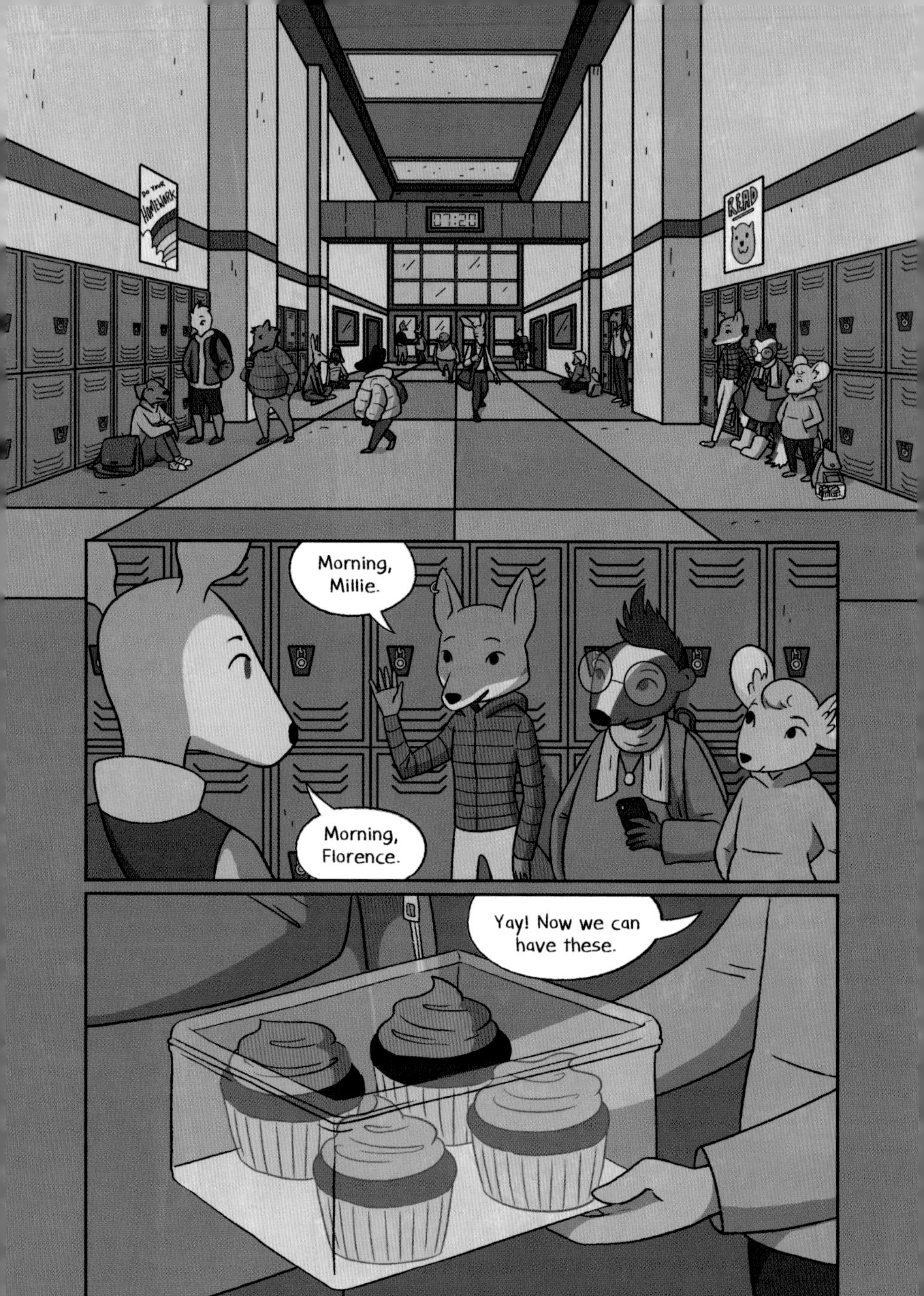
DO YOUR HOMEWORK
READ
Morning, Millie.
Morning, Florence.
Yay! Now we can have these.

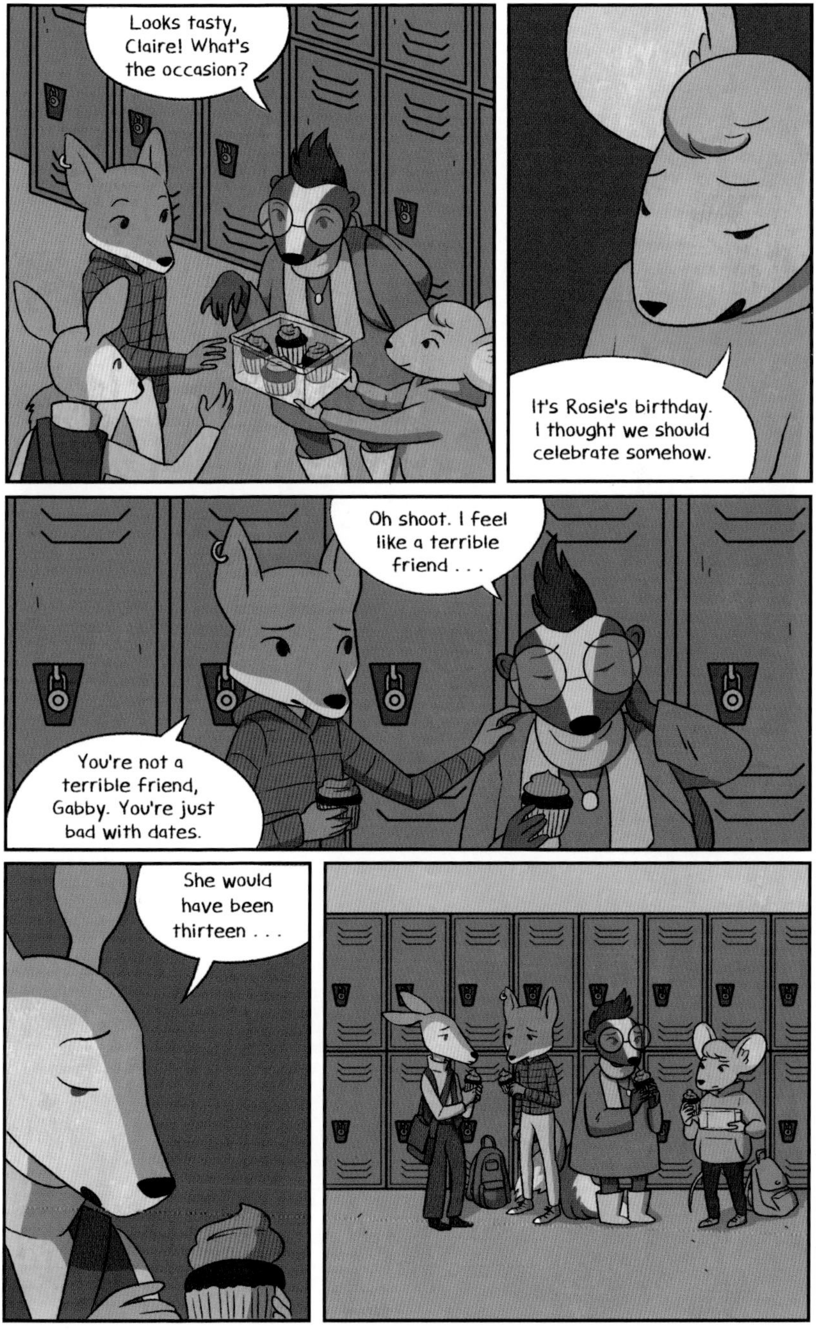
Looks tasty, Claire! What's the occasion?
It's Rosie's birthday. I thought we should celebrate somehow.
Oh shoot. I feel like a terrible friend . . .
You're not a terrible friend, Gabby. You're just bad with dates.
She would have been thirteen . . .

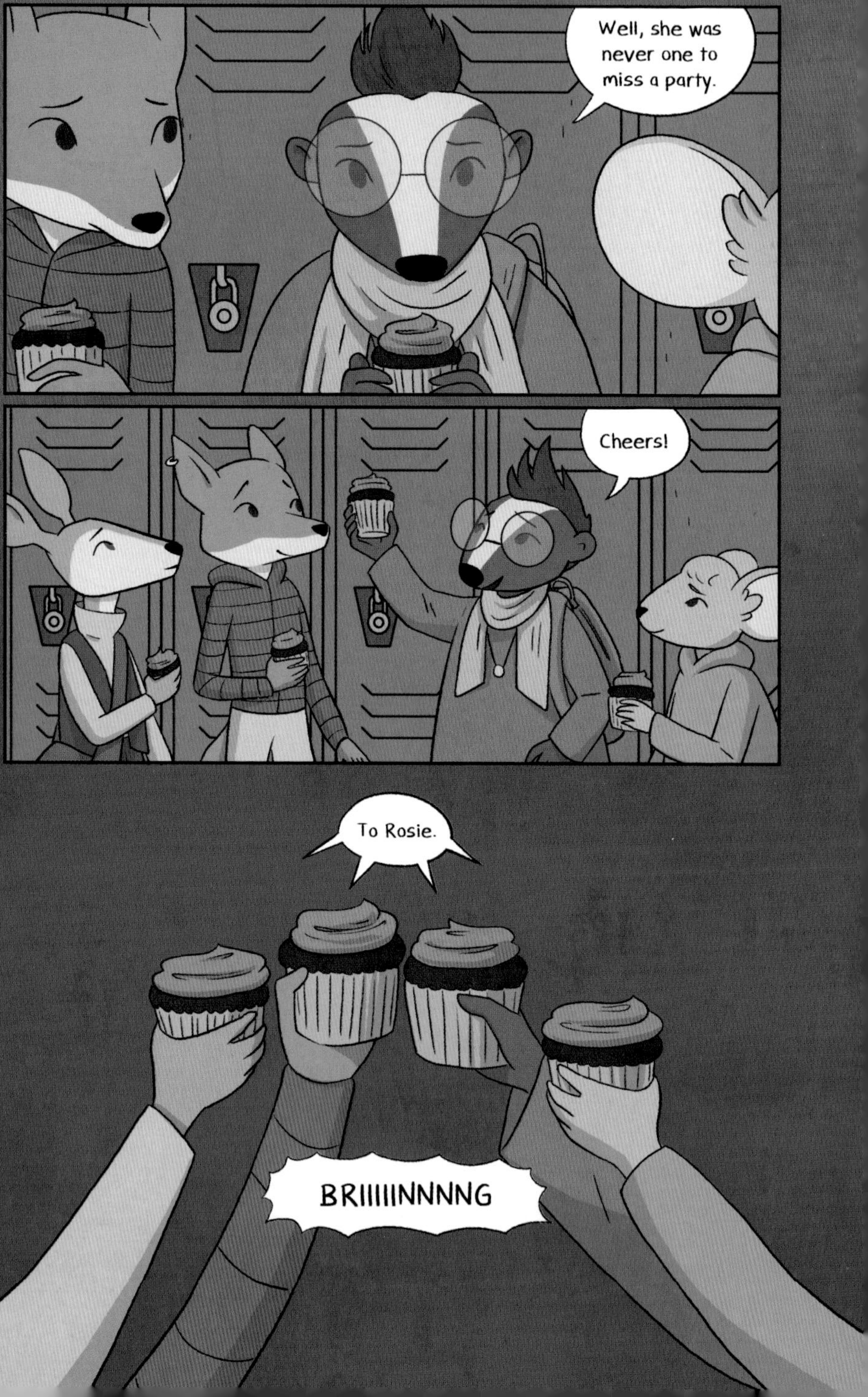
Well, she was never one to miss a party.
Cheers!
To Rosie.
BRIIIIINNNNG

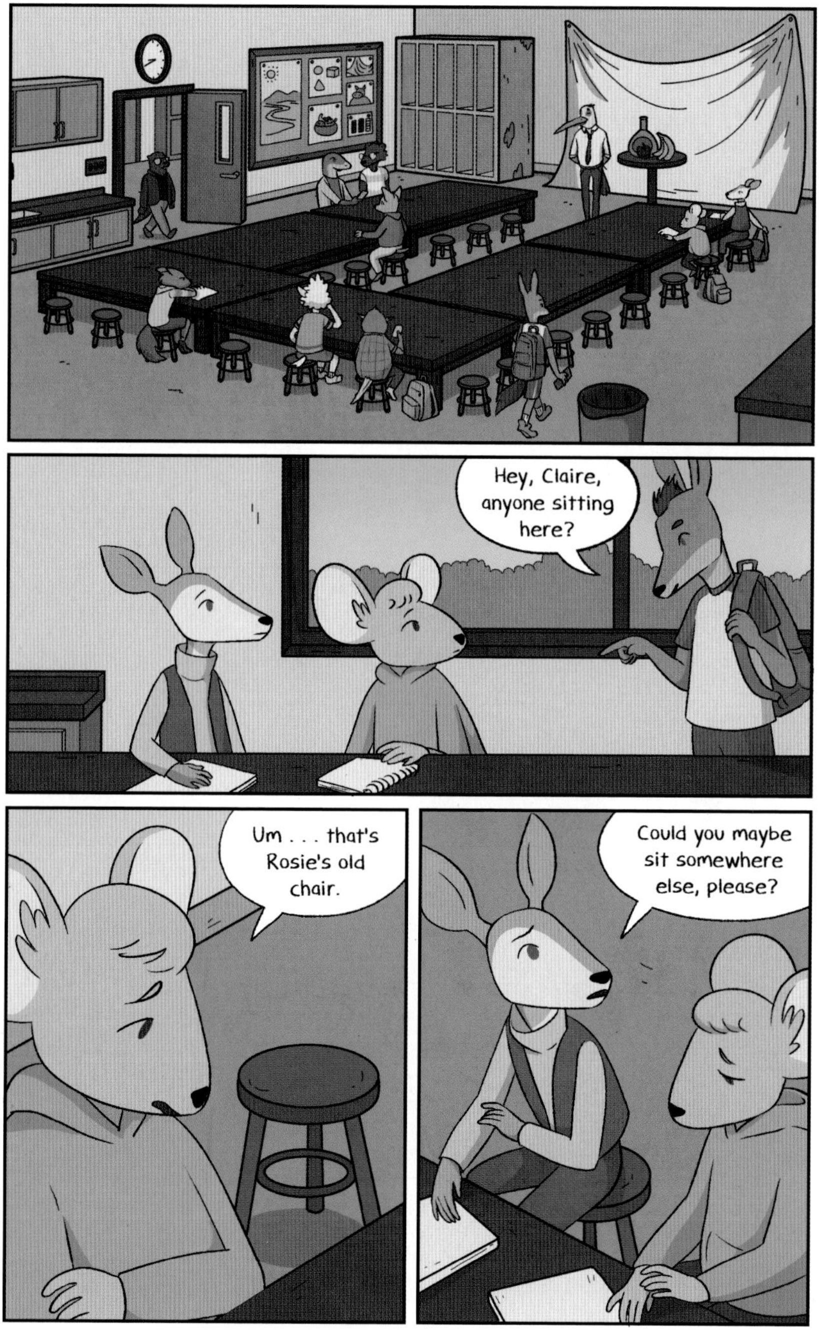
Hey, Claire, anyone sitting here?
Um . . . that's Rosie's old chair.
Could you maybe sit somewhere else, please?

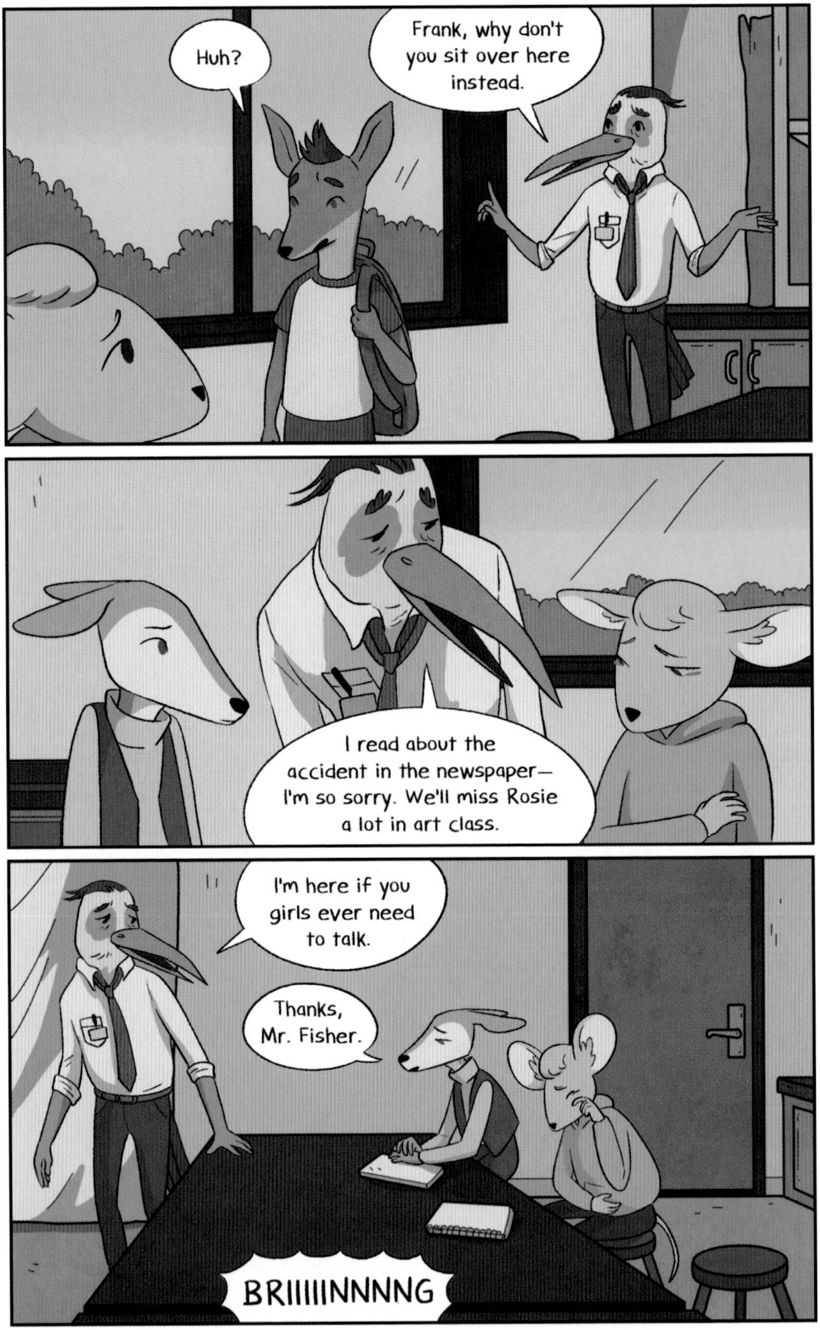
Huh?
Frank, why don't you sit over here instead.
I read about the accident in the newspaper— I'm so sorry. We'll miss Rosie a lot in art class.
I'm here if you girls ever need to talk.
Thanks, Mr. Fisher.
BRIIIIINNNNG

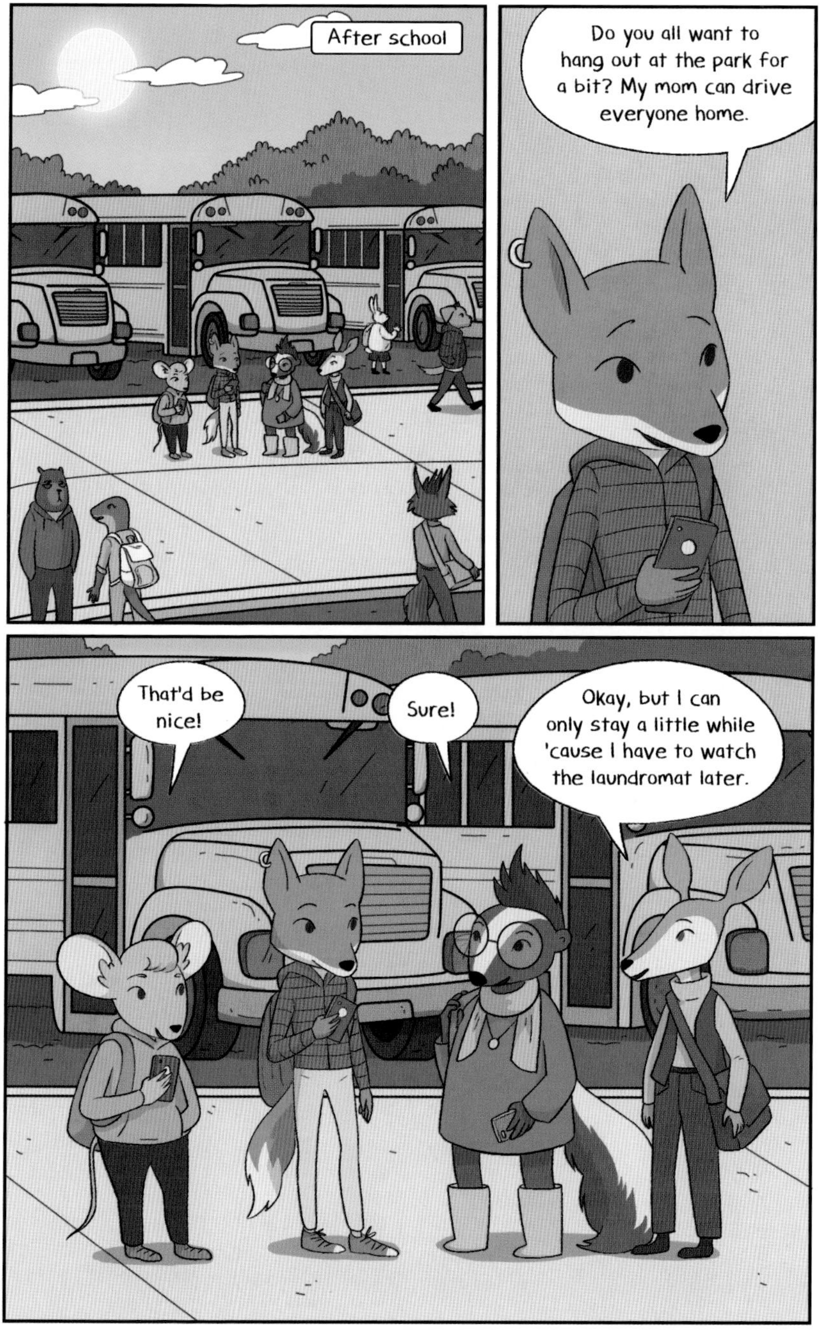
After school
Do you all want to hang out at the park for a bit? My mom can drive everyone home.
That'd be nice!
Sure!
Okay, but I can only stay a little while 'cause I have to watch the laundromat later.

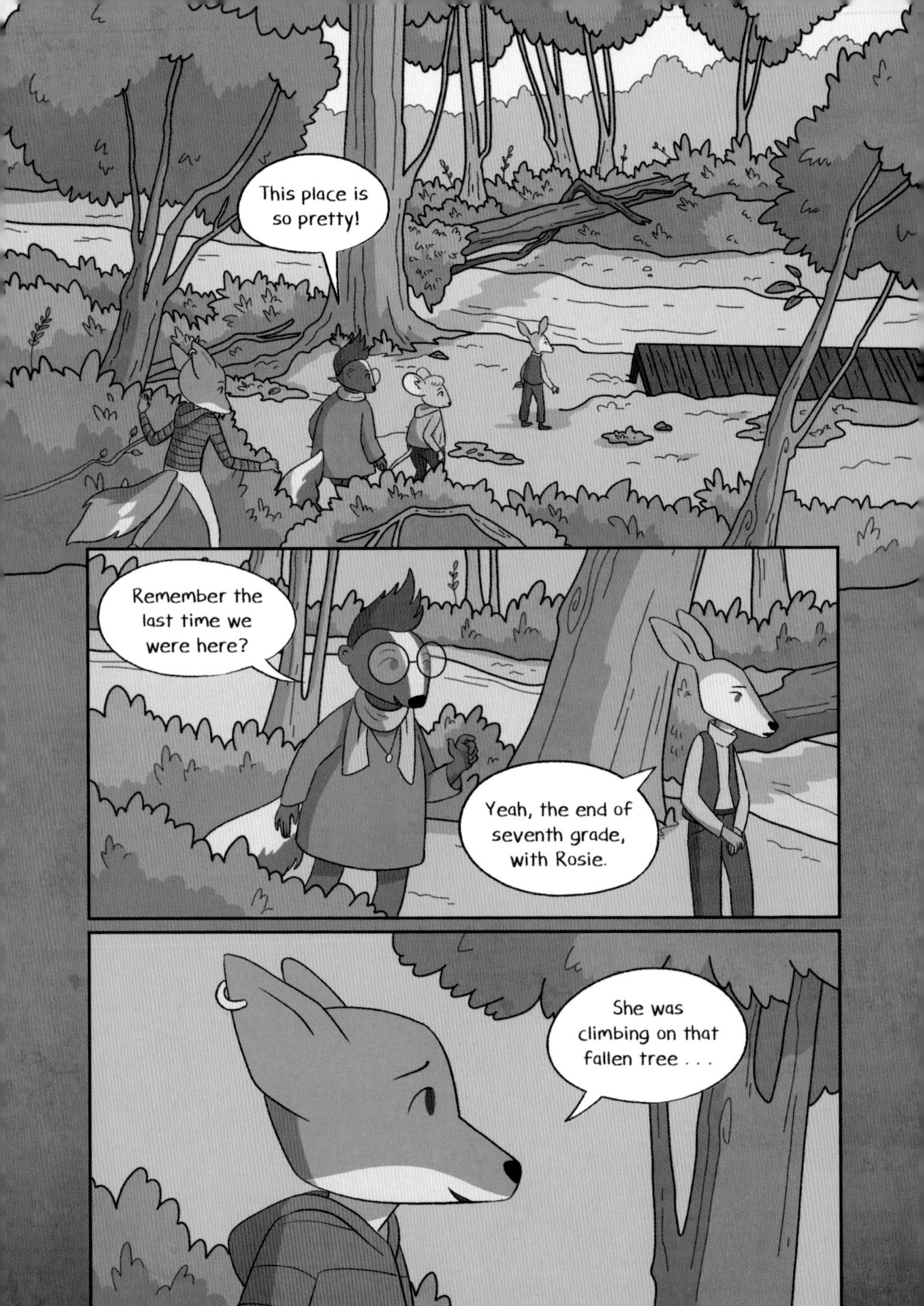
This place is so pretty!
Remember the last time we were here?
Yeah, the end of seventh grade, with Rosie.
She was climbing on that fallen tree . . .

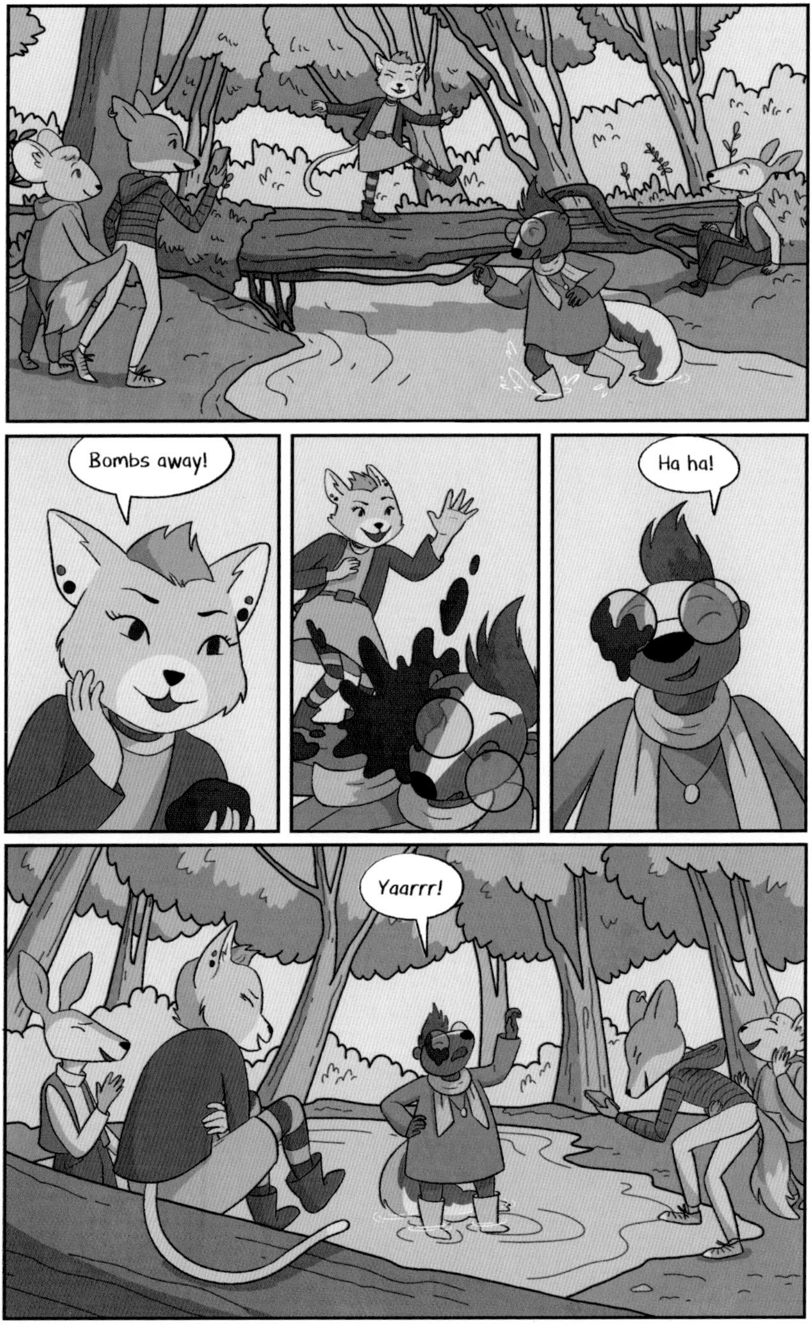
Bombs away!
Ha ha!
Yaarrr!

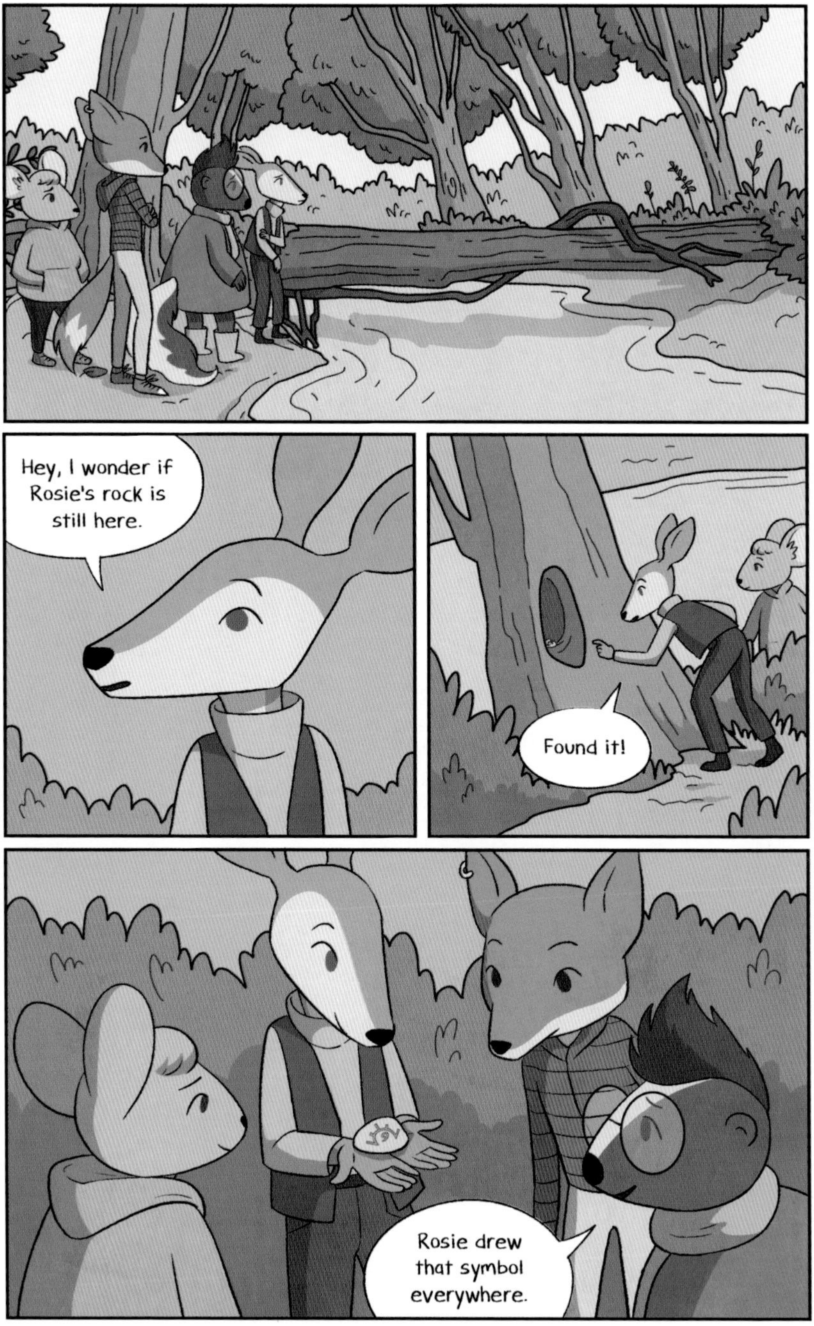
Hey, I wonder if Rosie's rock is still here.
Found it!
Rosie drew that symbol everywhere.

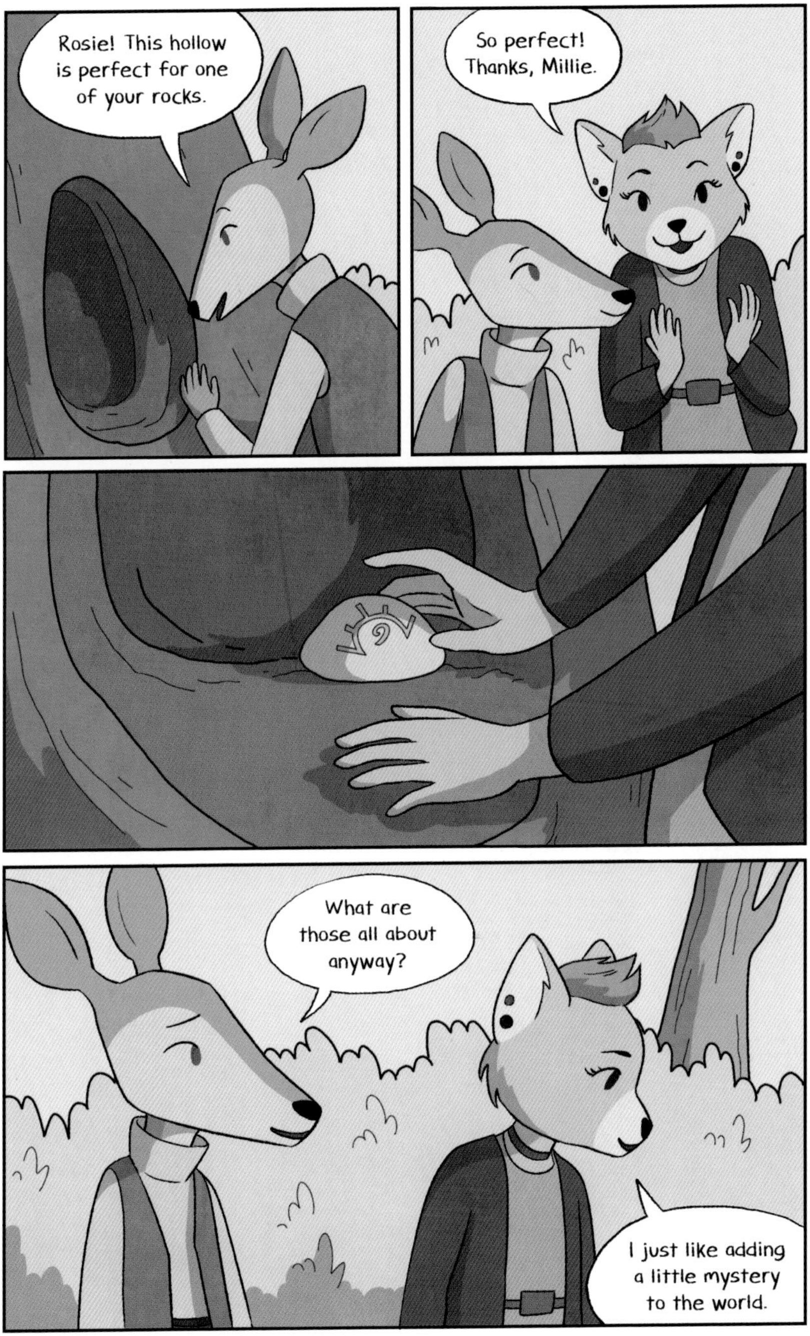
Rosie! This hollow is perfect for one of your rocks.
So perfect! Thanks, Millie.
What are those all about anyway?
I just like adding a little mystery to the world.

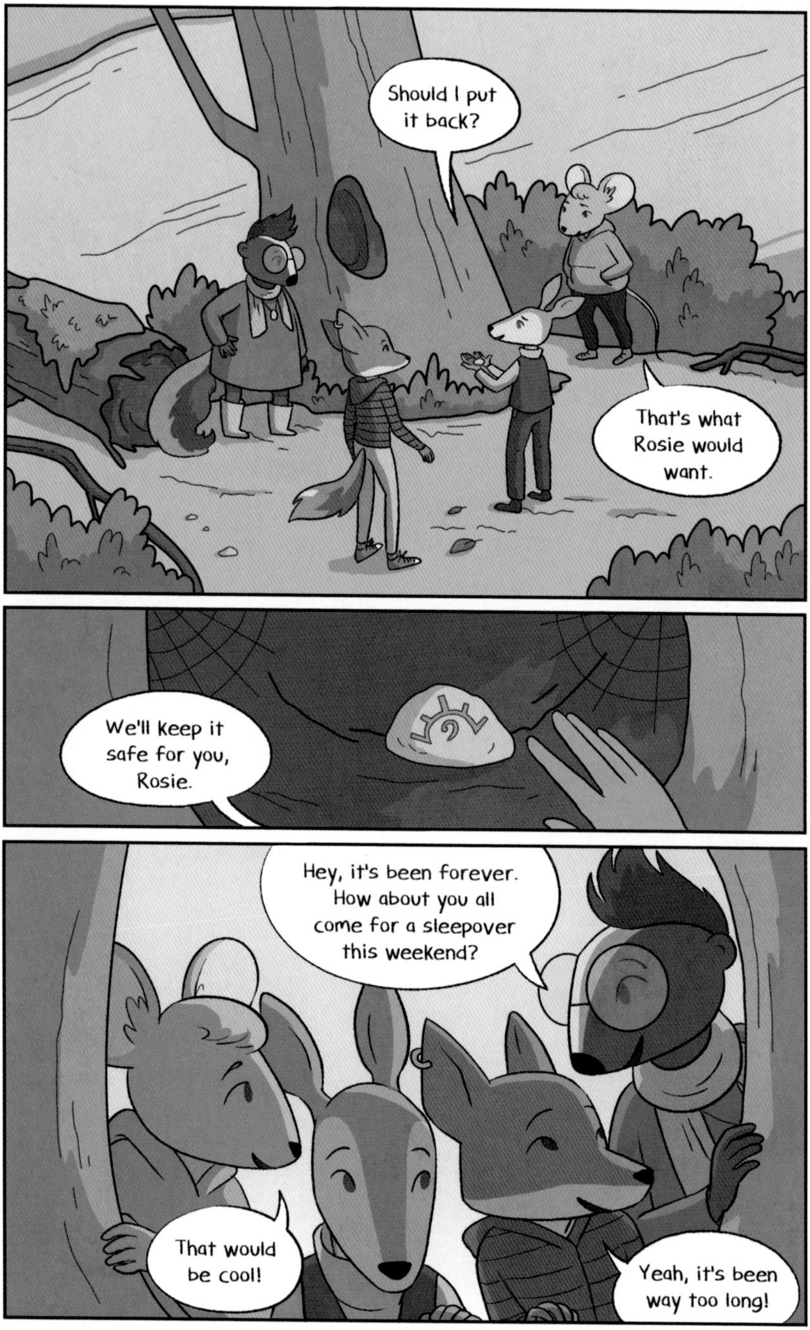
Should I put it back?
That's what Rosie would want.
We'll keep it safe for you, Rosie.
Hey, it's been forever. How about you all come for a sleepover this weekend?
That would be cool!
Yeah, it's been way too long!

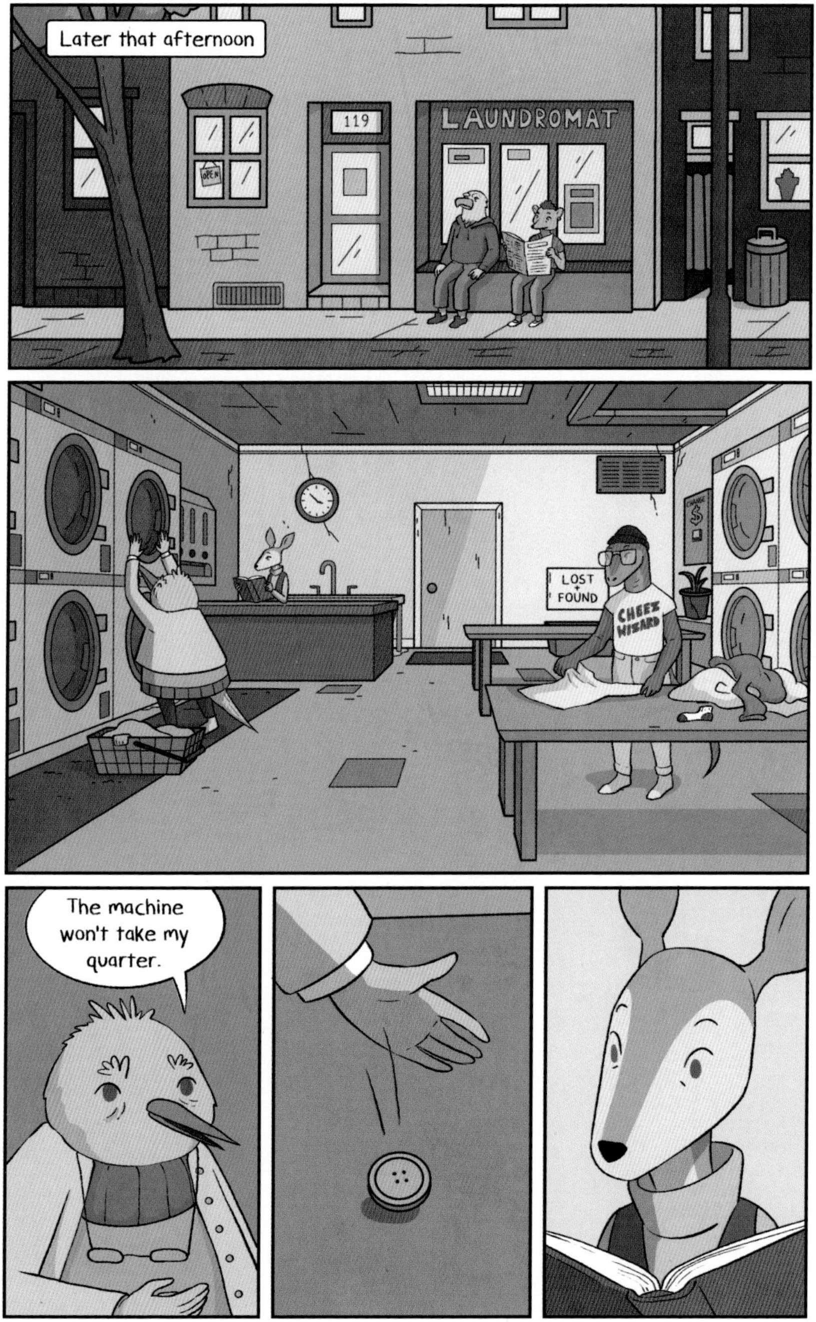
Later that afternoon
119
OPEN
LAUNDROMAT
LOST + FOUND
CHEEZ WIZARD
CHANGE $
The machine won't take my quarter.

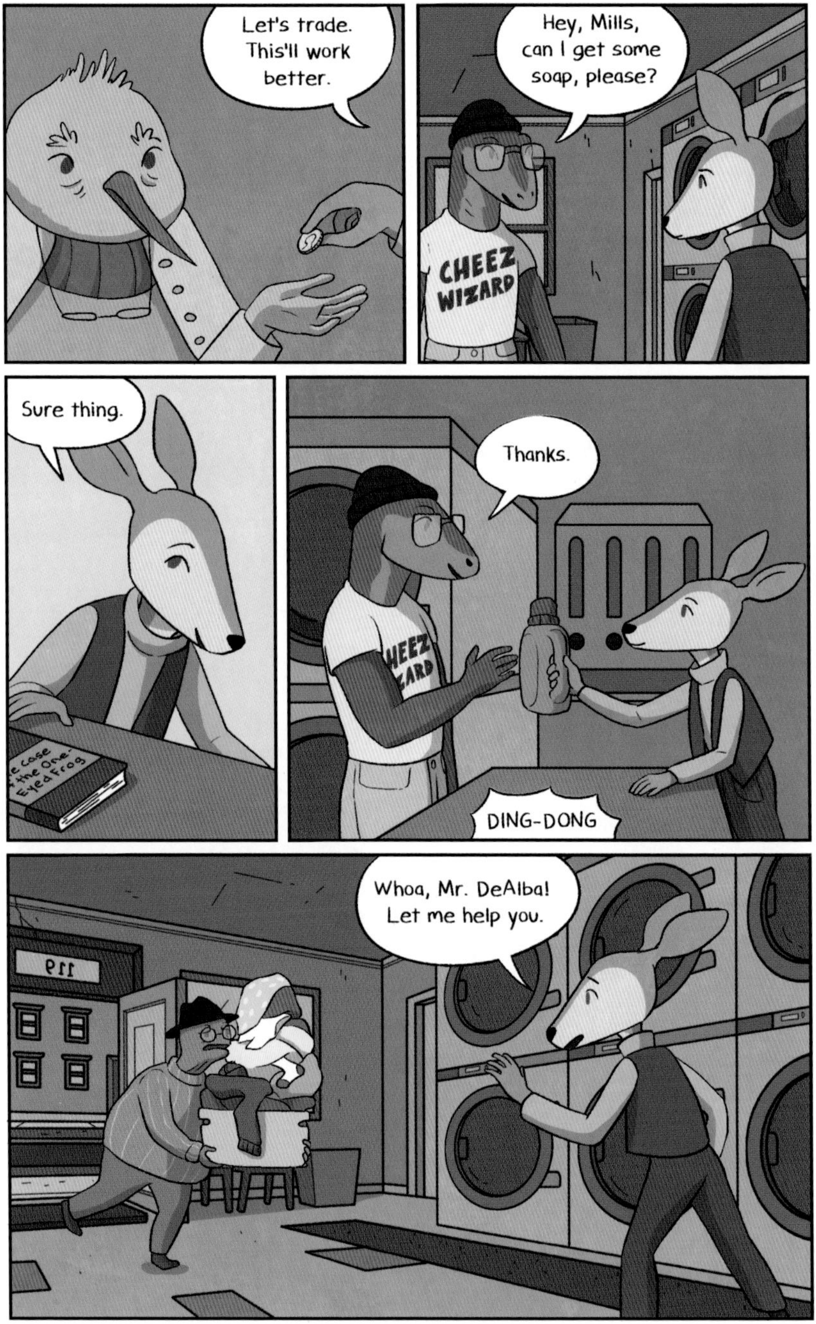
Let's trade. This'll work better.
Hey, Mills, can I get some soap, please?
CHEEZ WIZARD
Sure thing.
Thanks.
DING-DONG
Whoa, Mr. DeAlba! Let me help you.

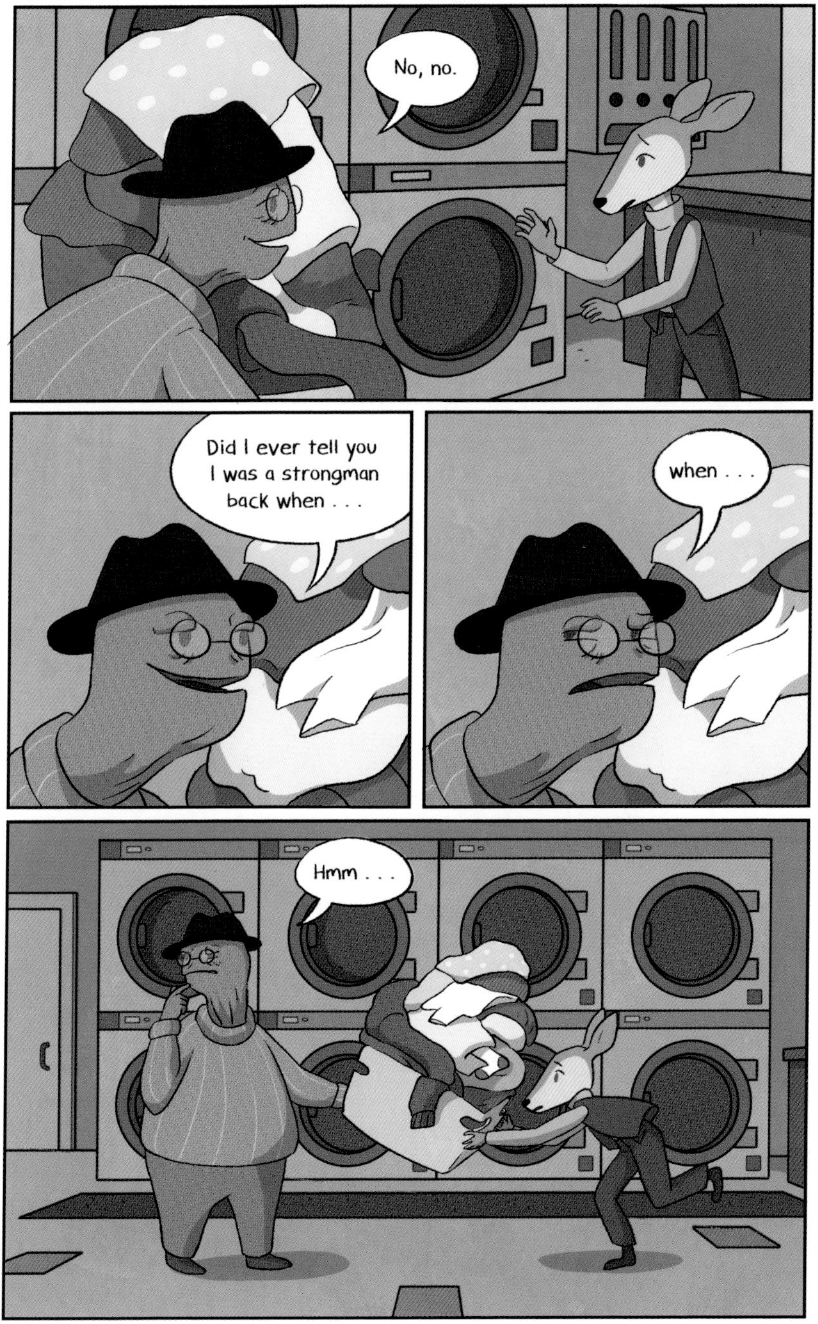
No, no.
Did I ever tell you I was a strongman back when . . .
when . . .
Hmm . . .

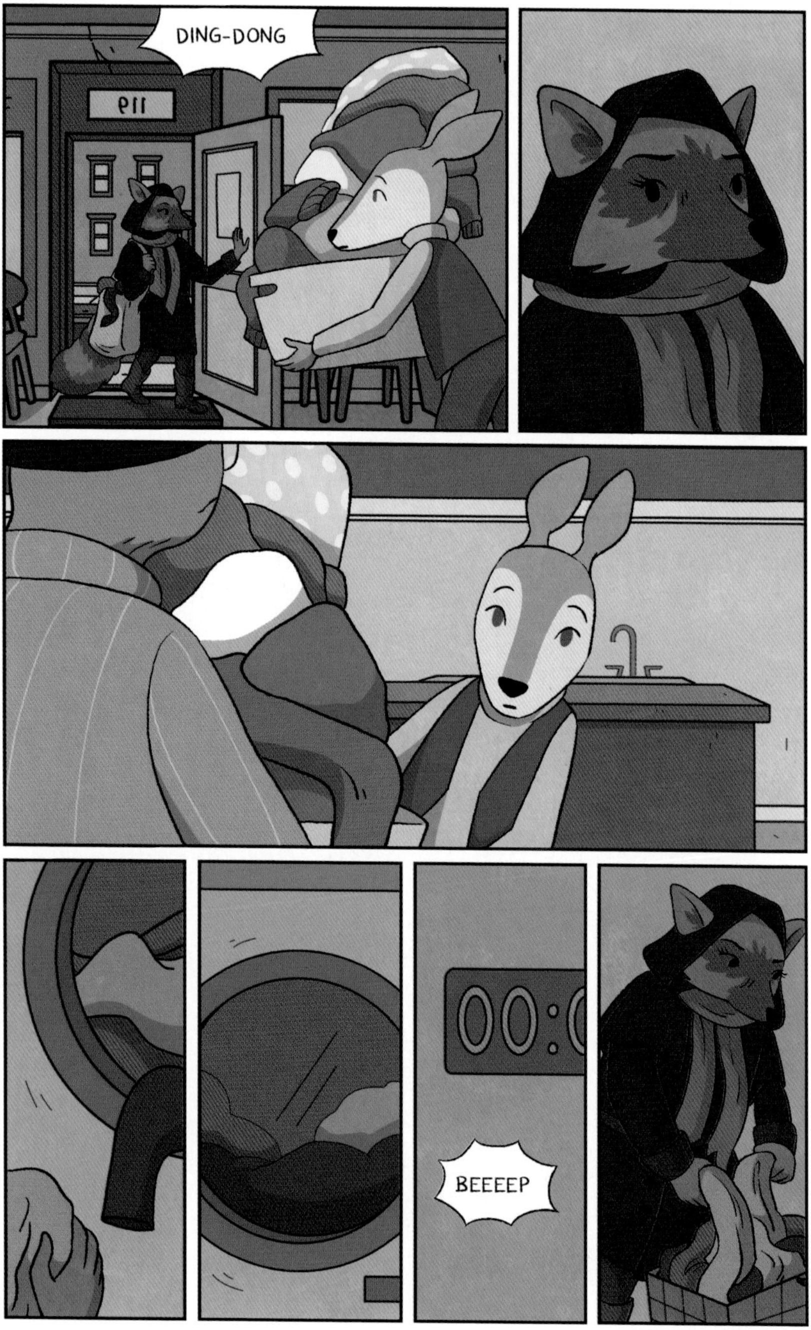
DING-DONG
BEEEEP

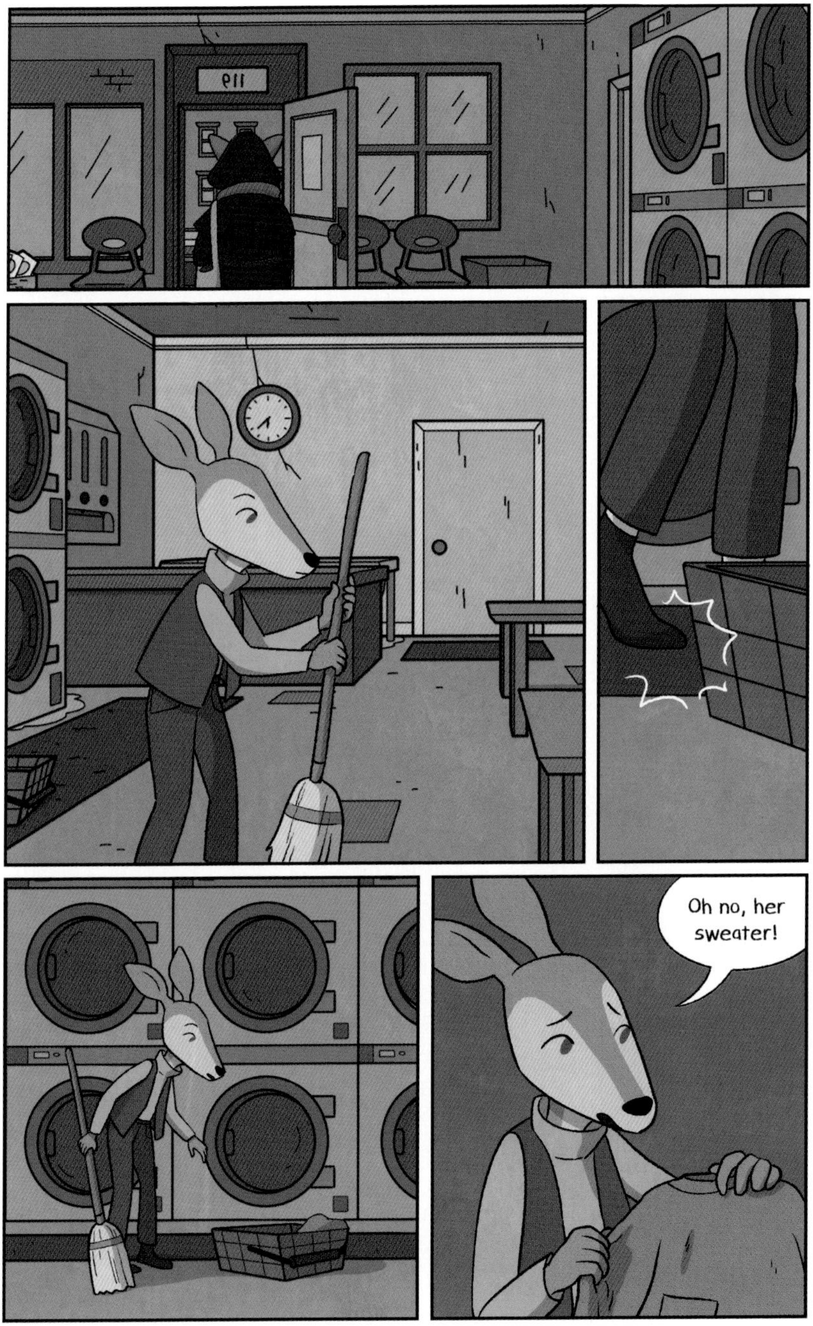

Oh no, her sweater!

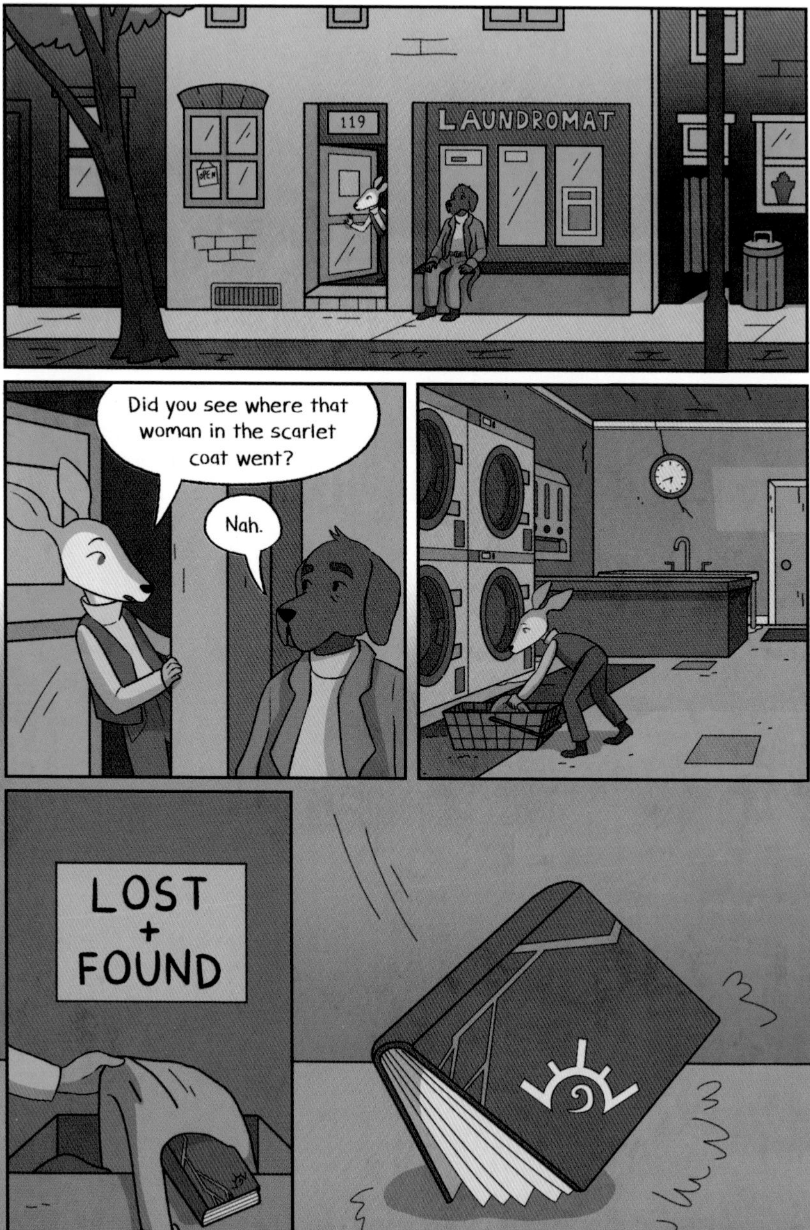
119
LAUNDROMAT
OPEN
Did you see where that woman in the scarlet coat went?
Nah.
LOST + FOUND

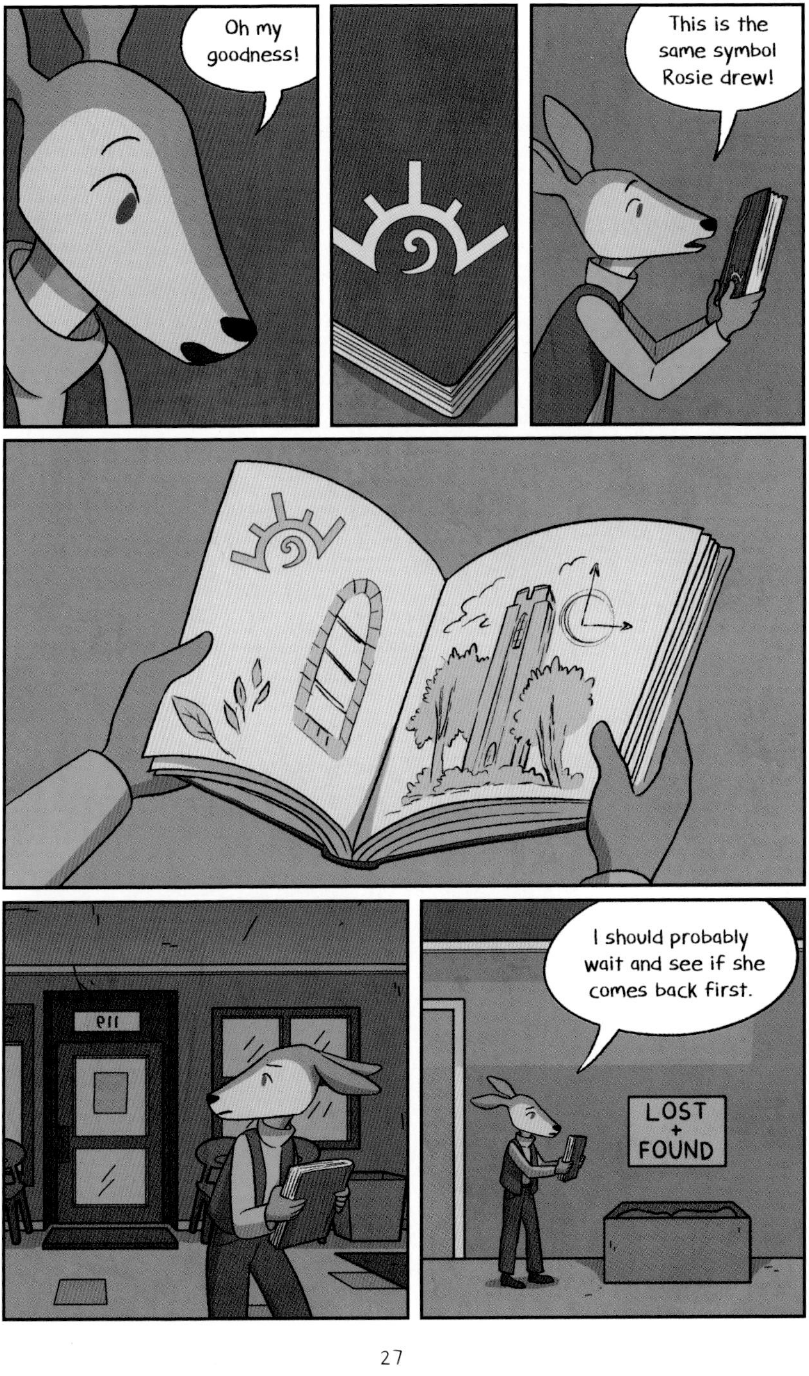
Oh my goodness!
This is the same symbol Rosie drew!
119
I should probably wait and see if she comes back first.
LOST + FOUND

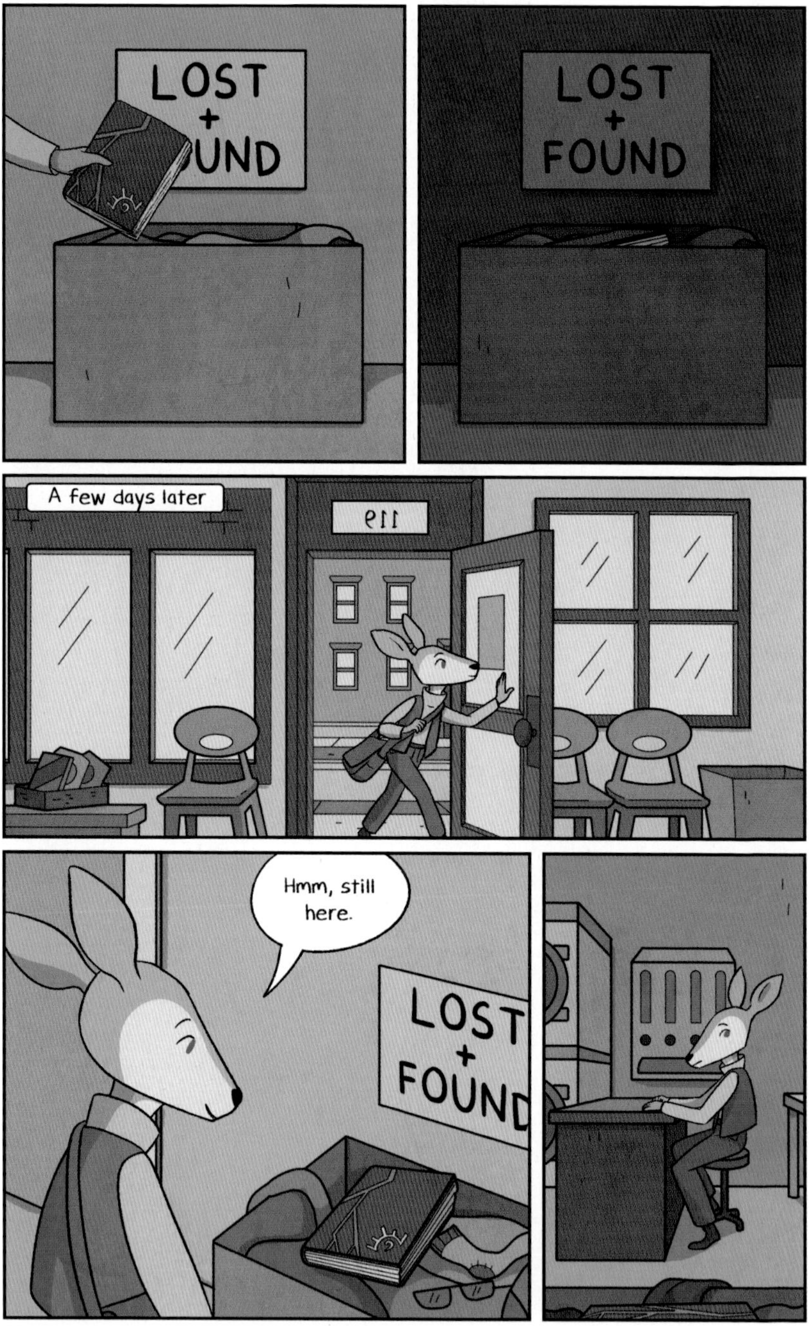
LOST
+
FOUND
LOST
+
FOUND
A few days later
119
Hmm, still here.
LOST
+
FOUND

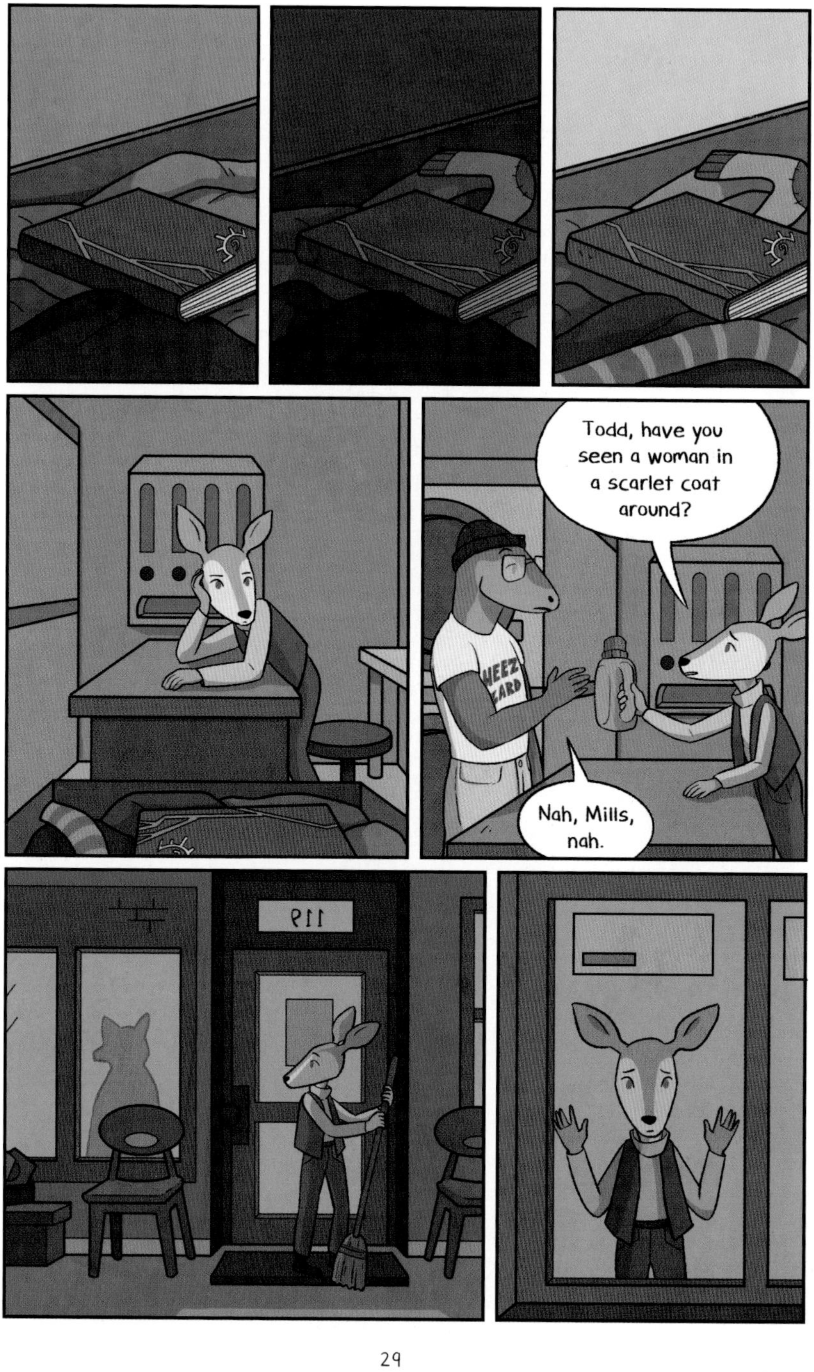
Todd, have you seen a woman in a scarlet coat around?
Nah, Mills, nah.
119

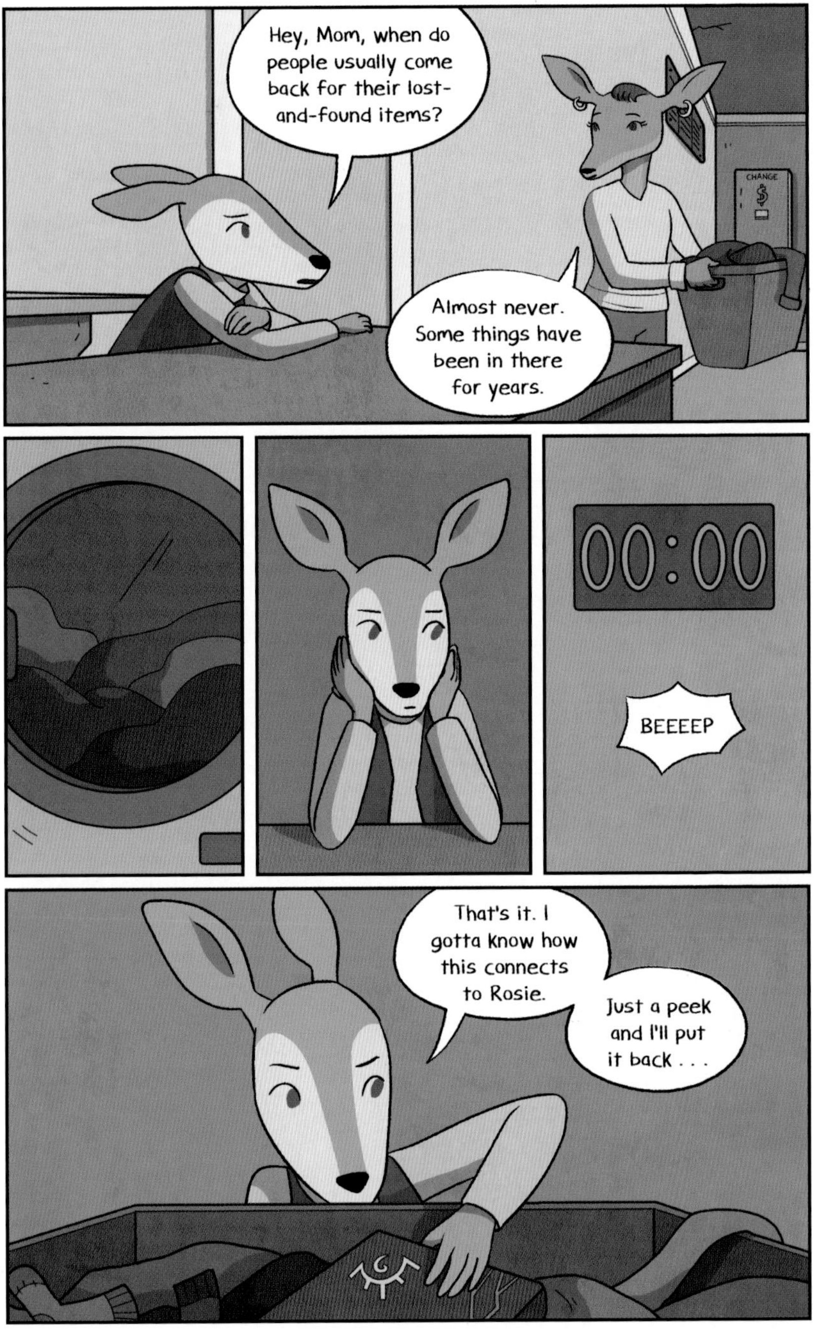
Hey, Mom, when do people usually come back for their lost-and-found items?
Almost never. Some things have been in there for years.
CHANGE
00:00
BEEEEP
That's it. I gotta know how this connects to Rosie.
Just a peek and I'll put it back . . .

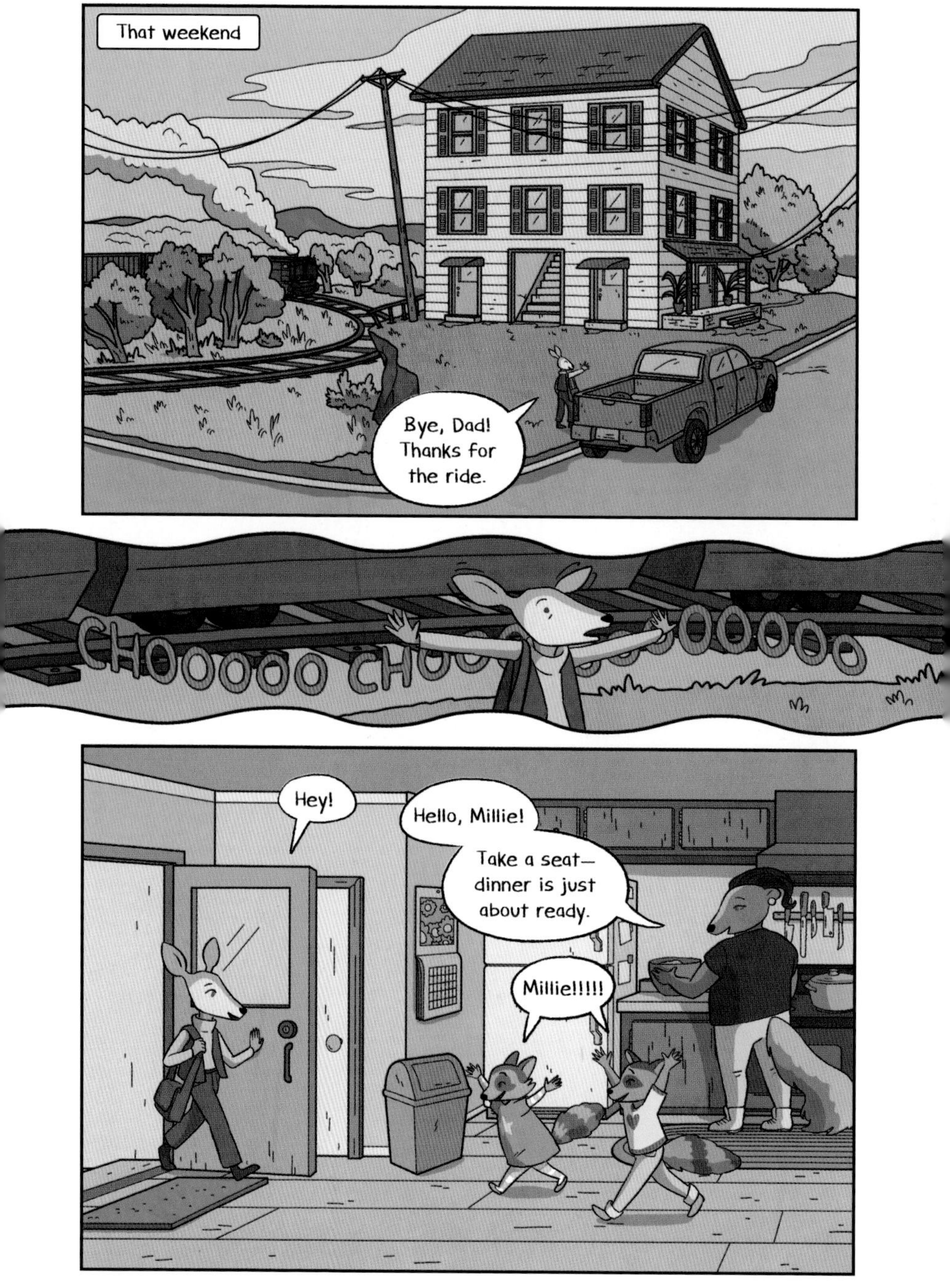
That weekend
Bye, Dad! Thanks for the ride.
CHOOOOO CHOO
Hey!
Hello, Millie!
Take a seat—dinner is just about ready.
Millie!!!!!

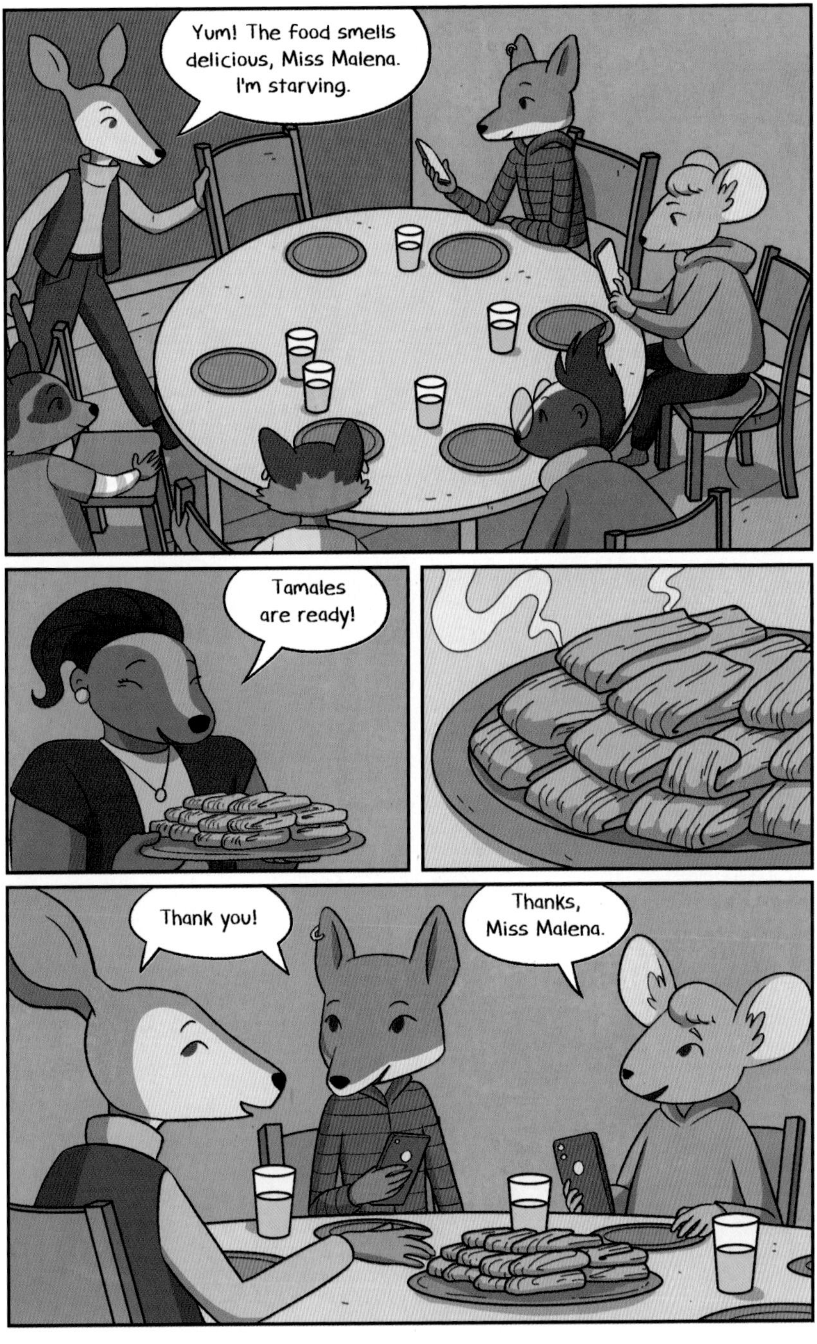
Yum! The food smells delicious, Miss Malena. I'm starving.
Tamales are ready!
Thank you!
Thanks, Miss Malena.

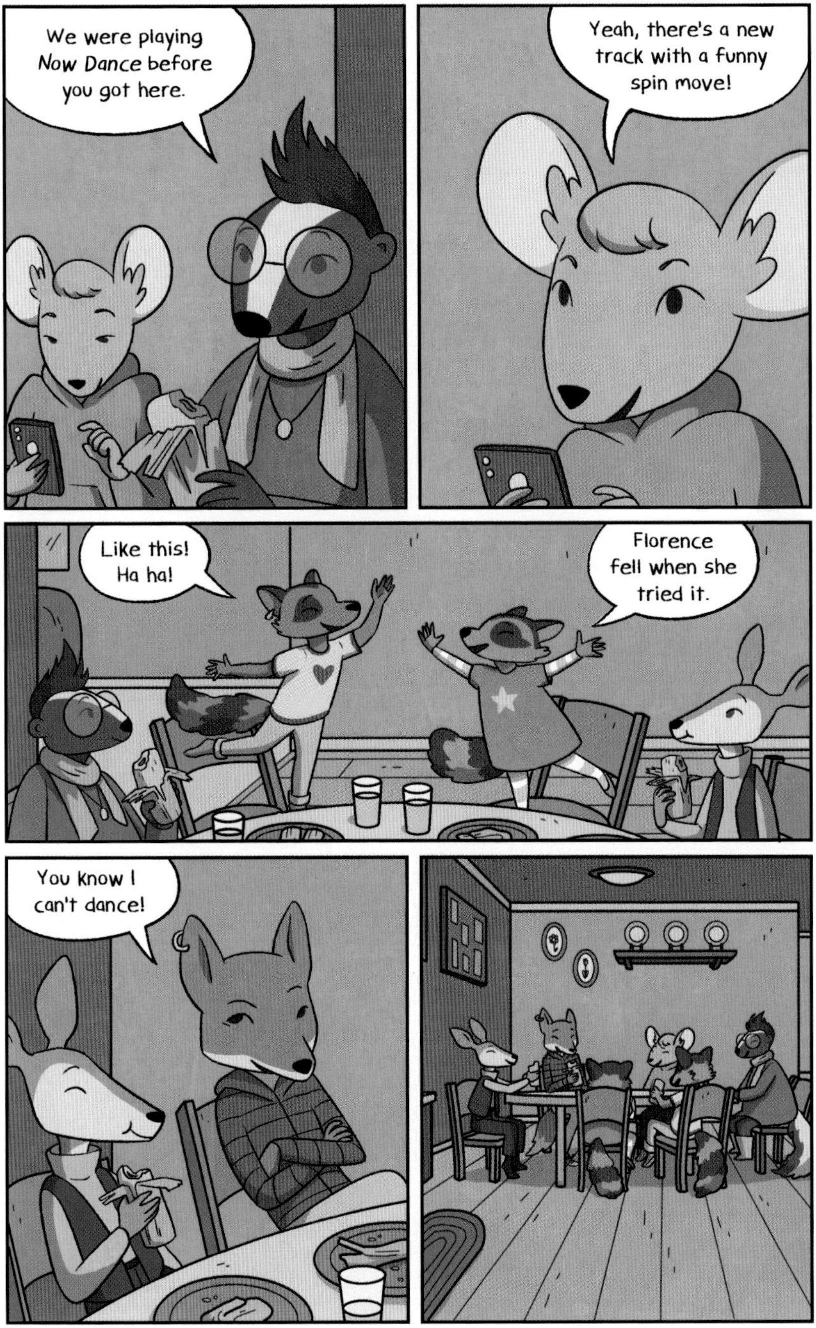
We were playing *Now Dance* before you got here.
Yeah, there's a new track with a funny spin move!
Like this! Ha ha!
Florence fell when she tried it.
You know I can't dance!

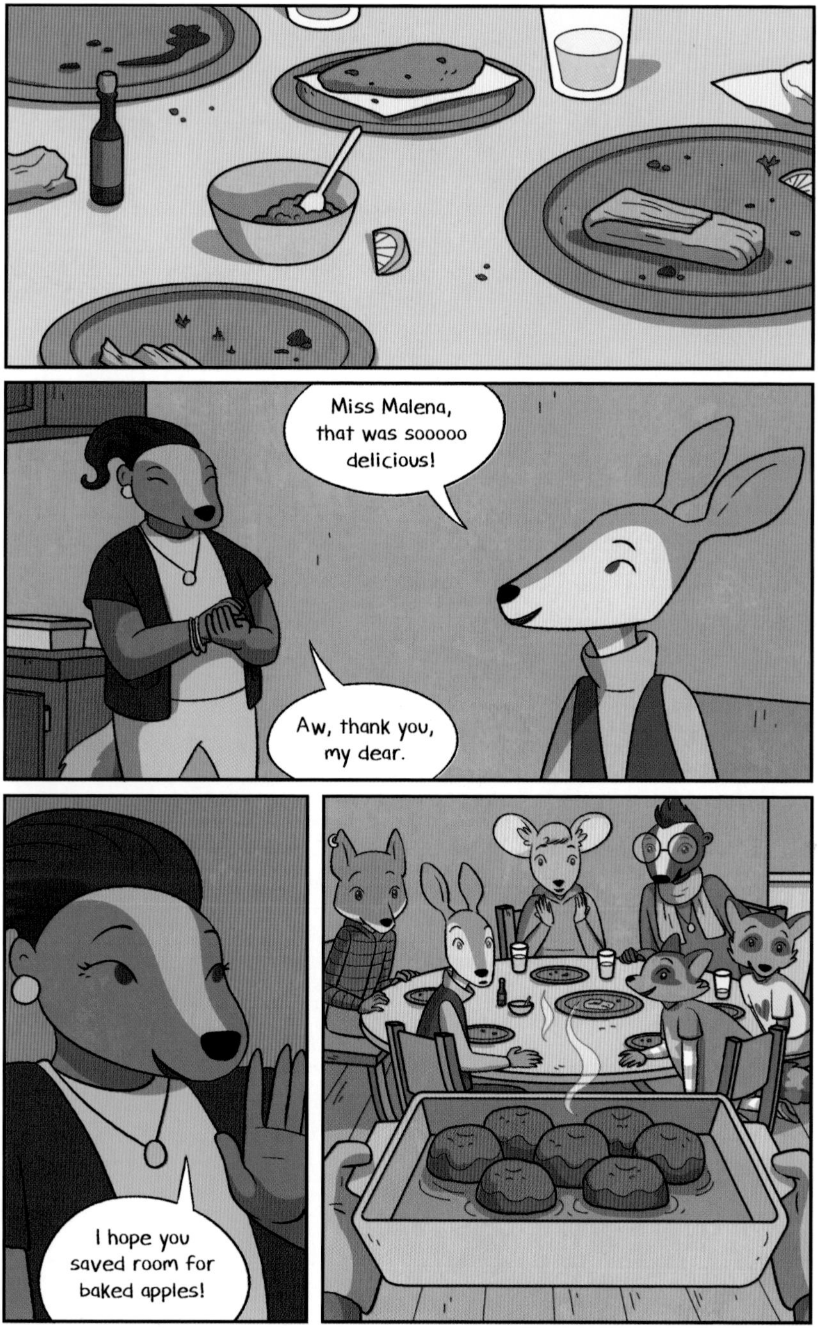
Miss Malena, that was sooooo delicious!
Aw, thank you, my dear.
I hope you saved room for baked apples!

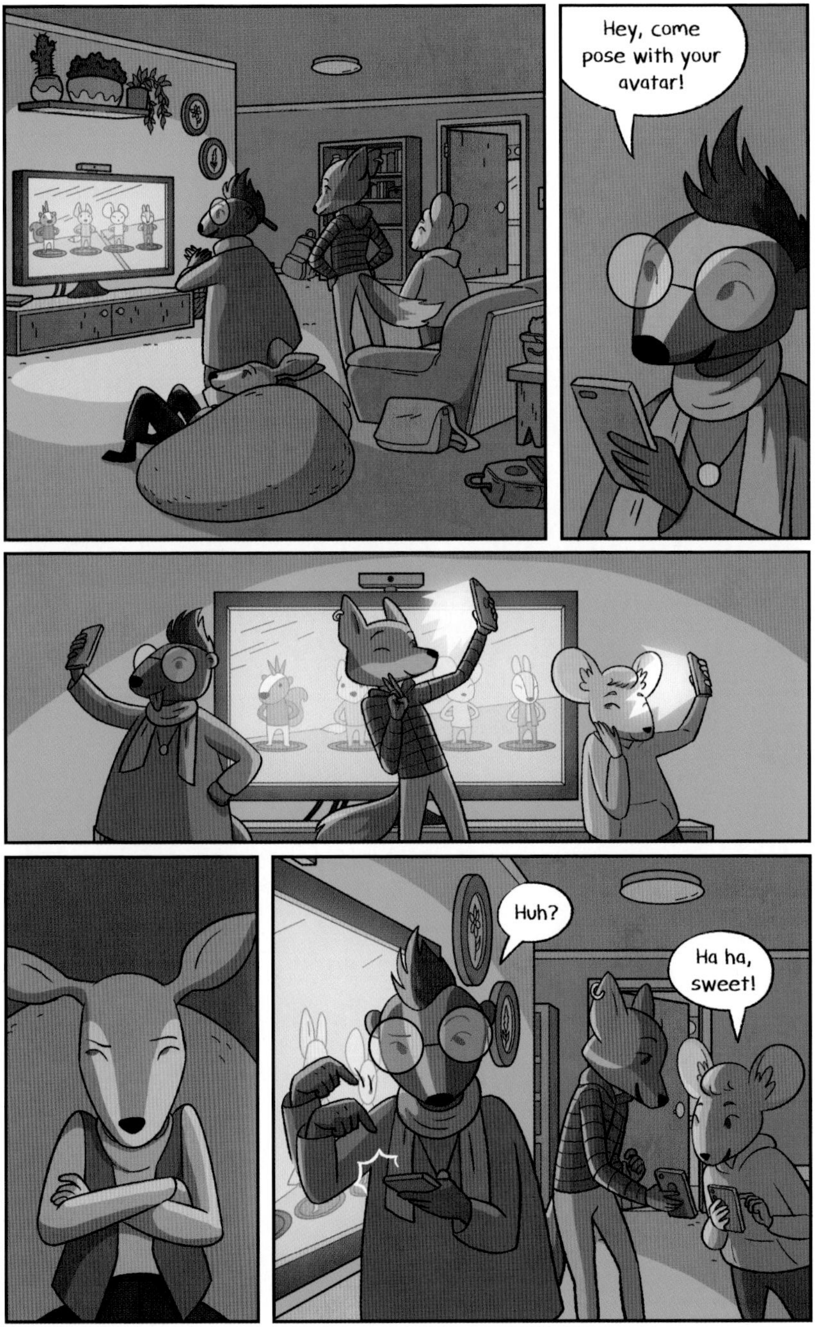
Hey, come pose with your avatar!
Huh?
Ha ha, sweet!

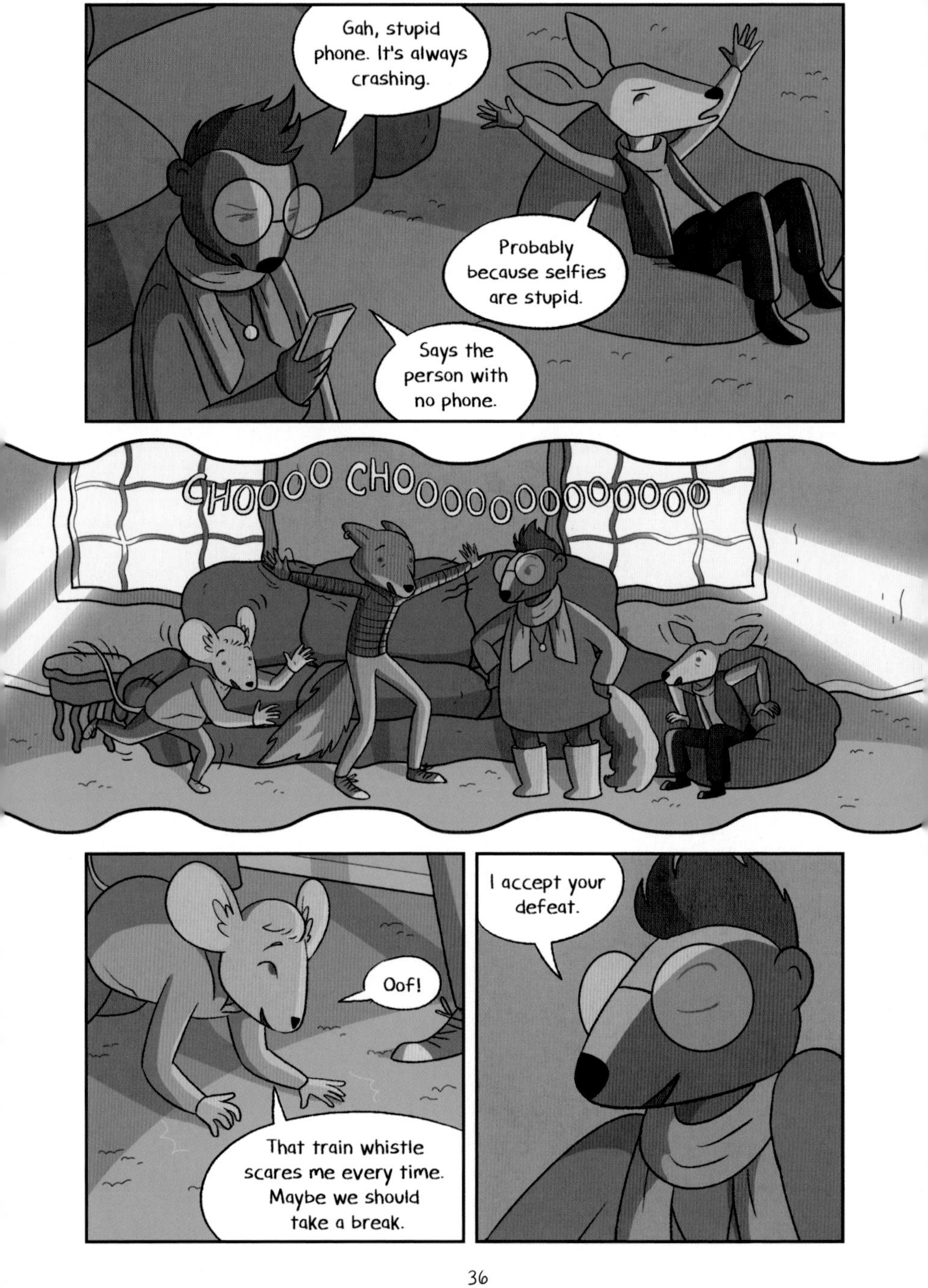
Gah, stupid phone. It's always crashing.
Probably because selfies are stupid.
Says the person with no phone.
CHOOOOO CHOOOOOOOOOOOOOOO
Oof!
That train whistle scares me every time. Maybe we should take a break.
I accept your defeat.

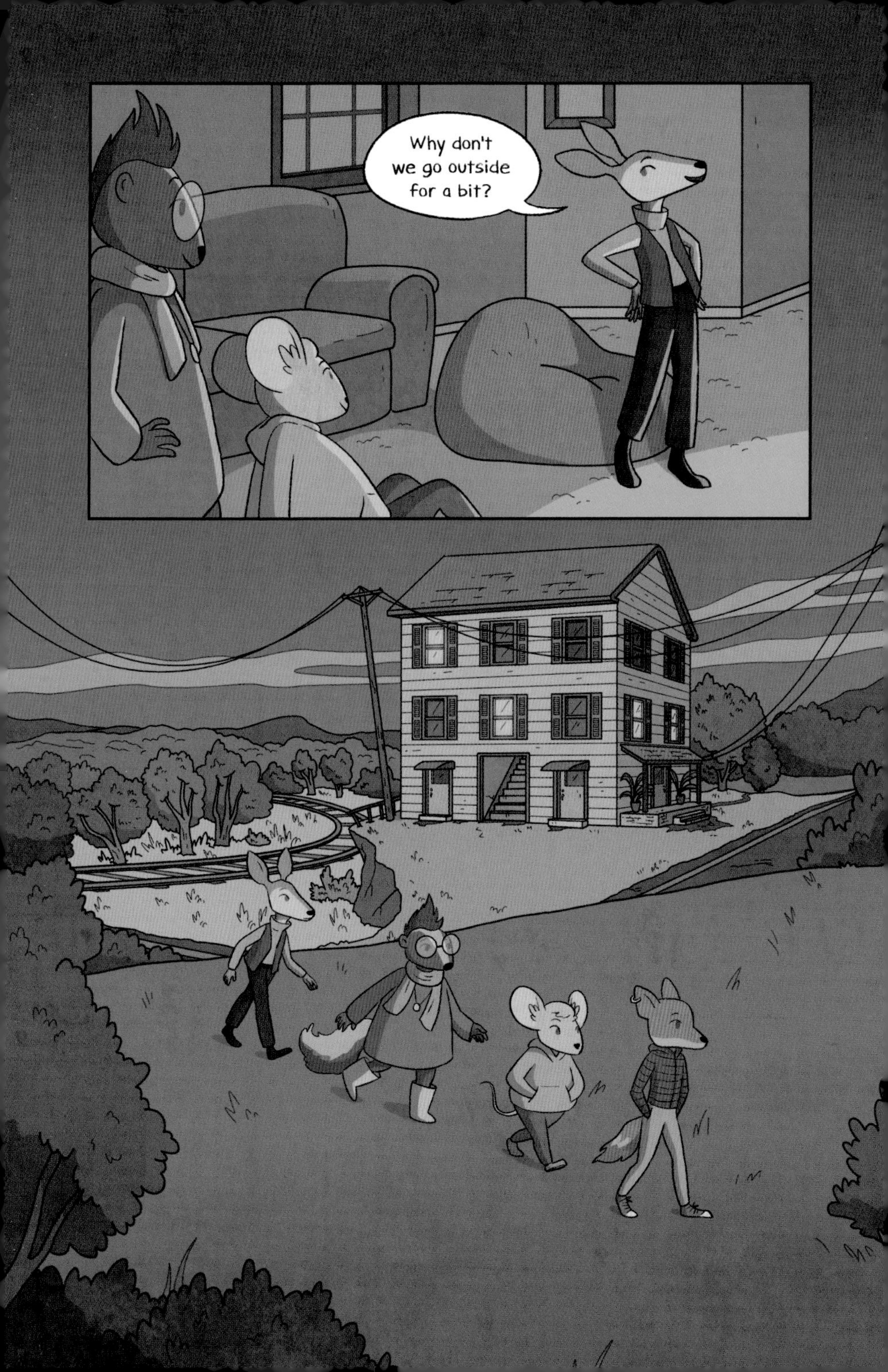
Why don't we go outside for a bit?

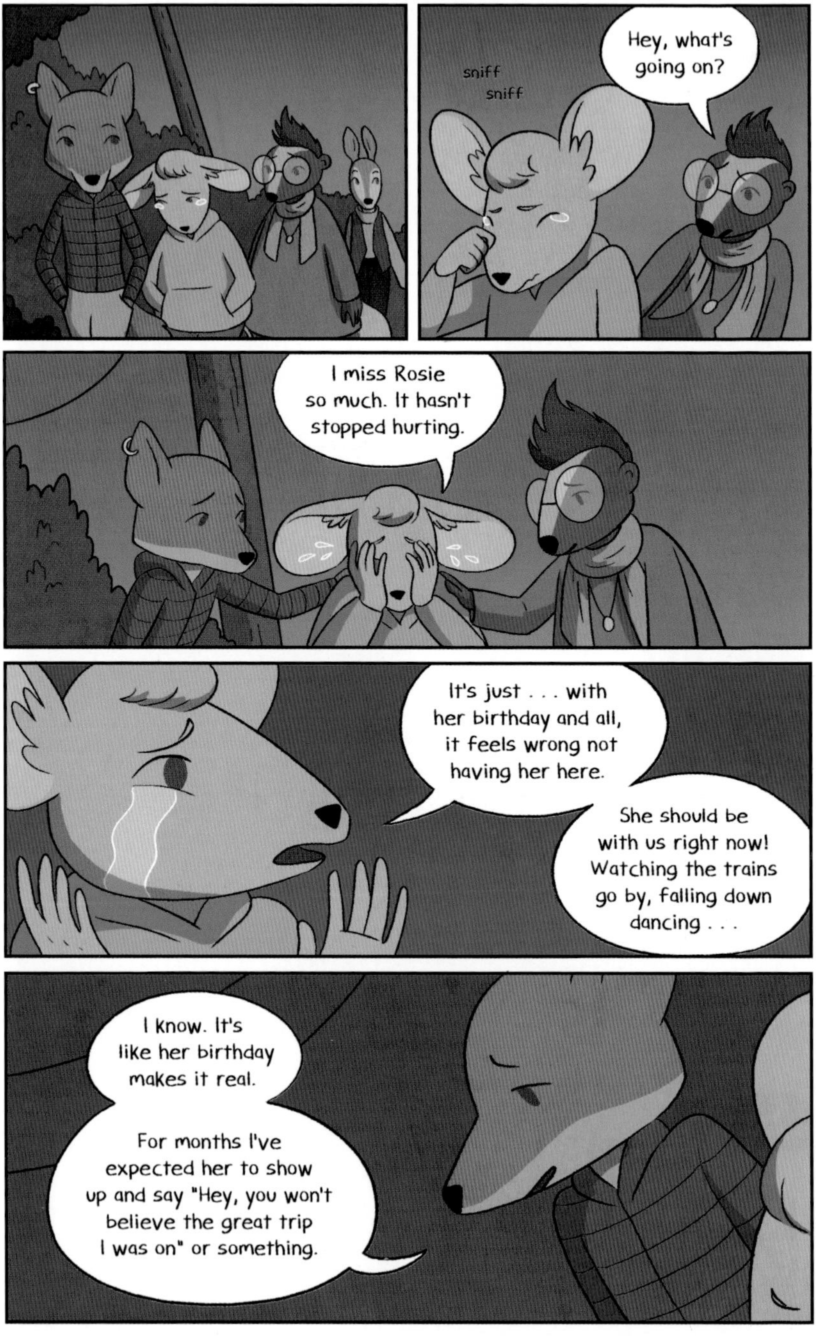

sniff
sniff
Hey, what's going on?
I miss Rosie so much. It hasn't stopped hurting.
It's just . . . with her birthday and all, it feels wrong not having her here.
She should be with us right now! Watching the trains go by, falling down dancing . . .
I know. It's like her birthday makes it real.
For months I've expected her to show up and say "Hey, you won't believe the great trip I was on" or something.

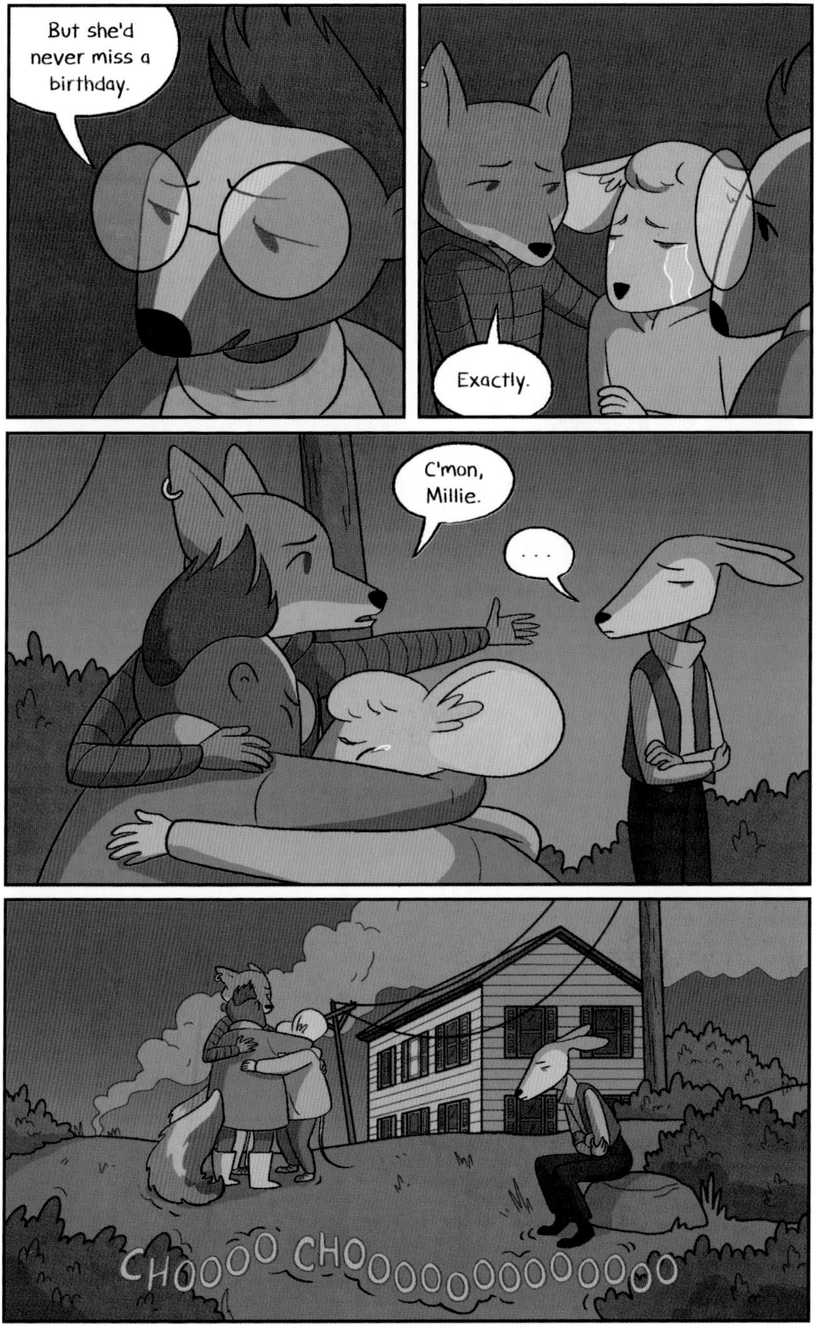
But she'd never miss a birthday.
Exactly.
C'mon, Millie.
...
CHOOOO CHOOOOOOOOOOOOO

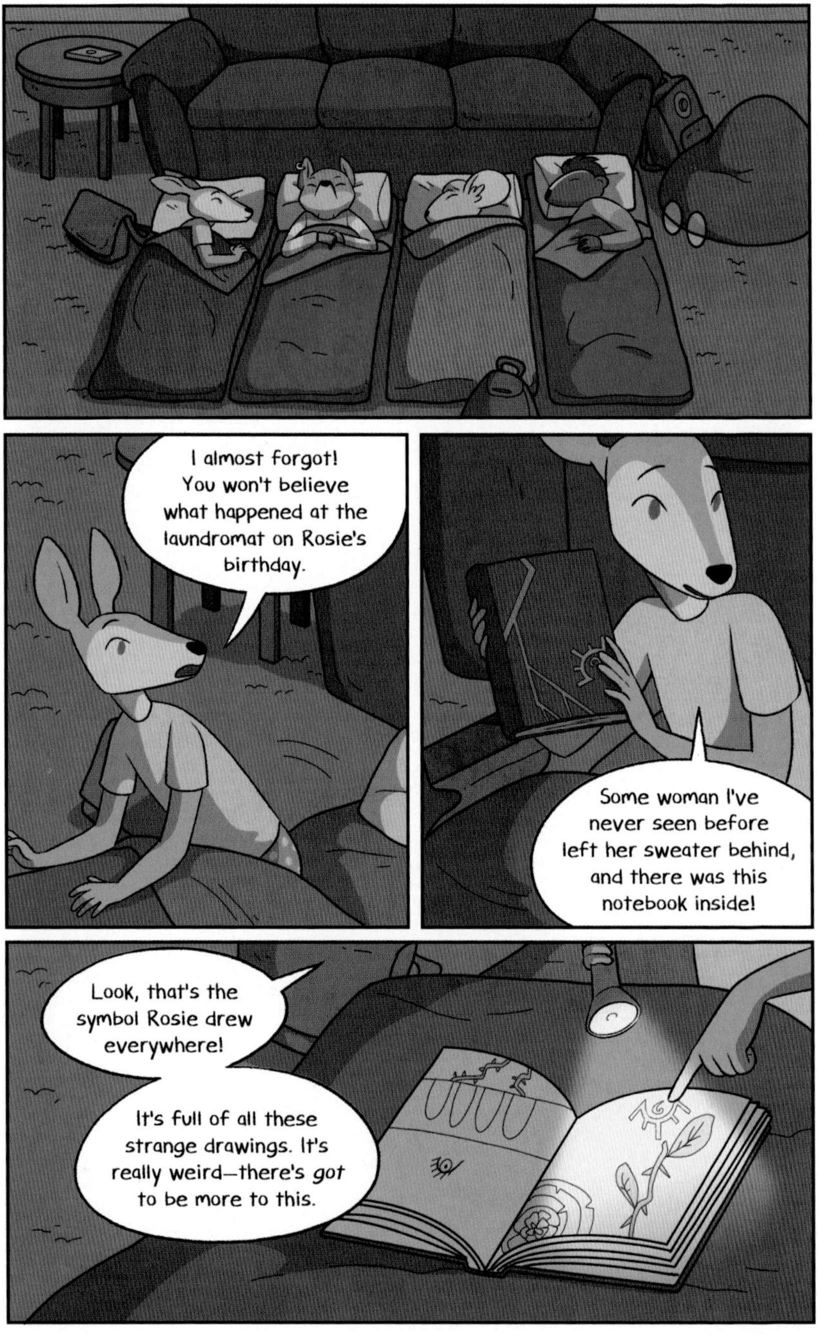
I almost forgot! You won't believe what happened at the laundromat on Rosie's birthday.
Some woman I've never seen before left her sweater behind, and there was this notebook inside!
Look, that's the symbol Rosie drew everywhere!
It's full of all these strange drawings. It's really weird—there's *got* to be more to this.

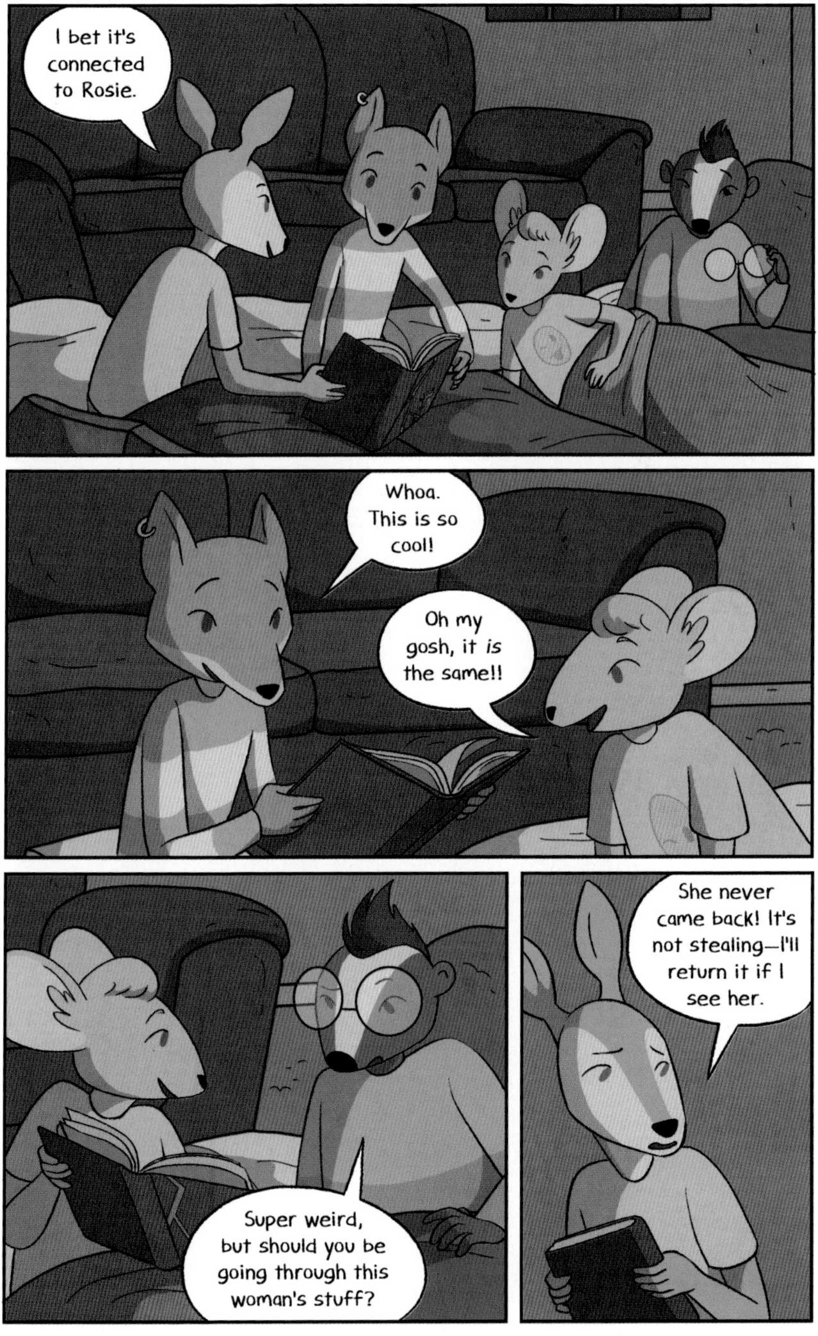
I bet it's connected to Rosie.
Whoa. This is so cool!
Oh my gosh, it *is* the same!!
Super weird, but should you be going through this woman's stuff?
She never came back! It's not stealing—I'll return it if I see her.

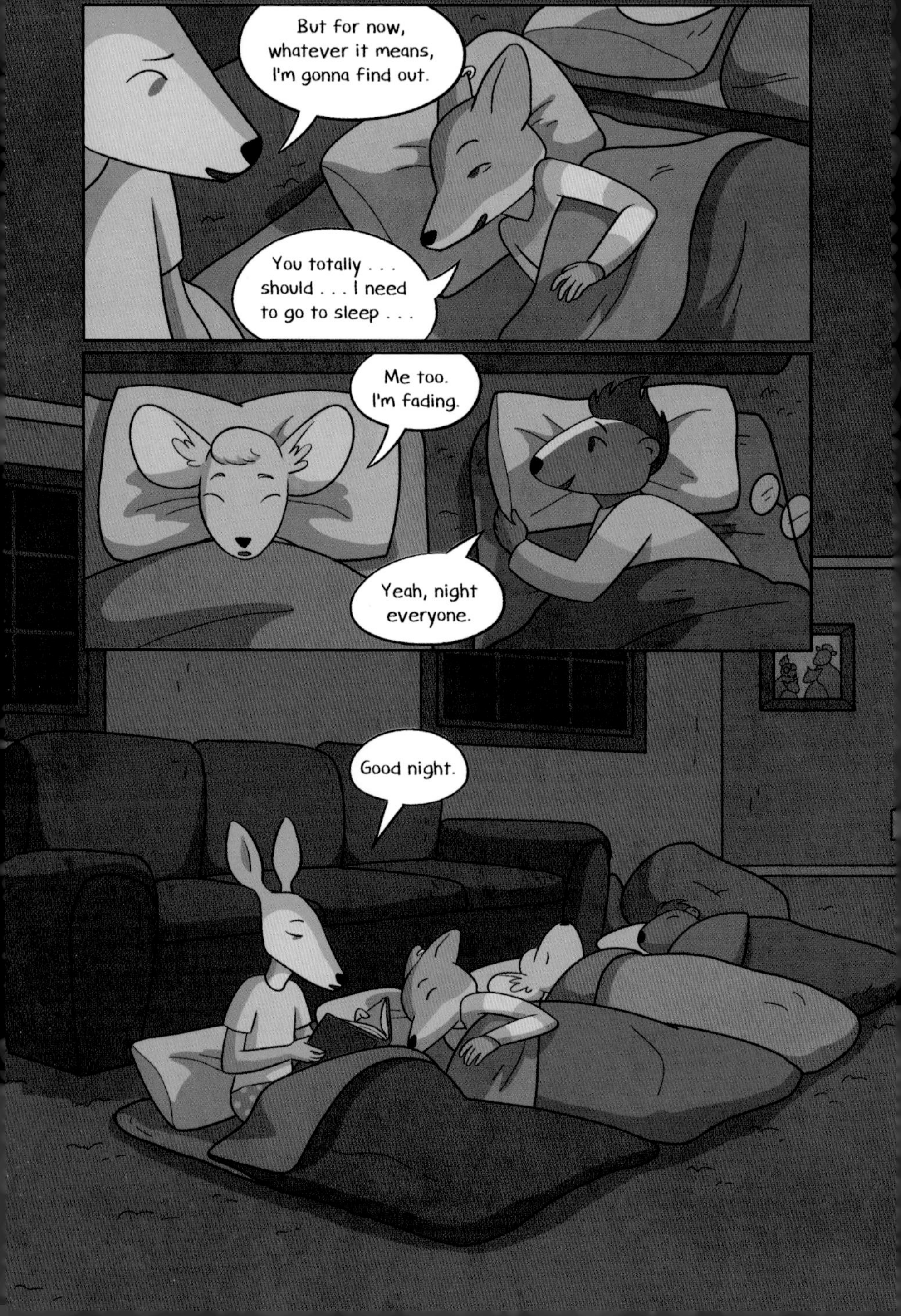
But for now, whatever it means, I'm gonna find out.
You totally . . . should . . . I need to go to sleep . . .
Me too. I'm fading.
Yeah, night everyone.
Good night.

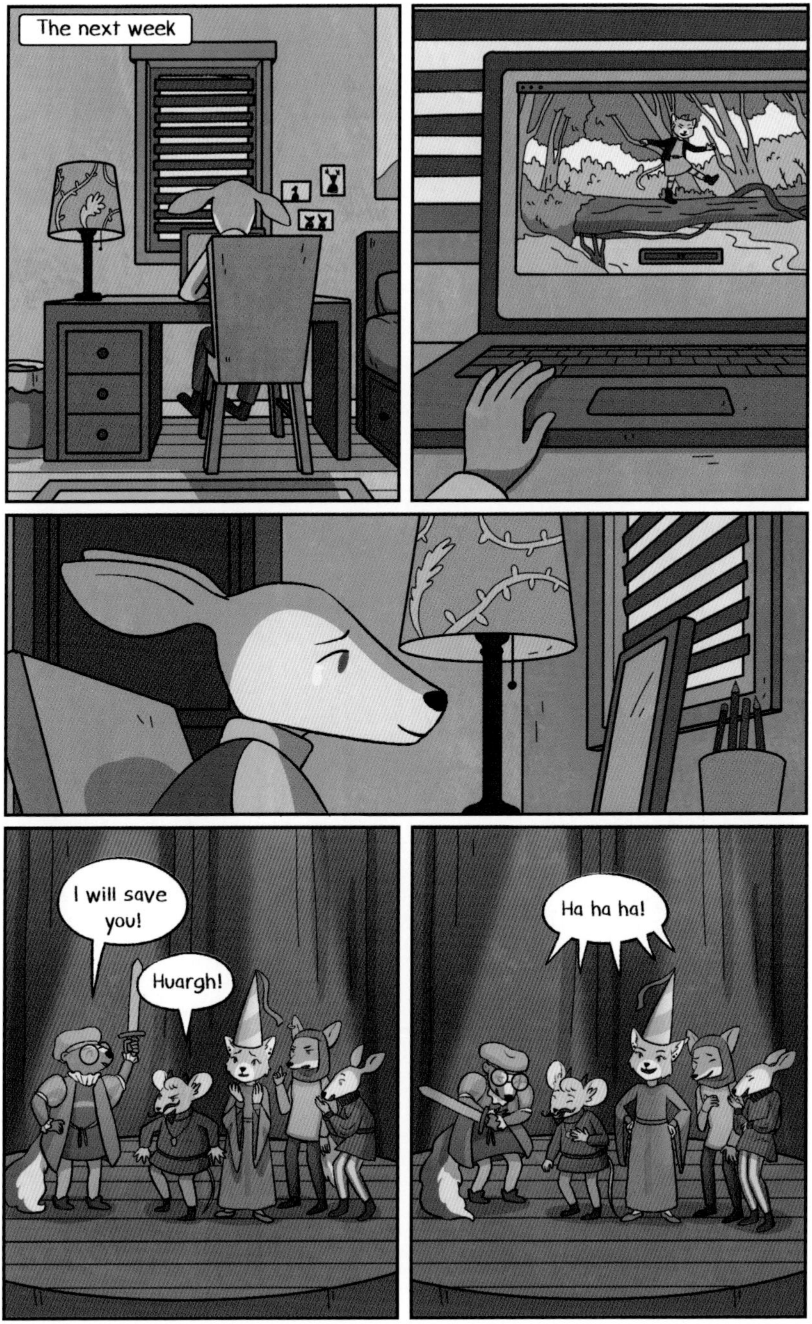
The next week
I will save you!
Huargh!
Ha ha ha!

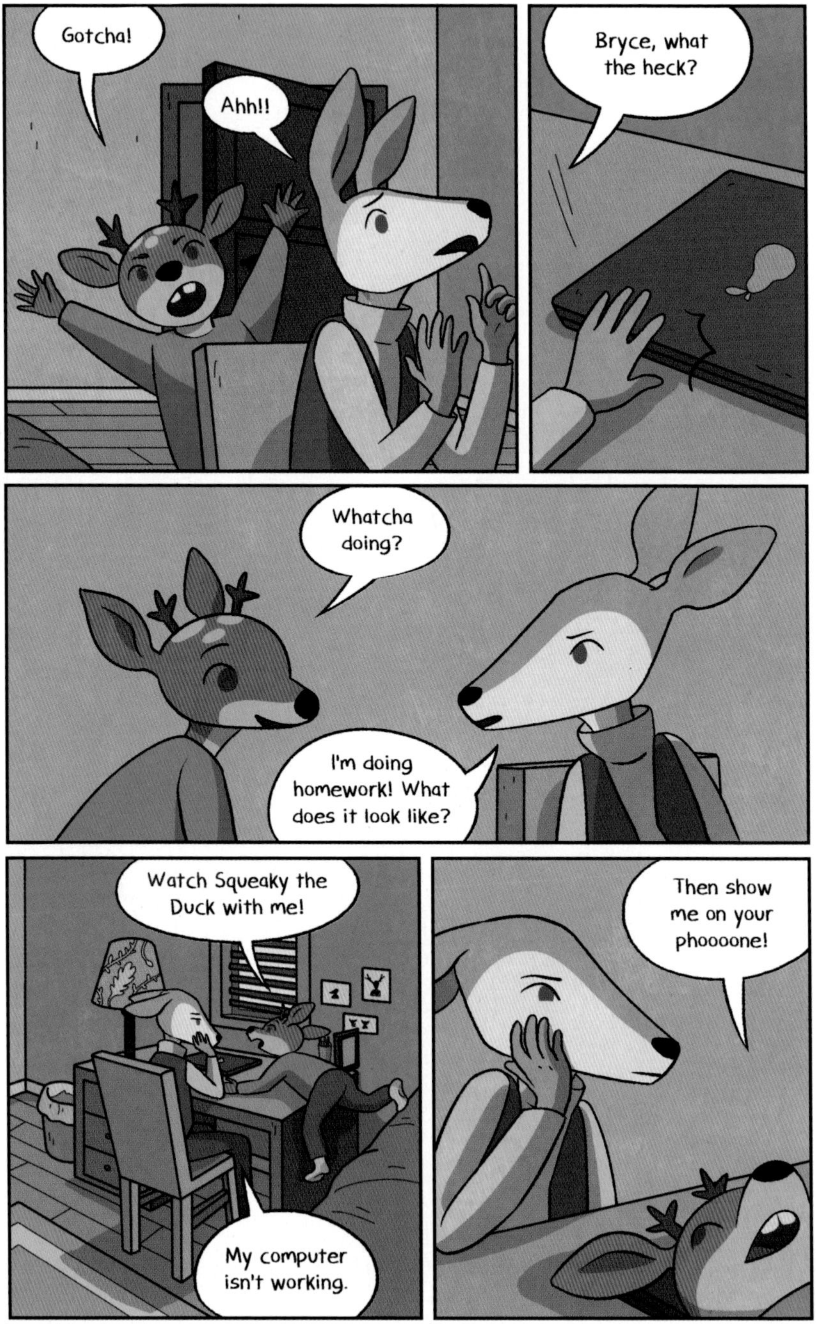
Gotcha!
Ahh!!
Bryce, what the heck?
Whatcha doing?
I'm doing homework! What does it look like?
Watch Squeaky the Duck with me!
My computer isn't working.
Then show me on your phoooone!

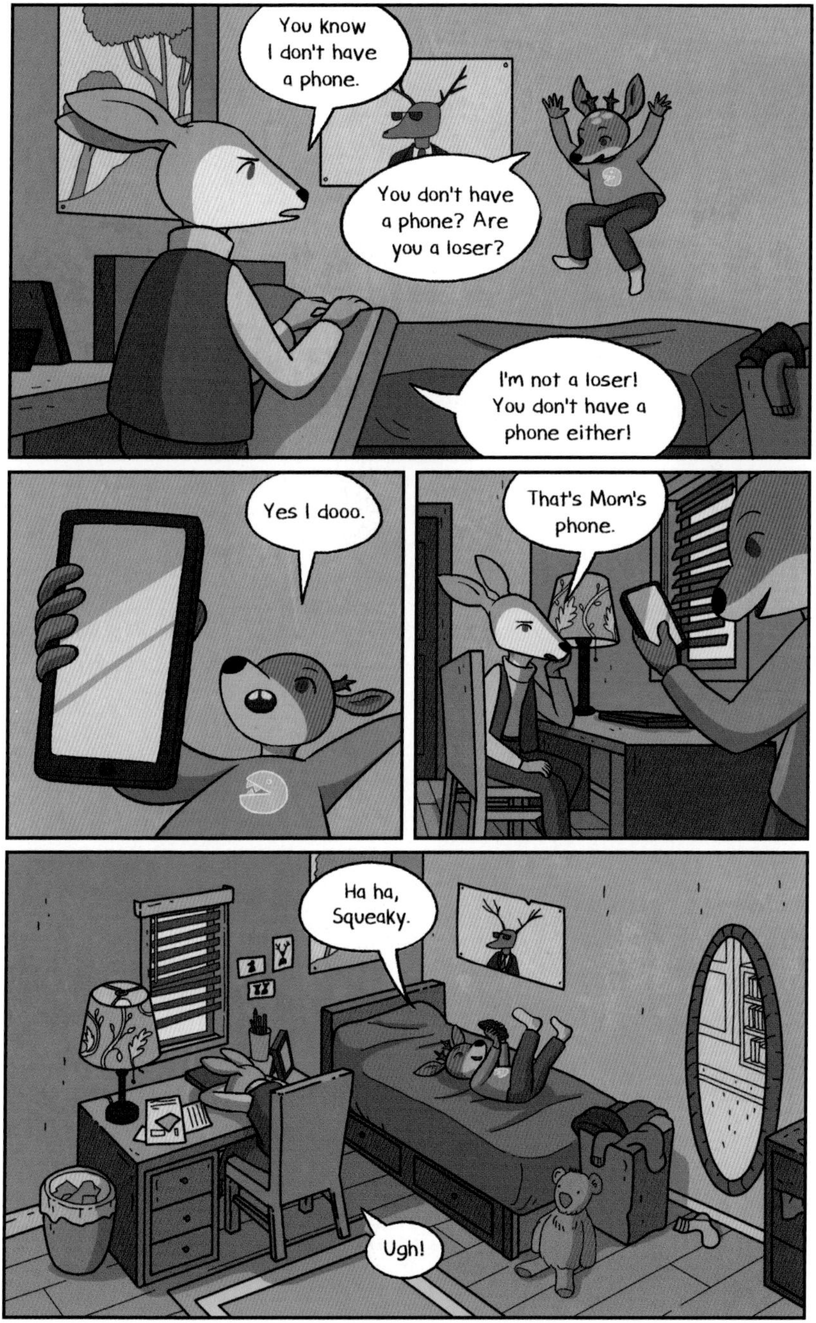
You know I don't have a phone.
You don't have a phone? Are you a loser?
I'm not a loser! You don't have a phone either!
Yes I dooo.
That's Mom's phone.
Ha ha, Squeaky.
Ugh!

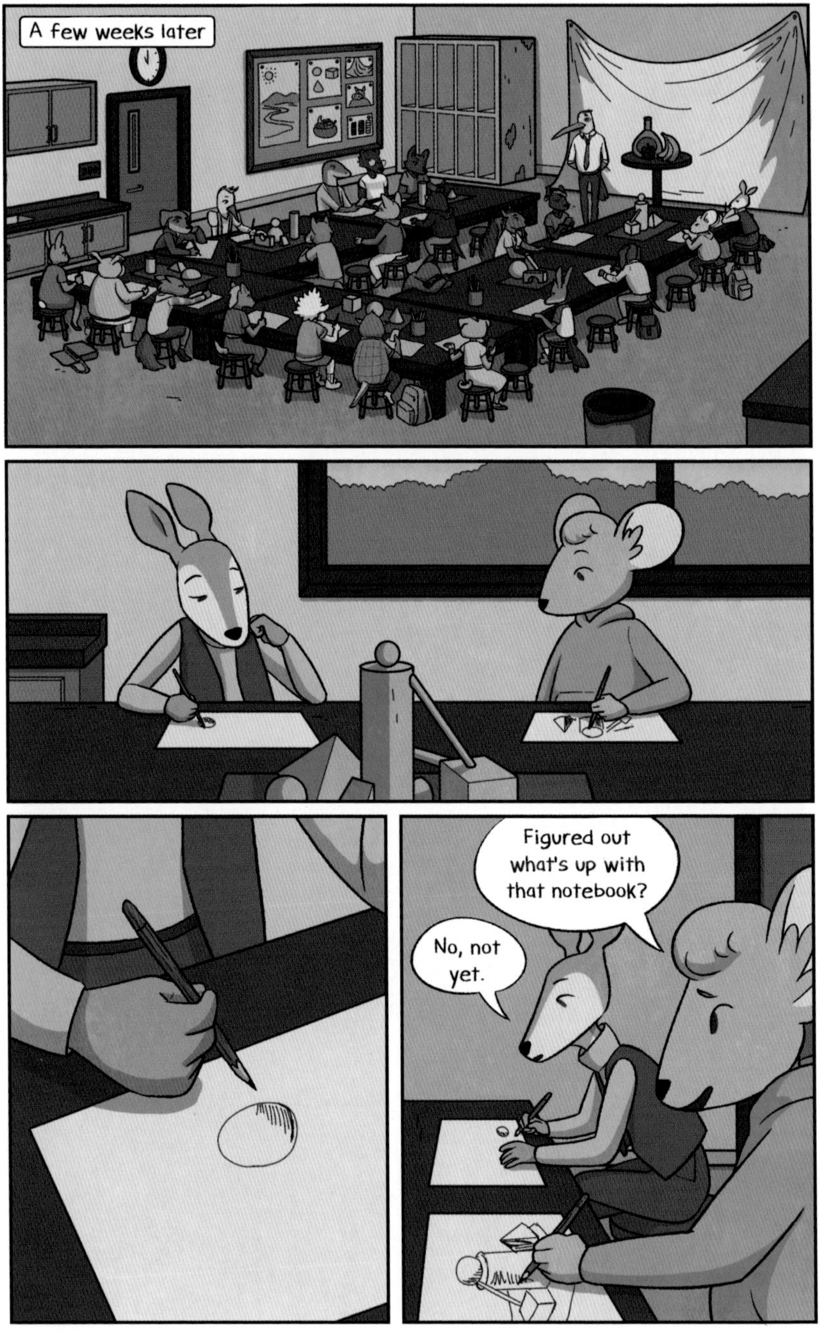

A few weeks later
Figured out what's up with that notebook?
No, not yet.

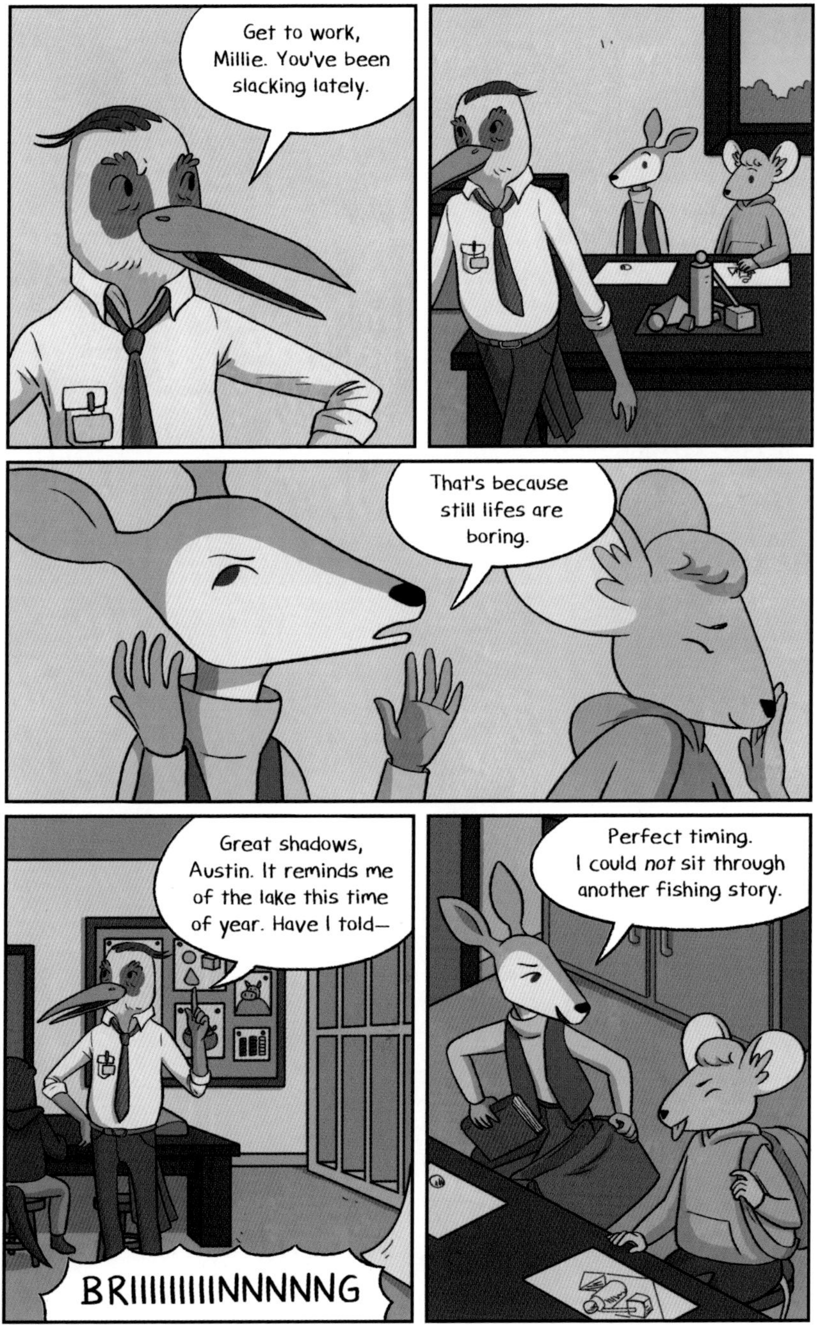
Get to work, Millie. You've been slacking lately.
That's because still lifes are boring.
Great shadows, Austin. It reminds me of the lake this time of year. Have I told—
BRIIIIIIIIINNNNNG
Perfect timing. I could *not* sit through another fishing story.

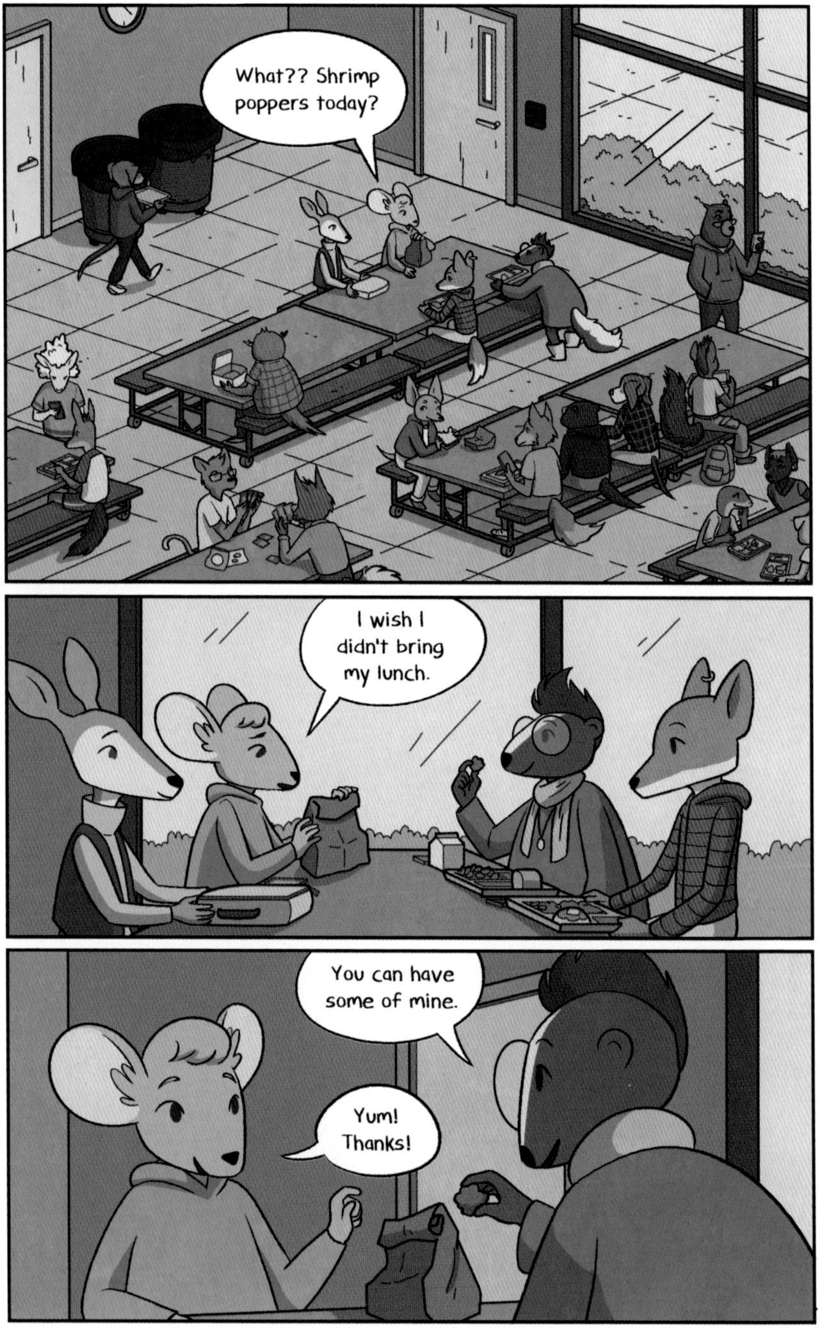
What?? Shrimp poppers today?
I wish I didn't bring my lunch.
You can have some of mine.
Yum! Thanks!

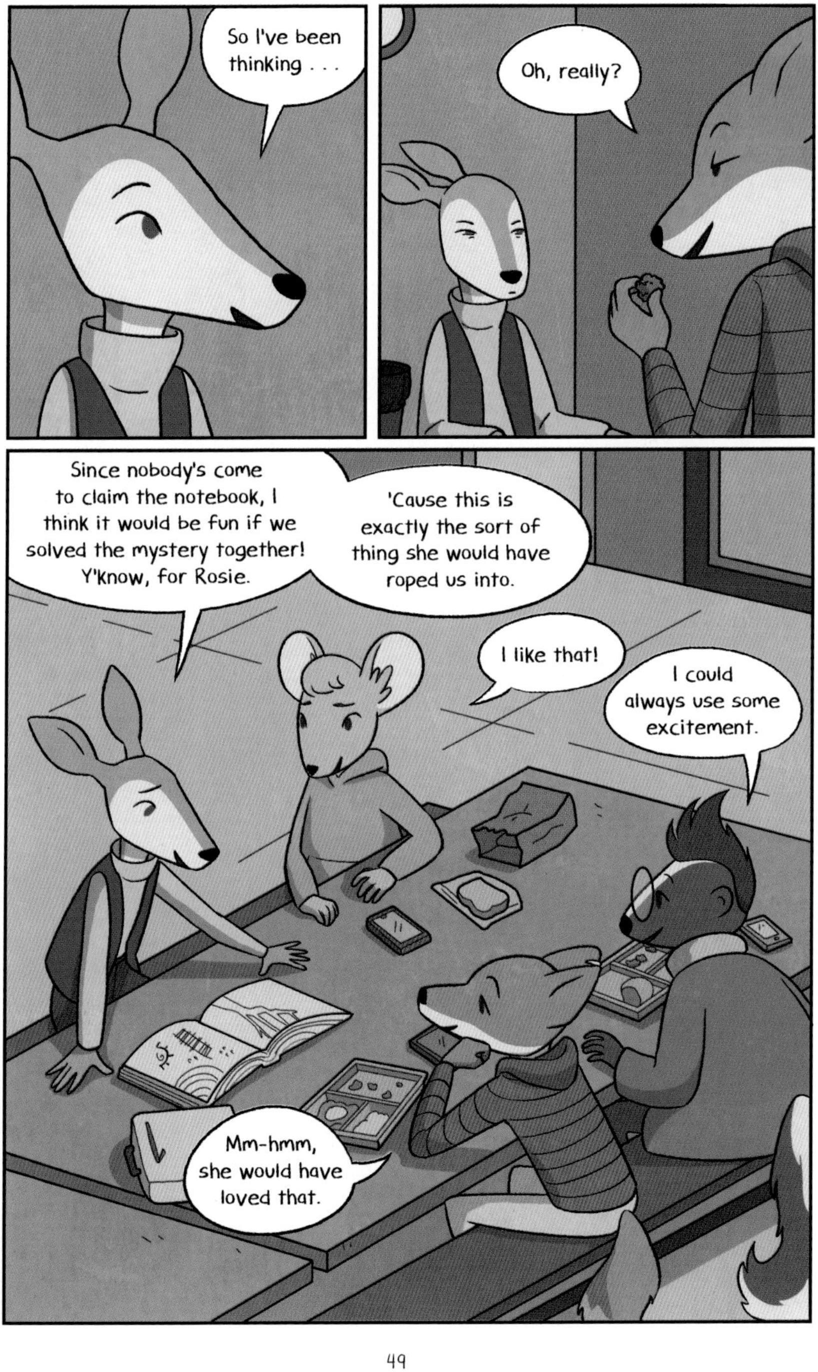
So I've been thinking . . .
Oh, really?
Since nobody's come to claim the notebook, I think it would be fun if we solved the mystery together! Y'know, for Rosie.
'Cause this is exactly the sort of thing she would have roped us into.
I like that!
I could always use some excitement.
Mm-hmm, she would have loved that.

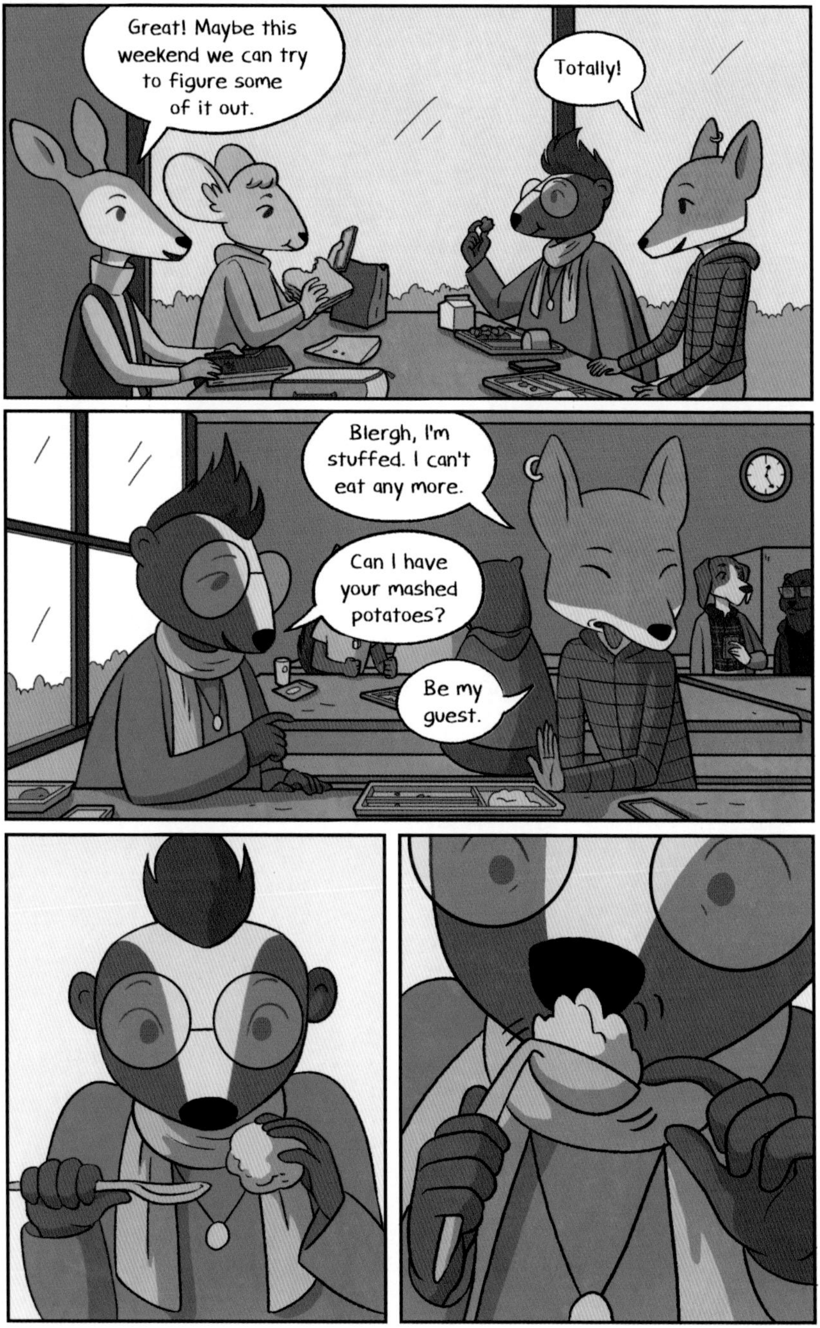
Great! Maybe this weekend we can try to figure some of it out.
Totally!
Blergh, I'm stuffed. I can't eat any more.
Can I have your mashed potatoes?
Be my guest.

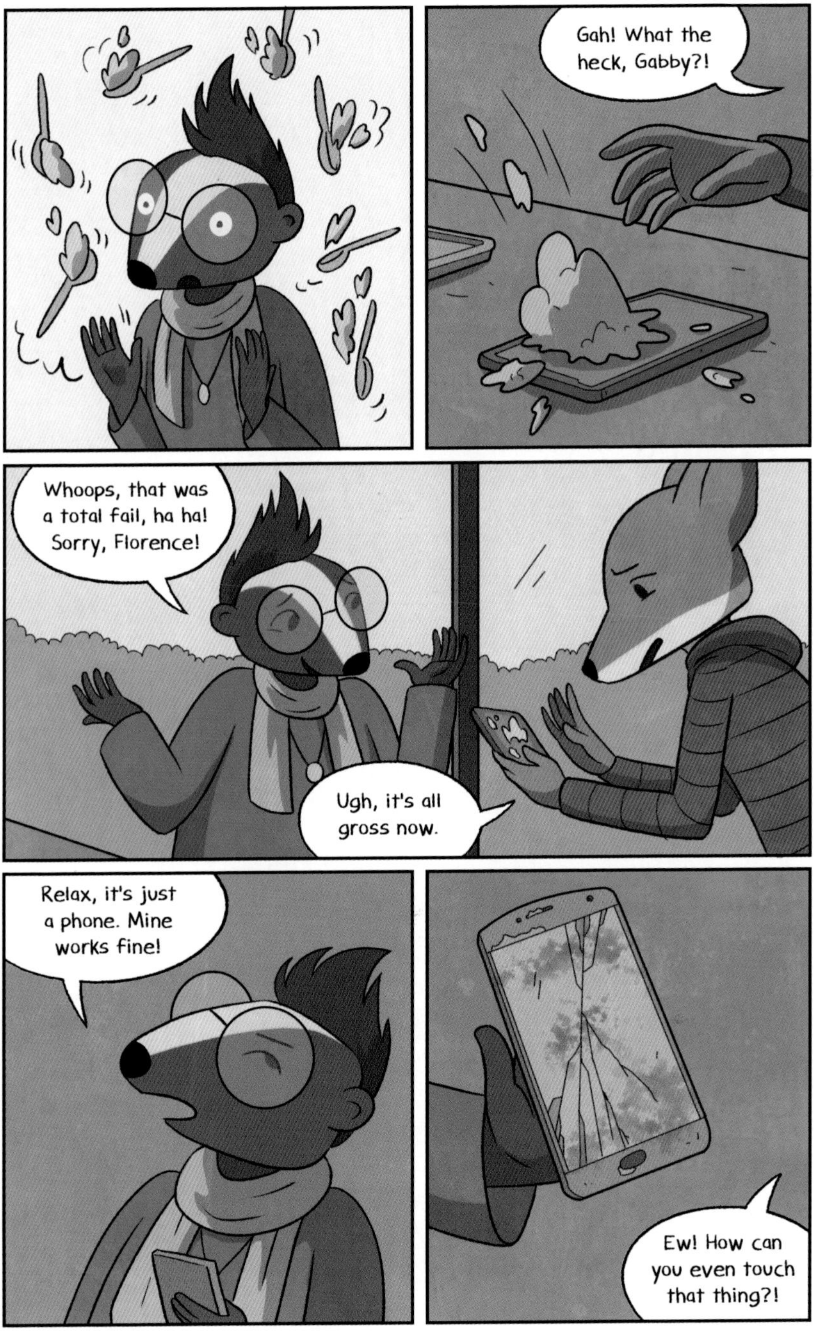
Gah! What the heck, Gabby?!
Whoops, that was a total fail, ha ha! Sorry, Florence!
Ugh, it's all gross now.
Relax, it's just a phone. Mine works fine!
Ew! How can you even touch that thing?!

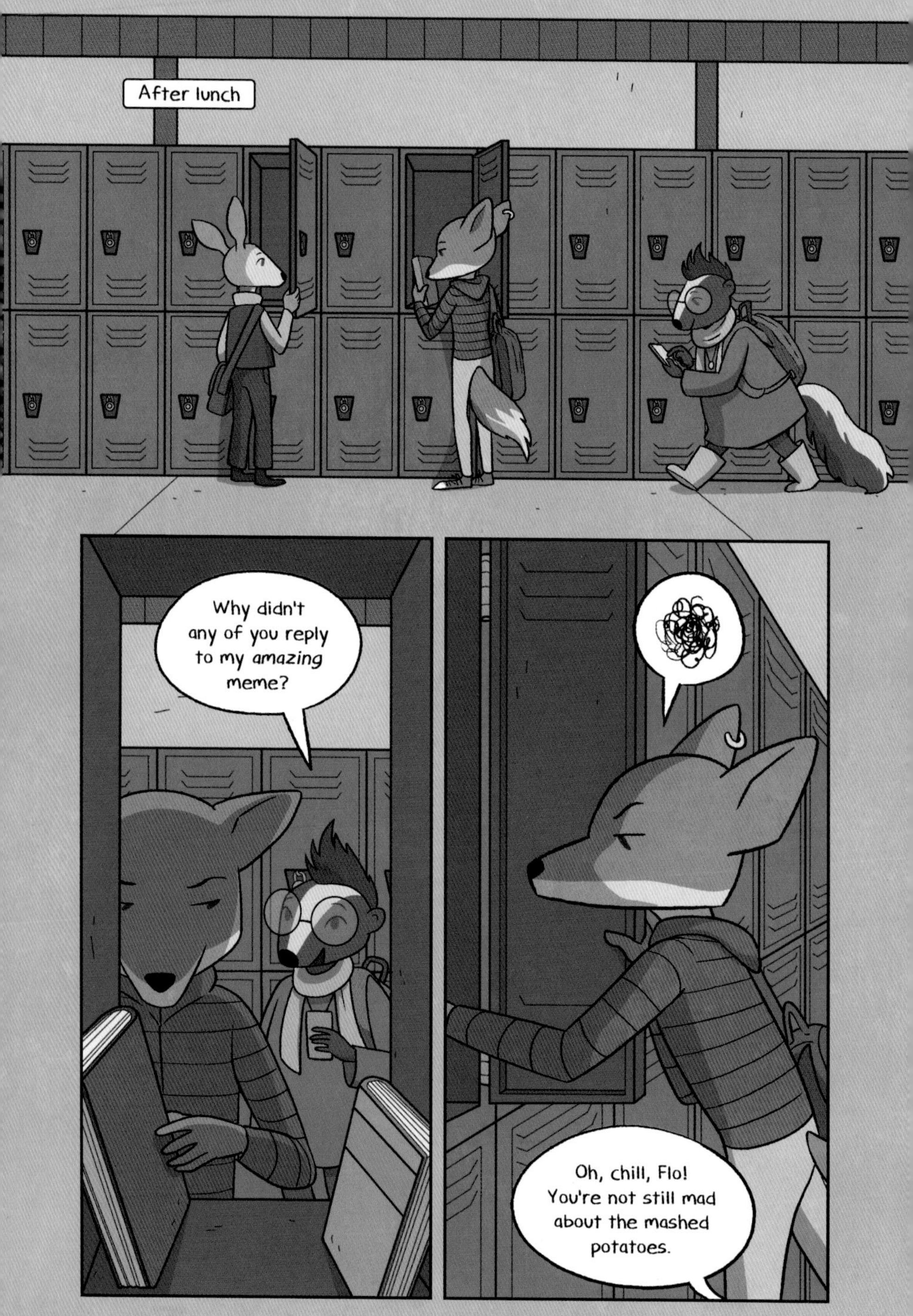
After lunch
Why didn't any of you reply to my amazing meme?
Oh, chill, Flo! You're not still mad about the mashed potatoes.

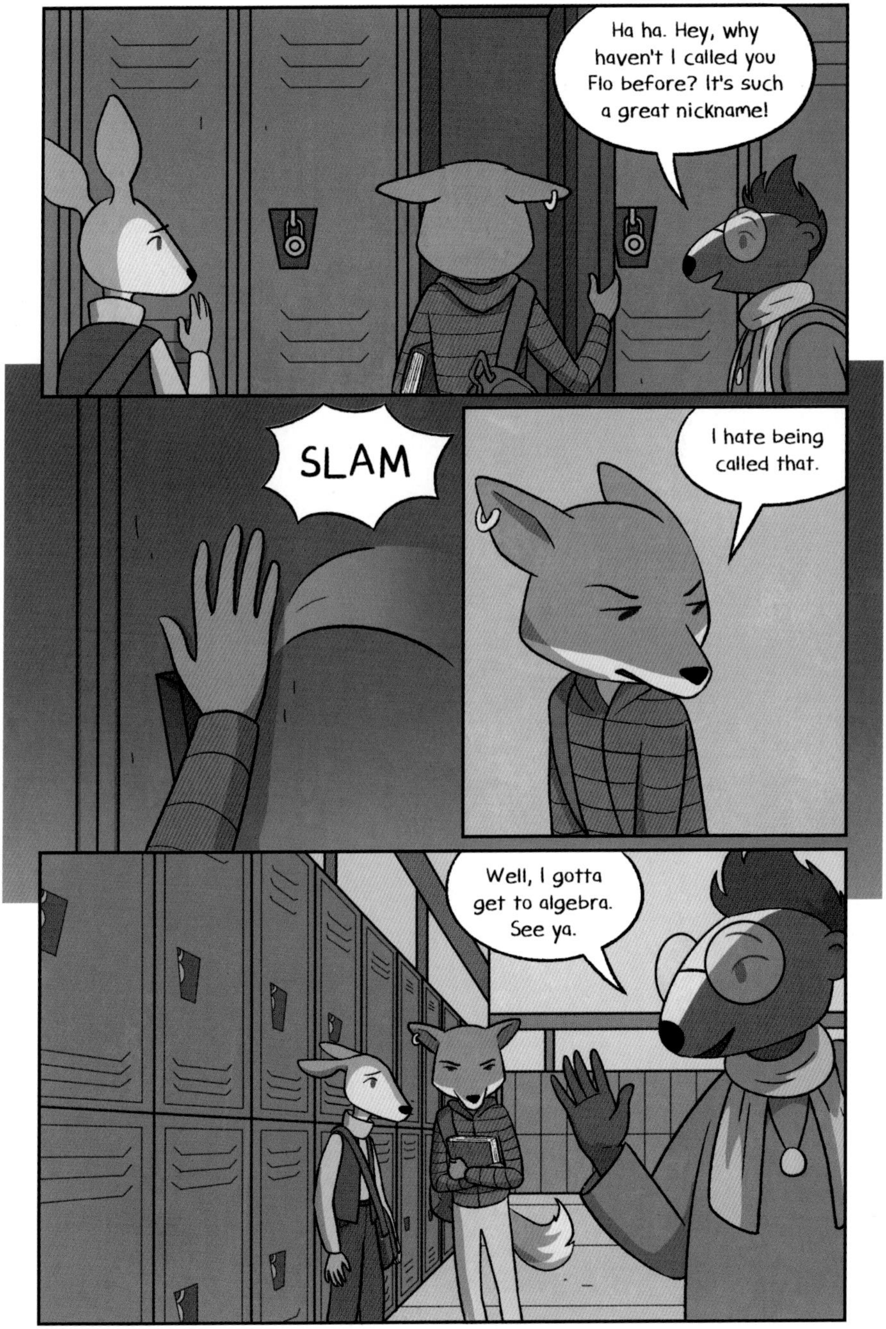

Ha ha. Hey, why haven't I called you Flo before? It's such a great nickname!
SLAM
I hate being called that.
Well, I gotta get to algebra. See ya.

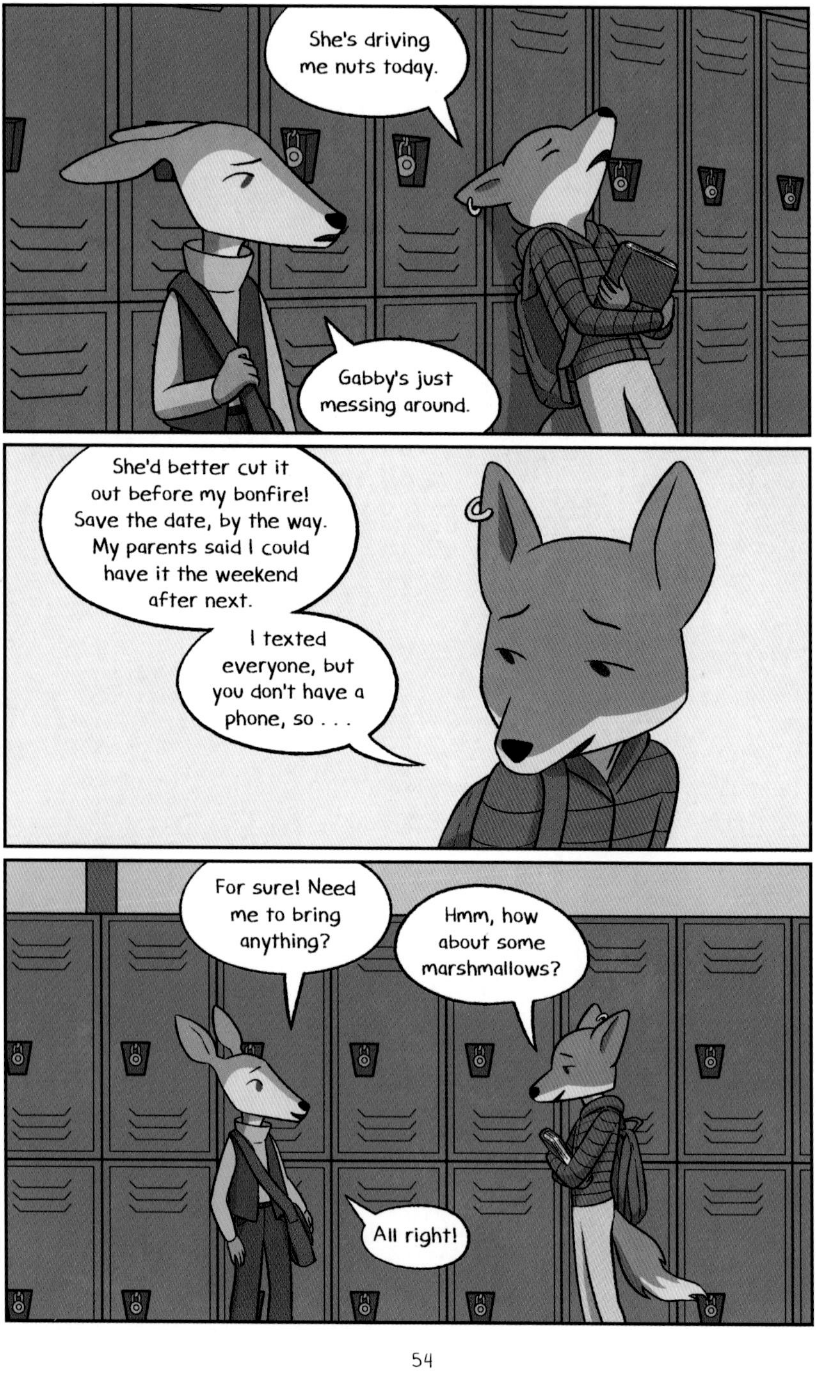
She's driving me nuts today.
Gabby's just messing around.
She'd better cut it out before my bonfire! Save the date, by the way. My parents said I could have it the weekend after next.
I texted everyone, but you don't have a phone, so . . .
For sure! Need me to bring anything?
Hmm, how about some marshmallows?
All right!

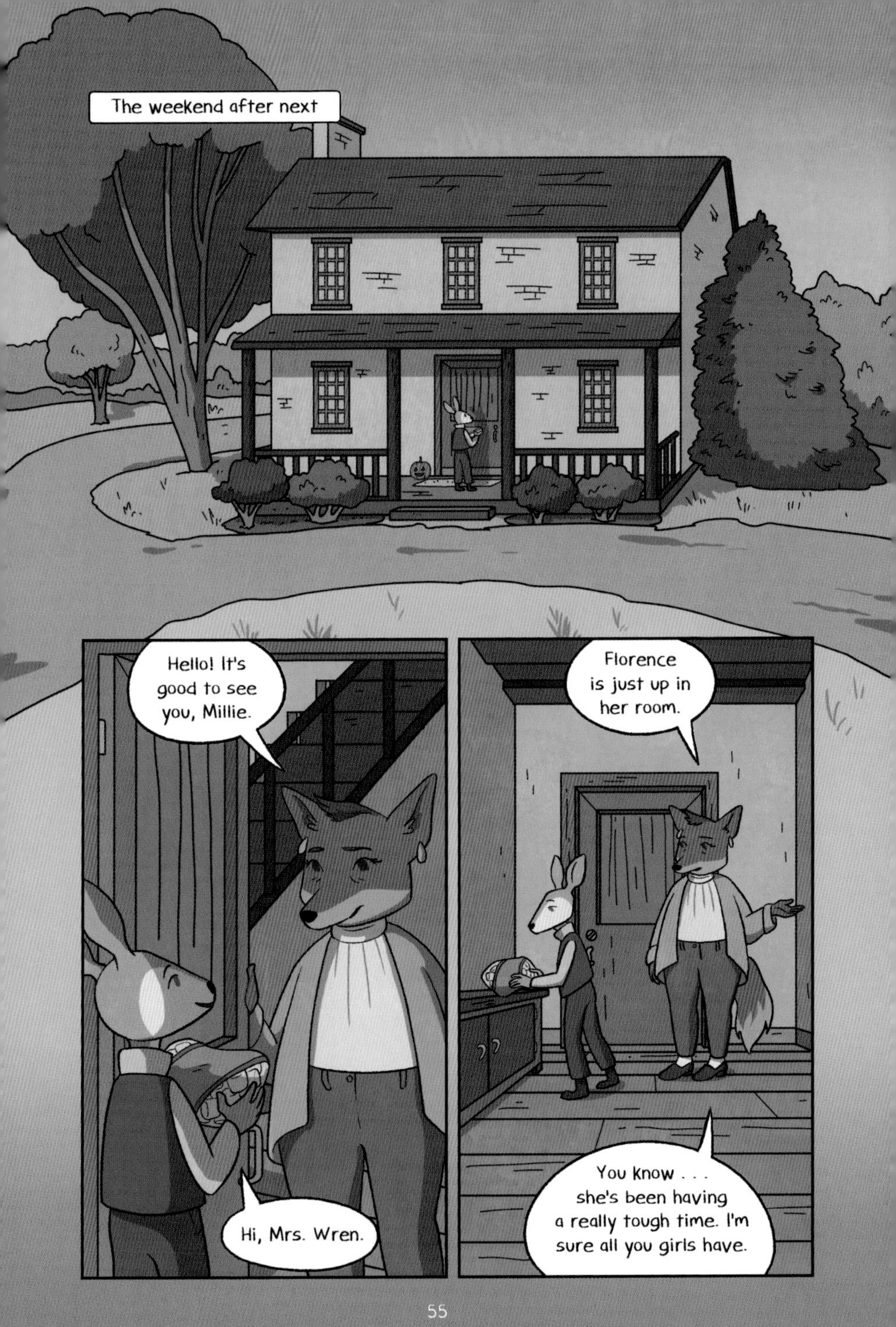
The weekend after next
Hello! It's good to see you, Millie.
Hi, Mrs. Wren.
Florence is just up in her room.
You know . . . she's been having a really tough time. I'm sure all you girls have.

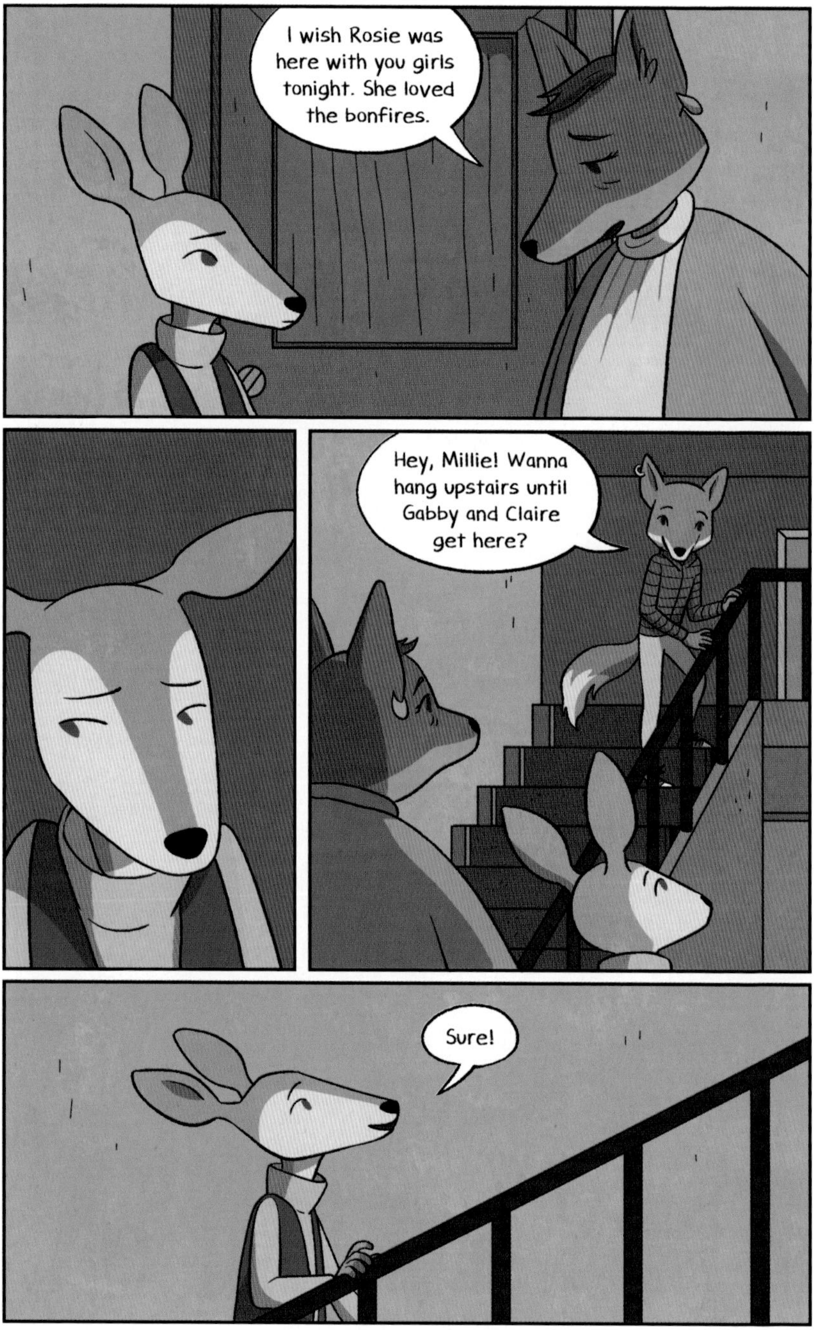
I wish Rosie was here with you girls tonight. She loved the bonfires.
Hey, Millie! Wanna hang upstairs until Gabby and Claire get here?
Sure!

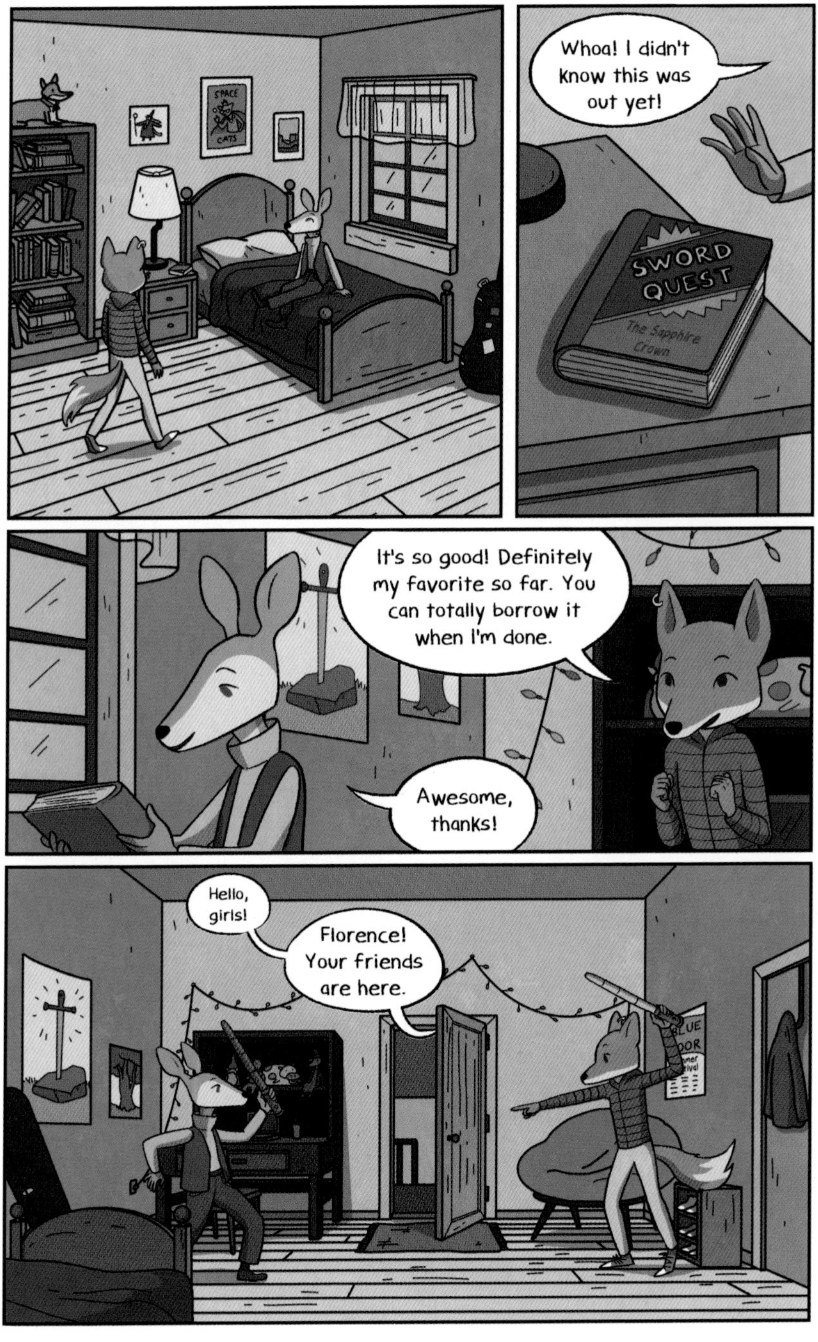
SPACE CATS
Whoa! I didn't know this was out yet!
SWORD QUEST
The Sapphire Crown
It's so good! Definitely my favorite so far. You can totally borrow it when I'm done.
Awesome, thanks!
Hello, girls!
Florence! Your friends are here.

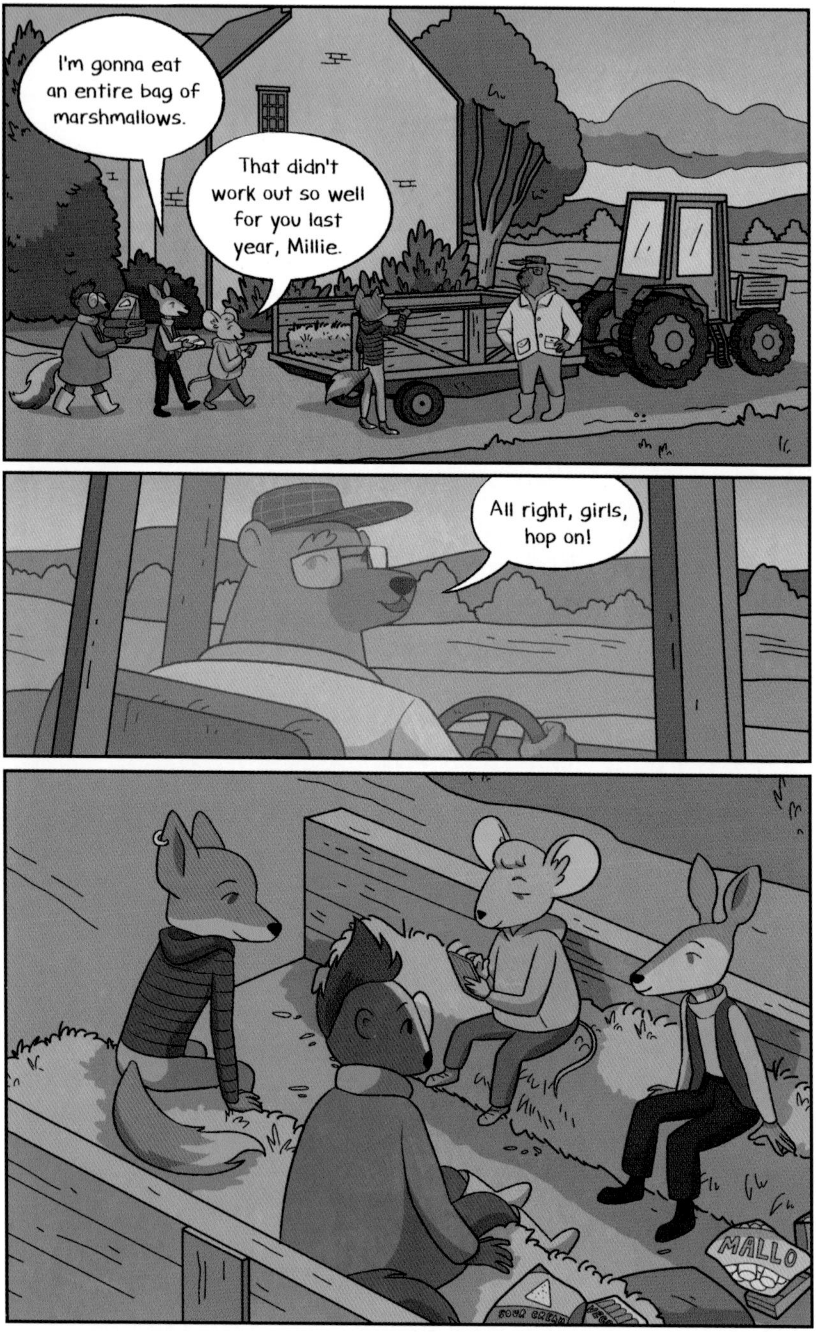
I'm gonna eat an entire bag of marshmallows.
That didn't work out so well for you last year, Millie.
All right, girls, hop on!
MALLO
SOUR CREAM

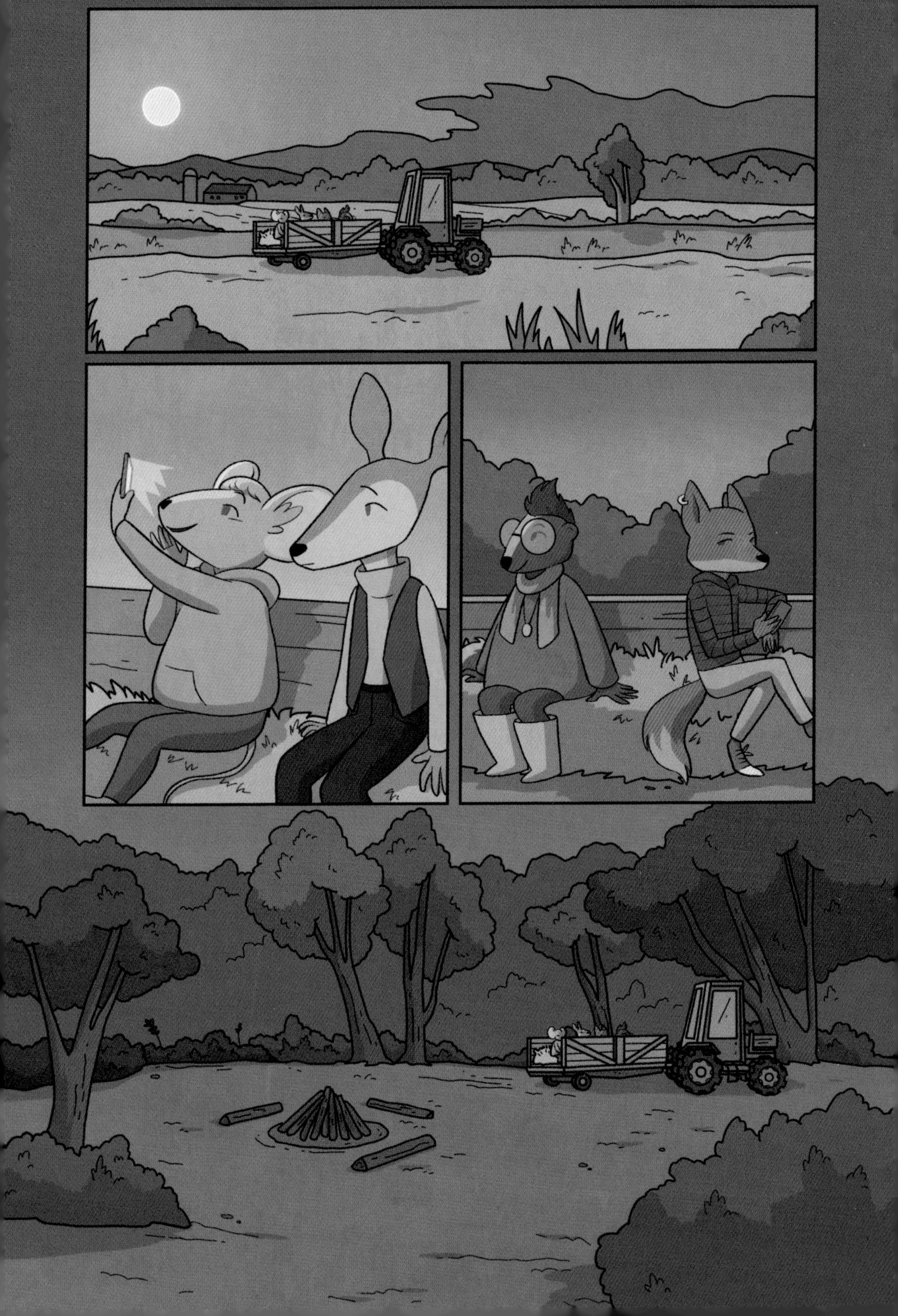

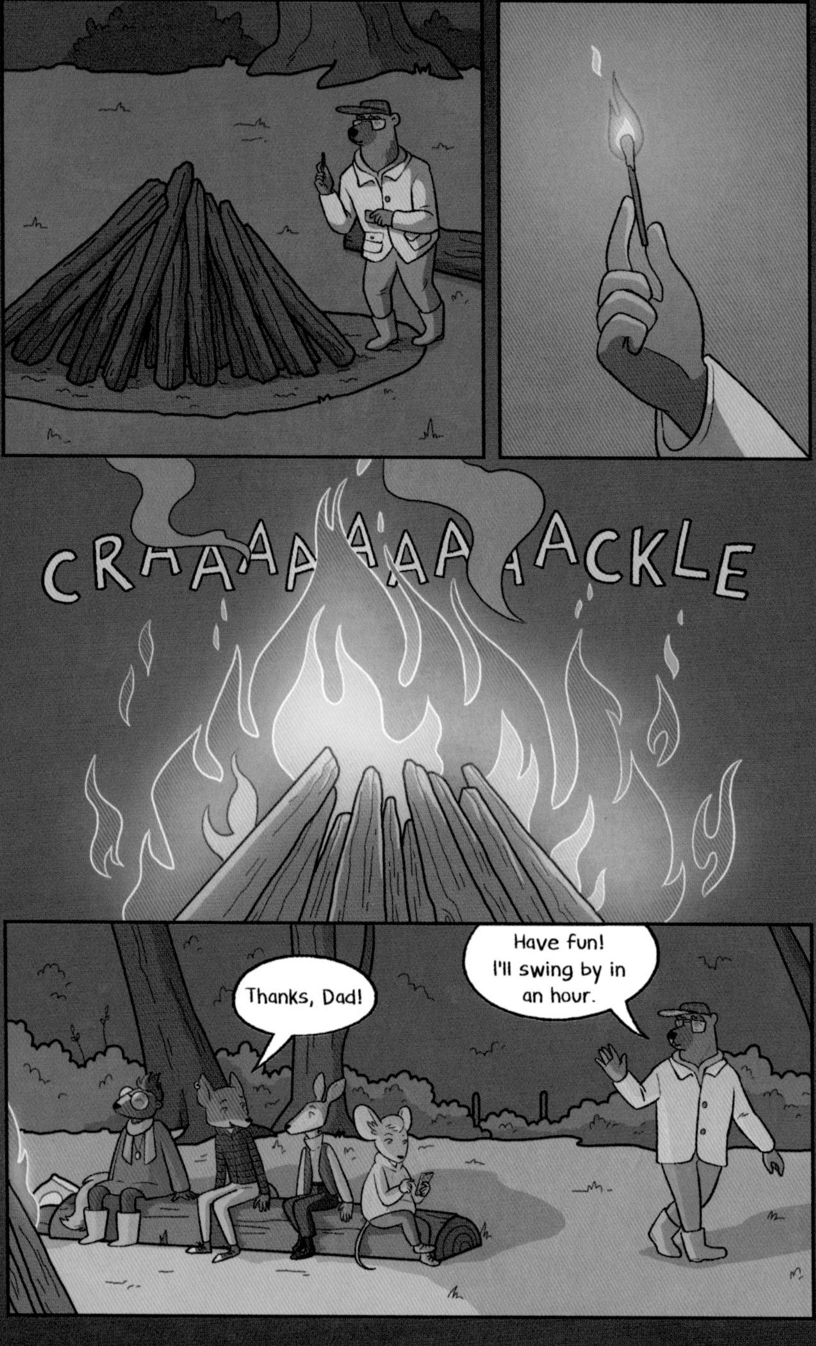
CRAAAAAAAACKLE
Thanks, Dad!
Have fun!
I'll swing by in
an hour.

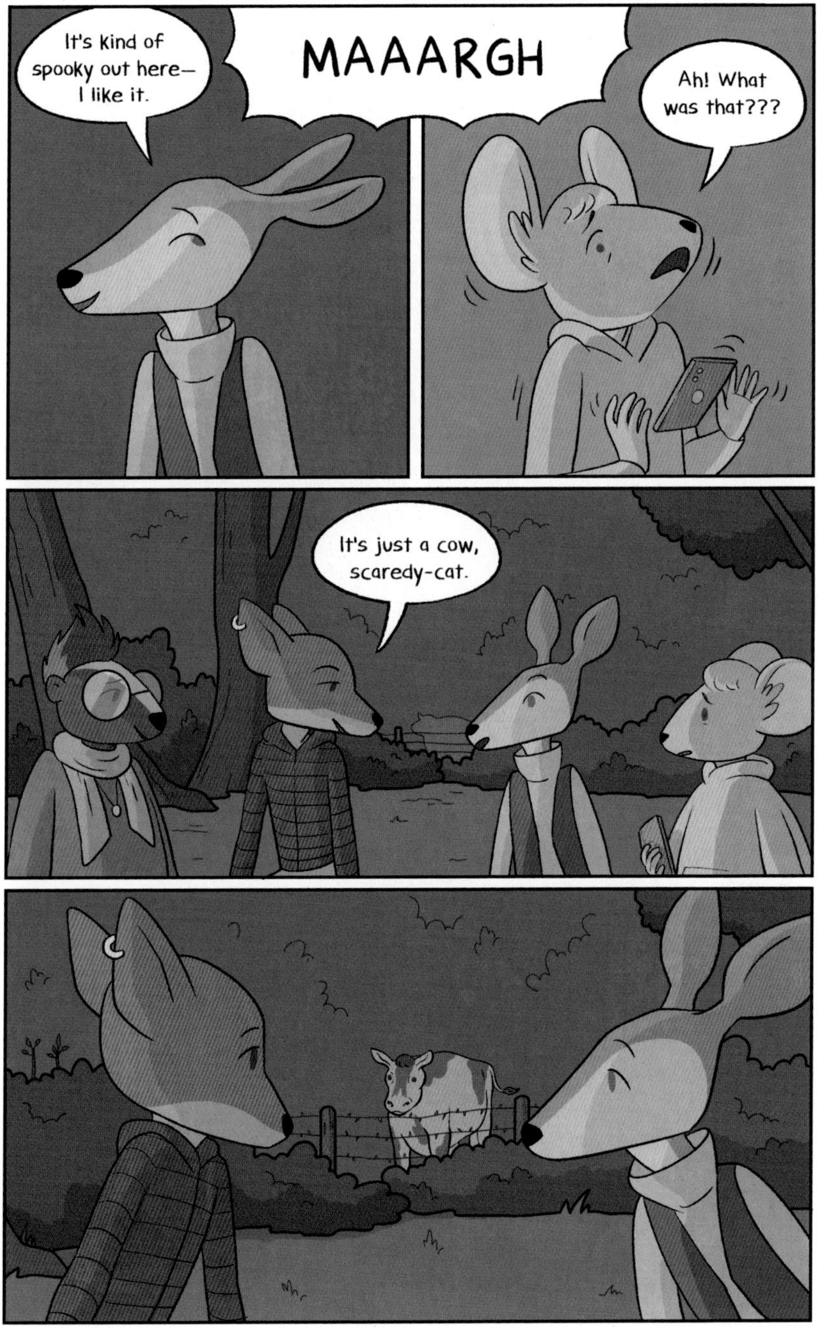
It's kind of spooky out here— I like it.
MAAARGH
Ah! What was that???
It's just a cow, scaredy-cat.

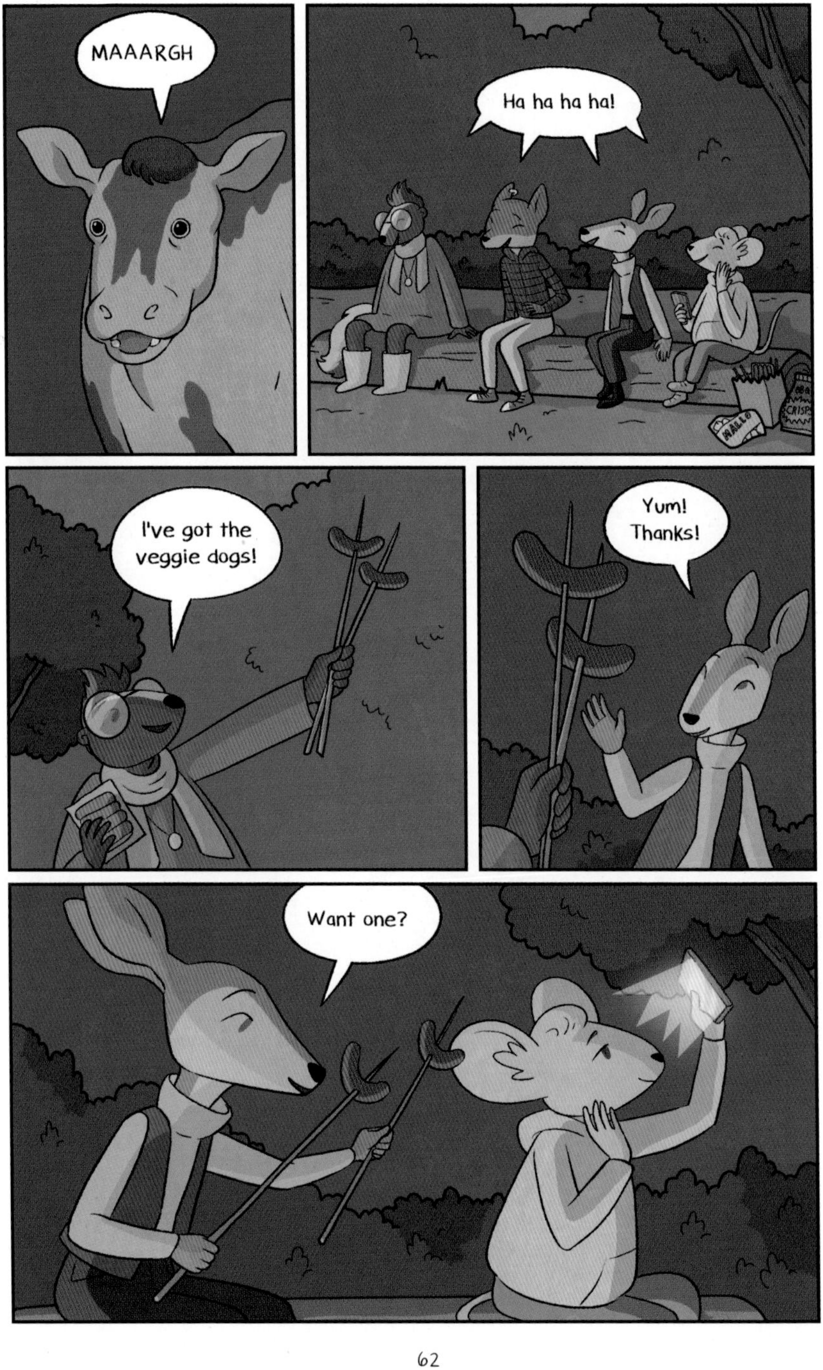
MAAARGH
Ha ha ha ha!
MALLO
CRISPS
I've got the veggie dogs!
Yum! Thanks!
Want one?

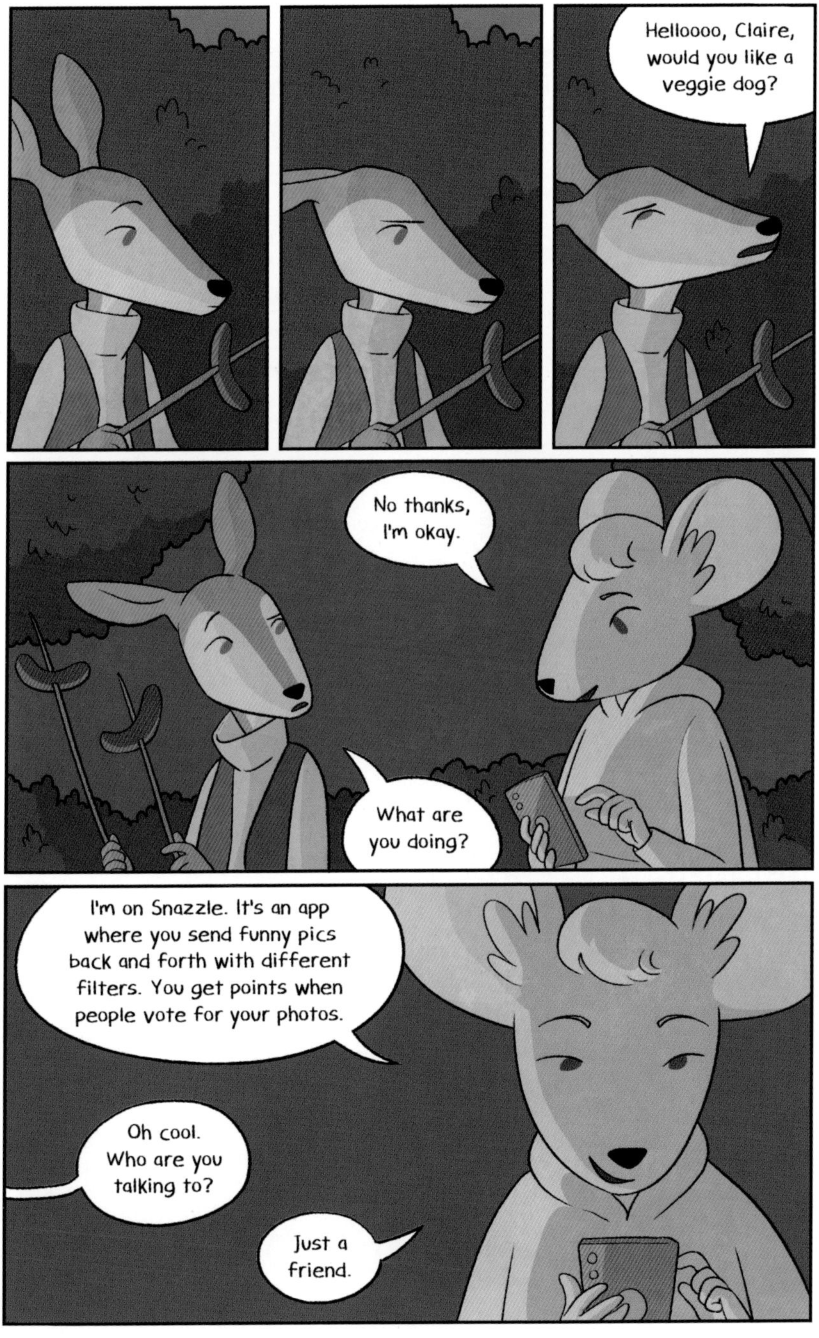
Helloooo, Claire, would you like a veggie dog?
No thanks, I'm okay.
What are you doing?
I'm on Snazzle. It's an app where you send funny pics back and forth with different filters. You get points when people vote for your photos.
Oh cool. Who are you talking to?
Just a friend.

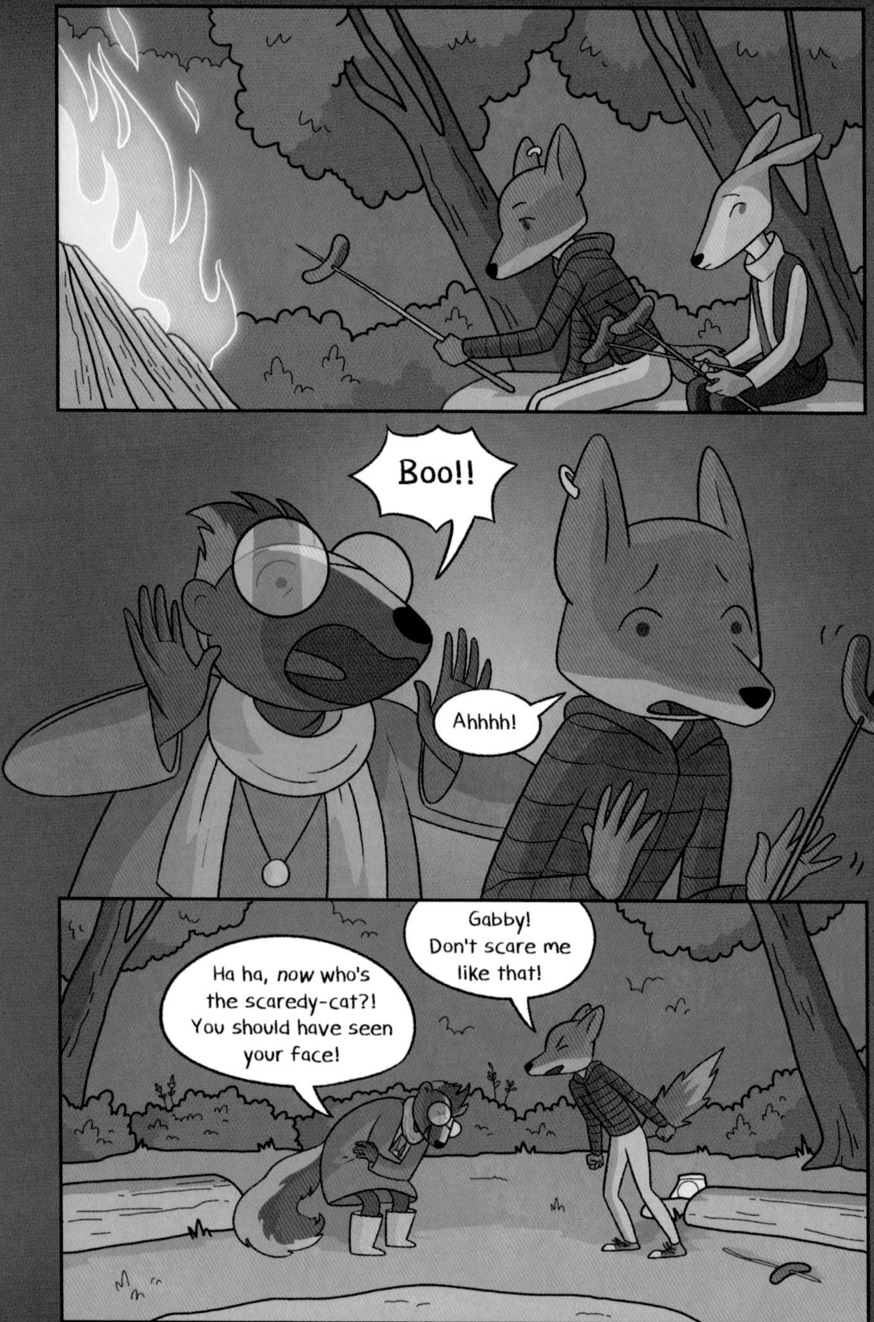
Boo!!
Ahhhh!
Ha ha, *now* who's the scaredy-cat?! You should have seen your face!
Gabby! Don't scare me like that!

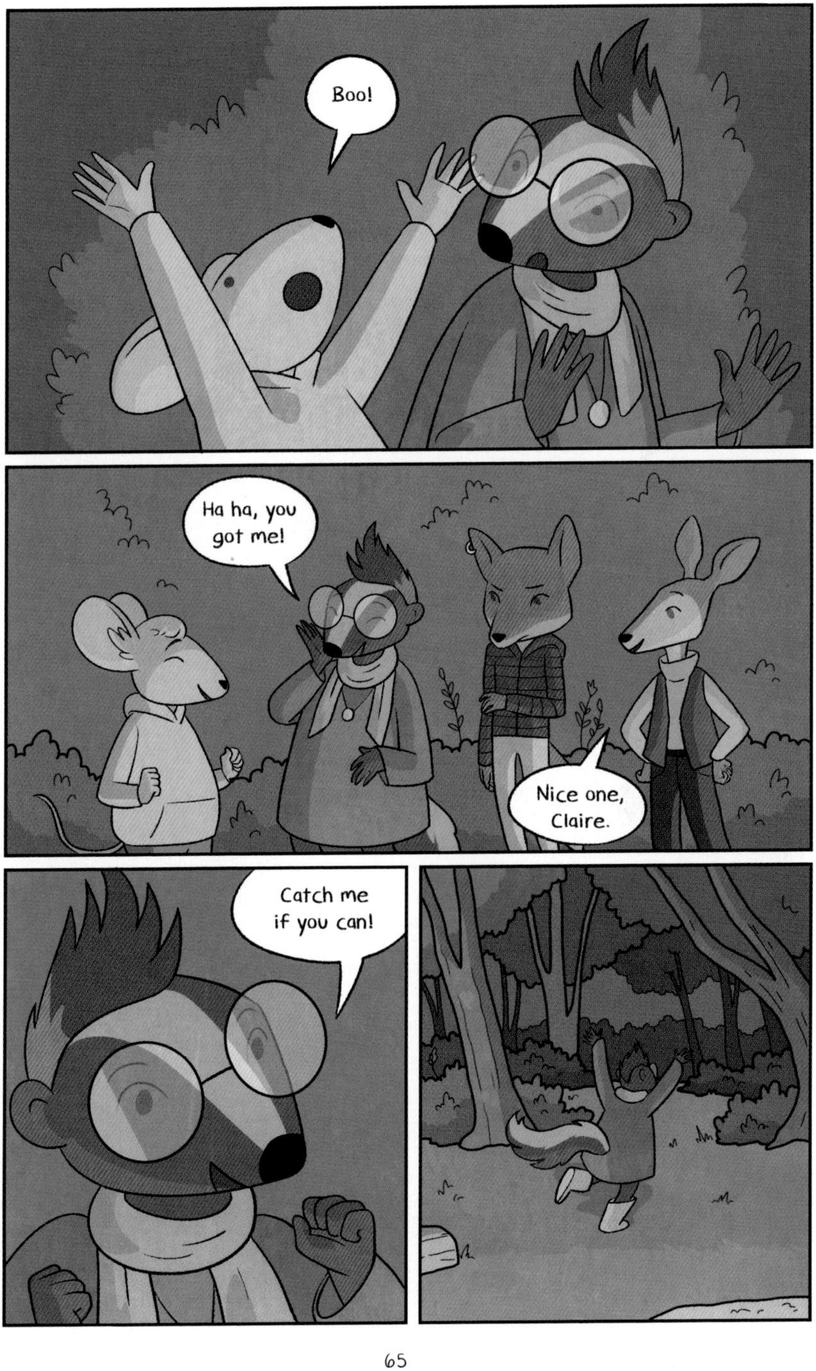
Boo!
Ha ha, you got me!
Nice one, Claire.
Catch me if you can!

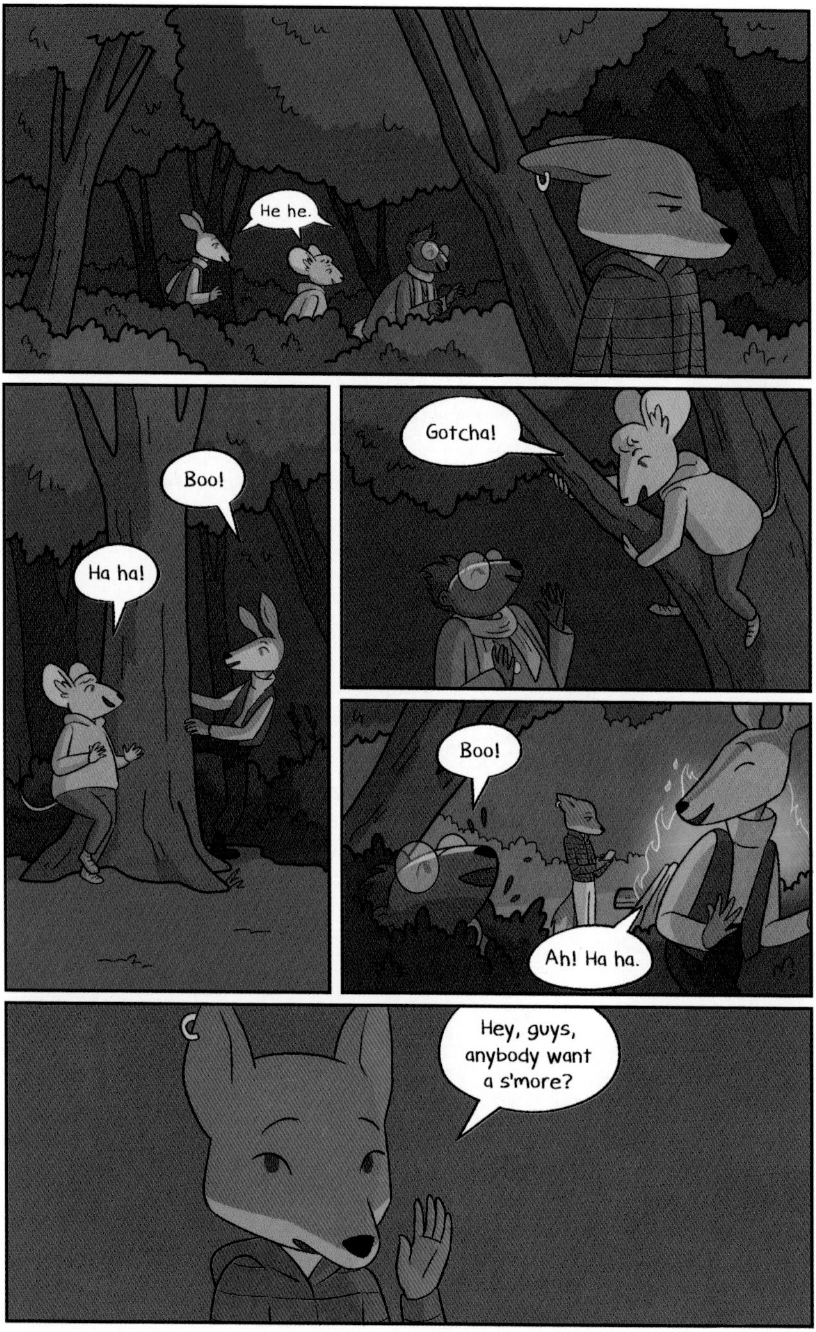
He he.
Boo!
Ha ha!
Gotcha!
Boo!
Ah! Ha ha.
Hey, guys, anybody want a s'more?

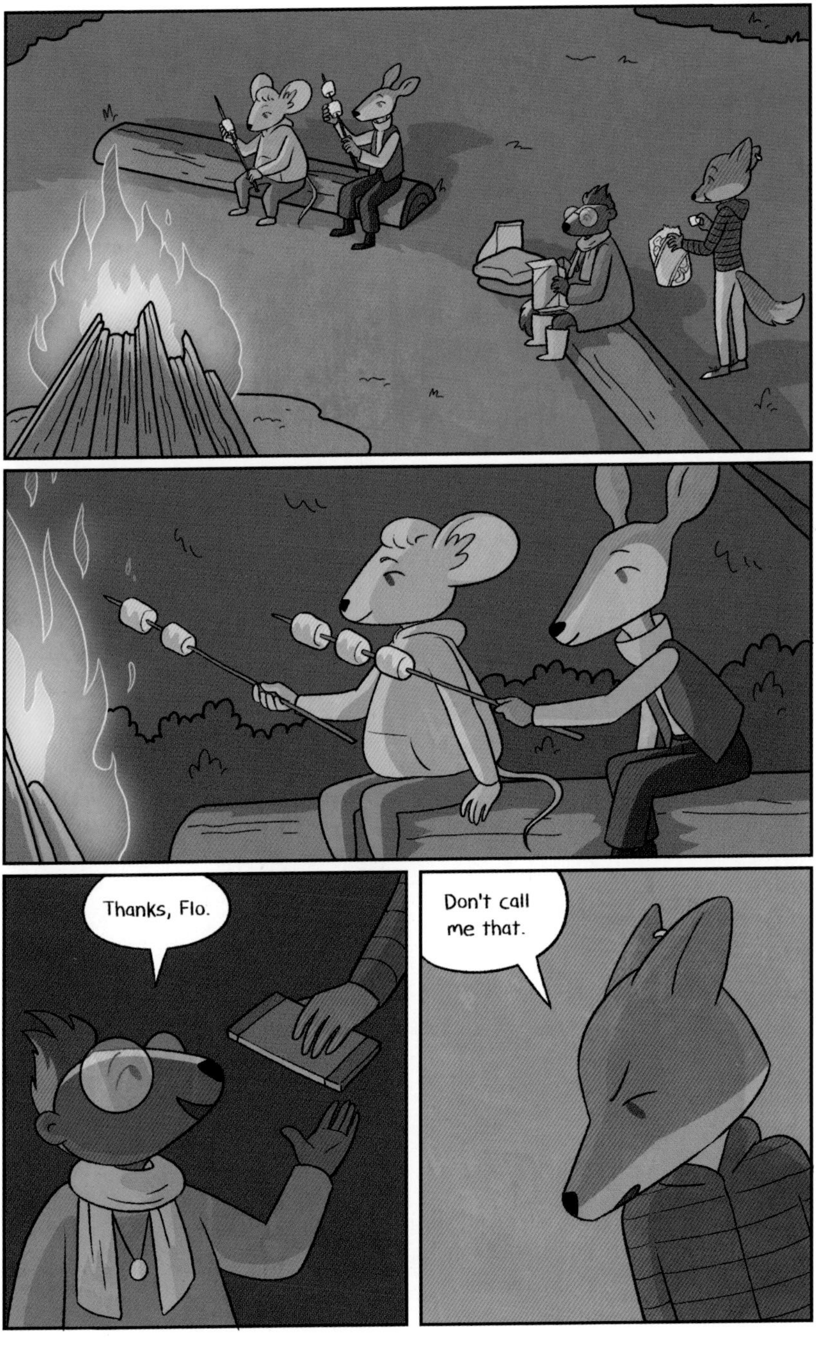
Thanks, Flo.
Don't call me that.

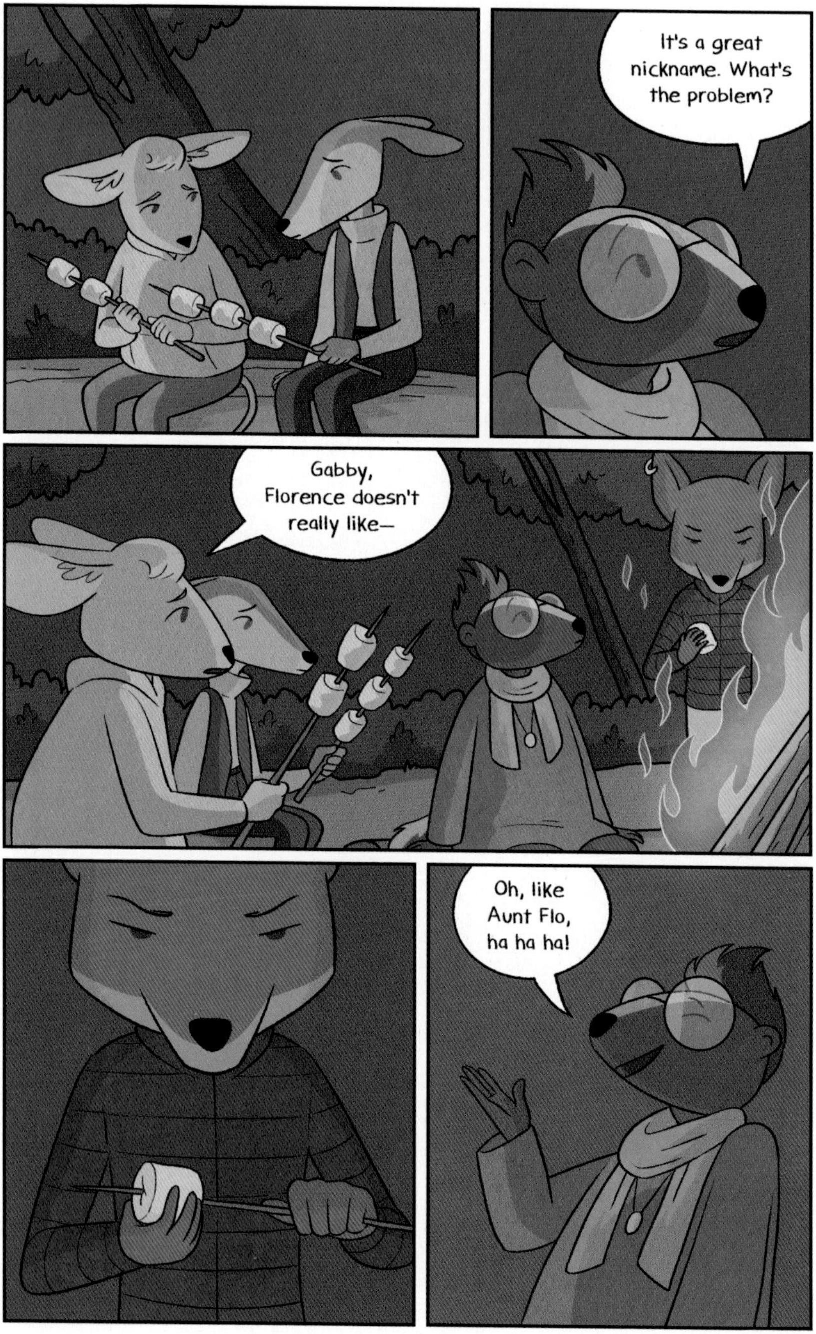

It's a great nickname. What's the problem?
Gabby, Florence doesn't really like—
Oh, like Aunt Flo, ha ha ha!

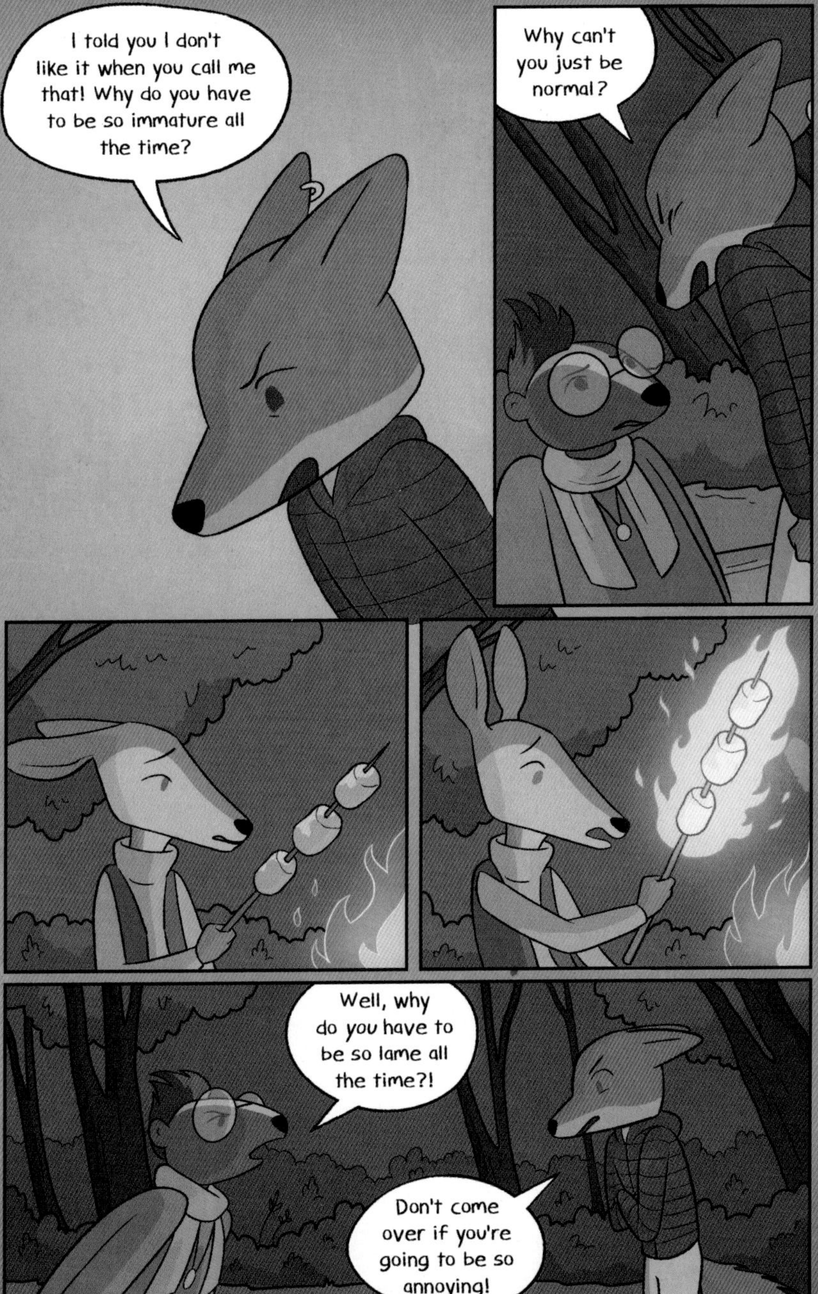
I told you I don't like it when you call me that! Why do you have to be so immature all the time?
Why can't you just be normal?
Well, why do you have to be so lame all the time?!
Don't come over if you're going to be so annoying!

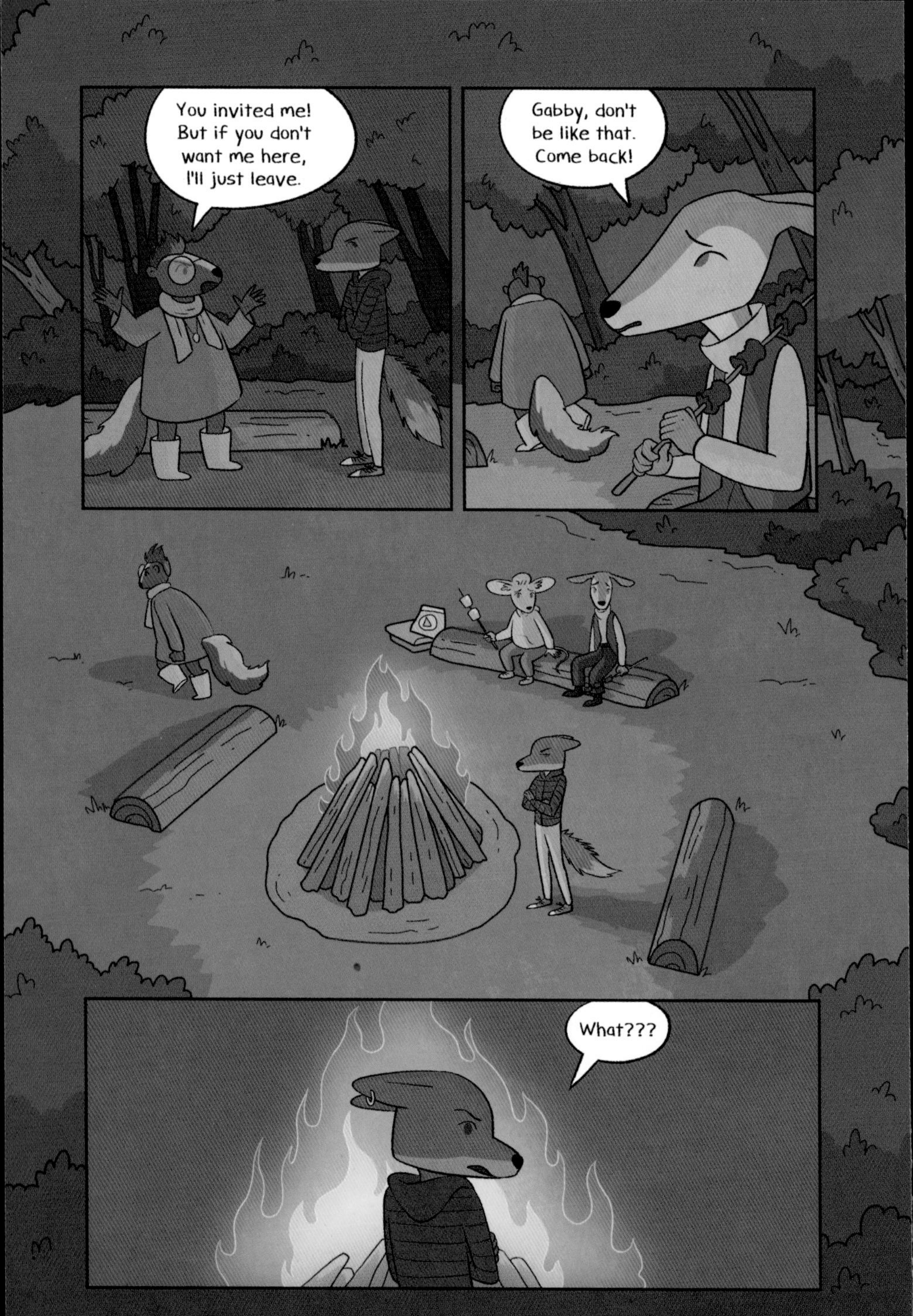
You invited me! But if you don't want me here, I'll just leave.
Gabby, don't be like that. Come back!
What???

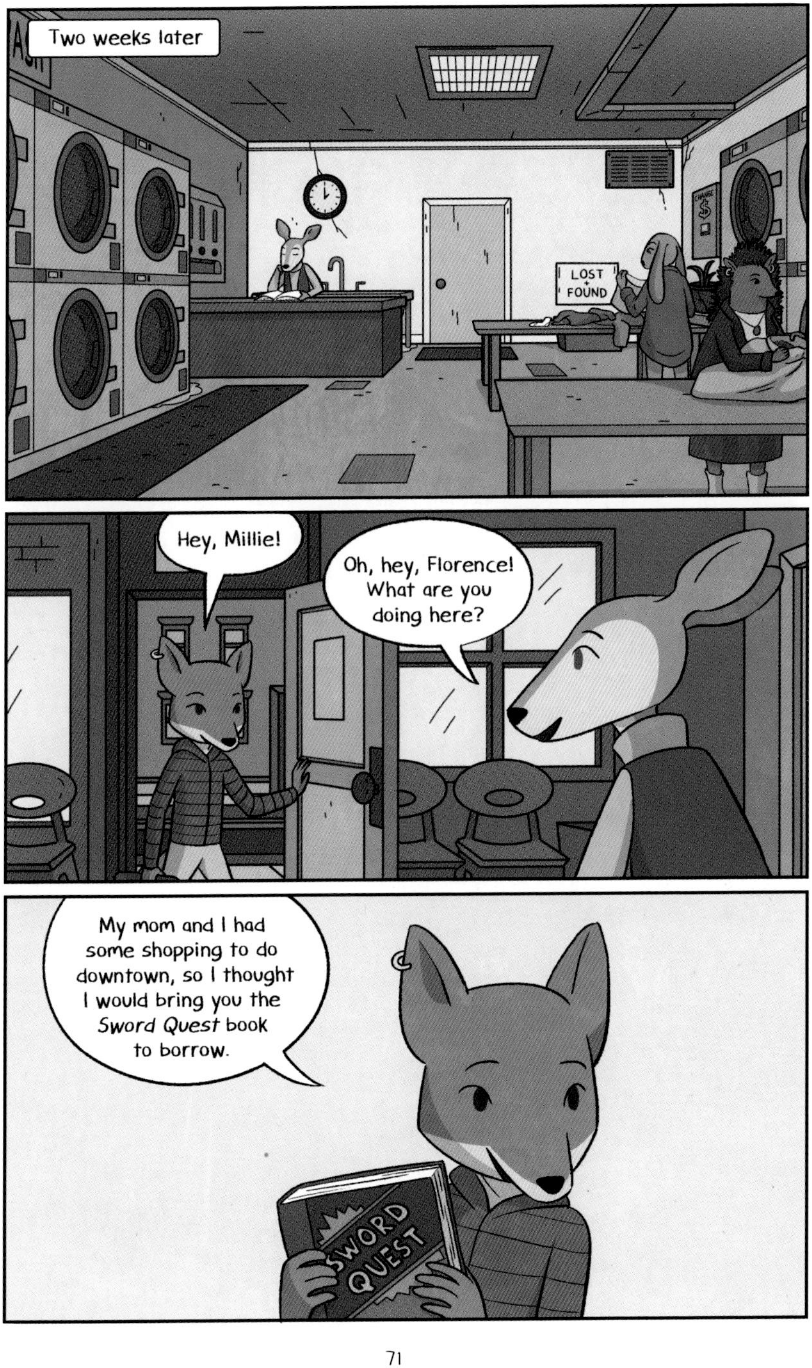

Two weeks later
LOST + FOUND
Hey, Millie!
Oh, hey, Florence! What are you doing here?
My mom and I had some shopping to do downtown, so I thought I would bring you the *Sword Quest* book to borrow.
SWORD QUEST

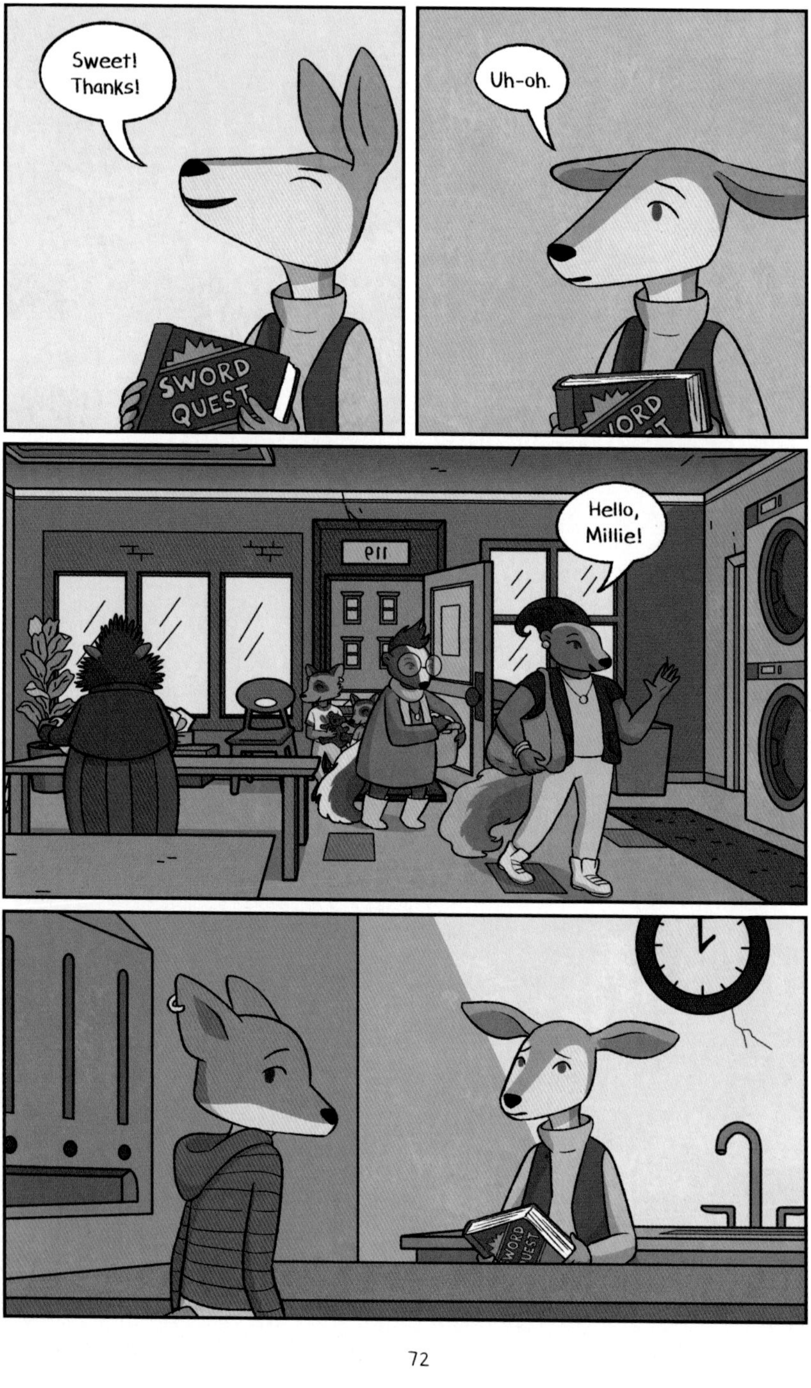
Sweet! Thanks!
SWORD QUEST
Uh-oh.
611
Hello, Millie!
SWORD QUEST

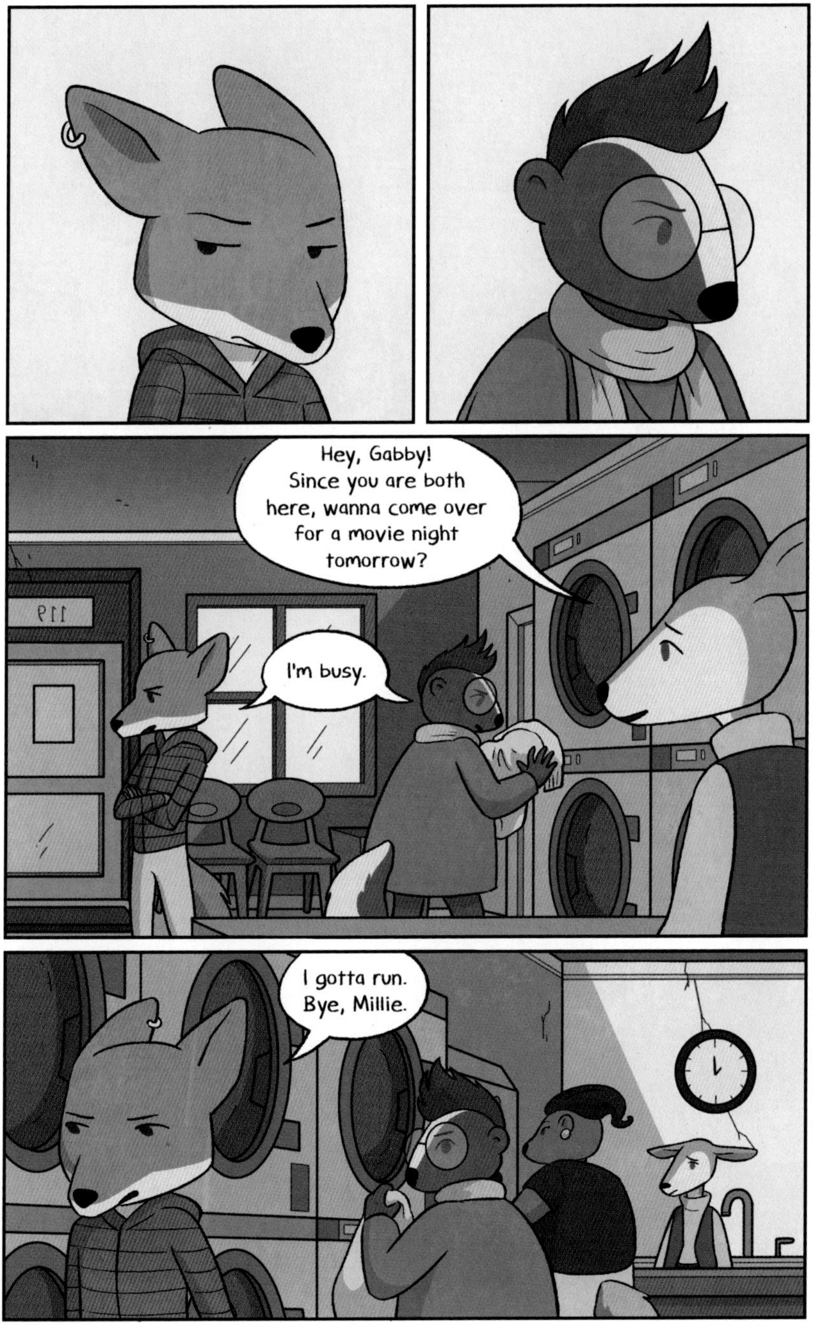
Hey, Gabby!
Since you are both here, wanna come over for a movie night tomorrow?
I'm busy.
I gotta run.
Bye, Millie.

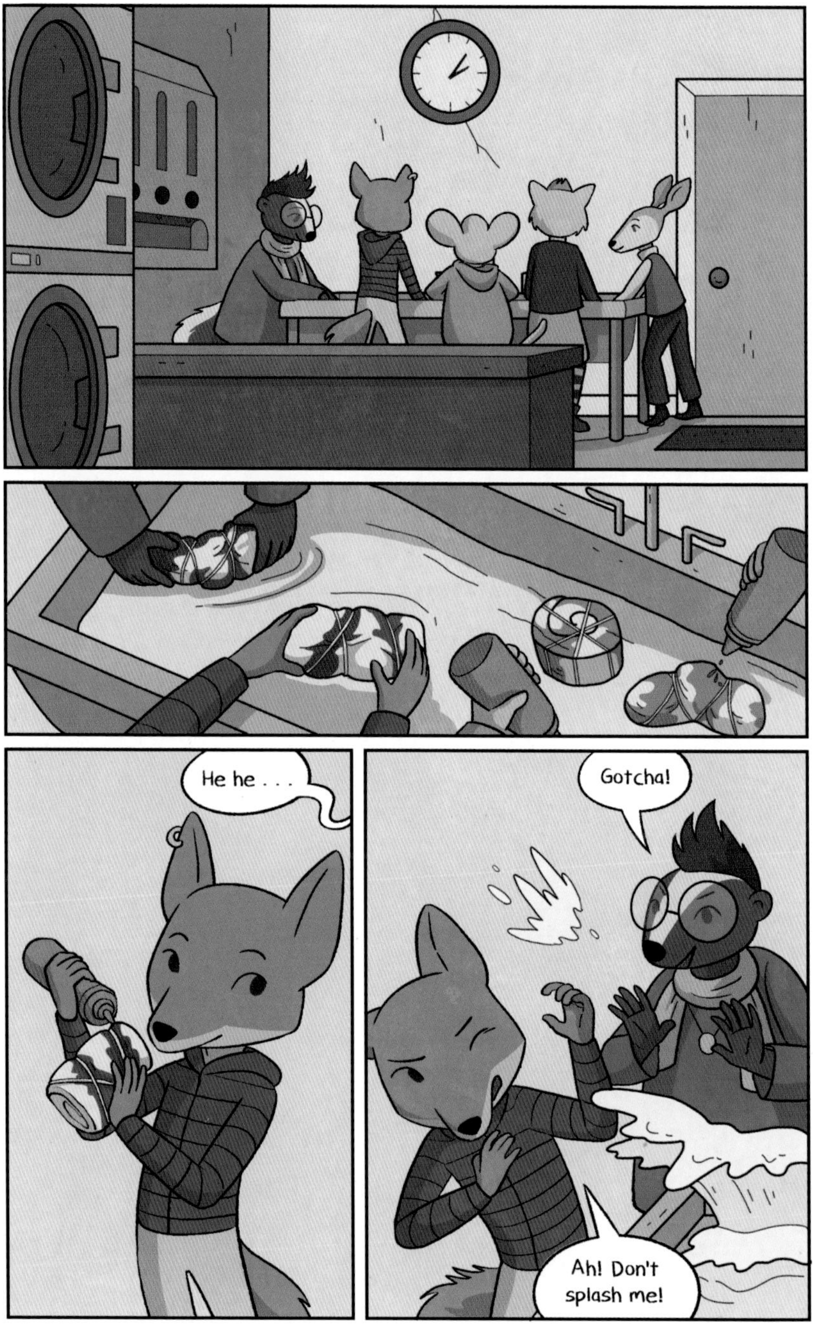
He he . . .
Gotcha!
Ah! Don't splash me!

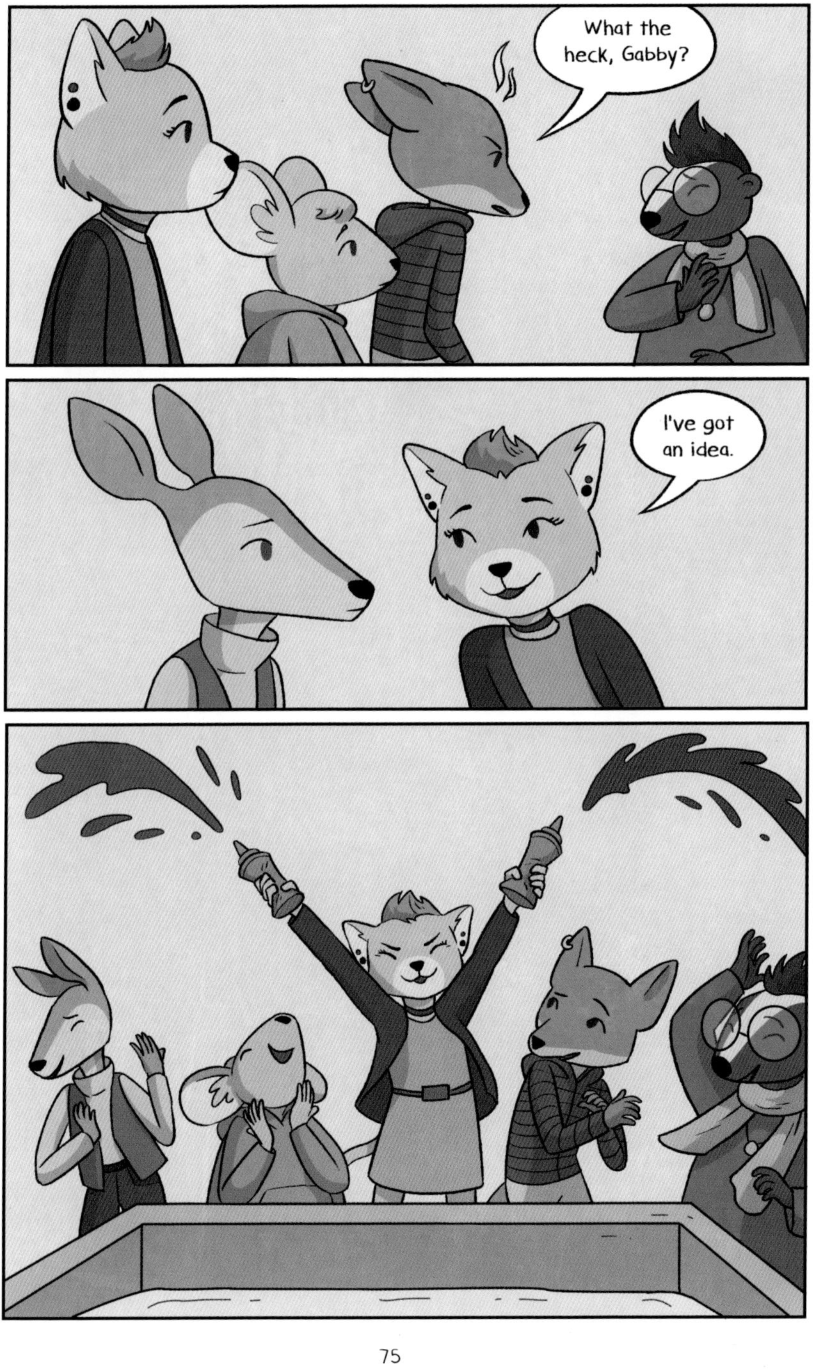
What the heck, Gabby?
I've got an idea.

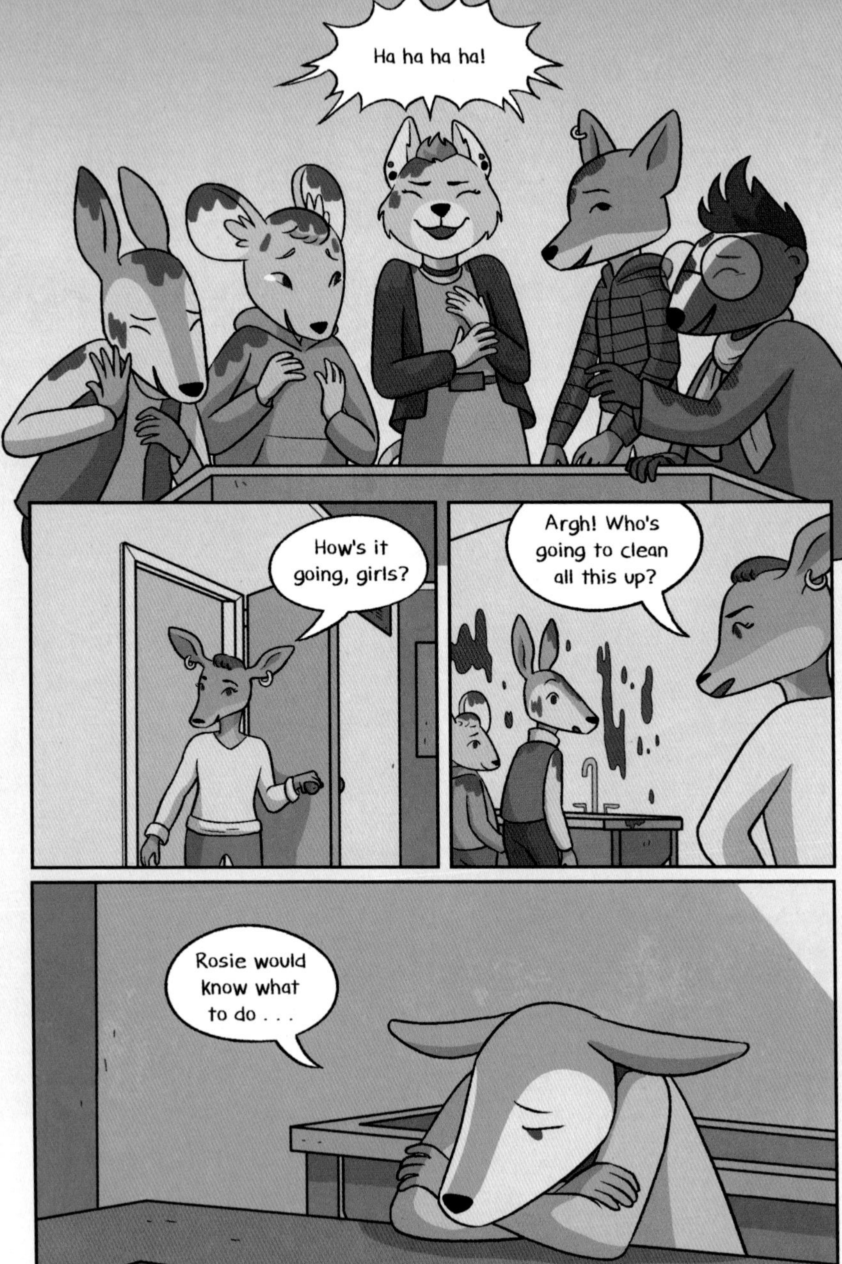
Ha ha ha ha!
How's it going, girls?
Argh! Who's going to clean all this up?
Rosie would know what to do . . .

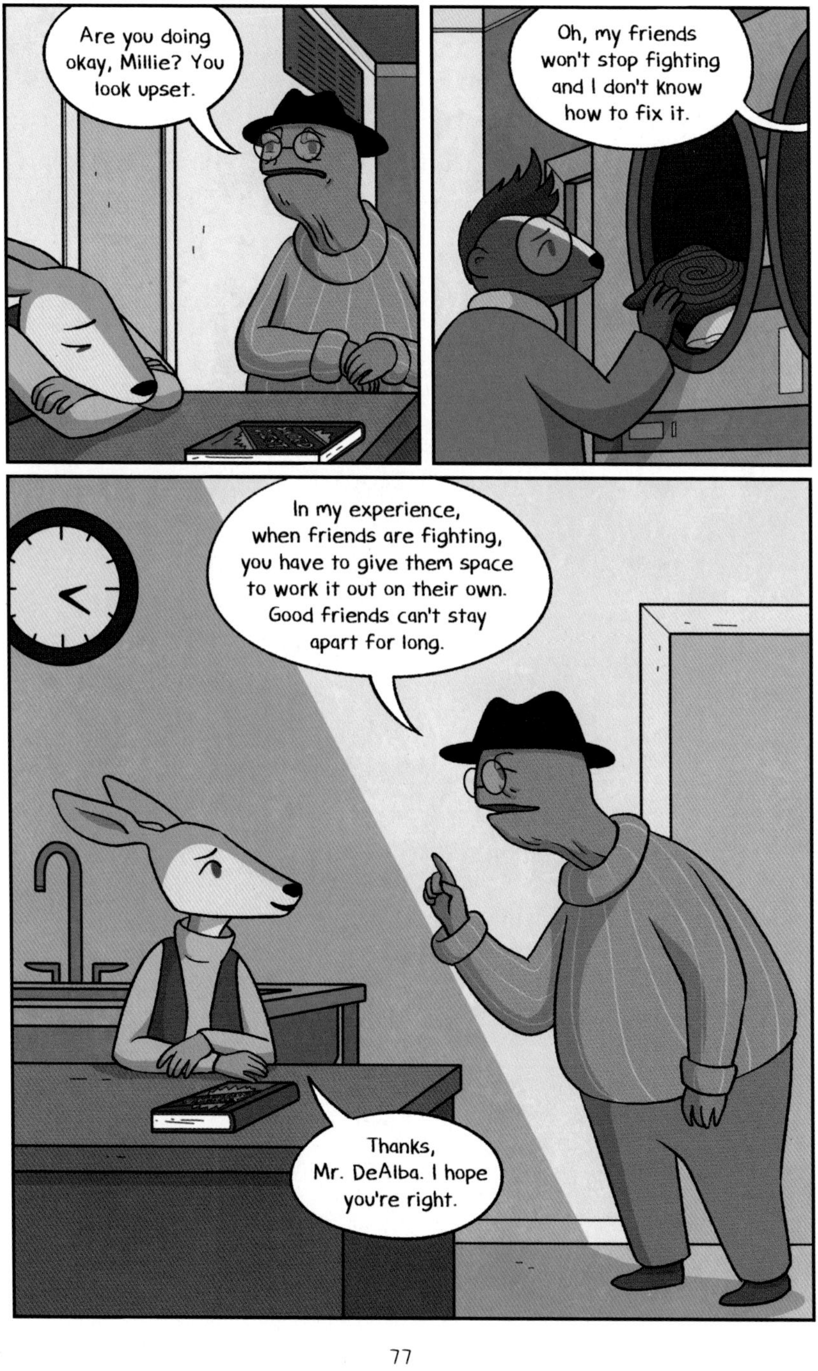
Are you doing okay, Millie? You look upset.
Oh, my friends won't stop fighting and I don't know how to fix it.
In my experience, when friends are fighting, you have to give them space to work it out on their own. Good friends can't stay apart for long.
Thanks, Mr. DeAlba. I hope you're right.

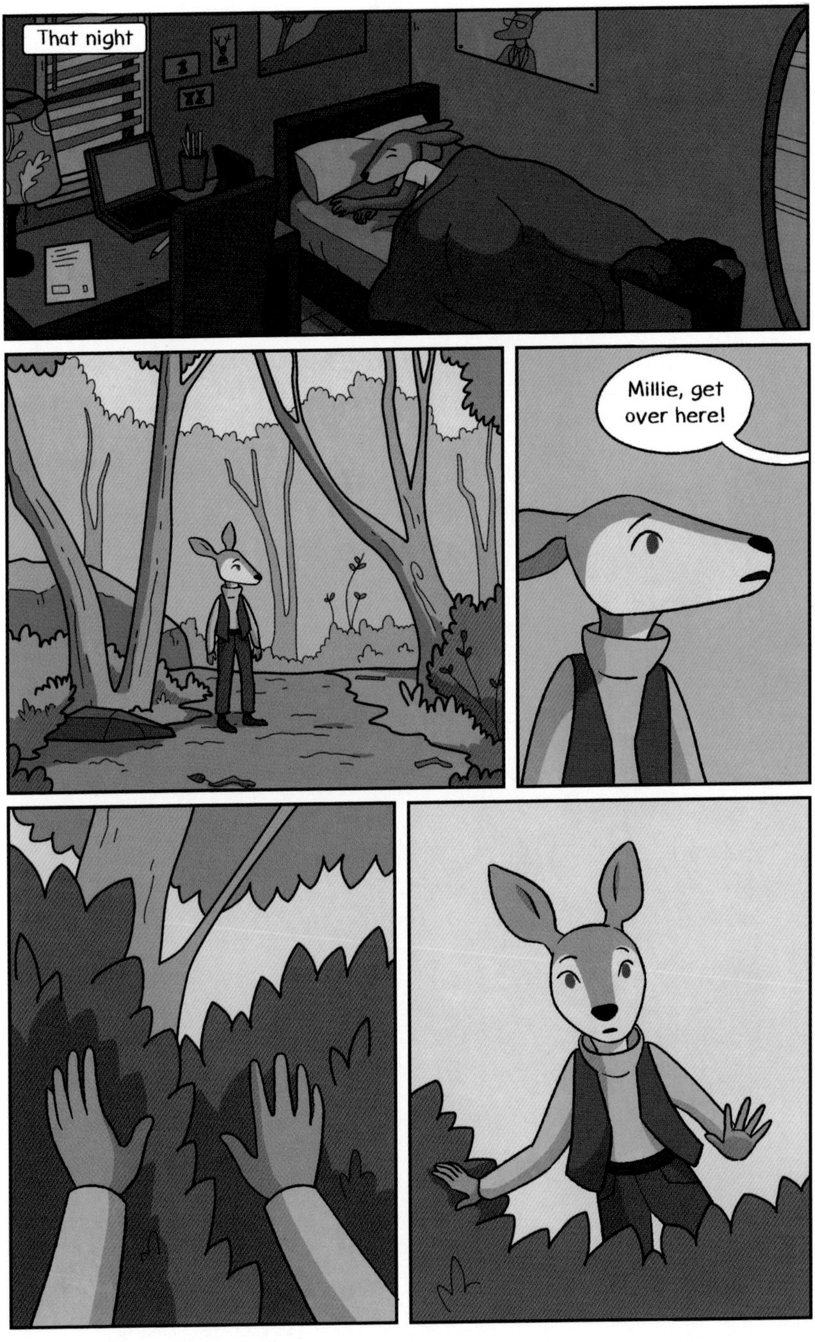
That night
Millie, get over here!

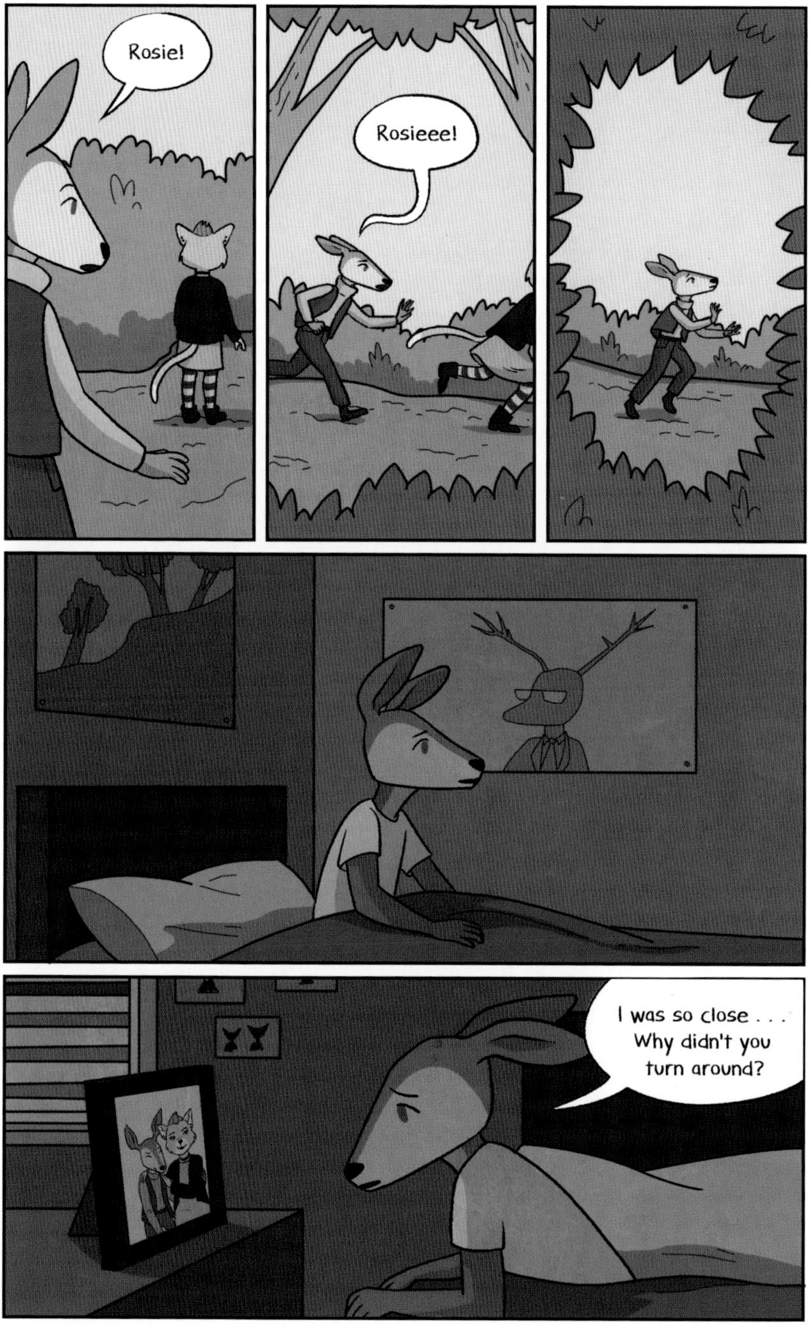
Rosie!
Rosieee!
I was so close . . .
Why didn't you
turn around?

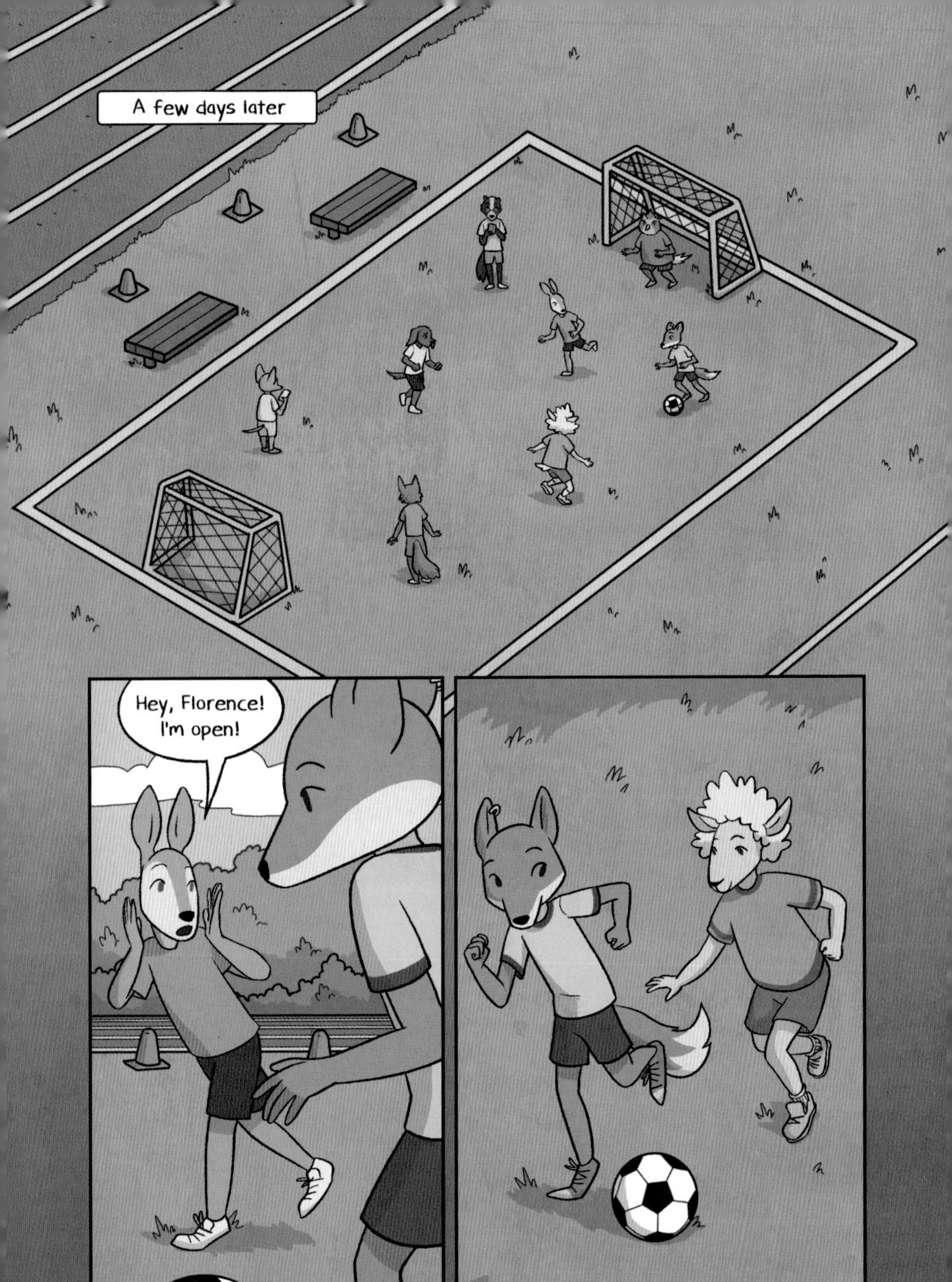
A few days later
Hey, Florence! I'm open!

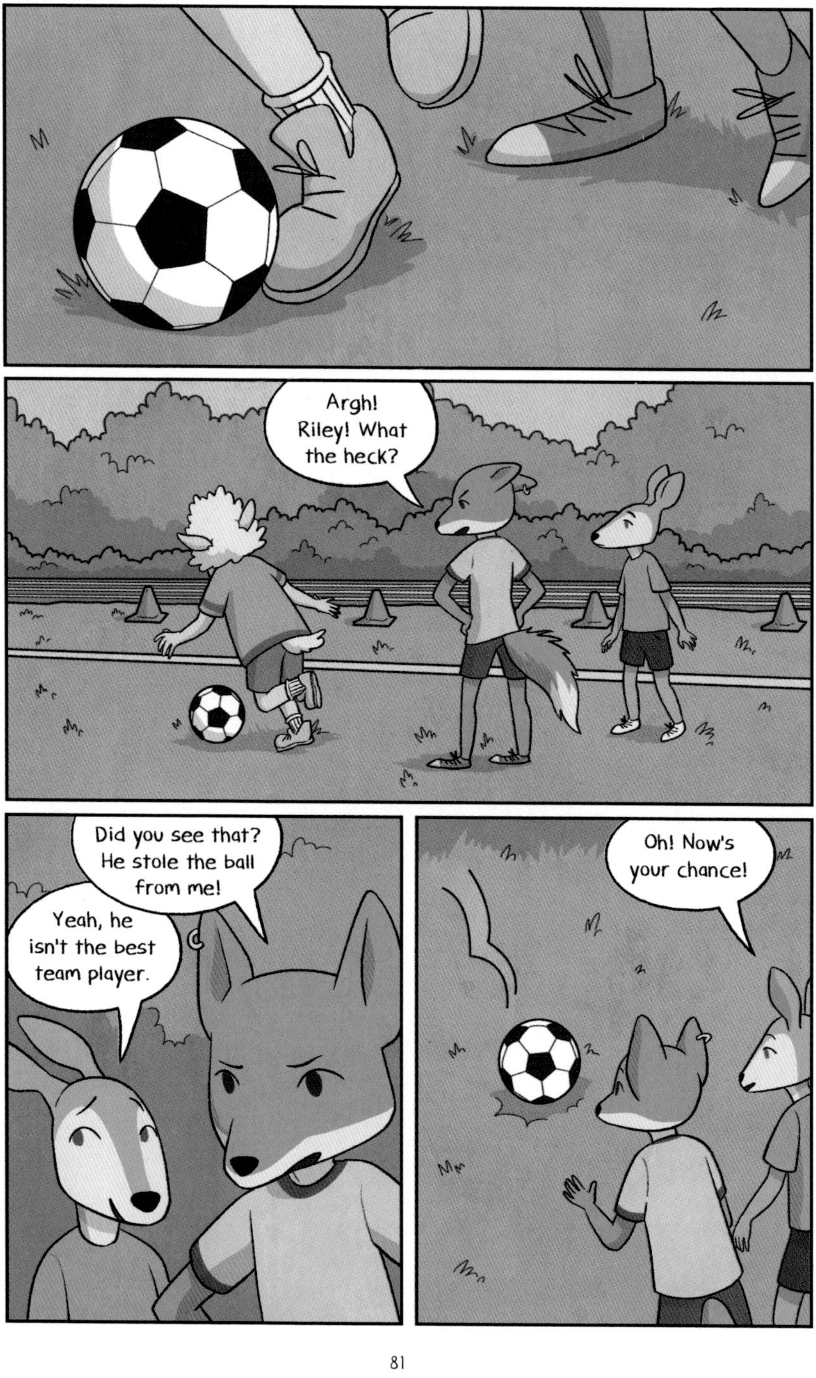
Argh! Riley! What the heck?
Did you see that? He stole the ball from me!
Yeah, he isn't the best team player.
Oh! Now's your chance!

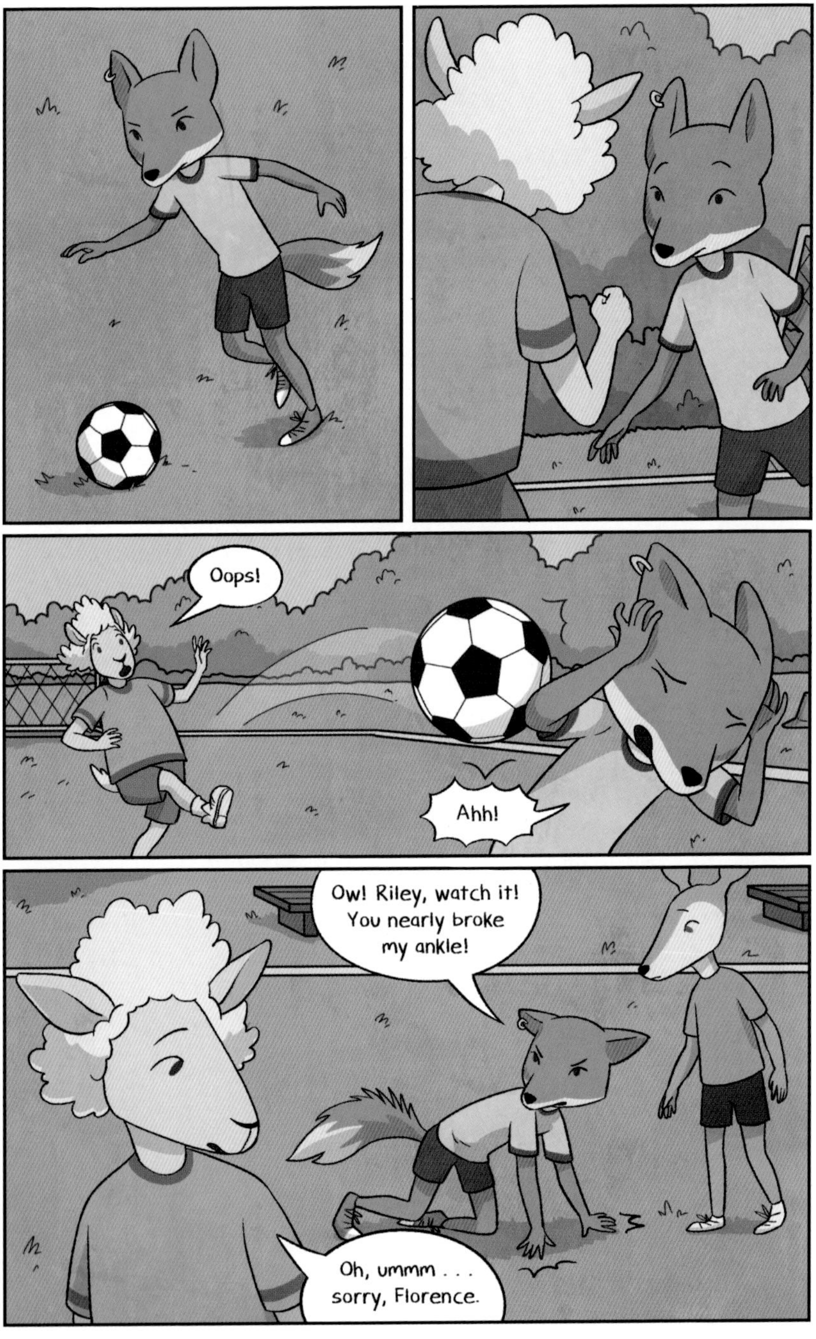
Oops!
Ahh!
Ow! Riley, watch it! You nearly broke my ankle!
Oh, ummm . . . sorry, Florence.

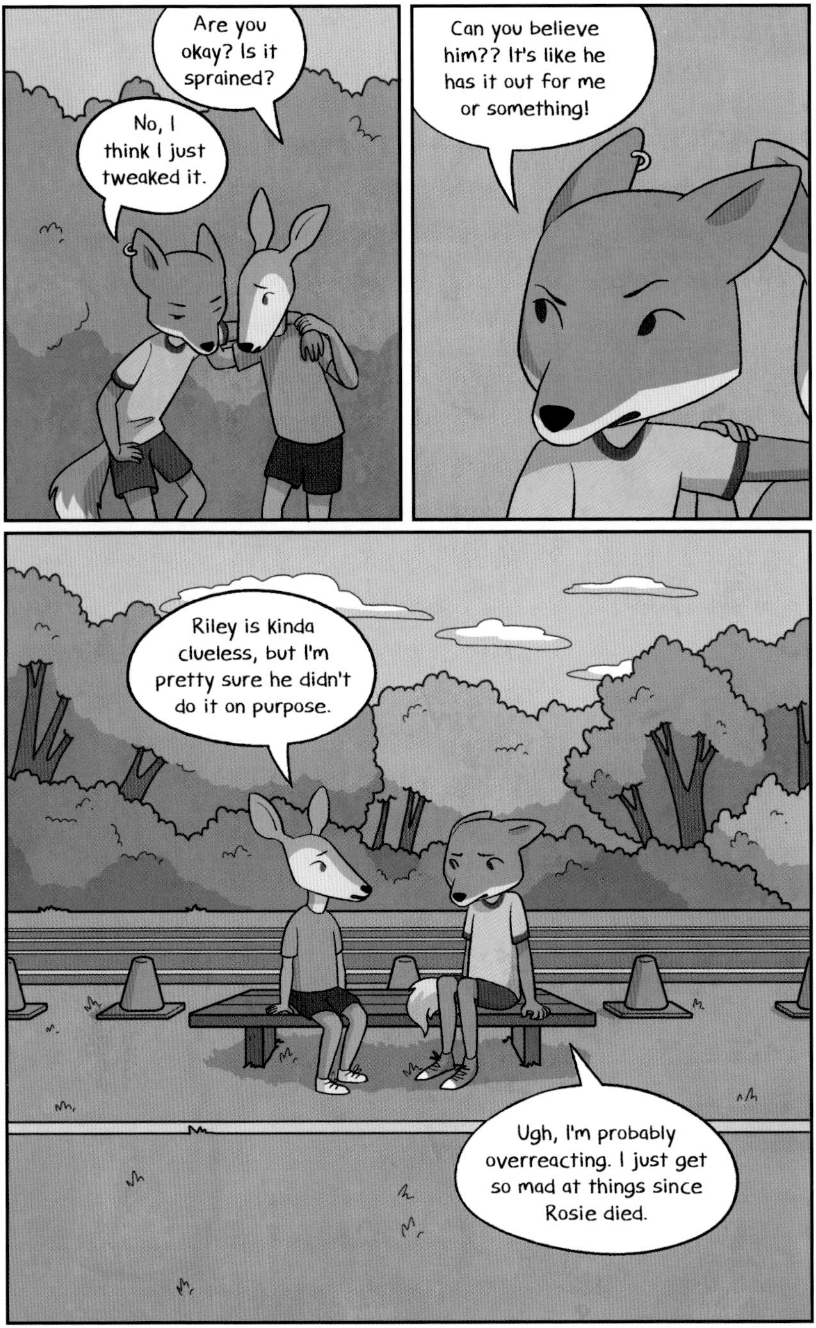
Are you okay? Is it sprained?
No, I think I just tweaked it.
Can you believe him?? It's like he has it out for me or something!
Riley is kinda clueless, but I'm pretty sure he didn't do it on purpose.
Ugh, I'm probably overreacting. I just get so mad at things since Rosie died.

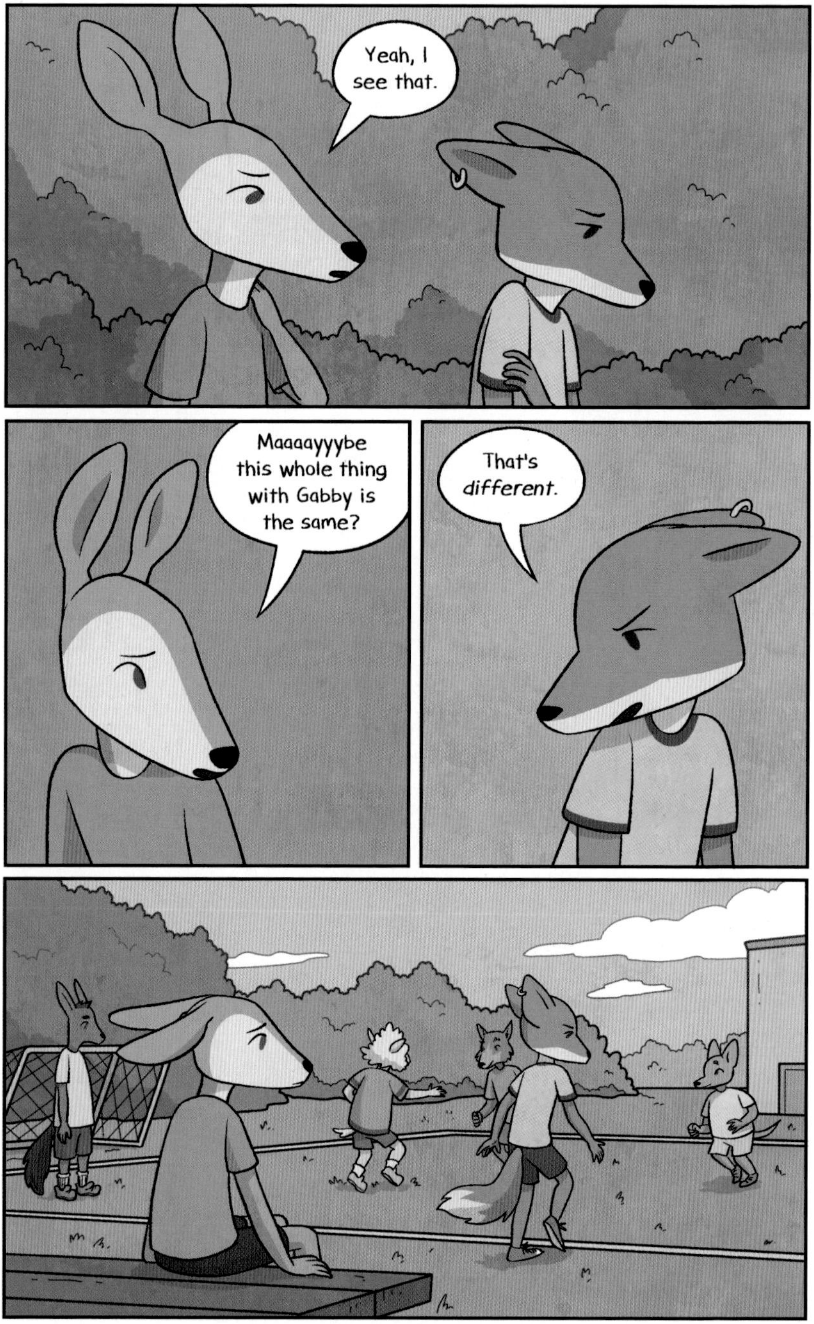
Yeah, I see that.
Maaaayyybe this whole thing with Gabby is the same?
That's *different.*

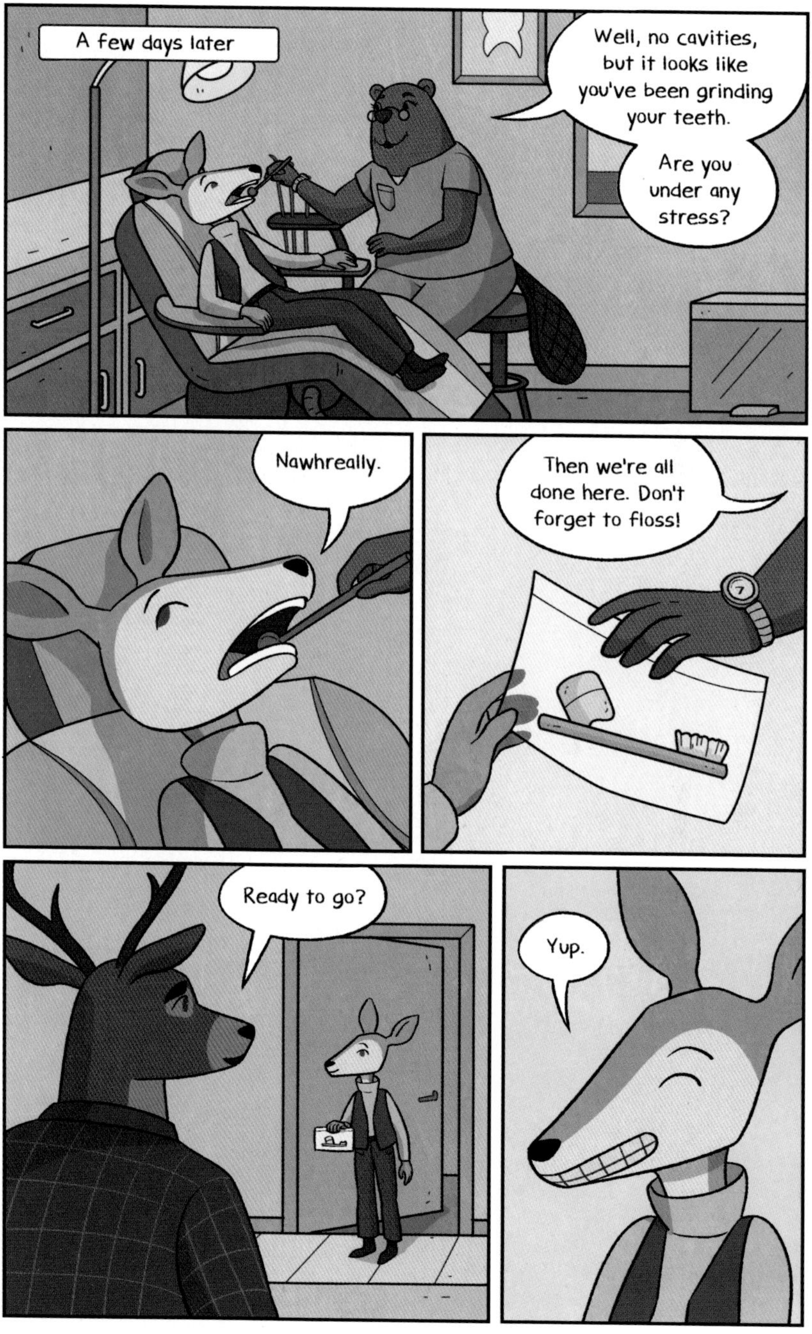
A few days later
Well, no cavities, but it looks like you've been grinding your teeth.
Are you under any stress?
Nawhreally.
Then we're all done here. Don't forget to floss!
Ready to go?
Yup.

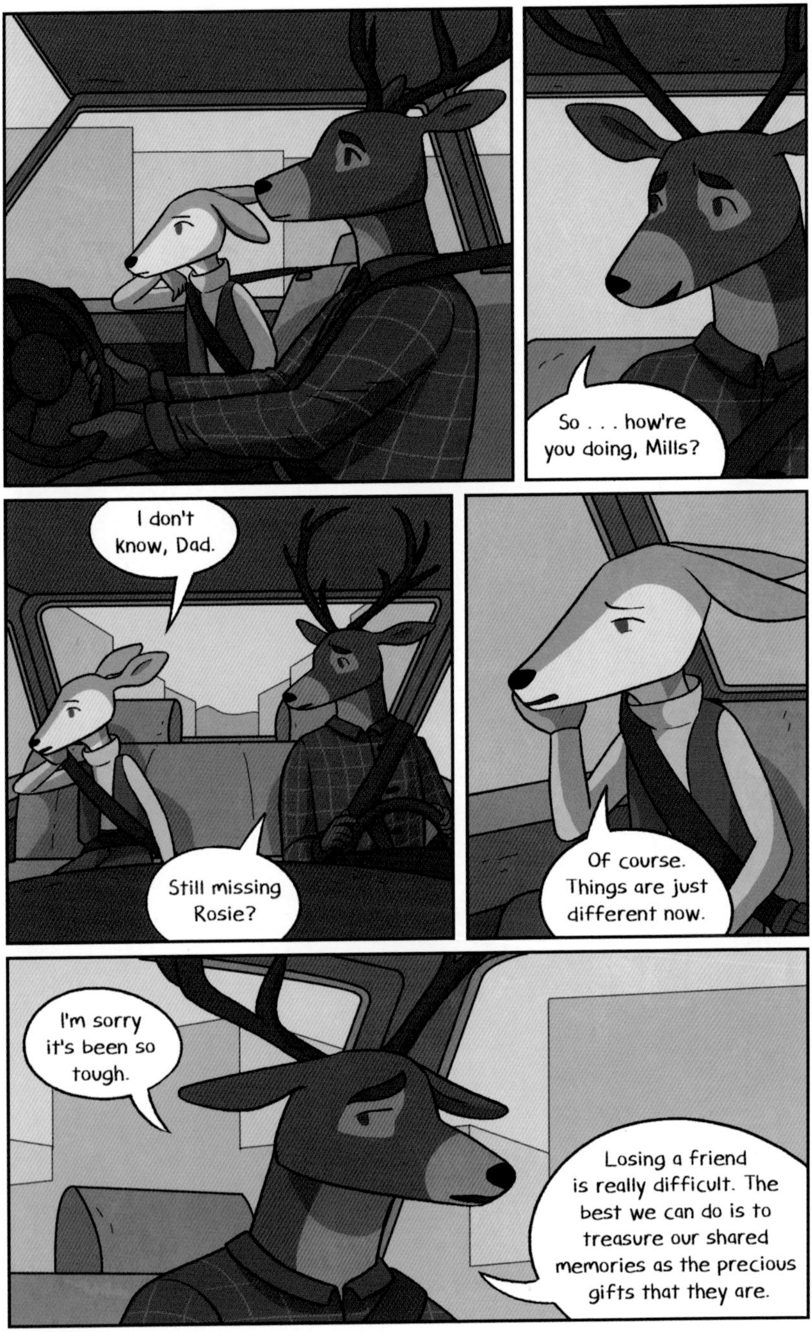
So . . . how're you doing, Mills?
I don't know, Dad.
Still missing Rosie?
Of course. Things are just different now.
I'm sorry it's been so tough.
Losing a friend is really difficult. The best we can do is to treasure our shared memories as the precious gifts that they are.

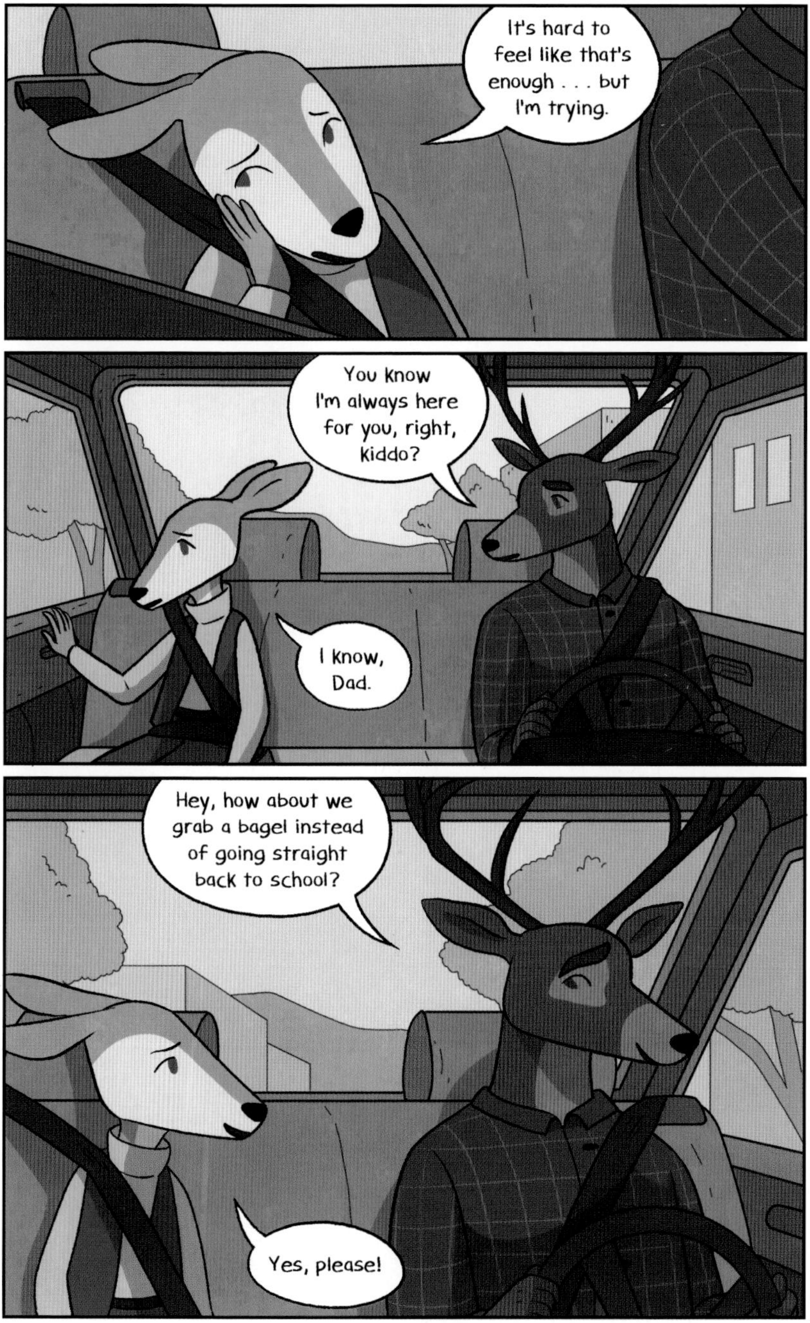
It's hard to feel like that's enough . . . but I'm trying.
You know I'm always here for you, right, kiddo?
I know, Dad.
Hey, how about we grab a bagel instead of going straight back to school?
Yes, please!

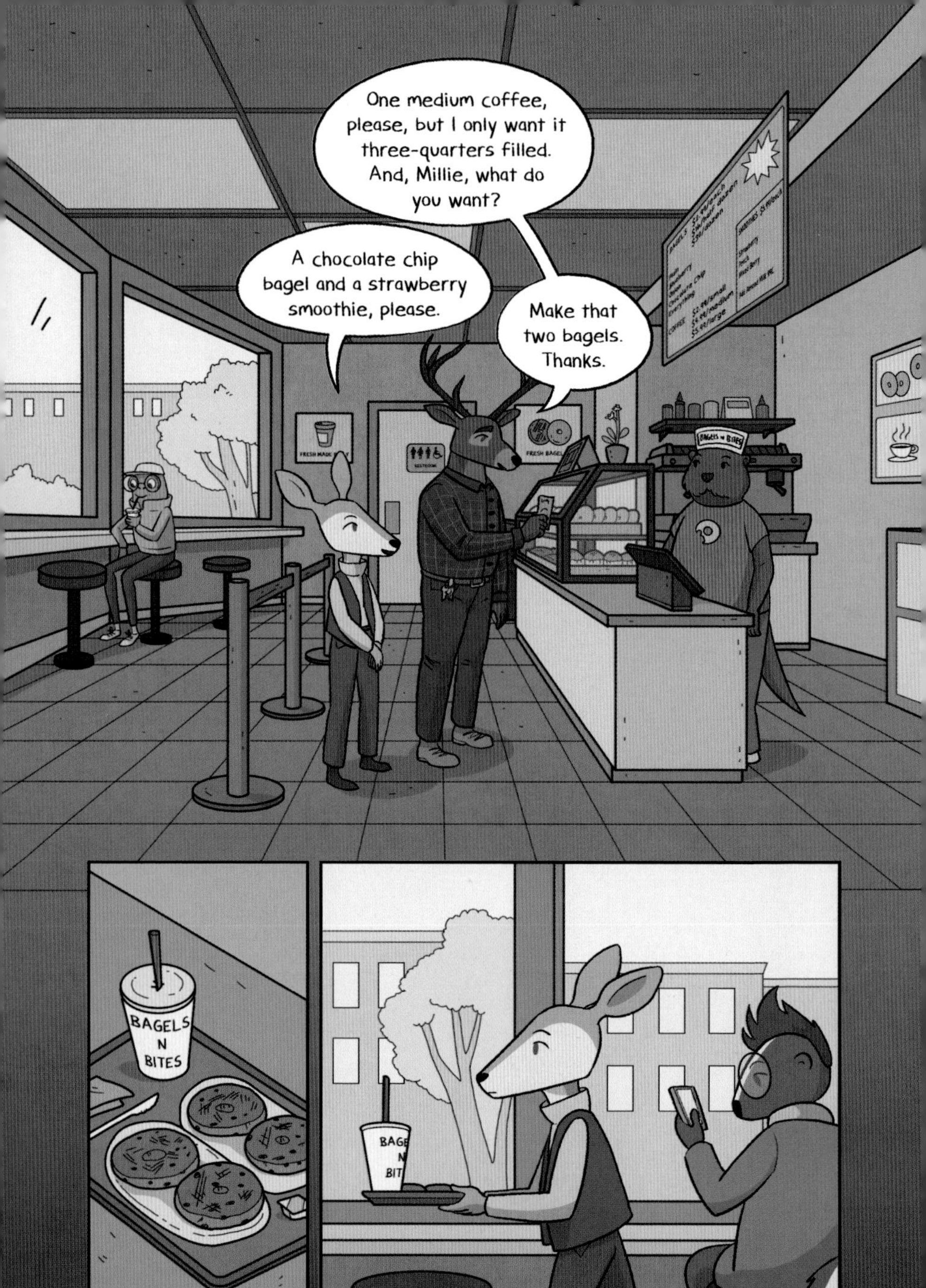
One medium coffee, please, but I only want it three-quarters filled. And, Millie, what do you want?
A chocolate chip bagel and a strawberry smoothie, please.
Make that two bagels. Thanks.
BAGELS N BITES

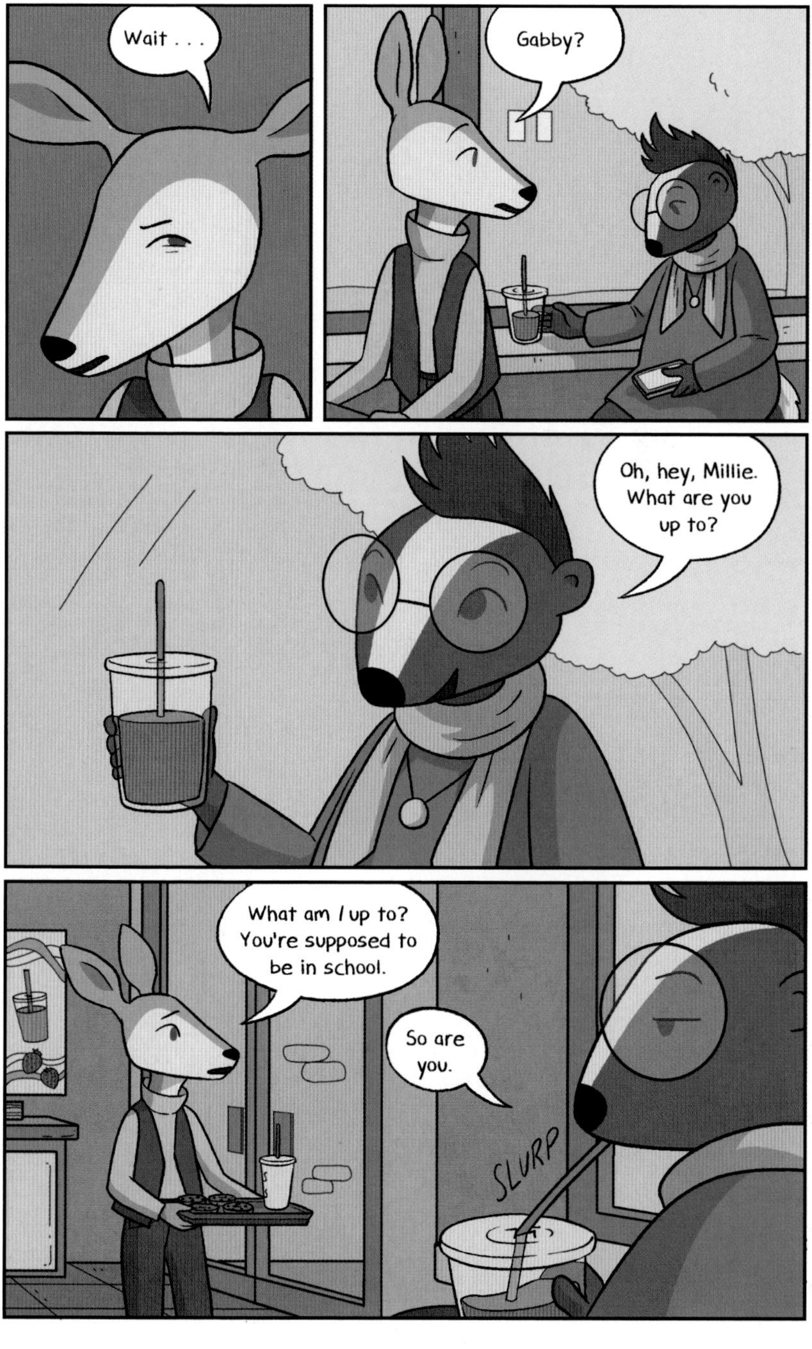
Wait . . .
Gabby?
Oh, hey, Millie. What are you up to?
What am I up to? You're supposed to be in school.
So are you.
SLURP

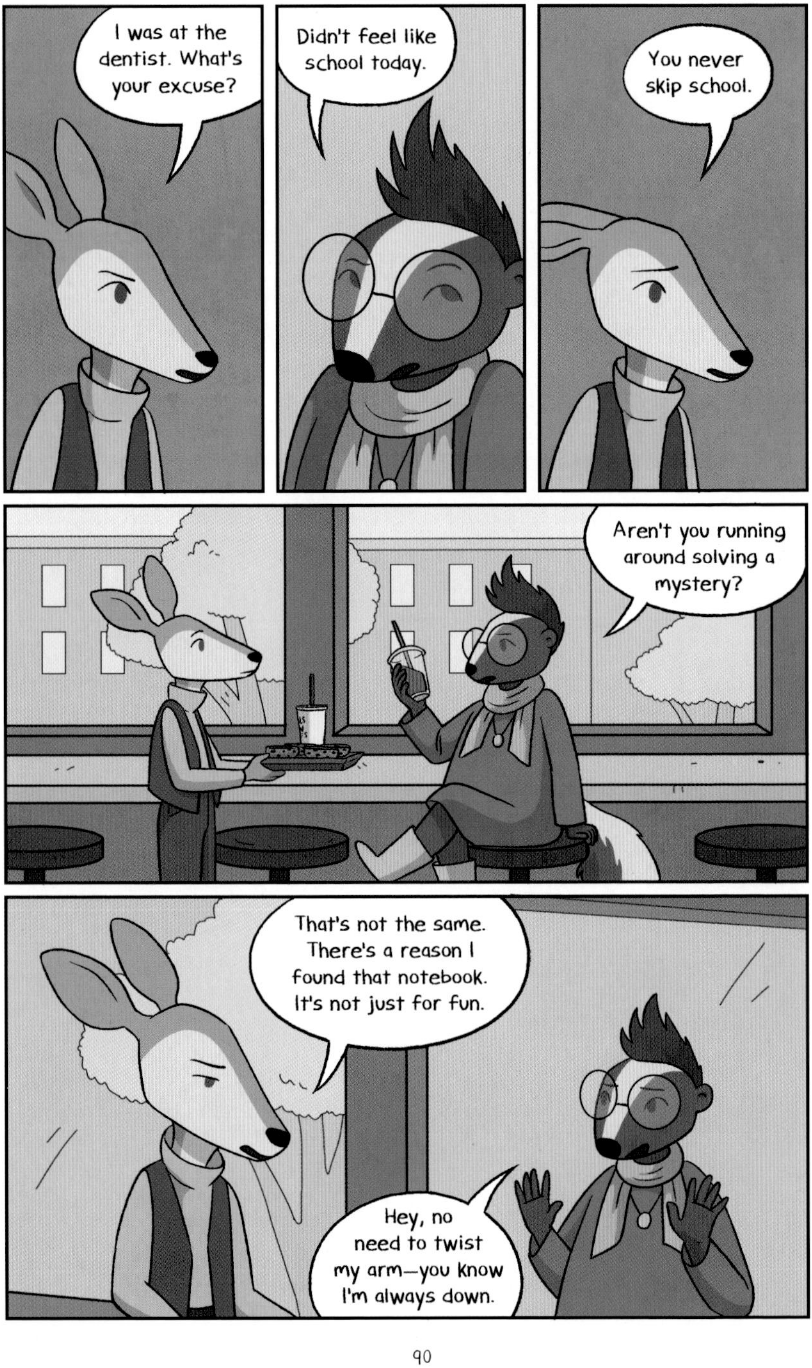

I was at the dentist. What's your excuse?
Didn't feel like school today.
You never skip school.
Aren't you running around solving a mystery?
That's not the same. There's a reason I found that notebook. It's not just for fun.
Hey, no need to twist my arm—you know I'm always down.

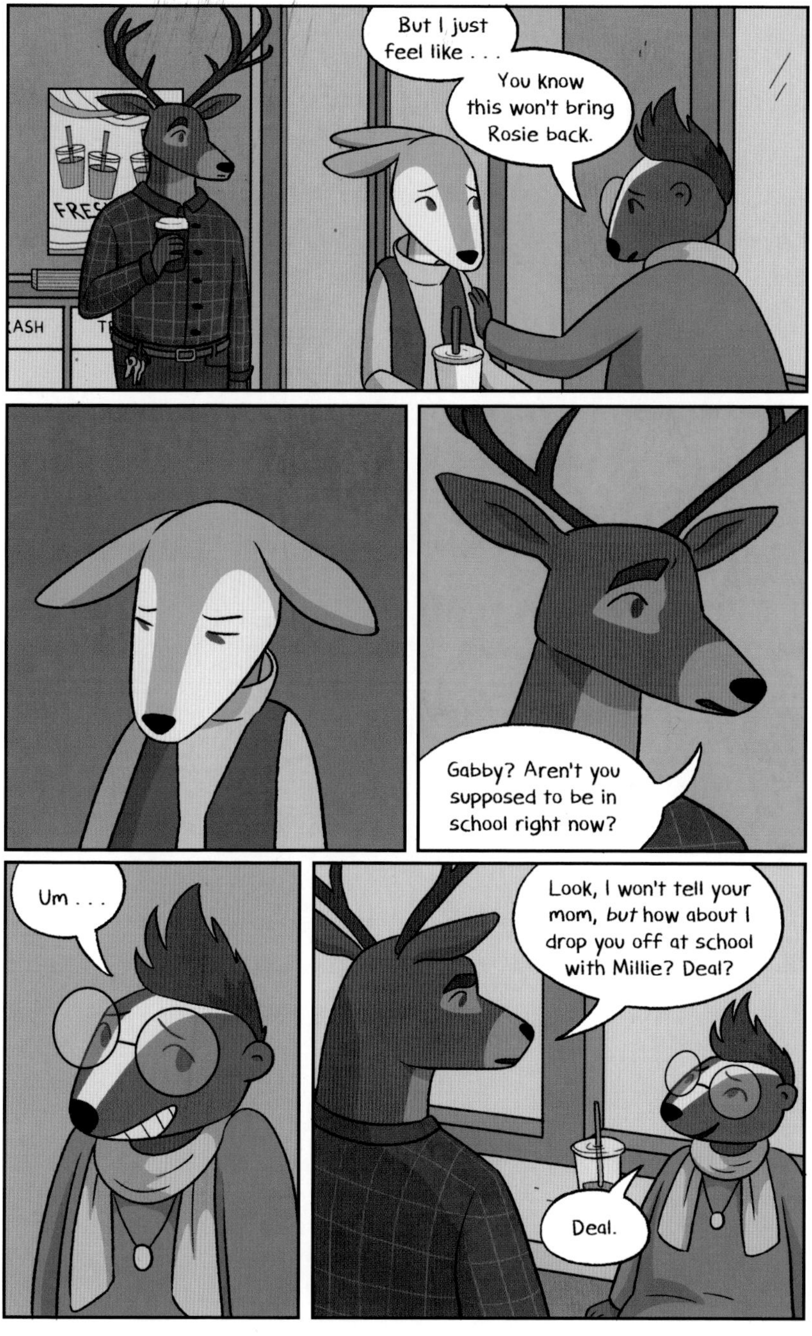
But I just feel like . . .
You know this won't bring Rosie back.
FRES
ASH
Gabby? Aren't you supposed to be in school right now?
Um . . .
Look, I won't tell your mom, *but* how about I drop you off at school with Millie? Deal?
Deal.

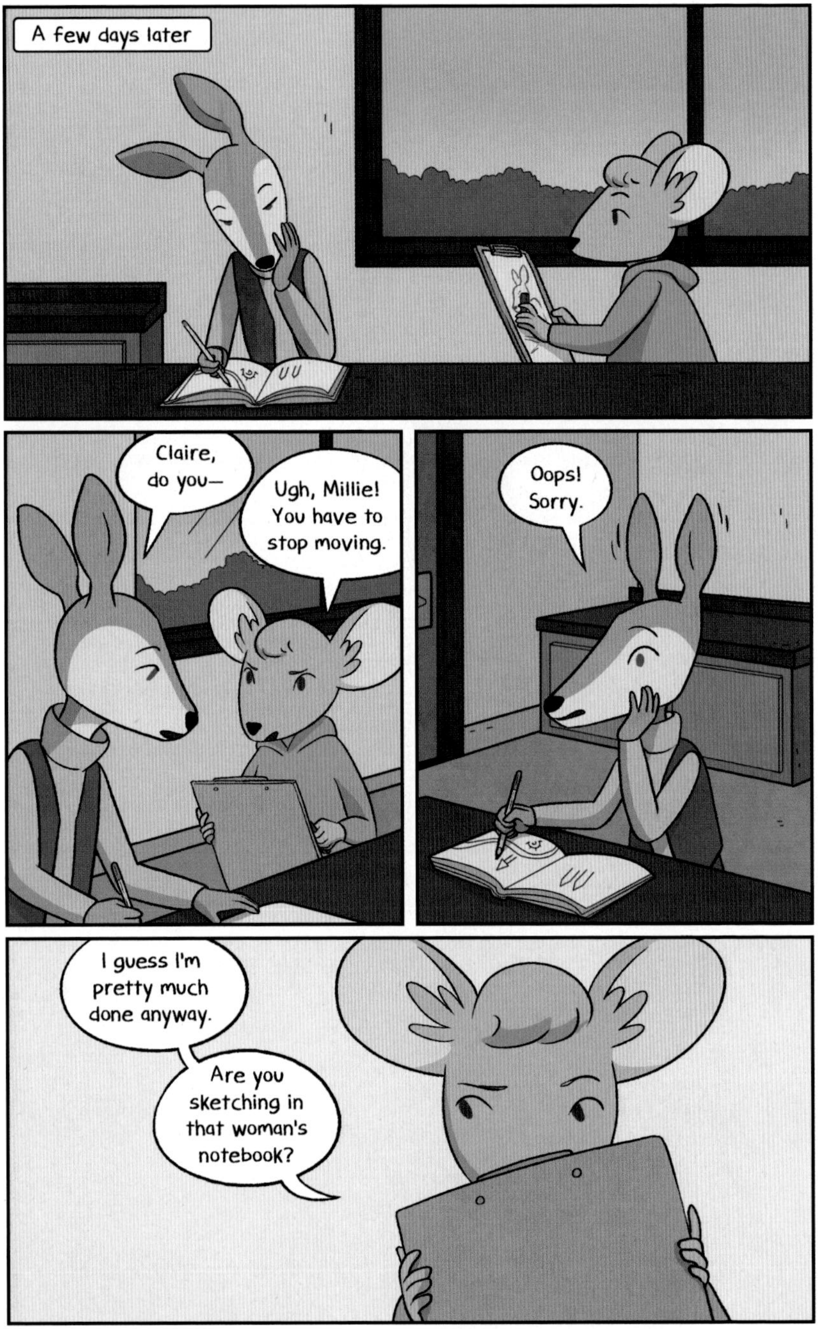
A few days later
Claire, do you—
Ugh, Millie! You have to stop moving.
Oops! Sorry.
I guess I'm pretty much done anyway.
Are you sketching in that woman's notebook?

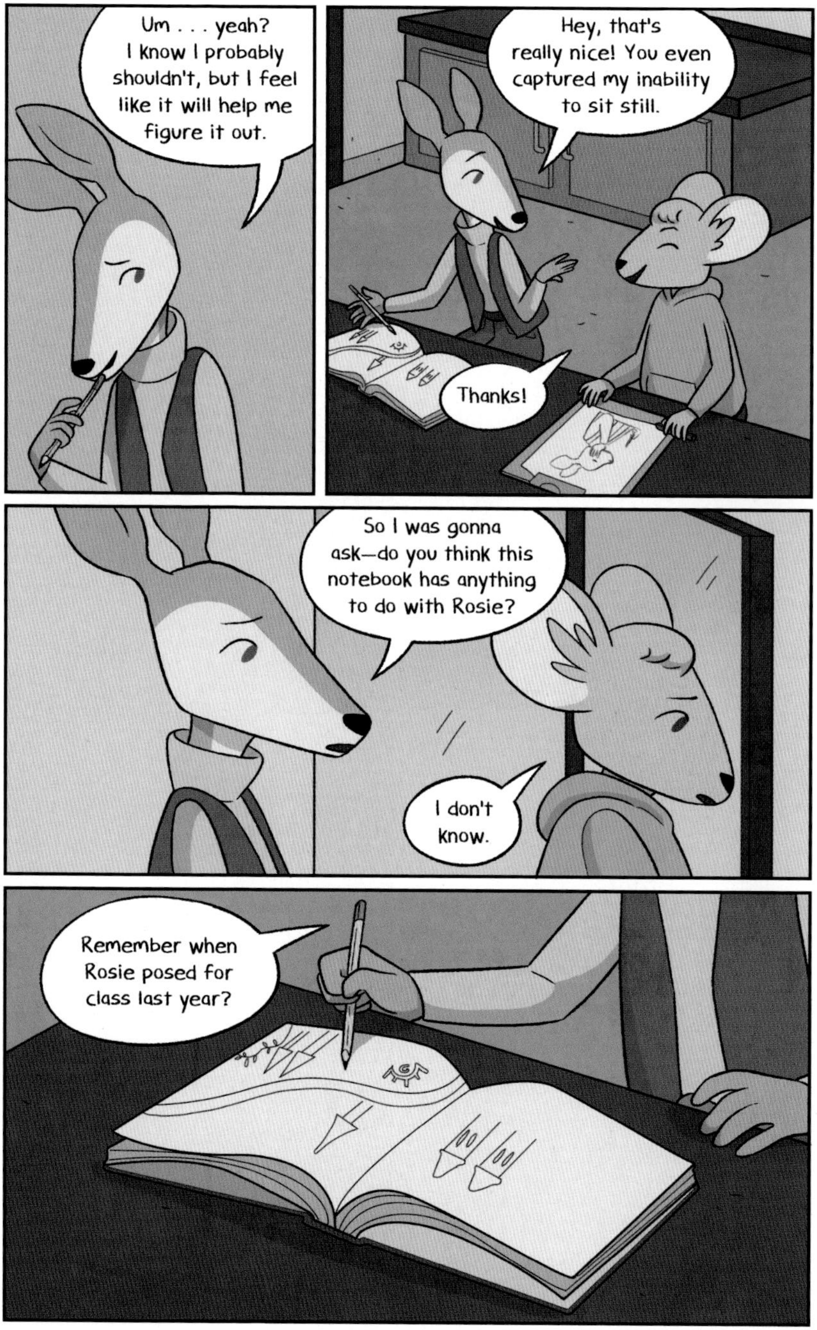
Um . . . yeah? I know I probably shouldn't, but I feel like it will help me figure it out.
Hey, that's really nice! You even captured my inability to sit still.
Thanks!
So I was gonna ask—do you think this notebook has anything to do with Rosie?
I don't know.
Remember when Rosie posed for class last year?

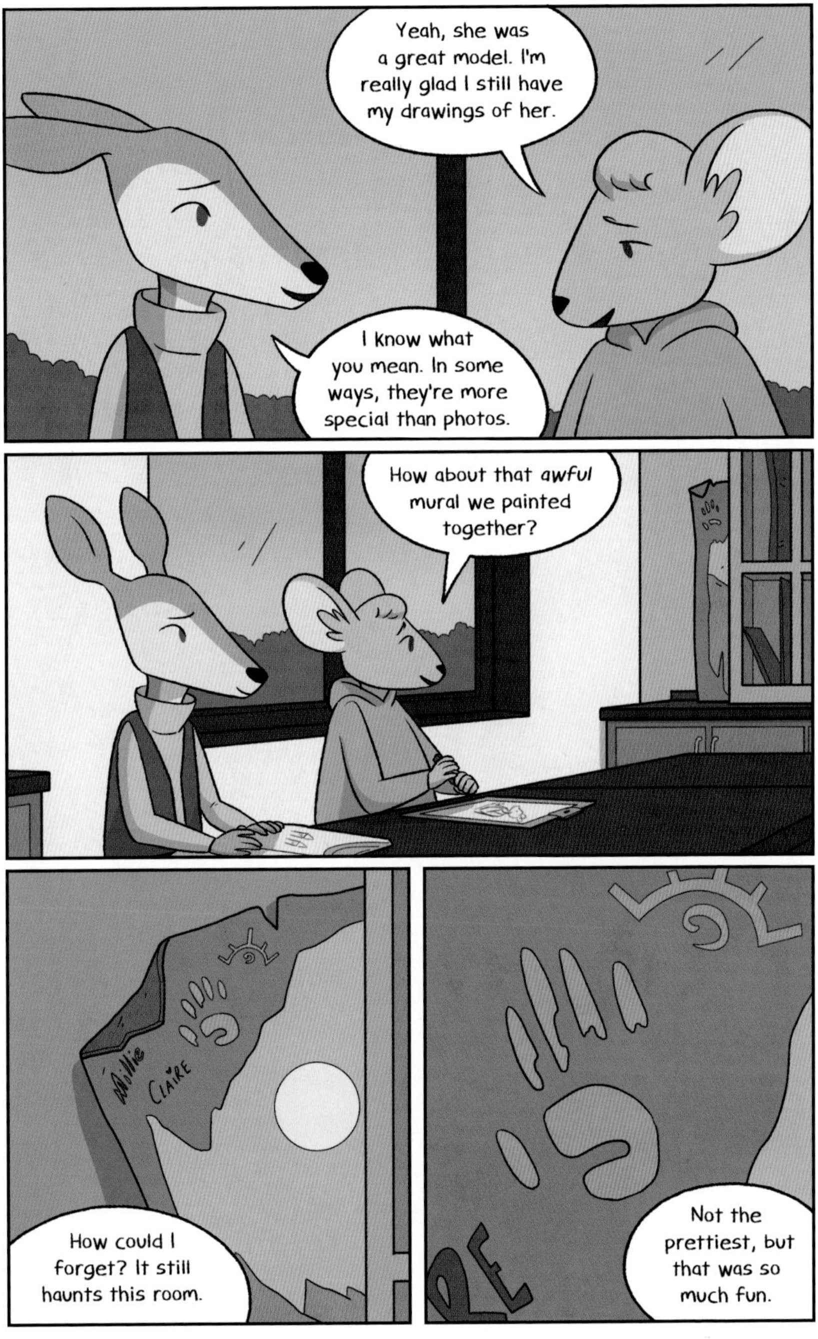
Yeah, she was a great model. I'm really glad I still have my drawings of her.
I know what you mean. In some ways, they're more special than photos.
How about that *awful* mural we painted together?
Millie
CLAIRE
How could I forget? It still haunts this room.
Not the prettiest, but that was so much fun.

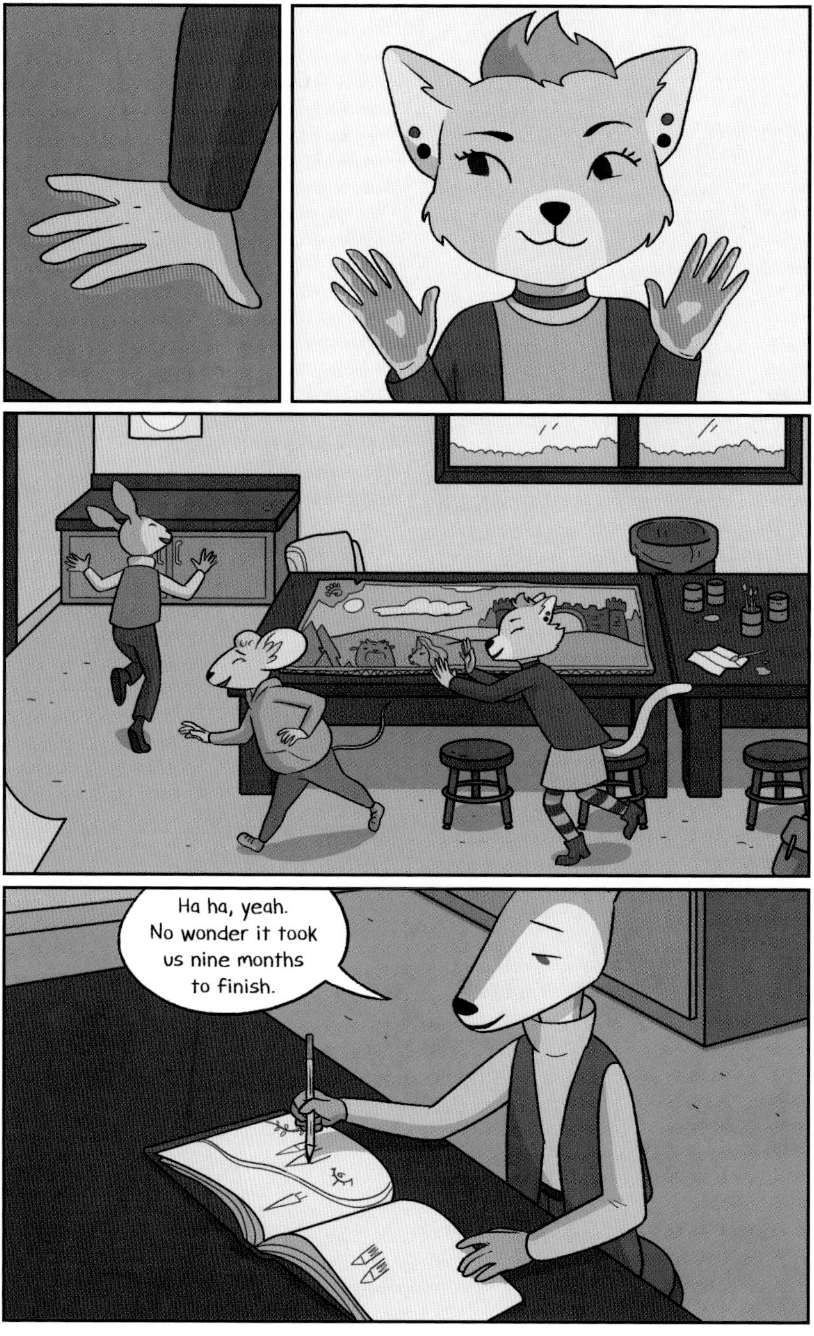
Ha ha, yeah. No wonder it took us nine months to finish.

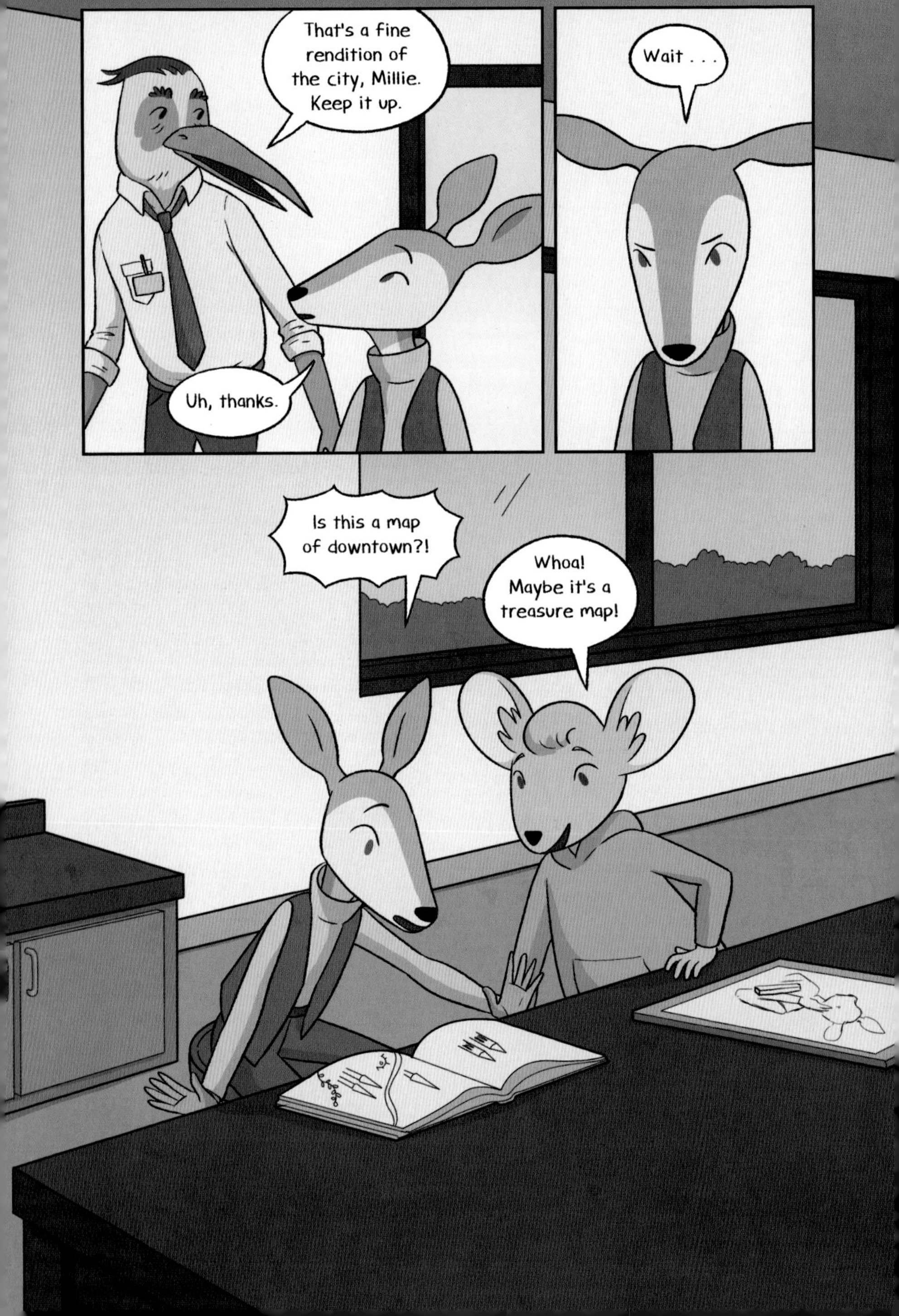

That's a fine rendition of the city, Millie. Keep it up.
Uh, thanks.
Wait . . .
Is this a map of downtown?!
Whoa! Maybe it's a treasure map!

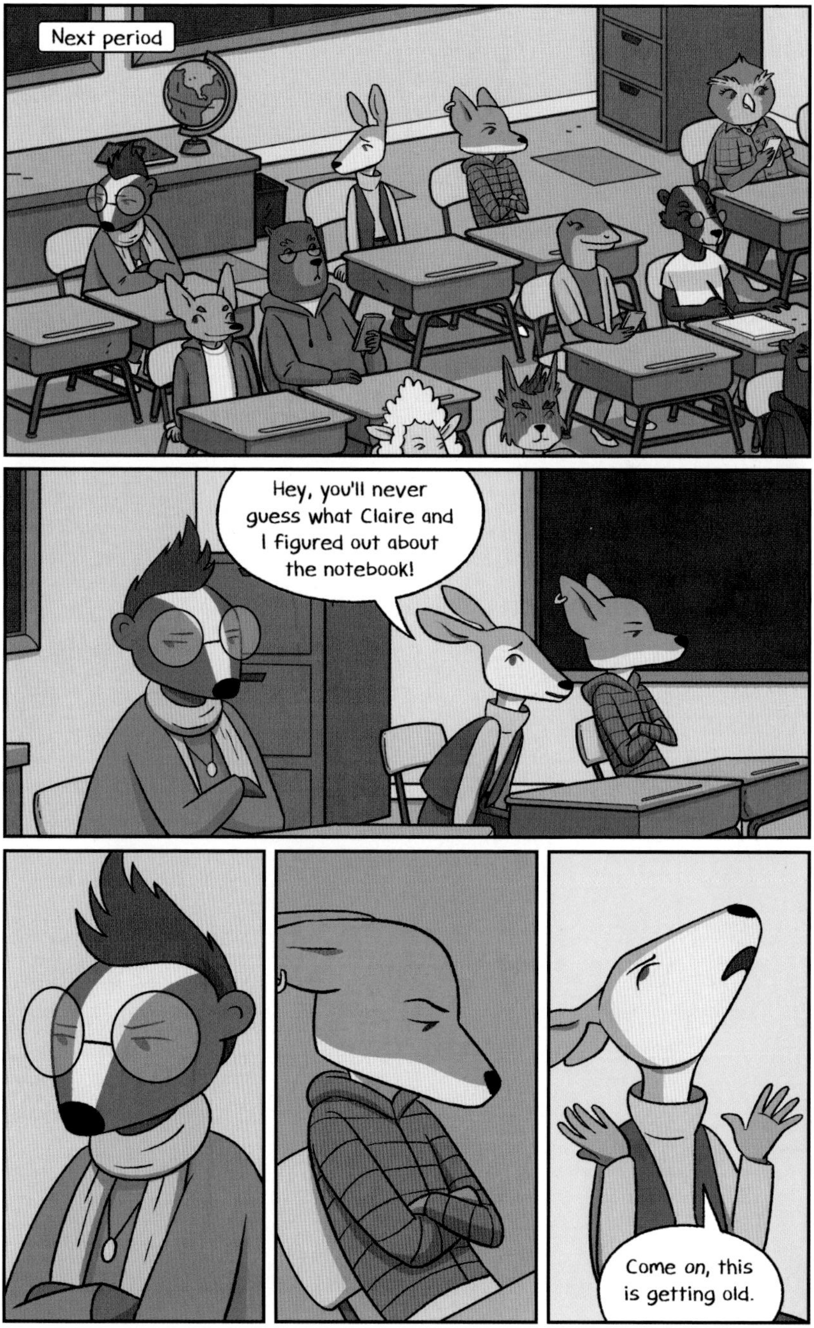
Next period
Hey, you'll never guess what Claire and I figured out about the notebook!
Come on, this is getting old.

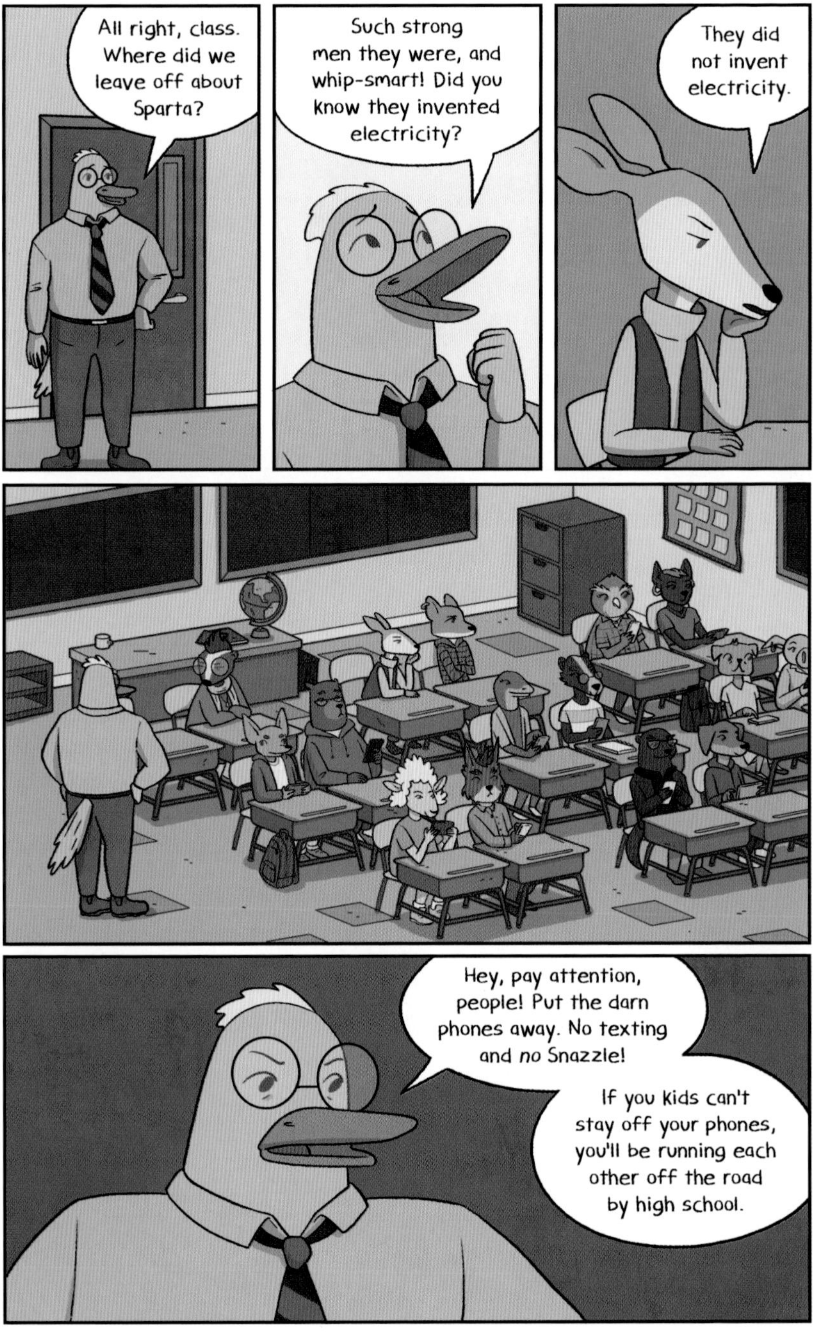
All right, class. Where did we leave off about Sparta?
Such strong men they were, and whip-smart! Did you know they invented electricity?
They did not invent electricity.
Hey, pay attention, people! Put the darn phones away. No texting and *no* Snazzle!
If you kids can't stay off your phones, you'll be running each other off the road by high school.

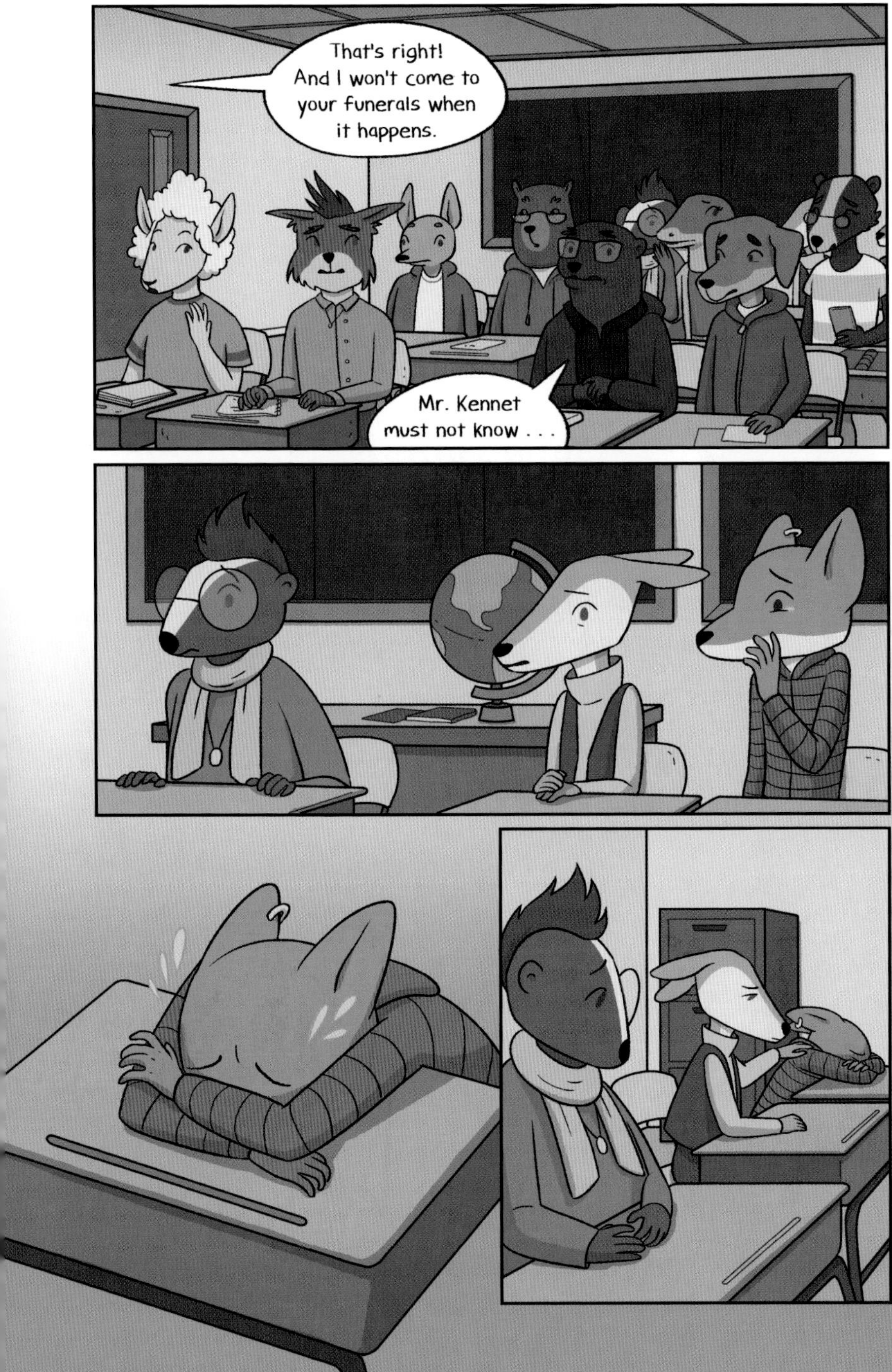
That's right! And I won't come to your funerals when it happens.
Mr. Kennet must not know . . .

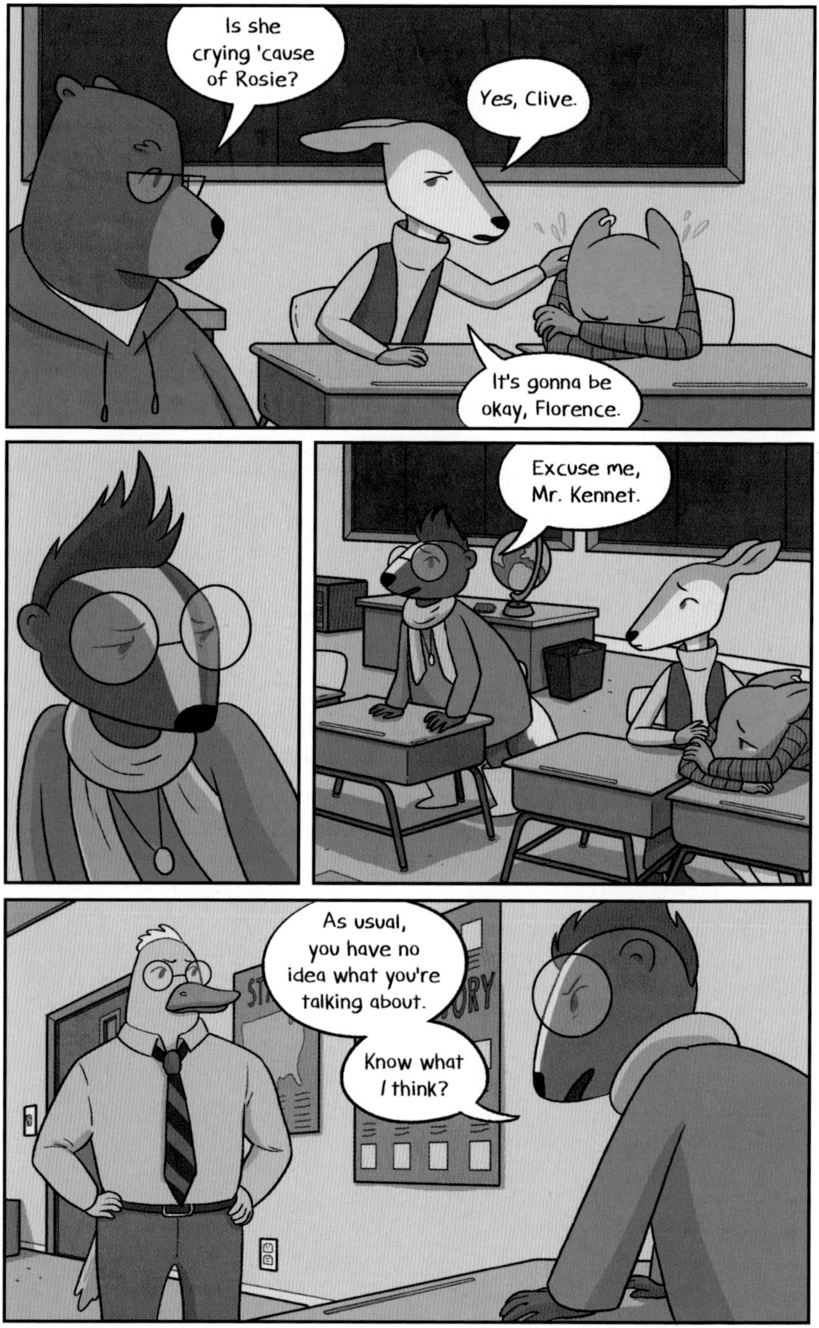
Is she crying 'cause of Rosie?
Yes, Clive.
It's gonna be okay, Florence.
Excuse me, Mr. Kennet.
As usual, you have no idea what you're talking about.
Know what I think?

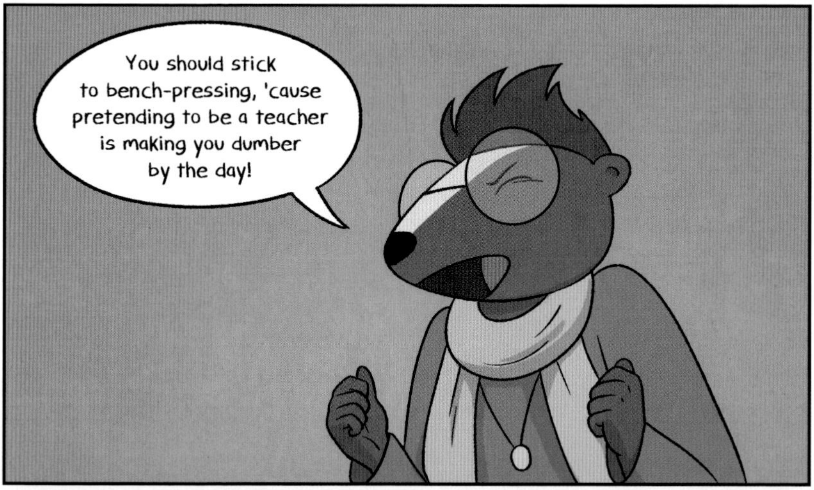
You should stick to bench-pressing, 'cause pretending to be a teacher is making you dumber by the day!

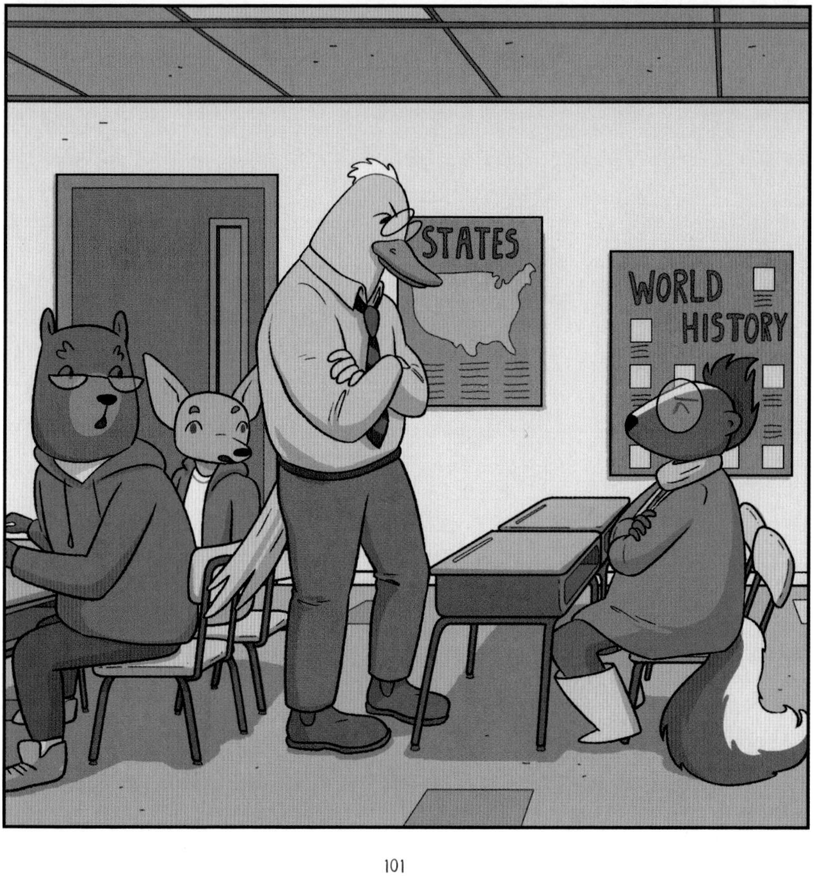
STATES
WORLD HISTORY

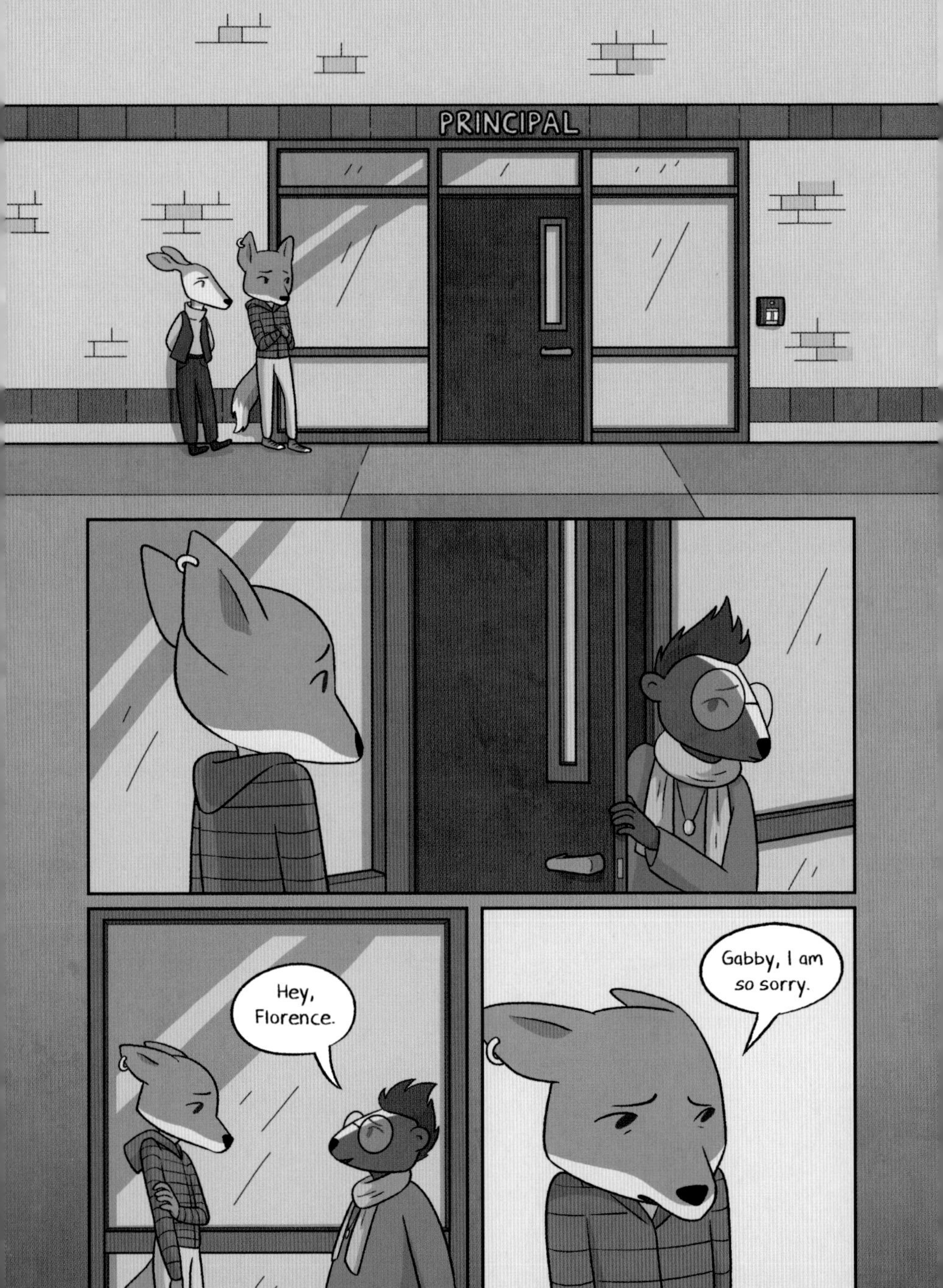
PRINCIPAL
Hey, Florence.
Gabby, I am so sorry.

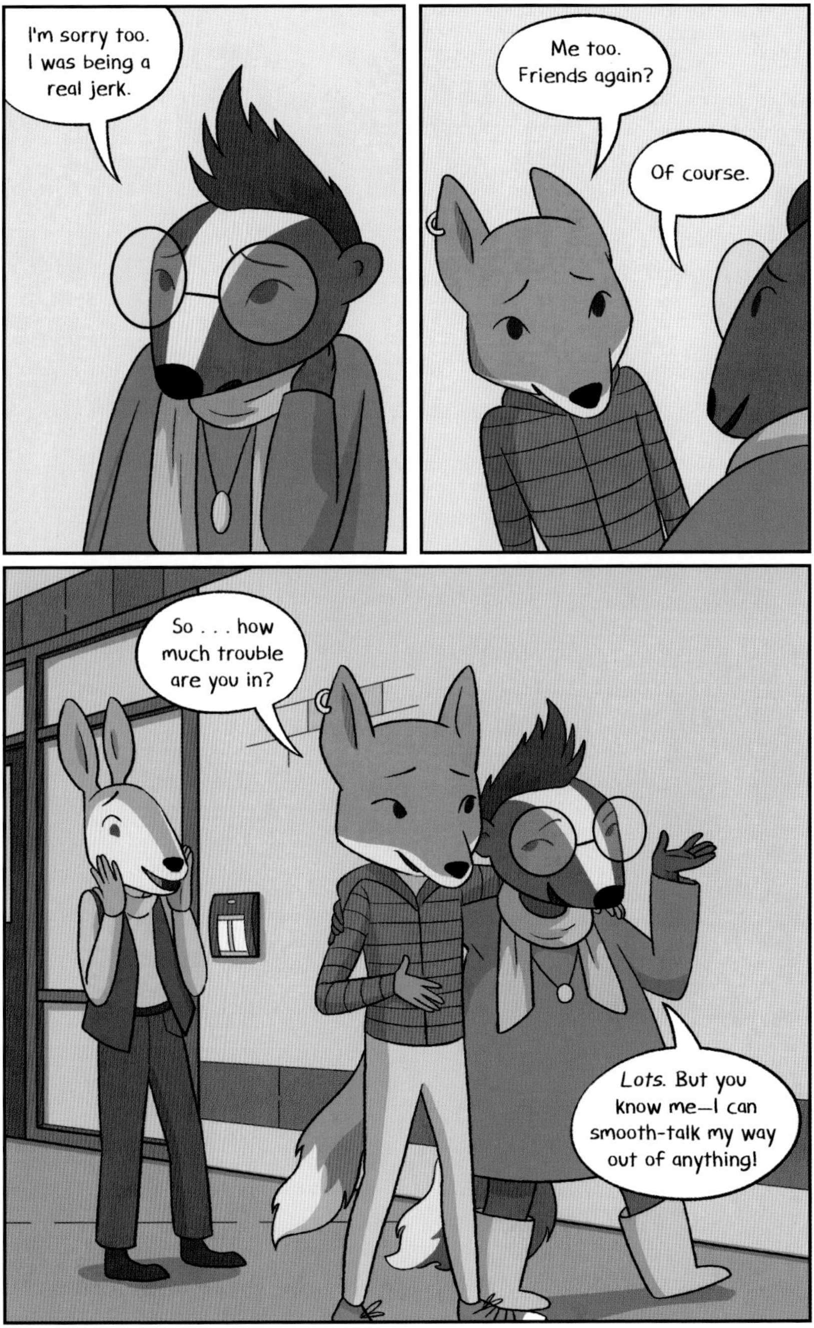
I'm sorry too. I was being a real jerk.
Me too. Friends again?
Of course.
So . . . how much trouble are you in?
Lots. But you know me—I can smooth-talk my way out of anything!

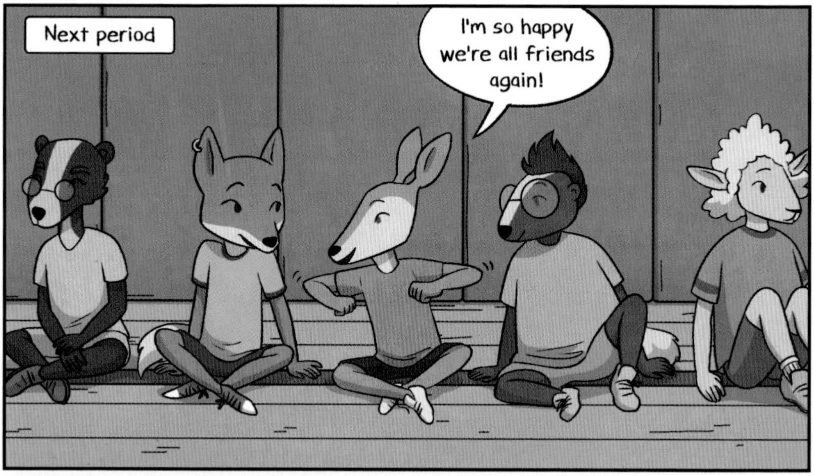
Next period
I'm so happy we're all friends again!

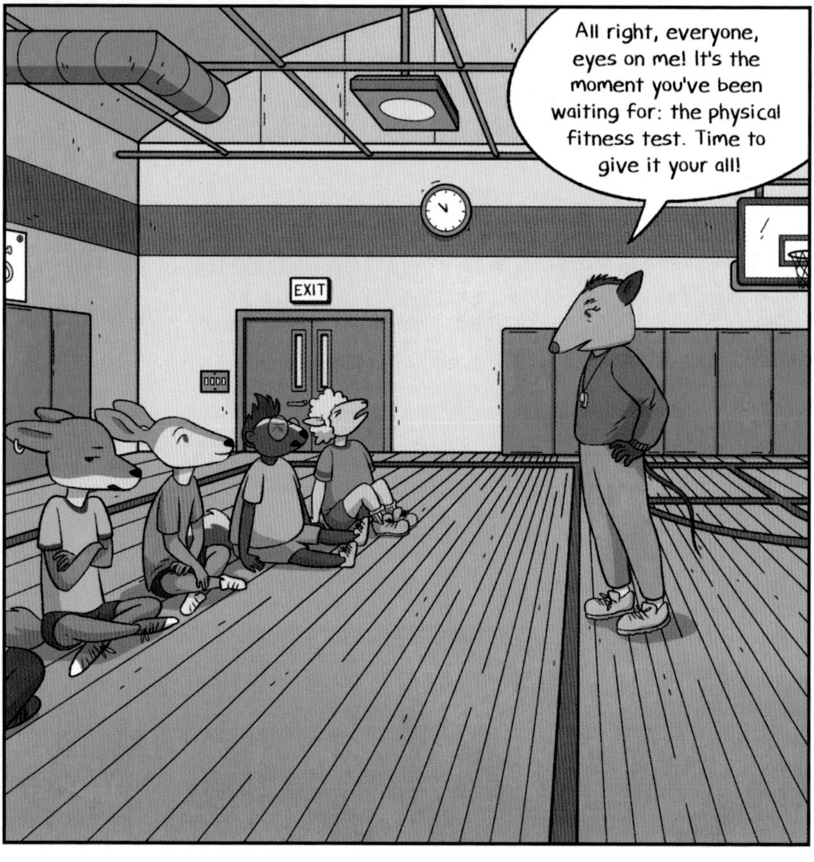
All right, everyone, eyes on me! It's the moment you've been waiting for: the physical fitness test. Time to give it your all!
EXIT

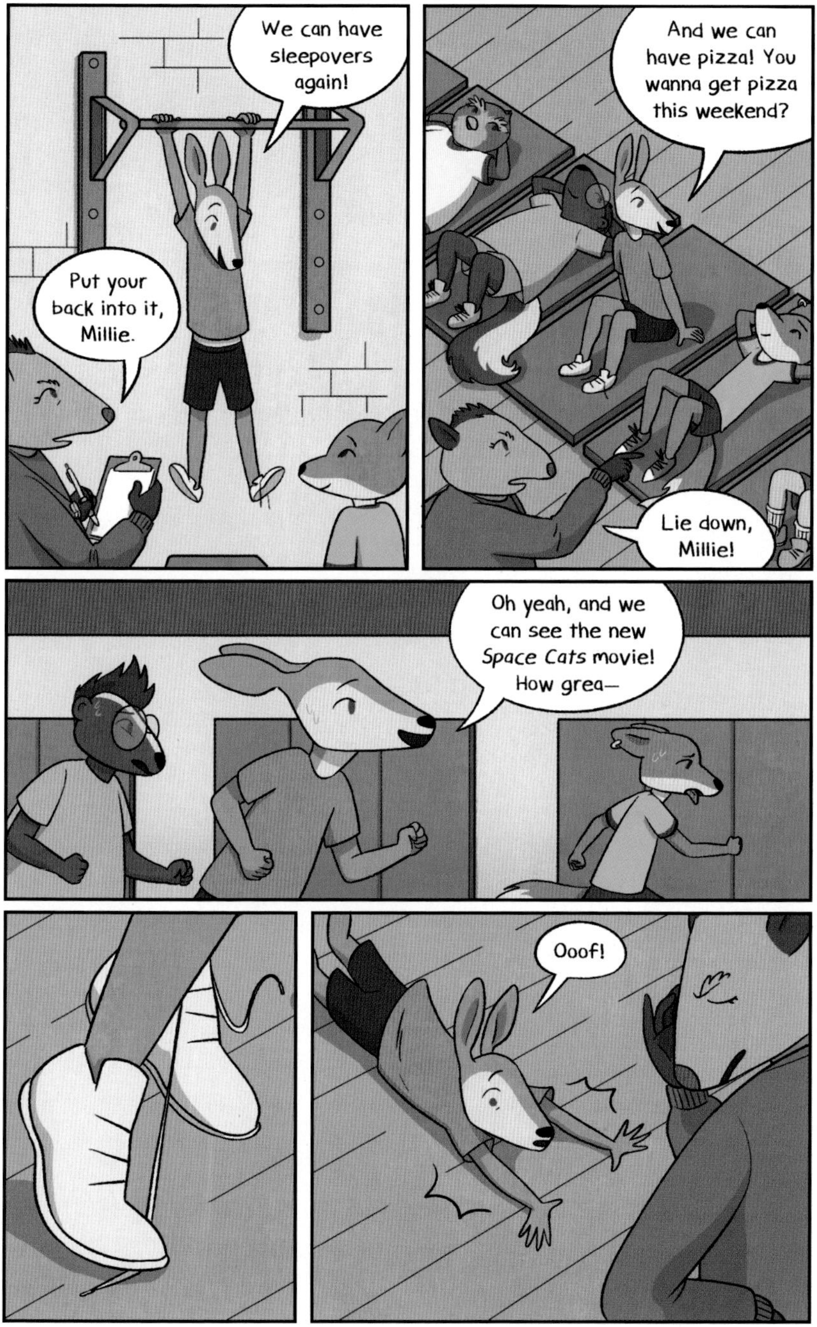
We can have sleepovers again!
Put your back into it, Millie.
And we can have pizza! You wanna get pizza this weekend?
Lie down, Millie!
Oh yeah, and we can see the new *Space Cats* movie! How grea—
Ooof!

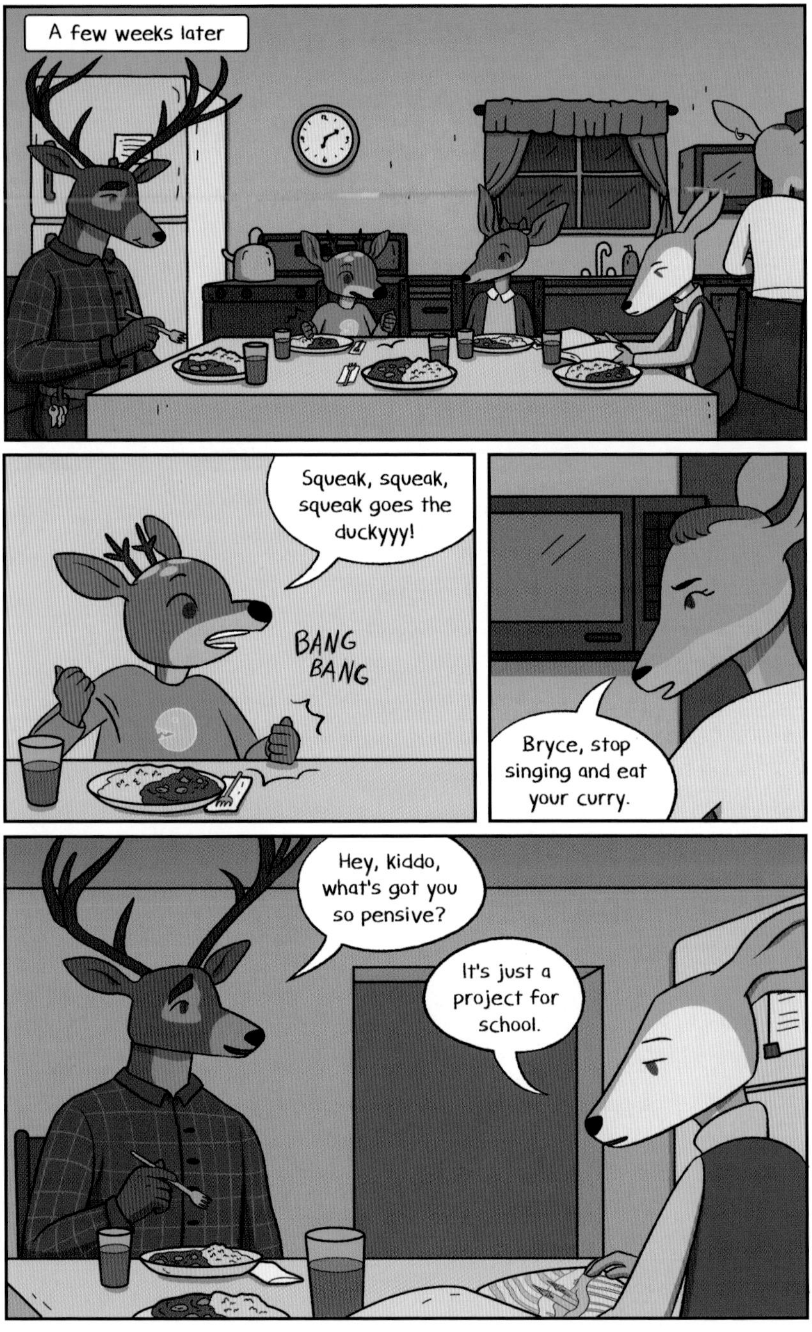
A few weeks later
Squeak, squeak, squeak goes the duckyyy!
BANG BANG
Bryce, stop singing and eat your curry.
Hey, kiddo, what's got you so pensive?
It's just a project for school.

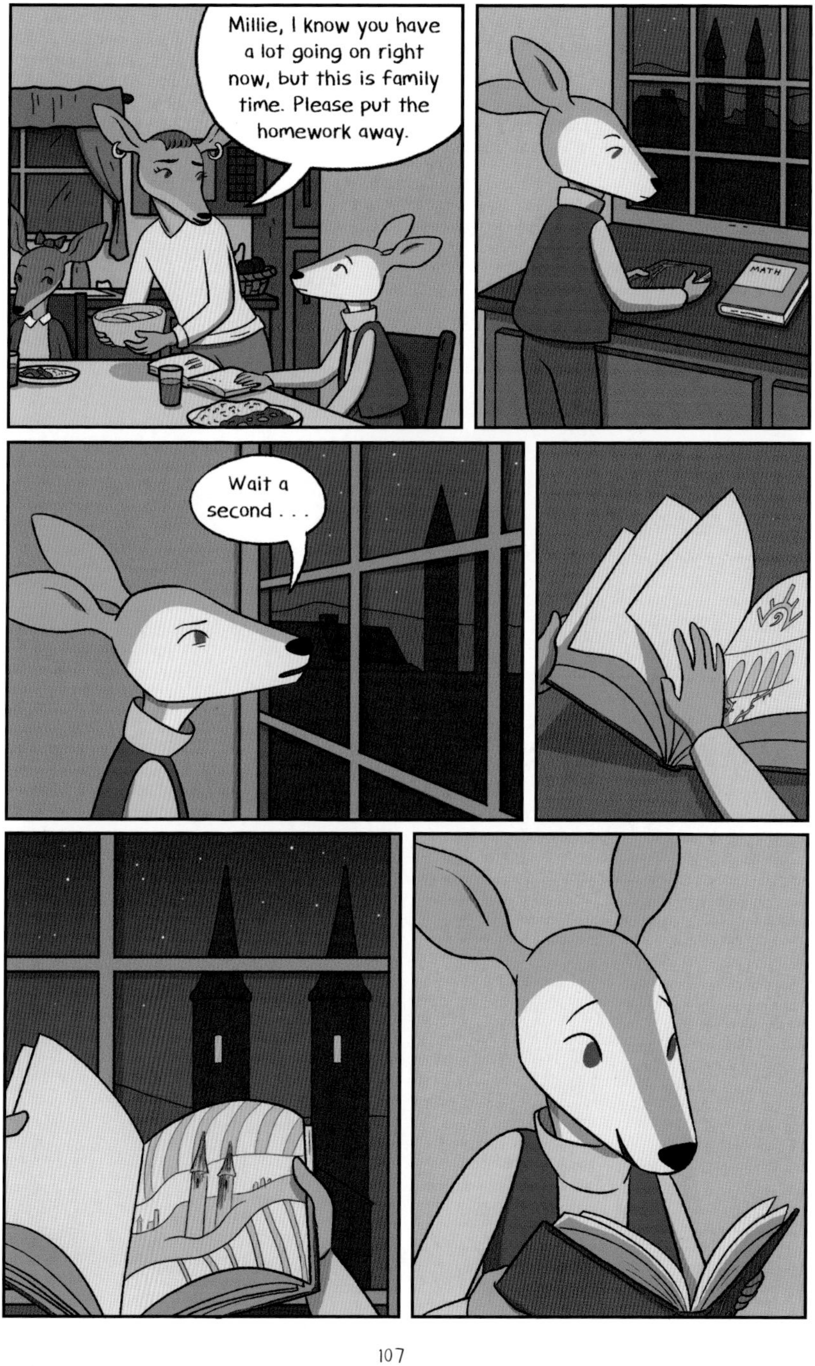
Millie, I know you have a lot going on right now, but this is family time. Please put the homework away.
MATH
Wait a second . . .

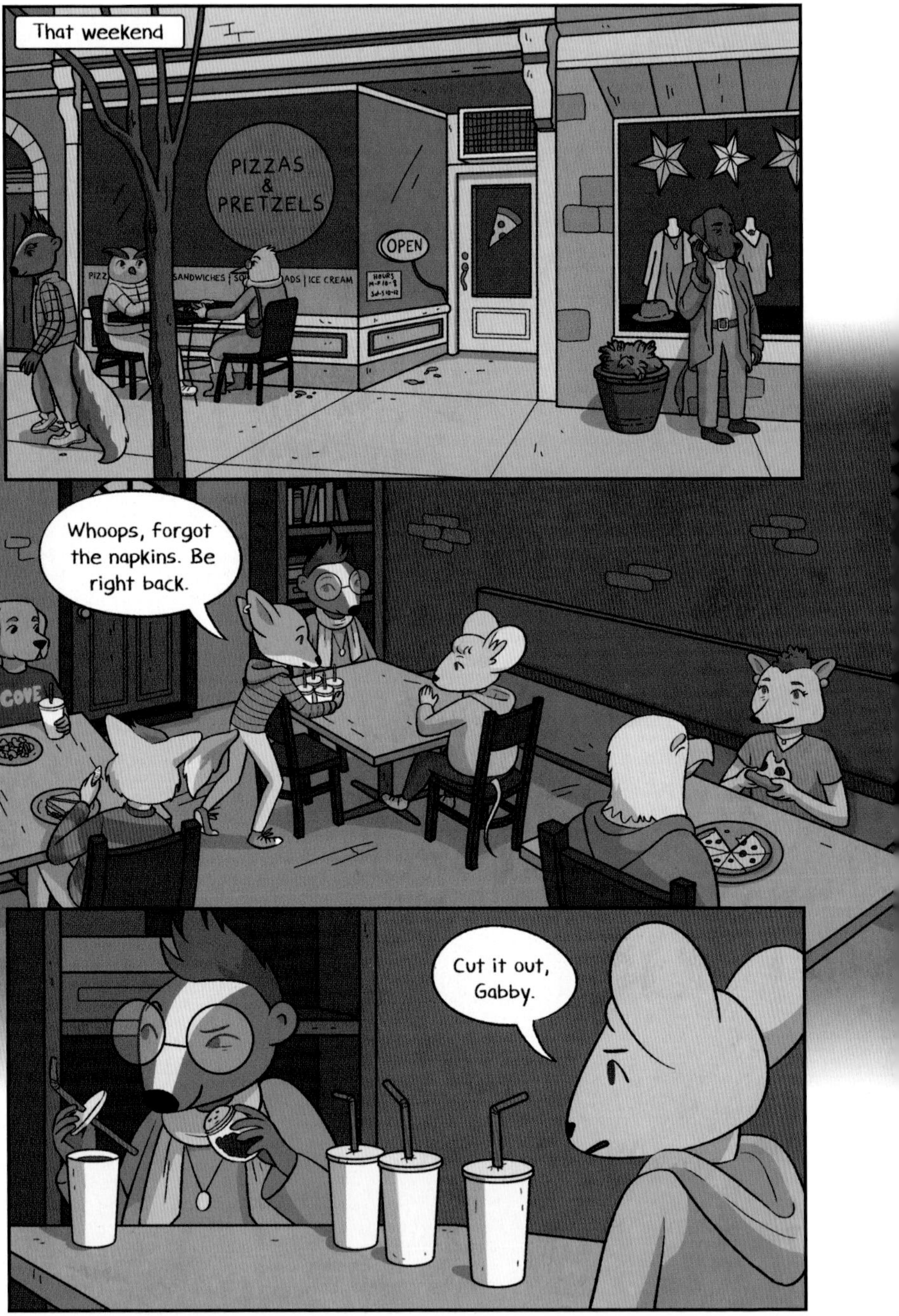
That weekend
PIZZAS & PRETZELS
OPEN
SANDWICHES
ICE CREAM
GOVE
Whoops, forgot the napkins. Be right back.
Cut it out, Gabby.

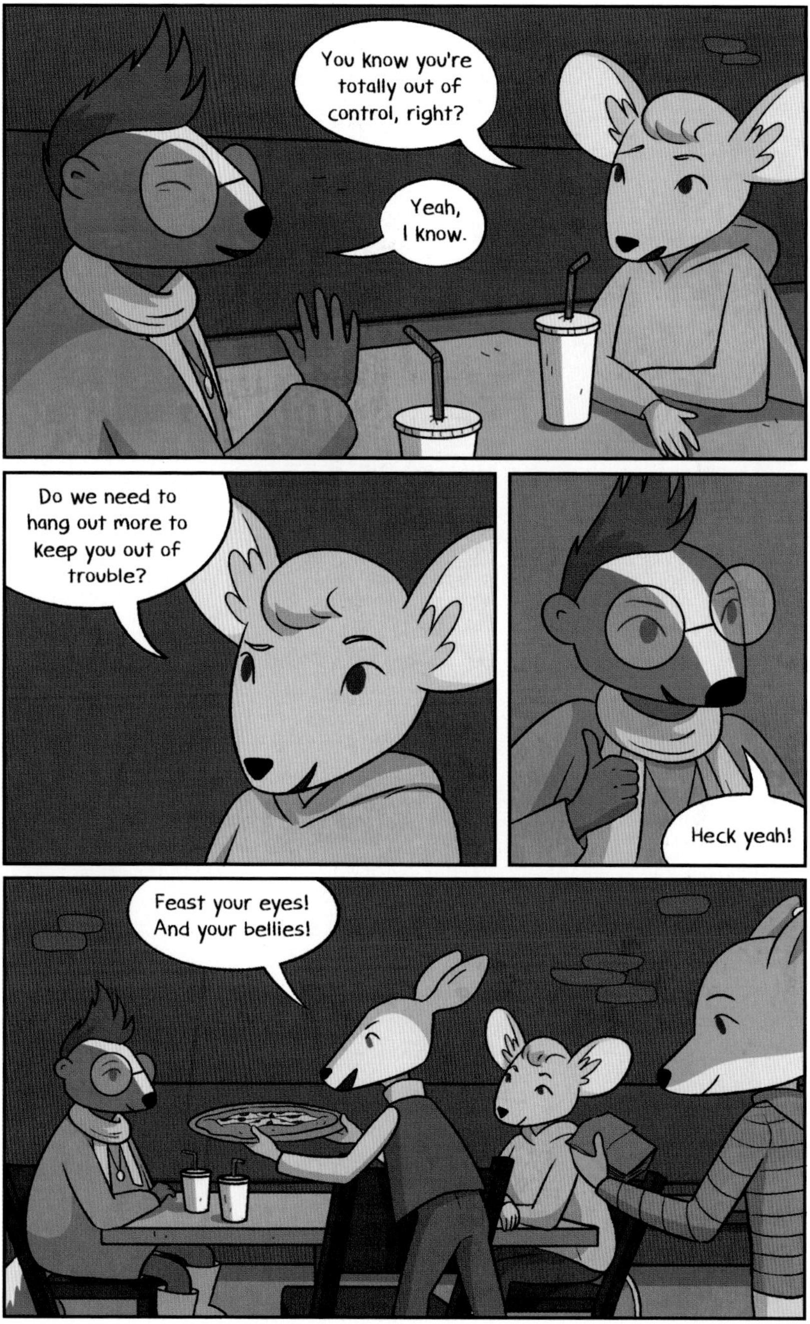
You know you're totally out of control, right?
Yeah, I know.
Do we need to hang out more to keep you out of trouble?
Heck yeah!
Feast your eyes! And your bellies!

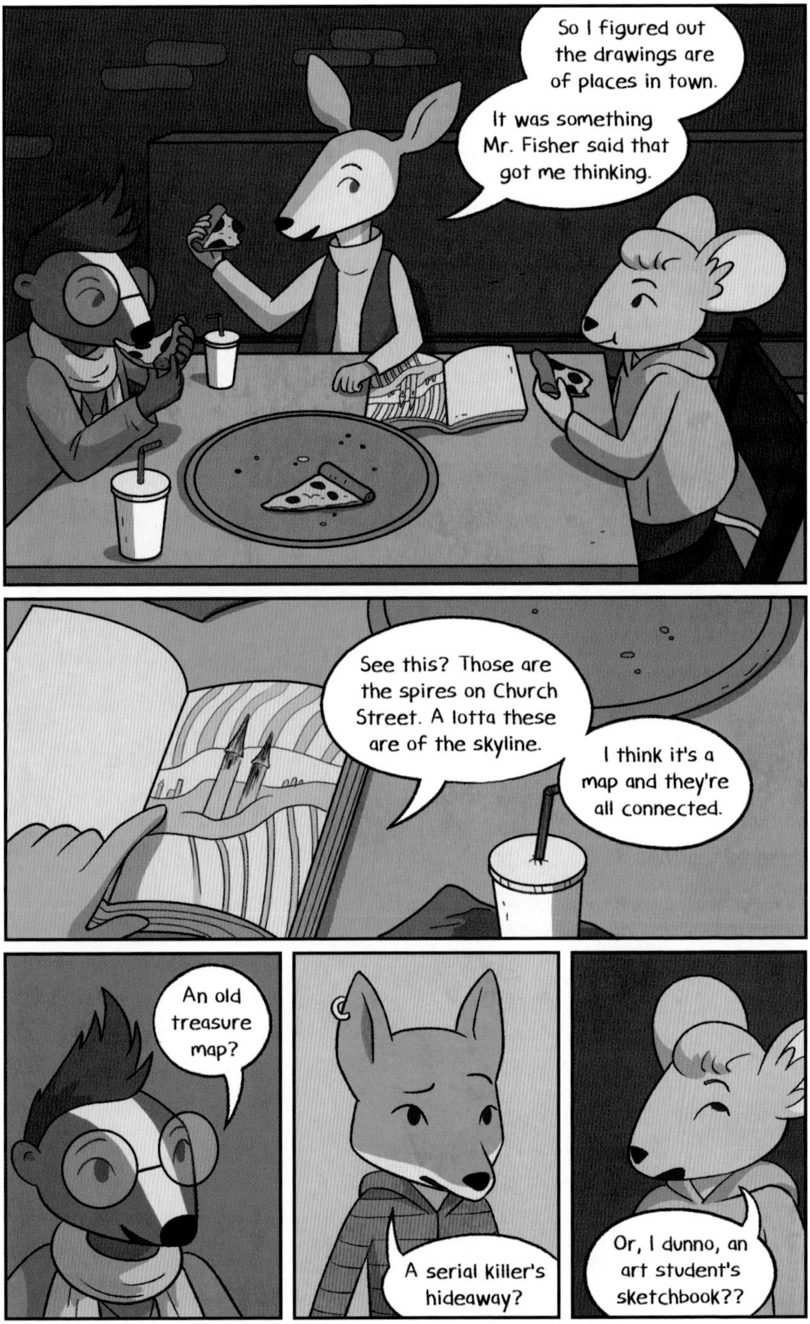
So I figured out the drawings are of places in town.
It was something Mr. Fisher said that got me thinking.
See this? Those are the spires on Church Street. A lotta these are of the skyline.
I think it's a map and they're all connected.
An old treasure map?
A serial killer's hideaway?
Or, I dunno, an art student's sketchbook??

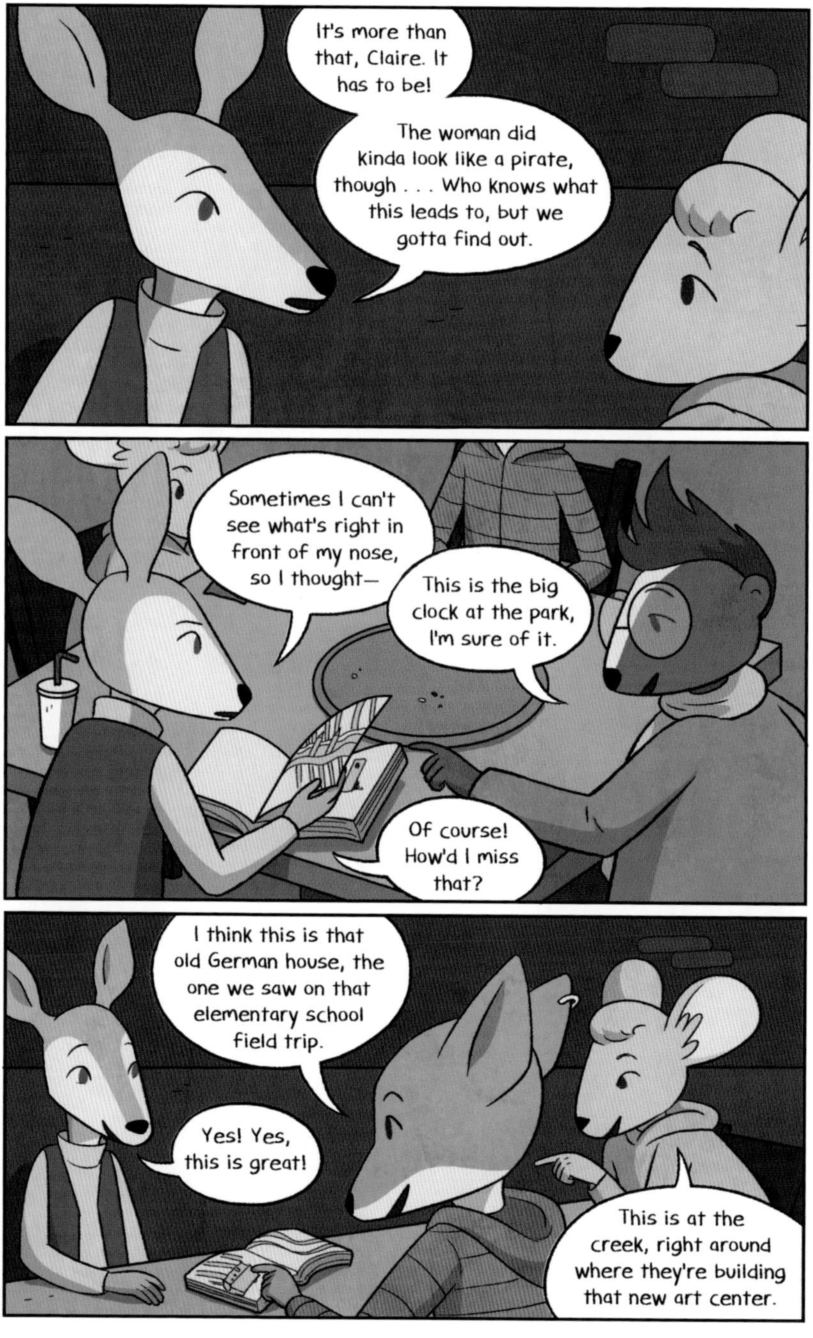
It's more than that, Claire. It has to be!
The woman did kinda look like a pirate, though . . . Who knows what this leads to, but we gotta find out.
Sometimes I can't see what's right in front of my nose, so I thought—
This is the big clock at the park, I'm sure of it.
Of course! How'd I miss that?
I think this is that old German house, the one we saw on that elementary school field trip.
Yes! Yes, this is great!
This is at the creek, right around where they're building that new art center.

I think that's most of them! Let me see . . .

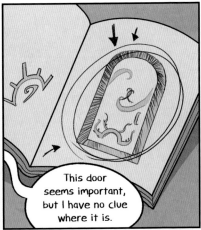

This door seems important, but I have no clue where it is.

We figured out a lot, though! *And* we'll keep our eyes peeled for that door.

Well, I'm going to get some ice cream to celebrate. Anybody else want some?

I could totally go for ice cream.

I gotta run to the bathroom.

BZZZ
BZZZ

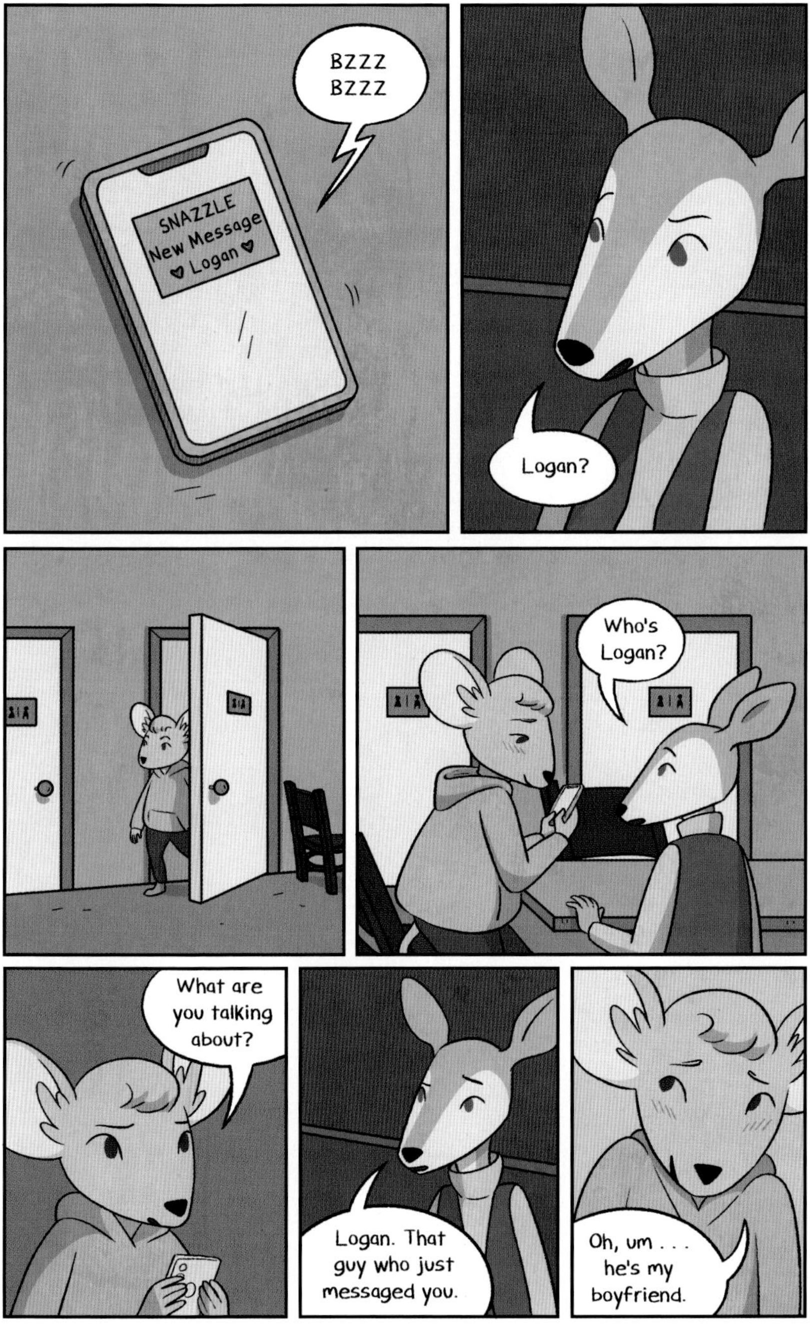

BZZZ
BZZZ
SNAZZLE
New Message
♥ Logan ♥
Logan?
Who's Logan?
What are you talking about?
Logan. That guy who just messaged you.
Oh, um . . . he's my boyfriend.

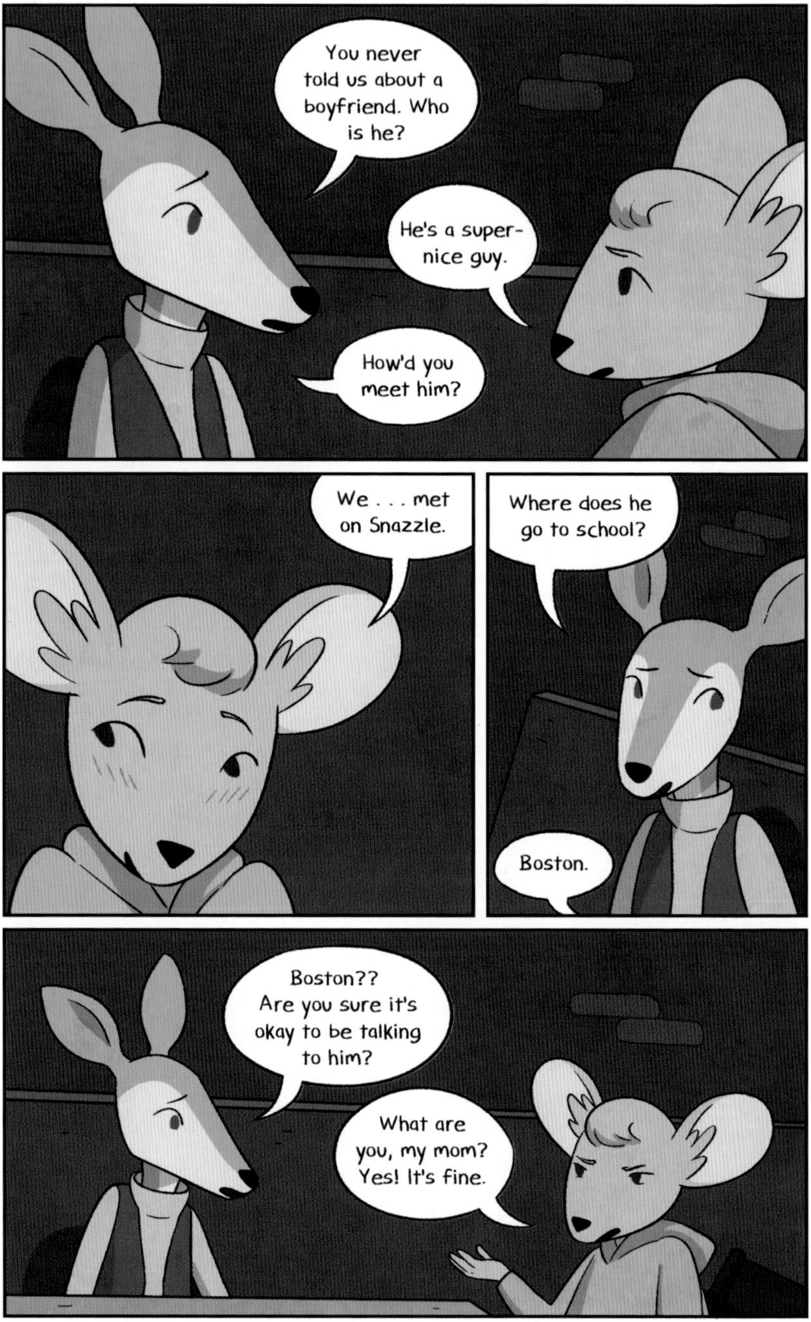
You never told us about a boyfriend. Who is he?
He's a super-nice guy.
How'd you meet him?
We . . . met on Snazzle.
Where does he go to school?
Boston.
Boston?? Are you sure it's okay to be talking to him?
What are you, my mom? Yes! It's fine.

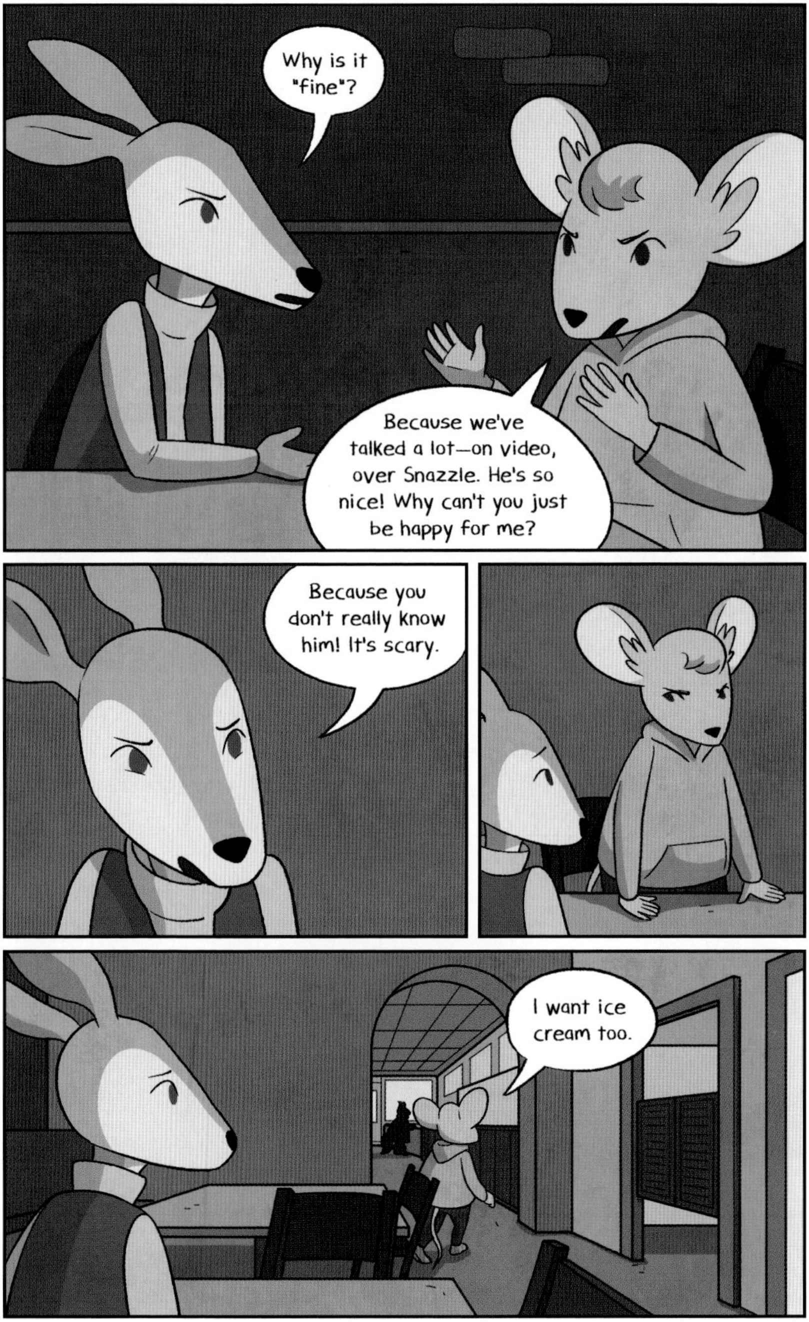
Why is it "fine"?
Because we've talked a lot—on video, over Snazzle. He's so nice! Why can't you just be happy for me?
Because you don't really know him! It's scary.
I want ice cream too.

A few weeks later

Mr. DeAlba! You've lived here for a long time—

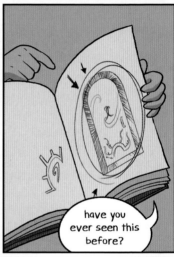

have you ever seen this before?

Hmm . . . it could be the front door of the old All Saints Church, the one tucked away behind the library.

But if I'm not mistaken, that building is set to be demolished soon.

116

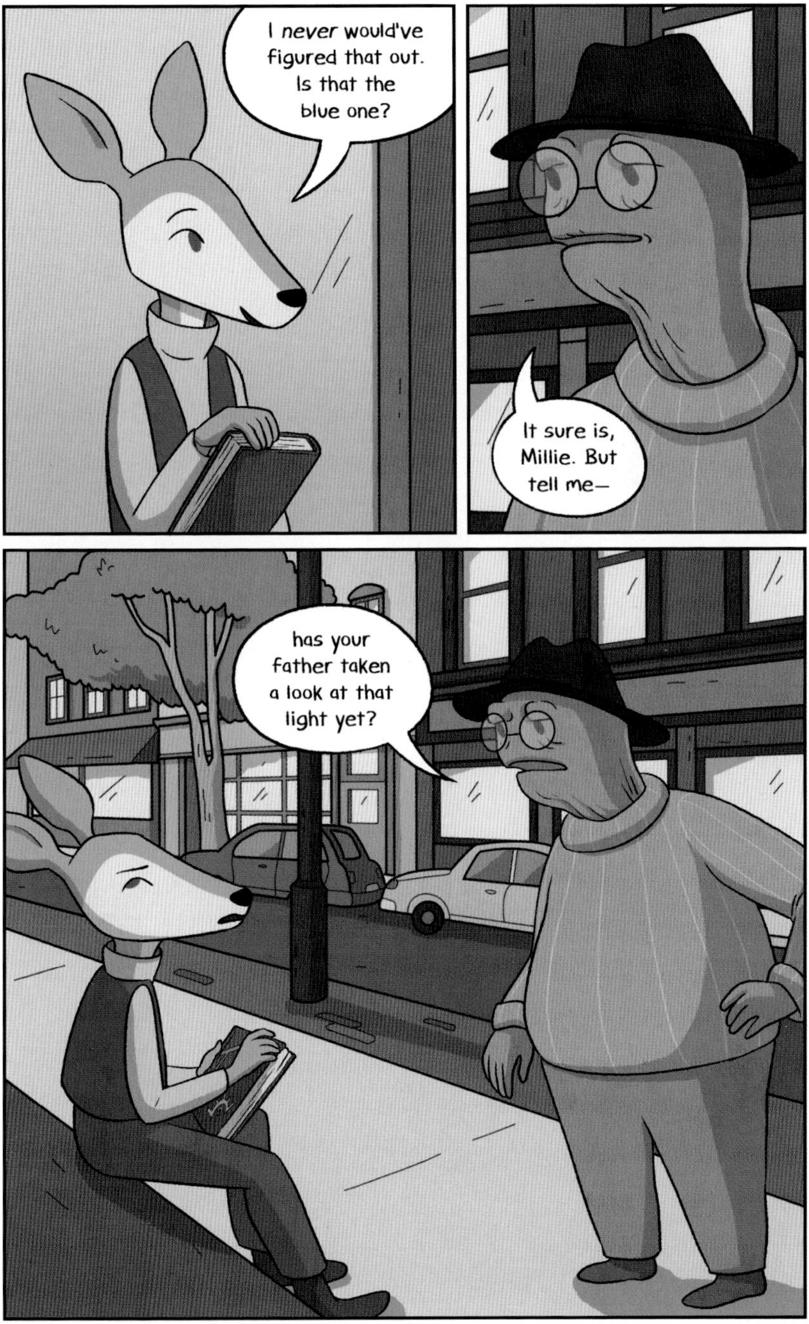
I *never* would've figured that out. Is that the blue one?
It sure is, Millie. But tell me—
has your father taken a look at that light yet?

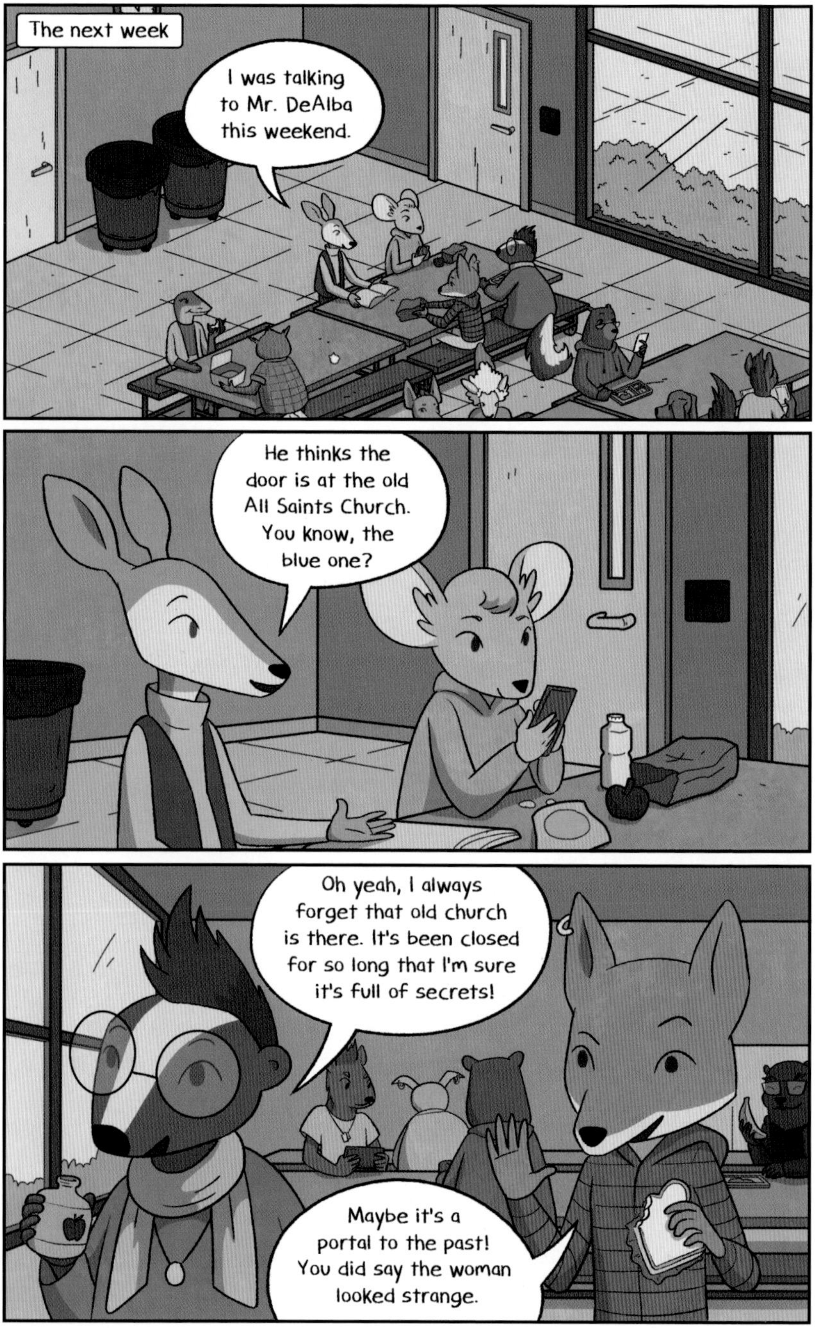

The next week
I was talking to Mr. DeAlba this weekend.
He thinks the door is at the old All Saints Church. You know, the blue one?
Oh yeah, I always forget that old church is there. It's been closed for so long that I'm sure it's full of secrets!
Maybe it's a portal to the past! You did say the woman looked strange.

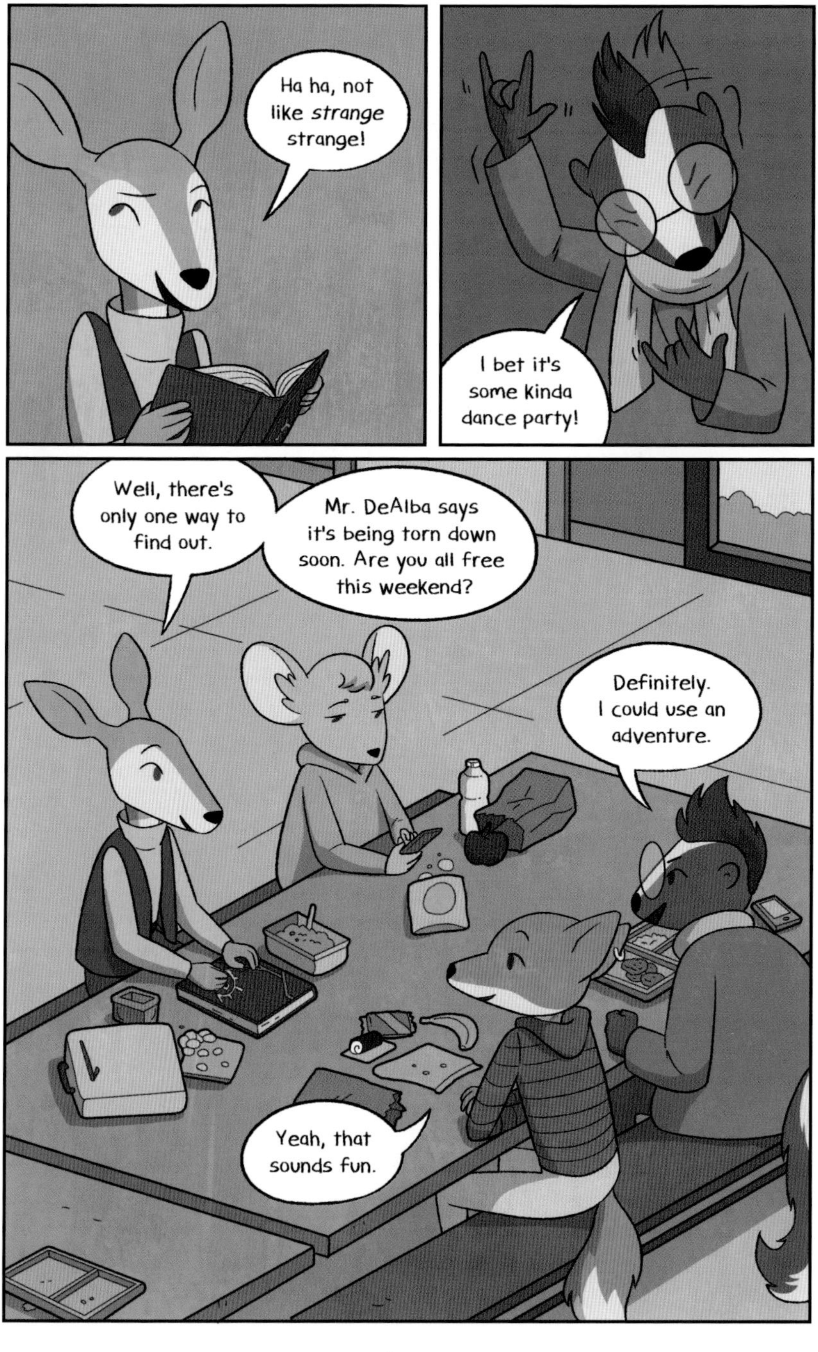
Ha ha, not like *strange* strange!
I bet it's some kinda dance party!
Well, there's only one way to find out.
Mr. DeAlba says it's being torn down soon. Are you all free this weekend?
Definitely. I could use an adventure.
Yeah, that sounds fun.

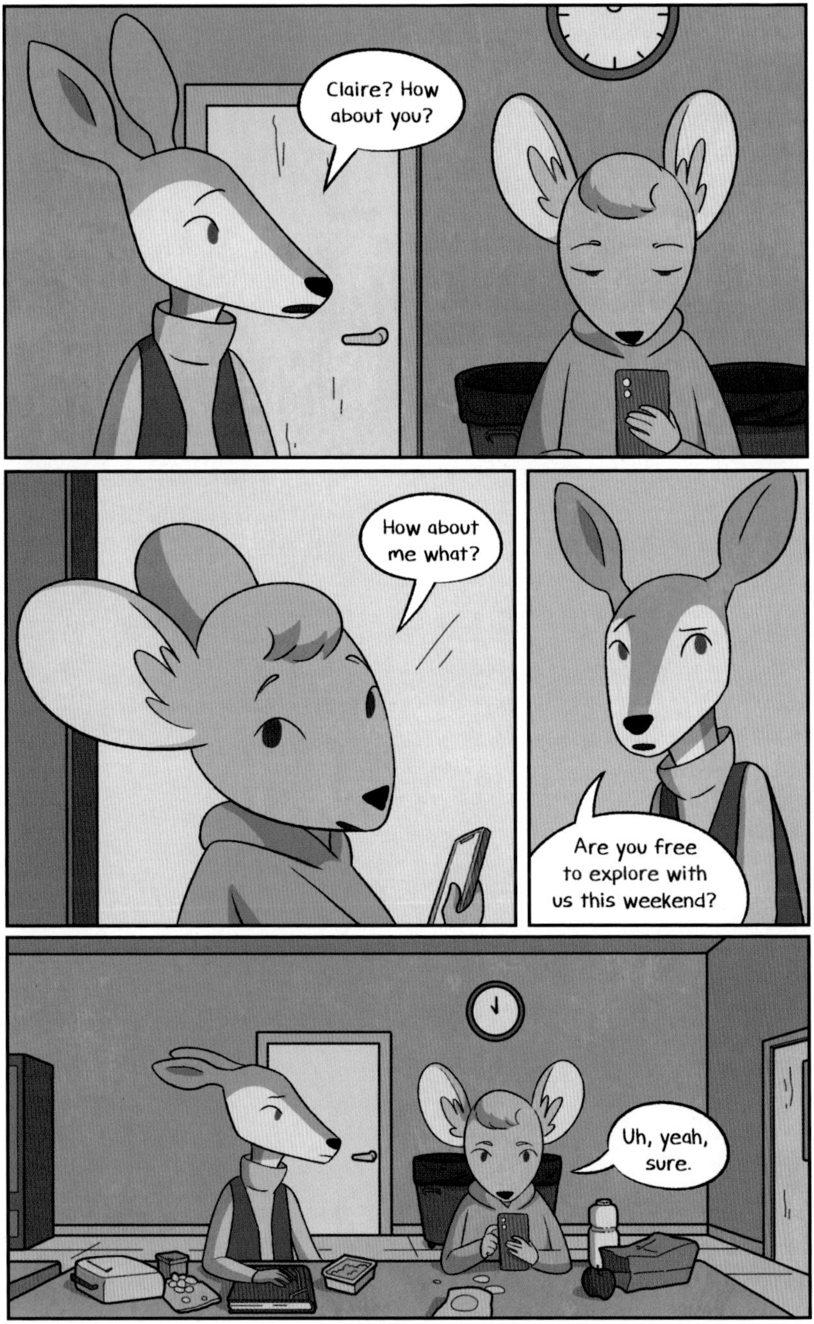
Claire? How about you?
How about me what?
Are you free to explore with us this weekend?
Uh, yeah, sure.

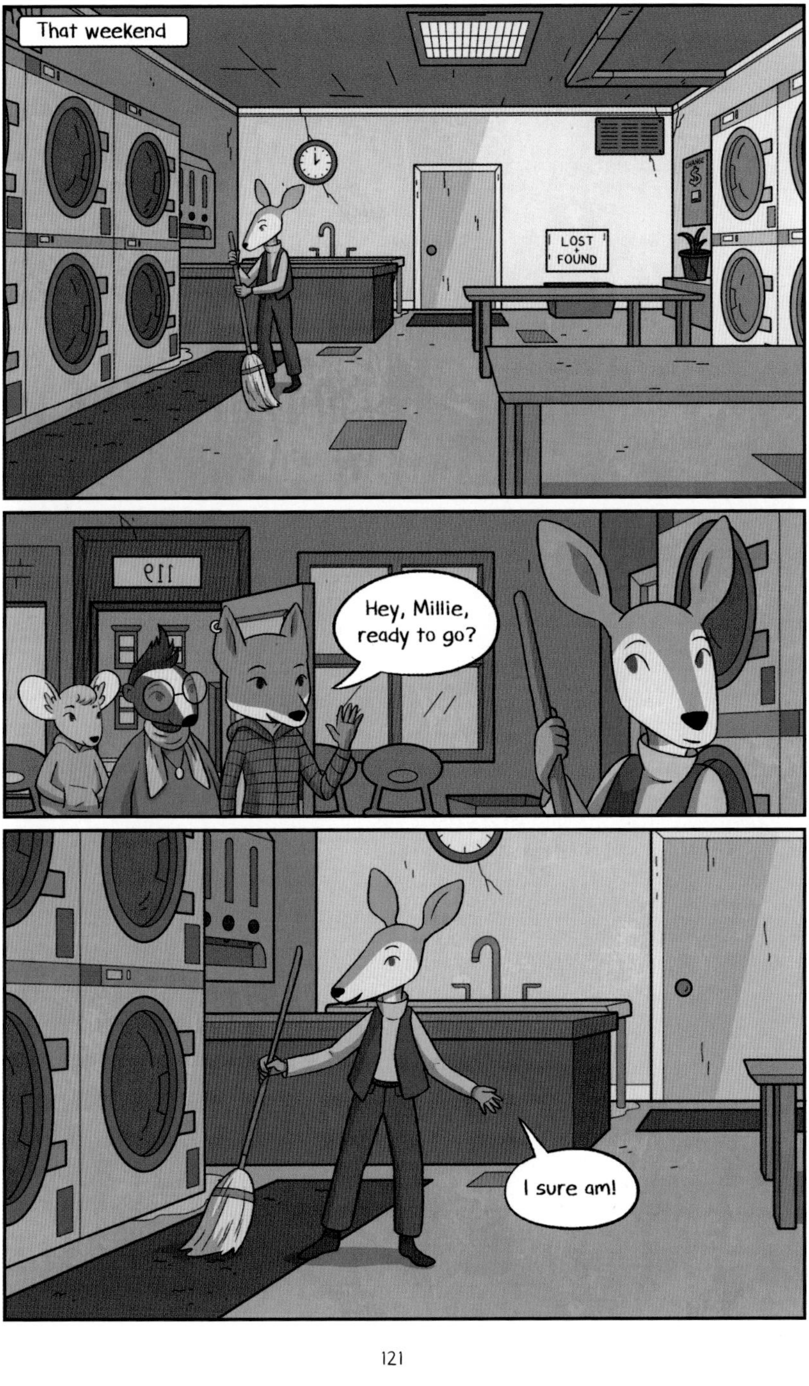
That weekend
LOST + FOUND
119
Hey, Millie, ready to go?
I sure am!

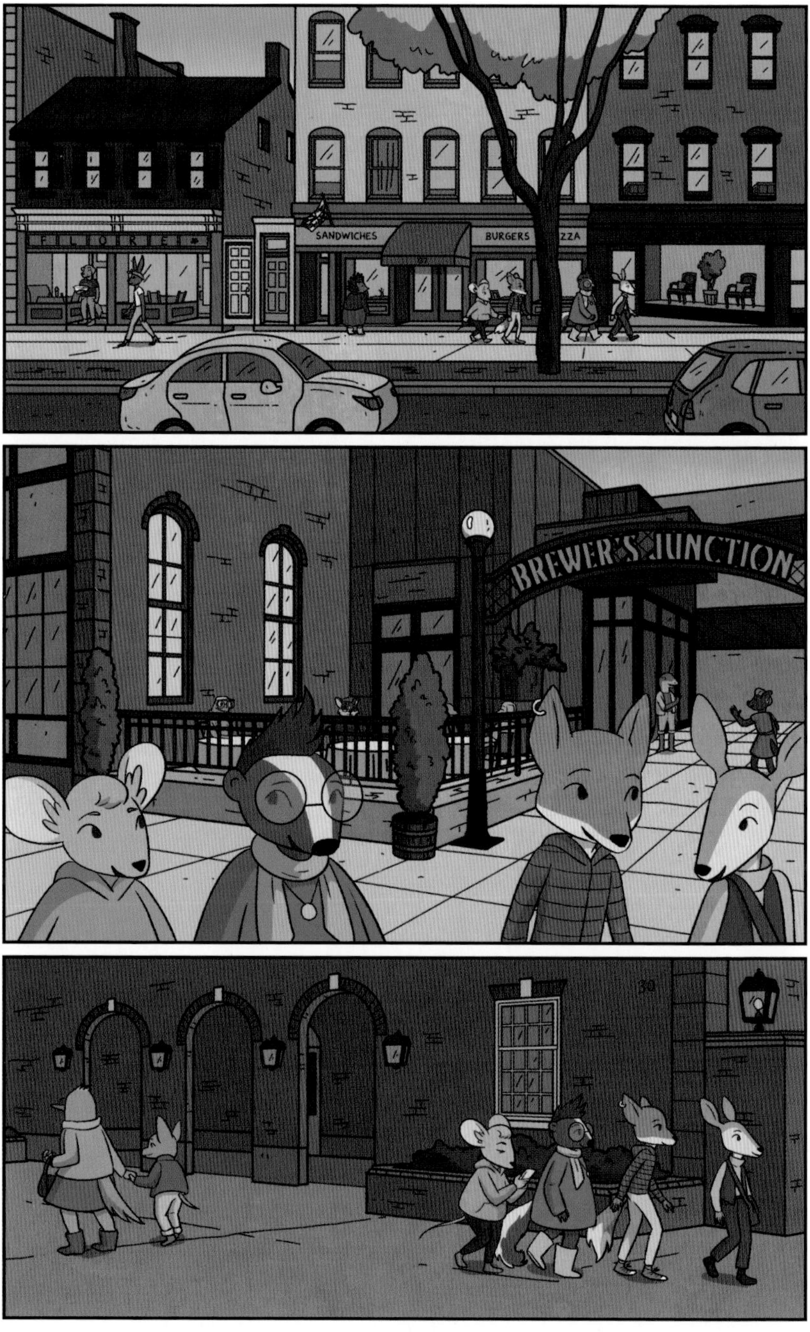
SANDWICHES
BURGERS
BREWER'S JUNCTION

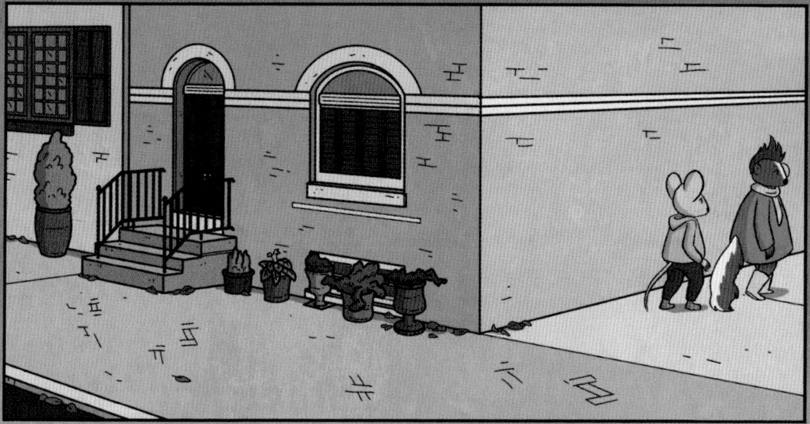
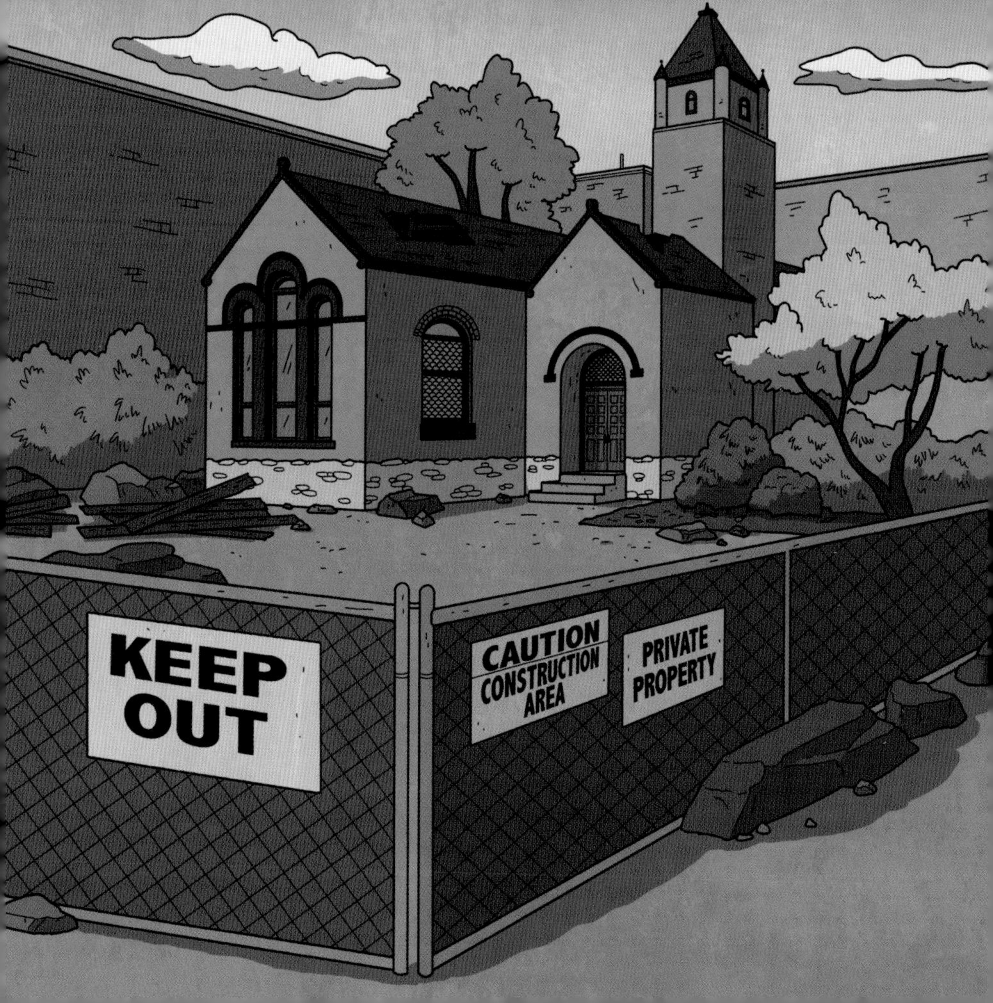
KEEP OUT
CAUTION CONSTRUCTION AREA
PRIVATE PROPERTY

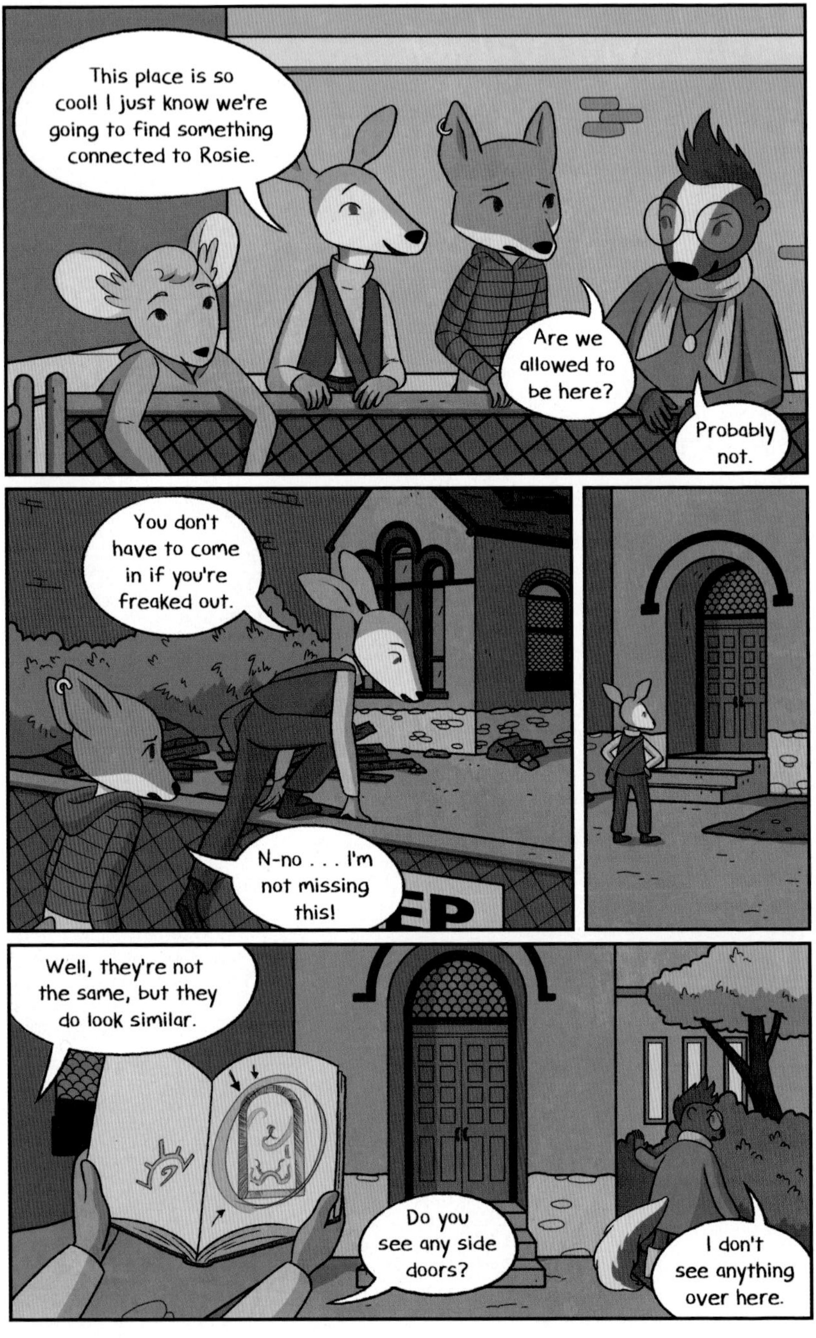
This place is so cool! I just know we're going to find something connected to Rosie.
Are we allowed to be here?
Probably not.
You don't have to come in if you're freaked out.
N-no . . . I'm not missing this!
Well, they're not the same, but they do look similar.
Do you see any side doors?
I don't see anything over here.

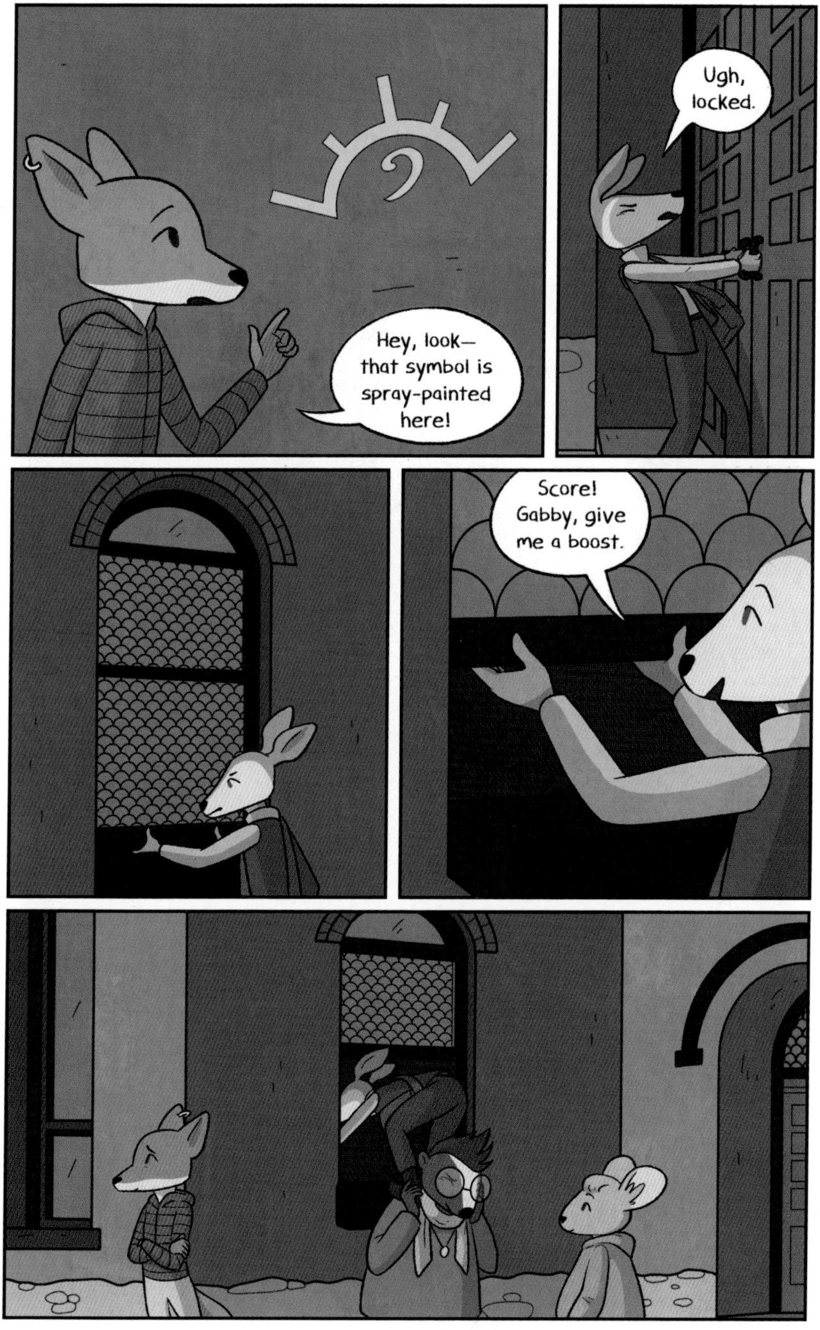
Hey, look—
that symbol is
spray-painted
here!
Ugh,
locked.
Score!
Gabby, give
me a boost.

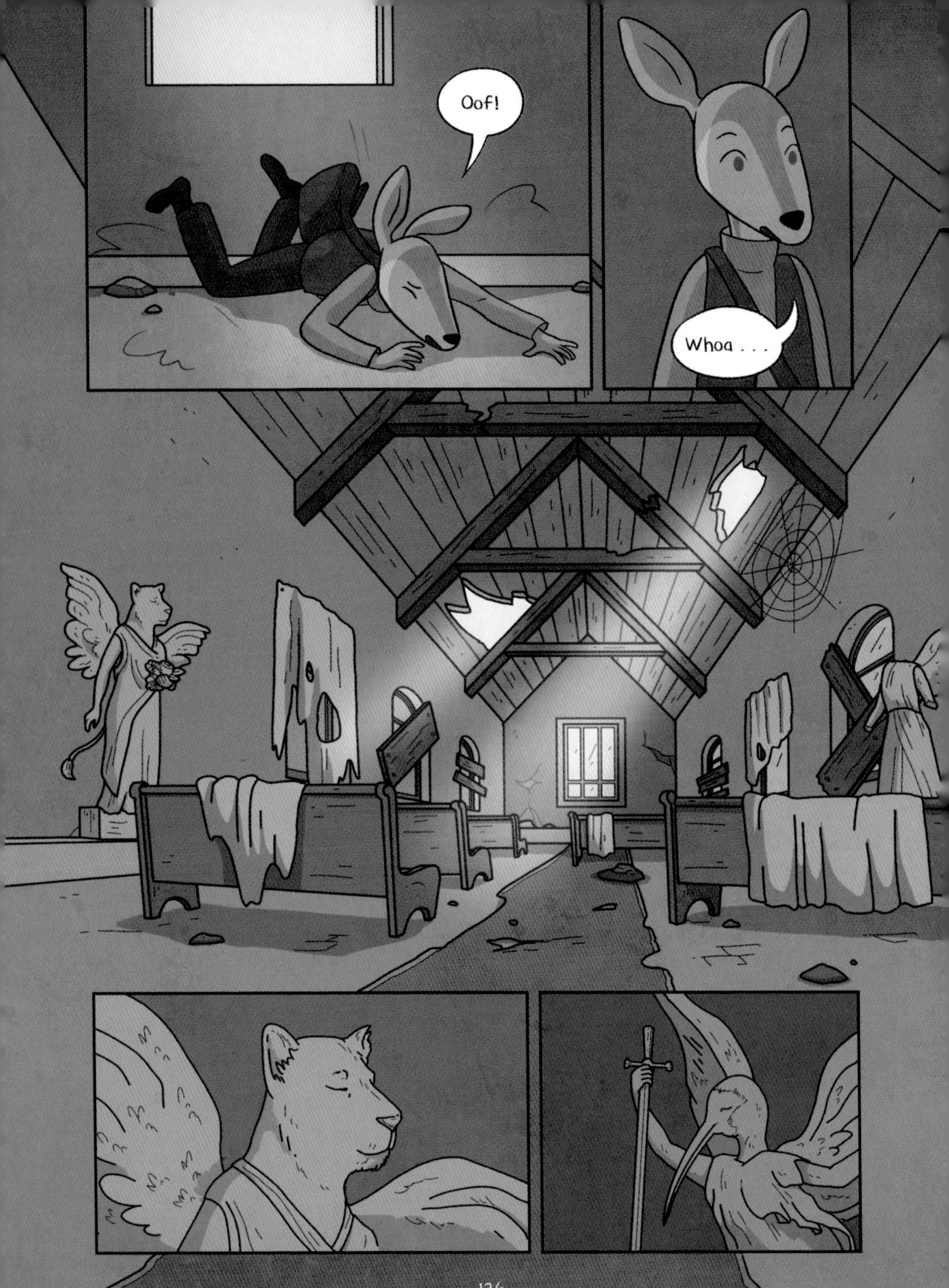
Oof!
Whoa . . .

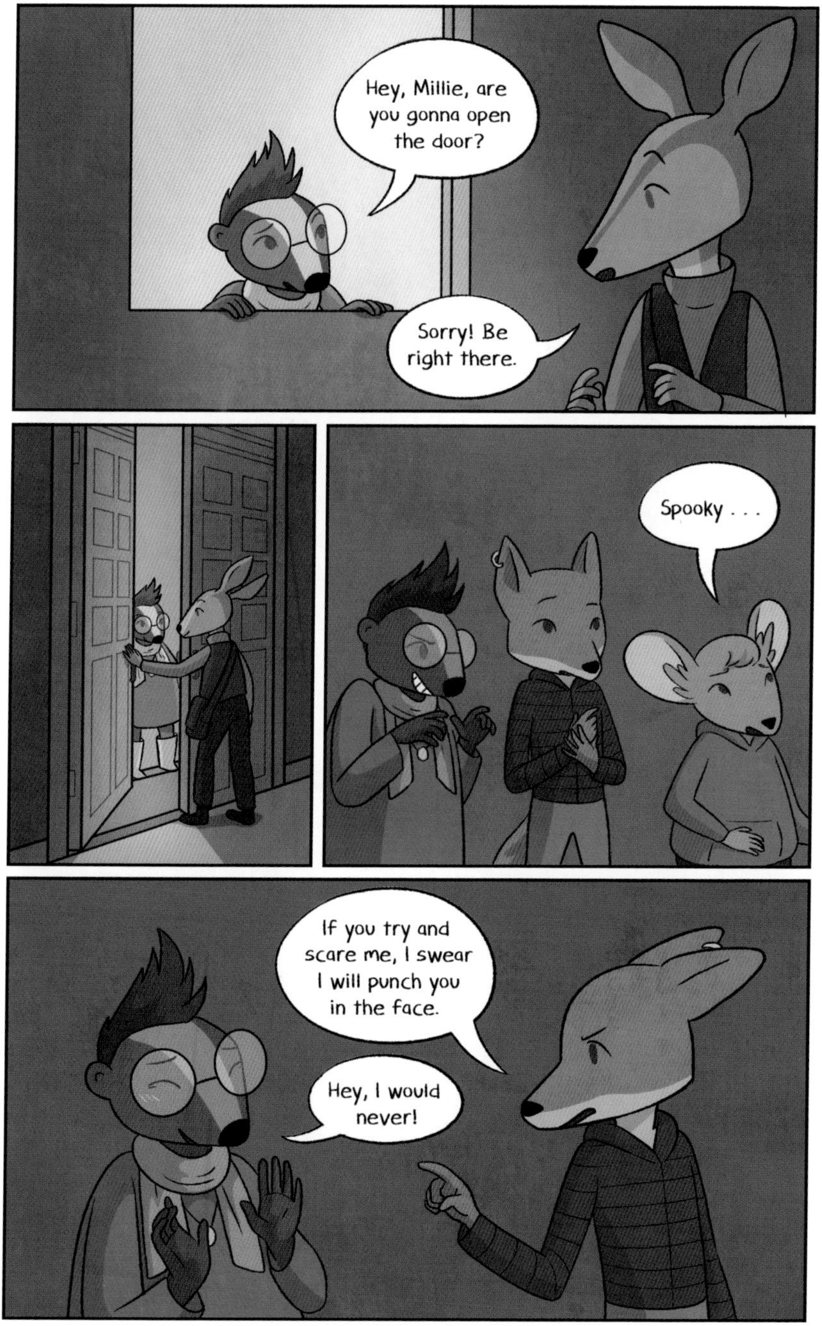
Hey, Millie, are you gonna open the door?
Sorry! Be right there.
Spooky . . .
If you try and scare me, I swear I will punch you in the face.
Hey, I would never!

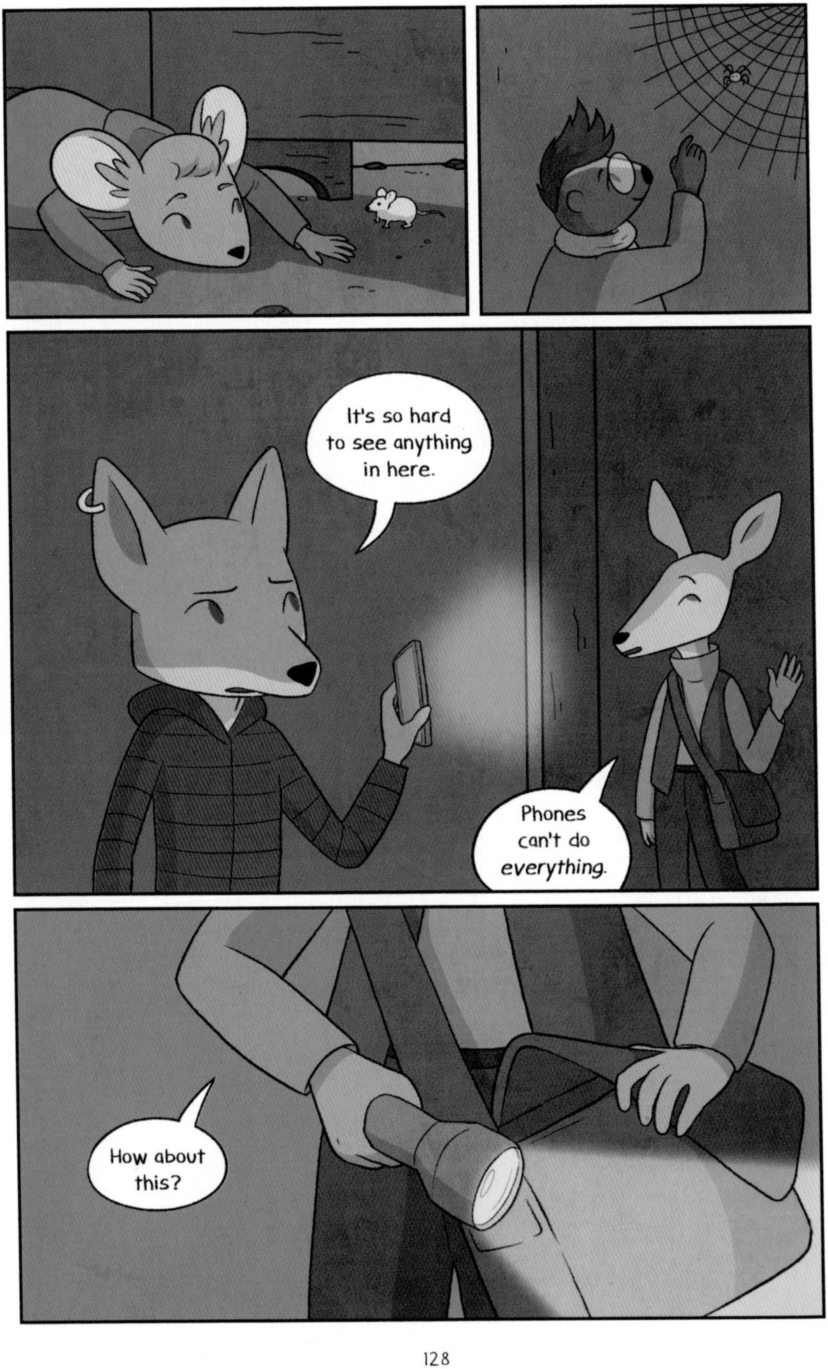

It's so hard to see anything in here.
Phones can't do *everything*.
How about this?

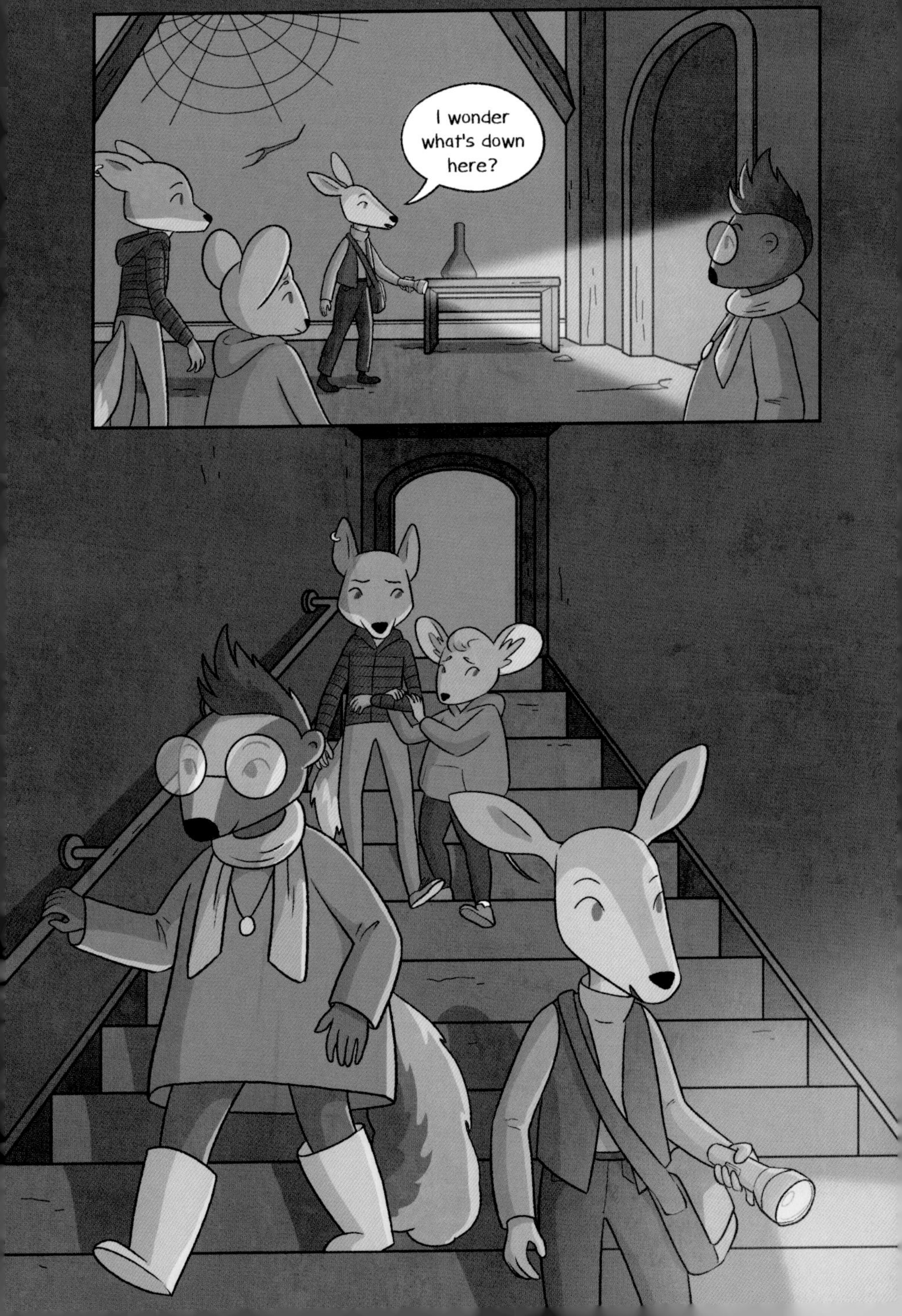
I wonder what's down here?

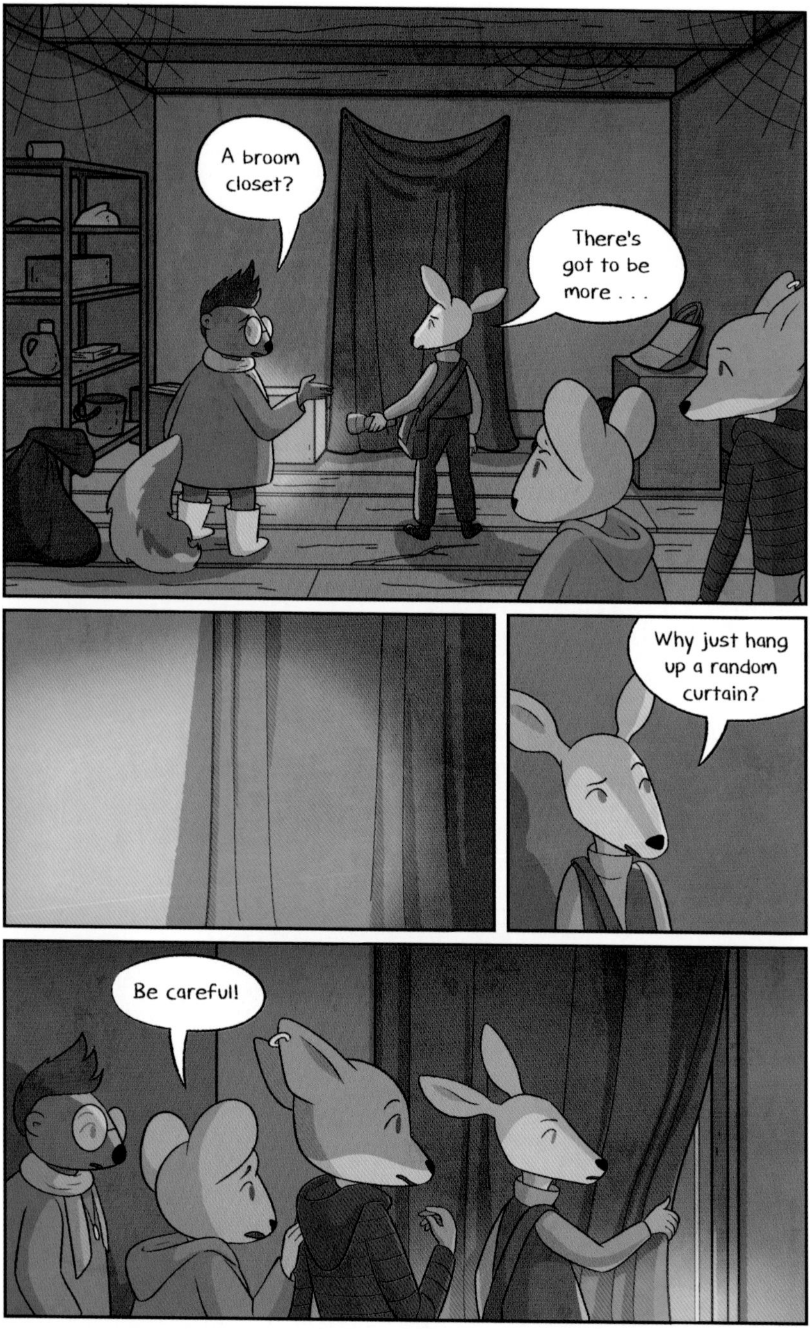
A broom closet?
There's got to be more . . .
Why just hang up a random curtain?
Be careful!

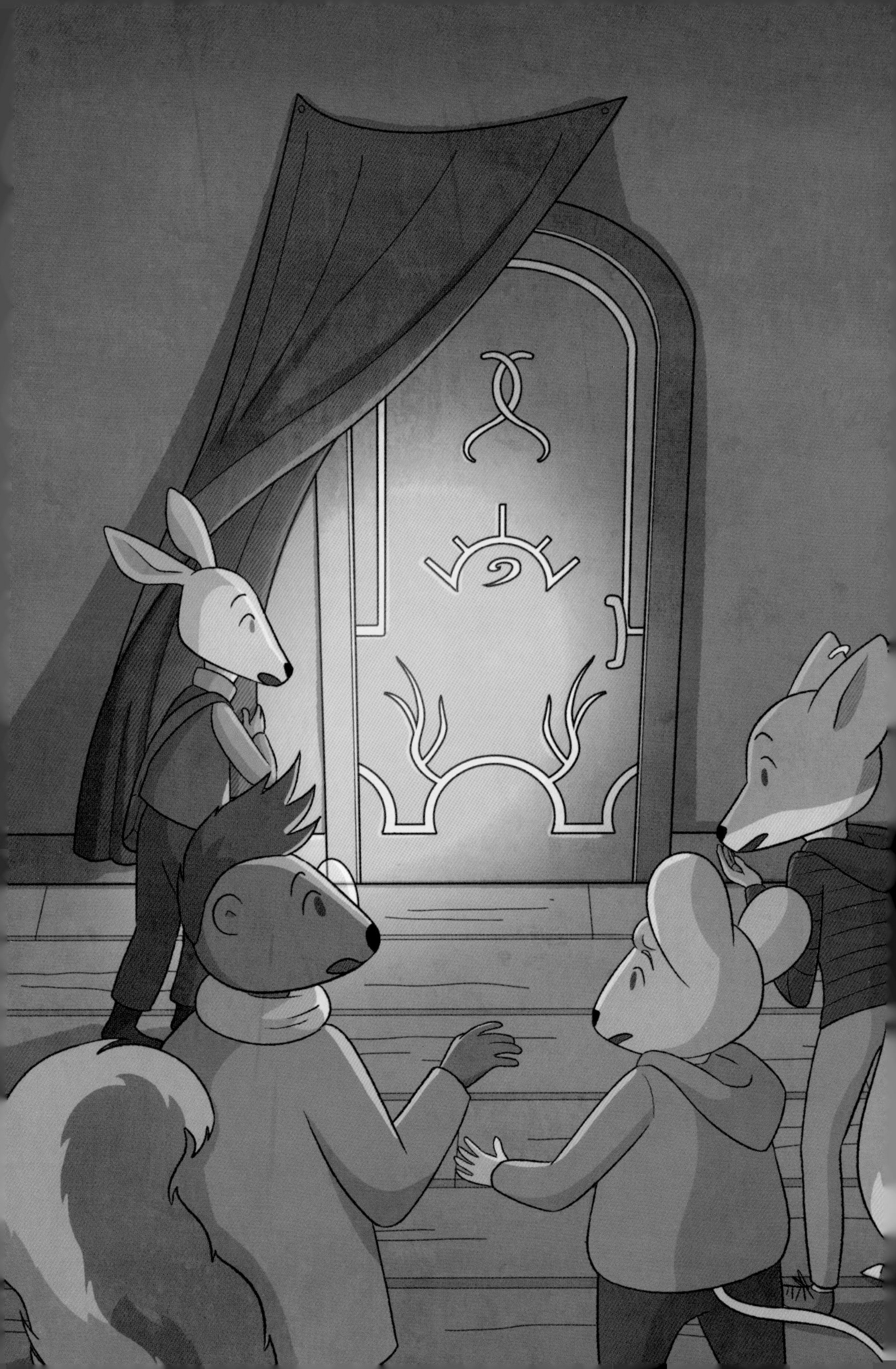

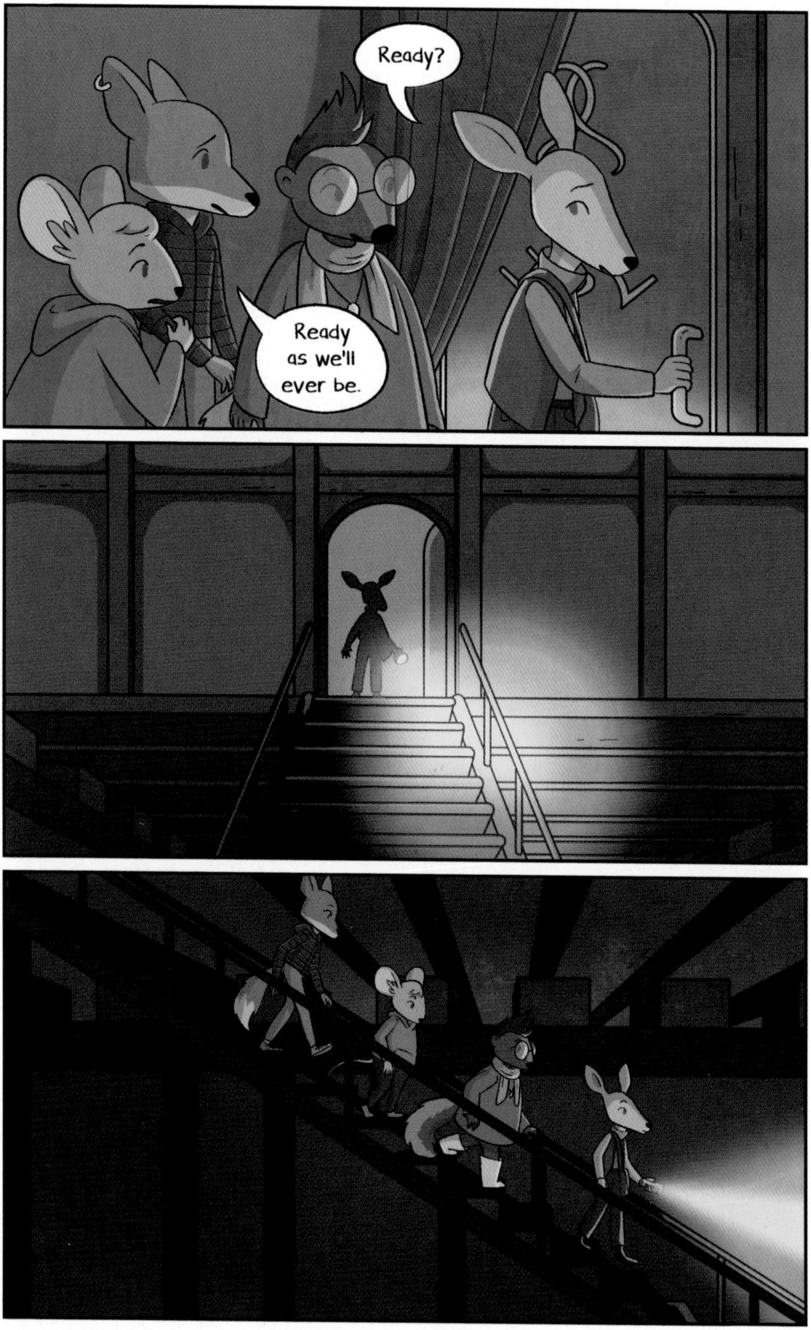
Ready?
Ready as we'll ever be.

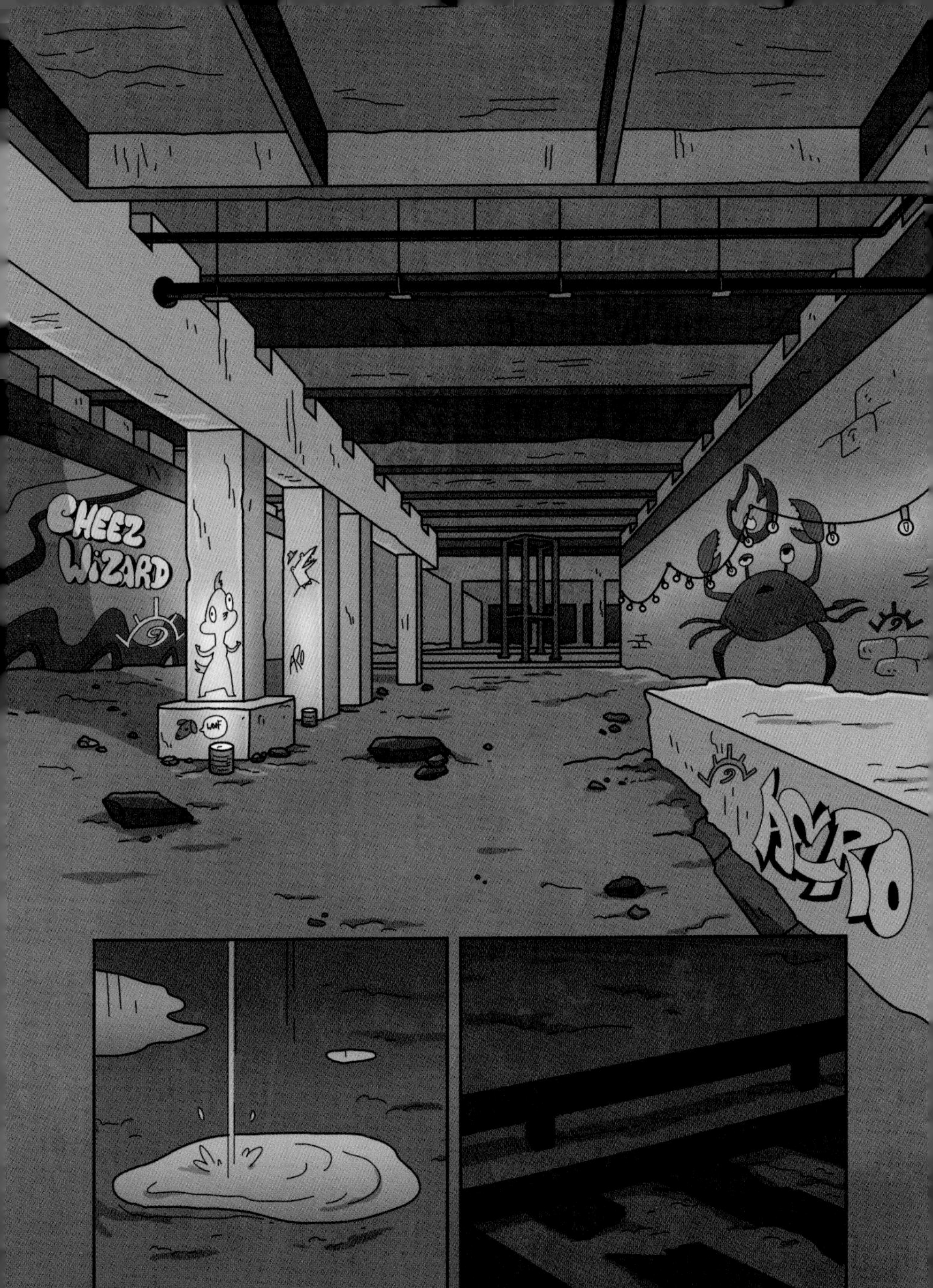
CHEEZ WIZARD

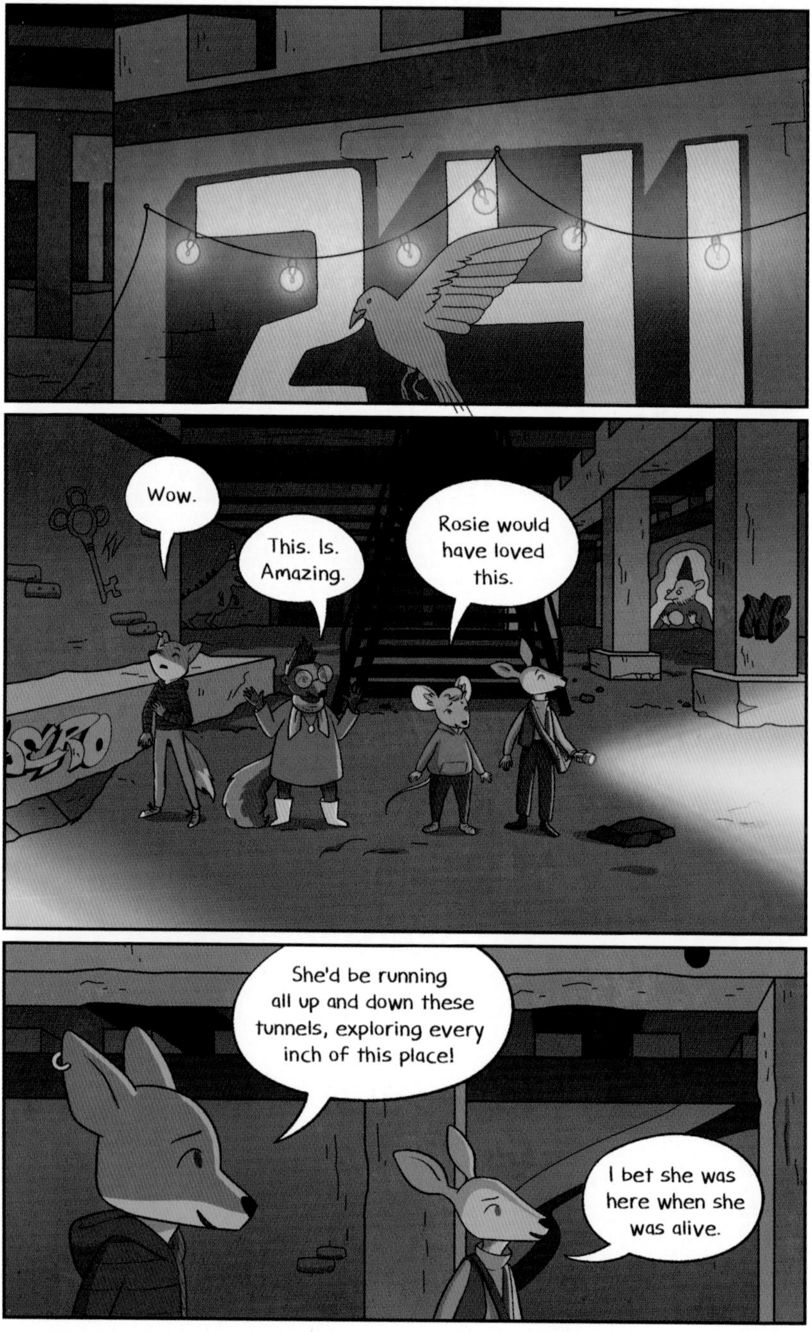
Wow.
This. Is. Amazing.
Rosie would have loved this.
She'd be running all up and down these tunnels, exploring every inch of this place!
I bet she was here when she was alive.

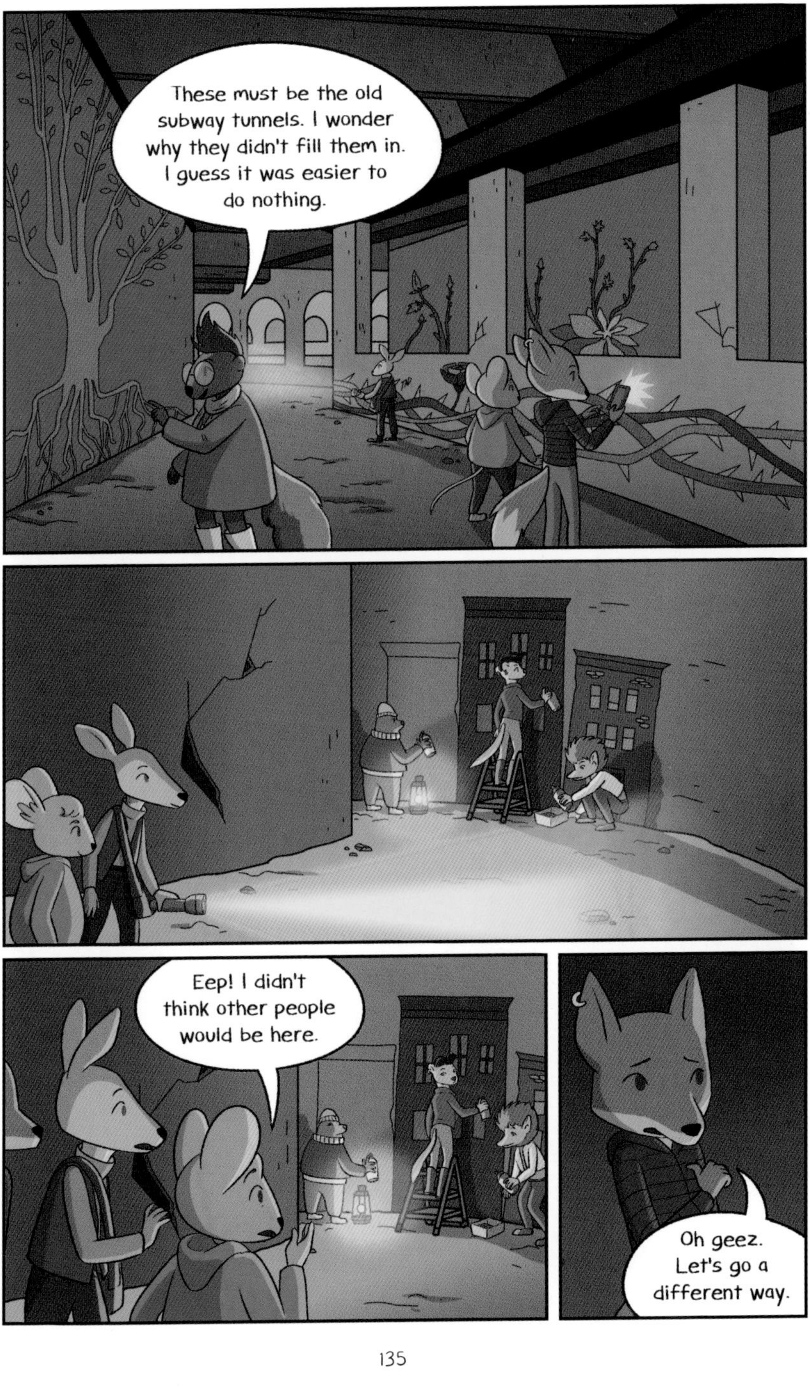
These must be the old subway tunnels. I wonder why they didn't fill them in. I guess it was easier to do nothing.
Eep! I didn't think other people would be here.
Oh geez. Let's go a different way.

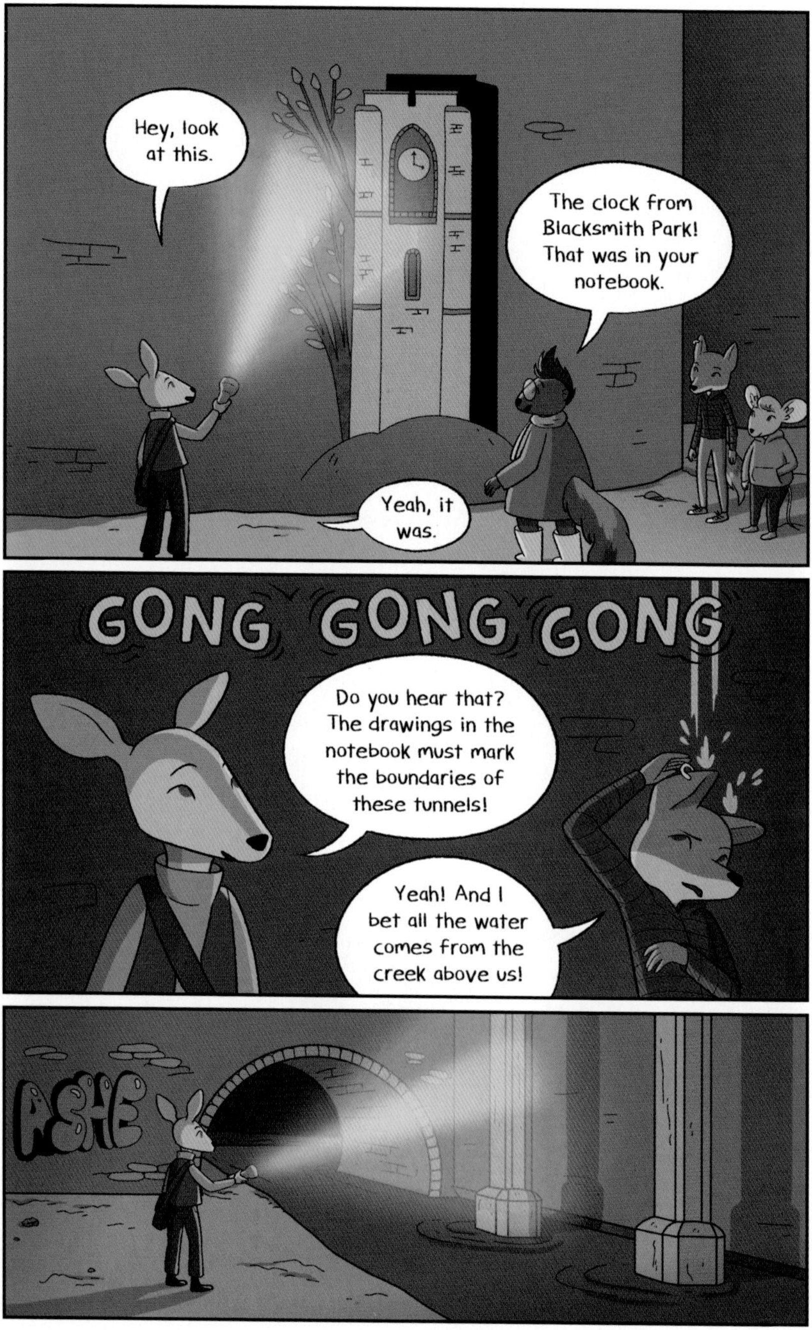
Hey, look at this.
The clock from Blacksmith Park! That was in your notebook.
Yeah, it was.
GONG GONG GONG
Do you hear that? The drawings in the notebook must mark the boundaries of these tunnels!
Yeah! And I bet all the water comes from the creek above us!
ASHE

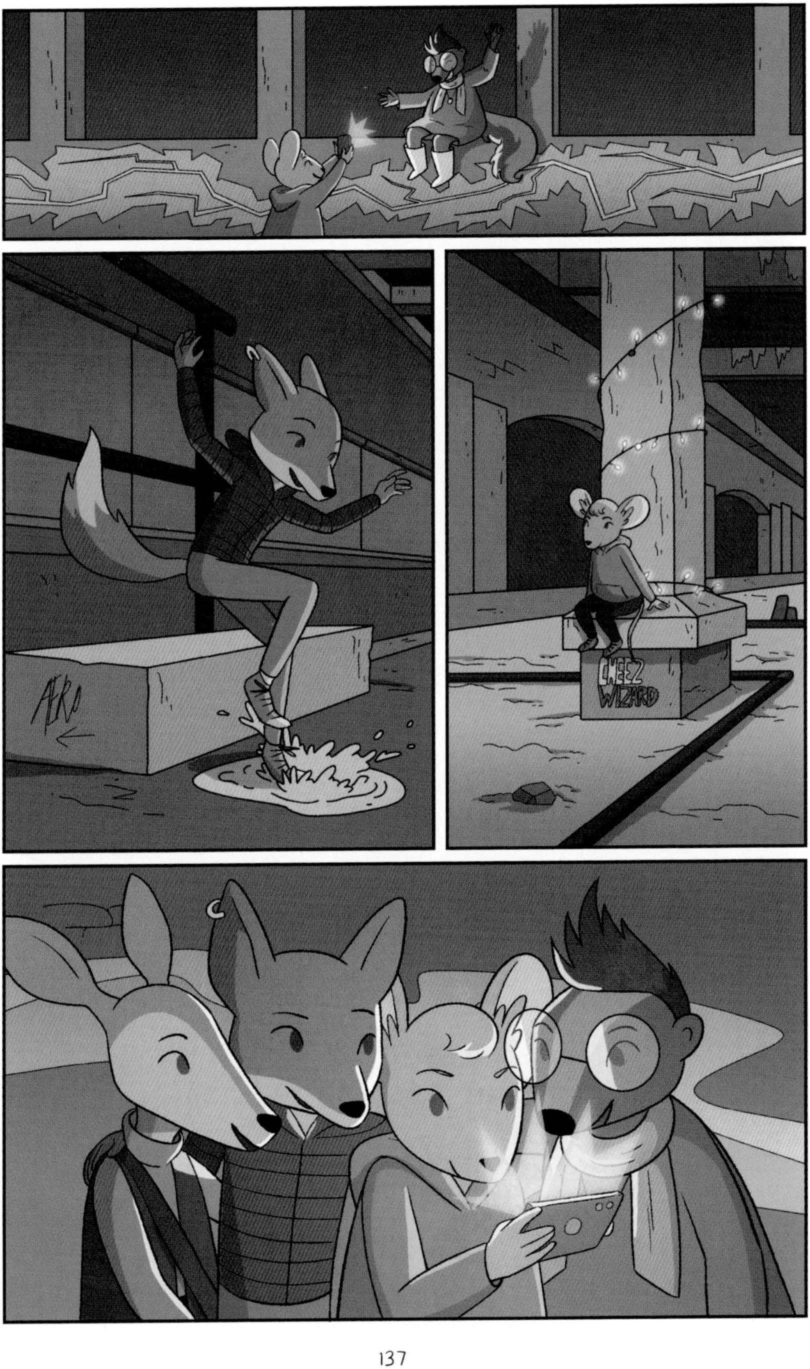
CHEEZ WIZARD

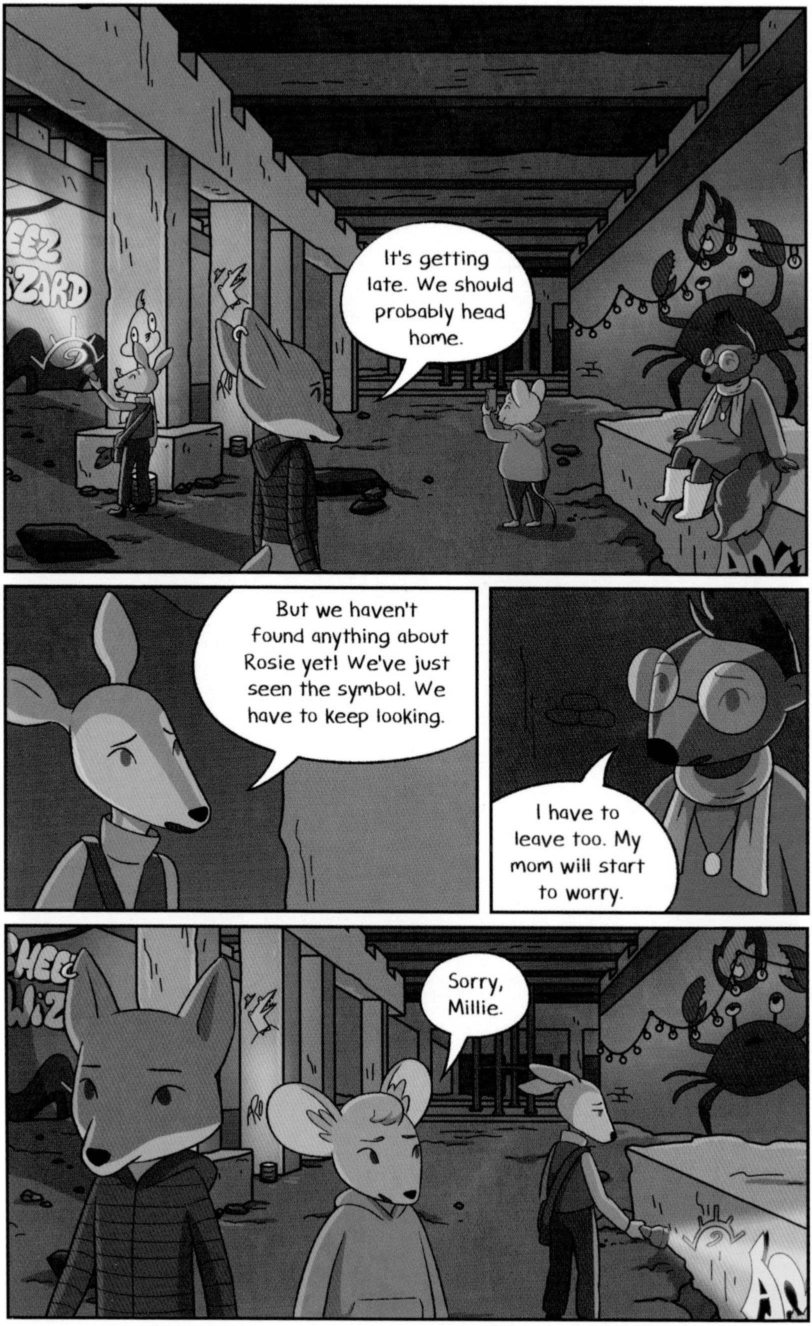
It's getting late. We should probably head home.
But we haven't found anything about Rosie yet! We've just seen the symbol. We have to keep looking.
I have to leave too. My mom will start to worry.
Sorry, Millie.

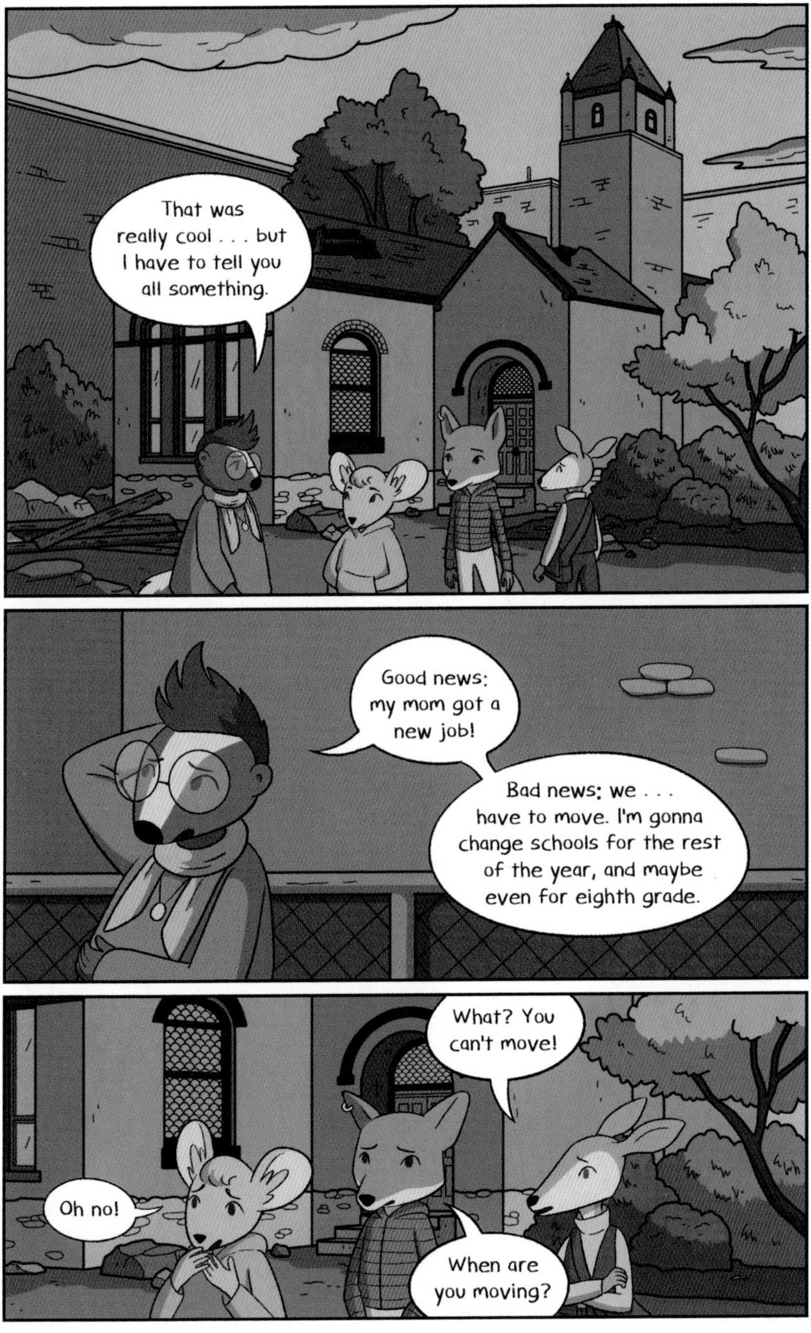
That was really cool . . . but I have to tell you all something.
Good news: my mom got a new job!
Bad news: we . . . have to move. I'm gonna change schools for the rest of the year, and maybe even for eighth grade.
What? You can't move!
Oh no!
When are you moving?

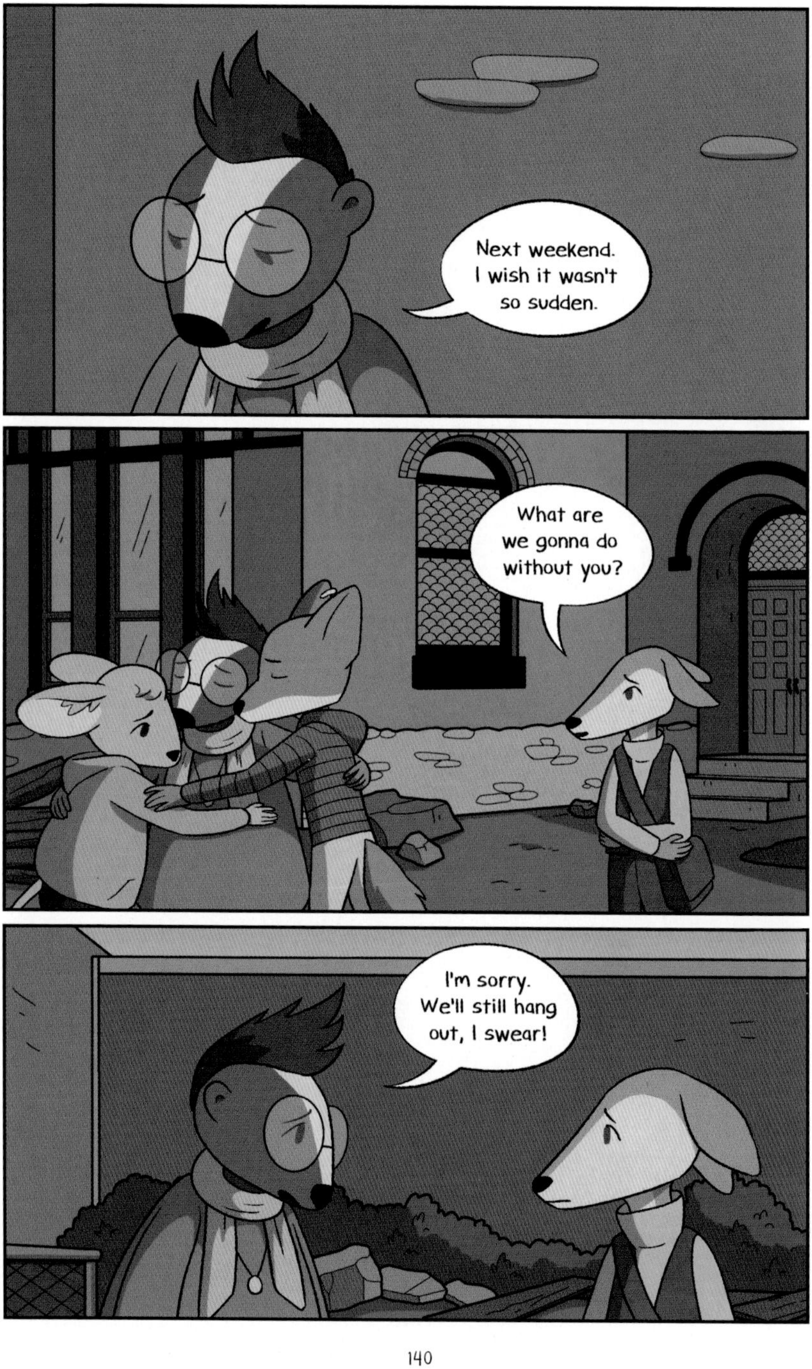
Next weekend. I wish it wasn't so sudden.
What are we gonna do without you?
I'm sorry. We'll still hang out, I swear!

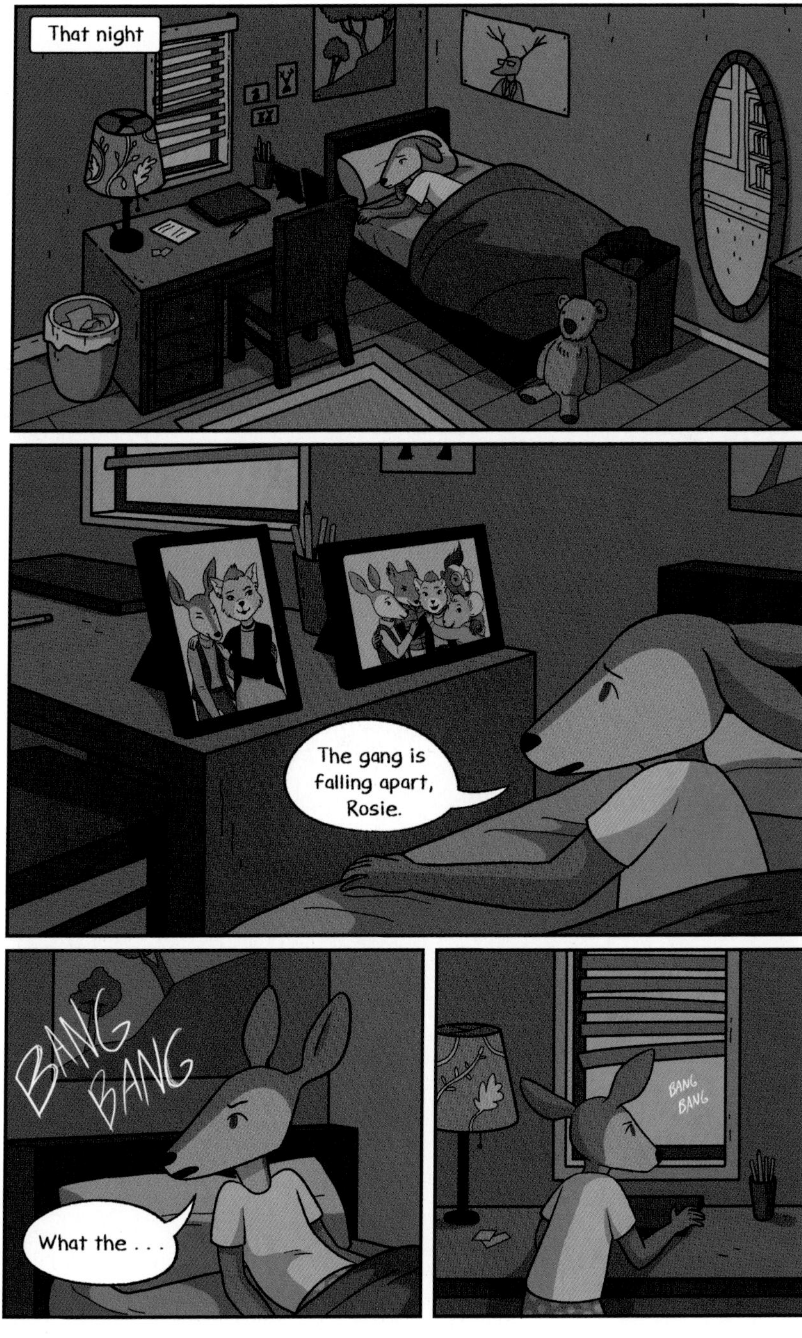
That night
The gang is falling apart, Rosie.
BANG BANG
What the . . .
BANG BANG

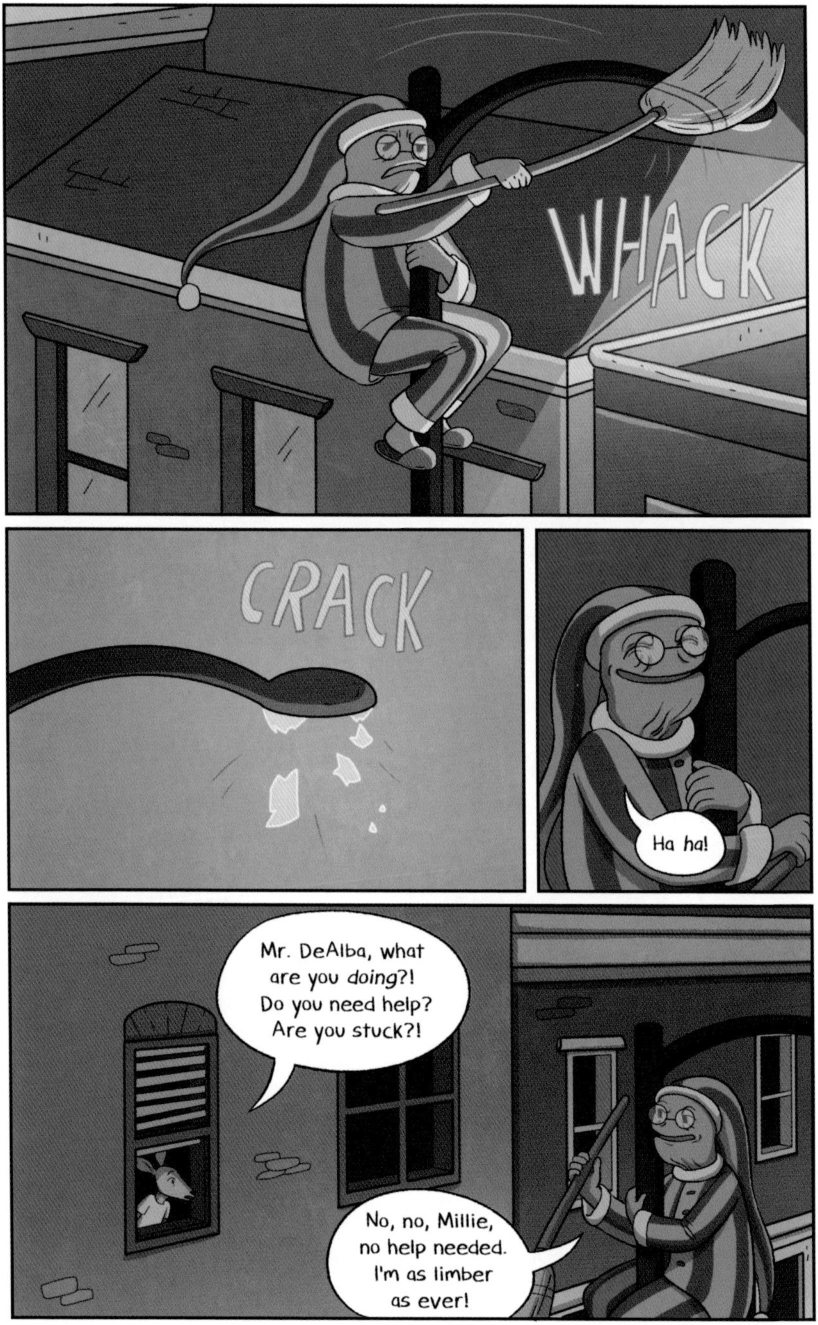
WHACK
CRACK
Ha ha!
Mr. DeAlba, what are you *doing*?! Do you need help? Are you stuck?!
No, no, Millie, no help needed. I'm as limber as ever!

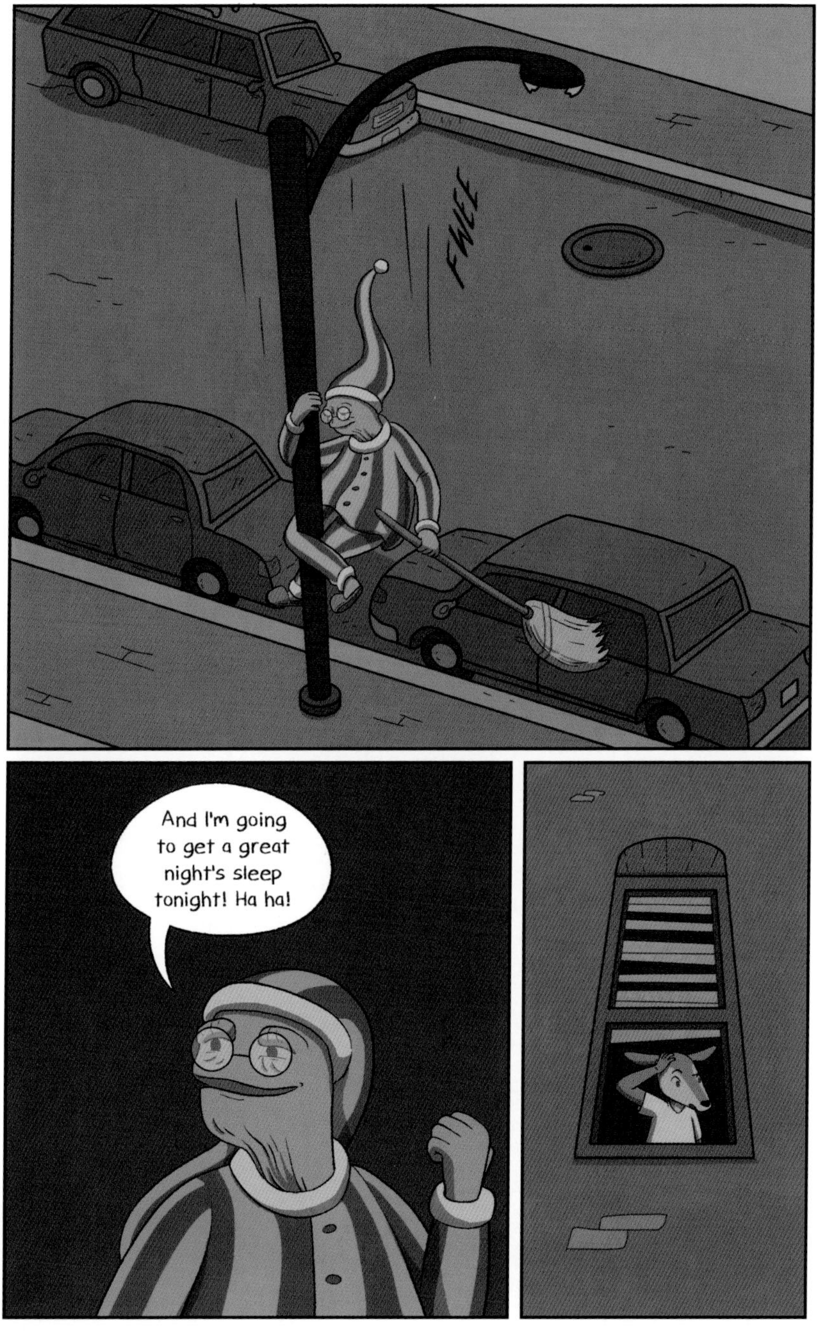
FWEE
And I'm going to get a great night's sleep tonight! Ha ha!

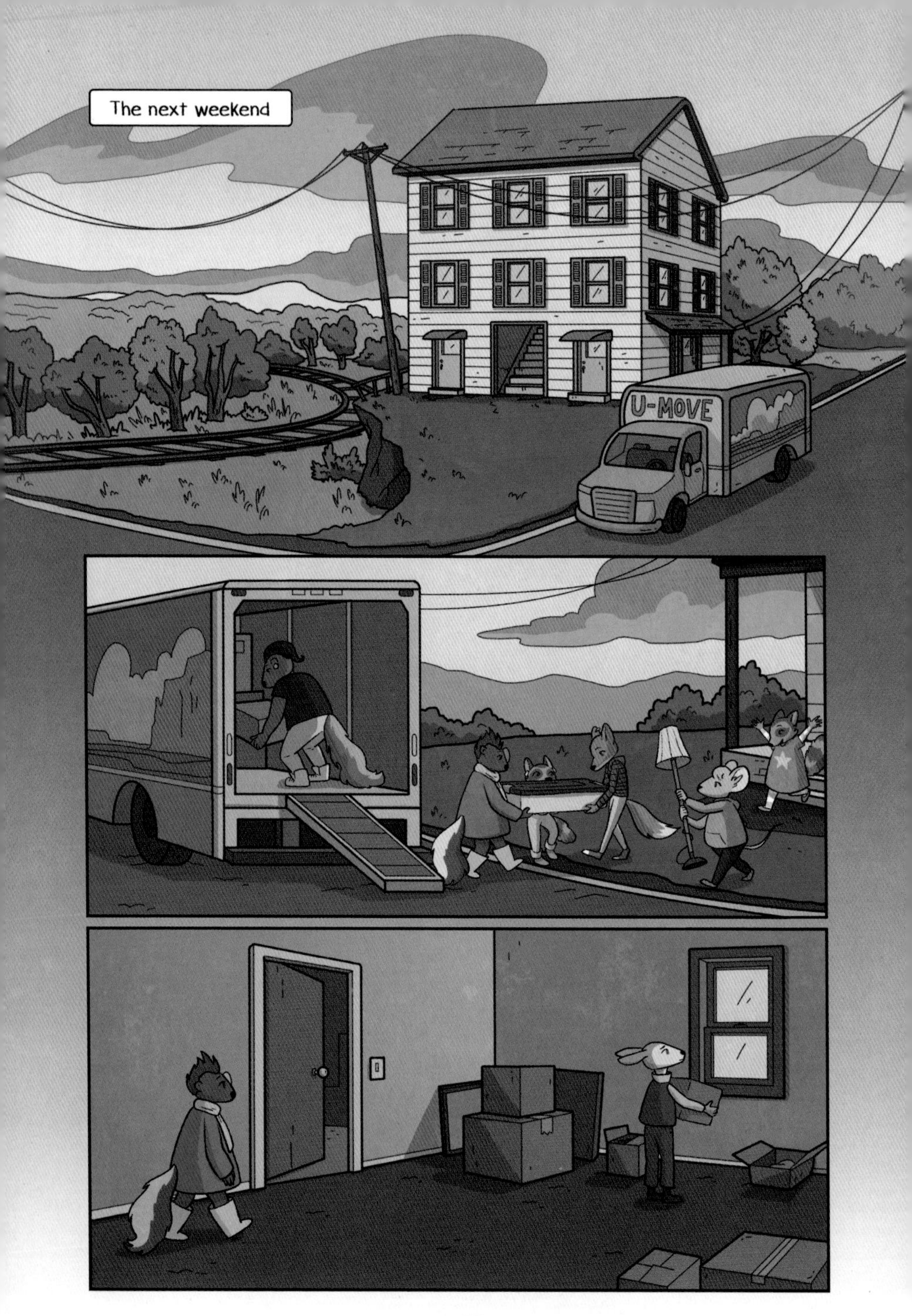
The next weekend
U-MOVE

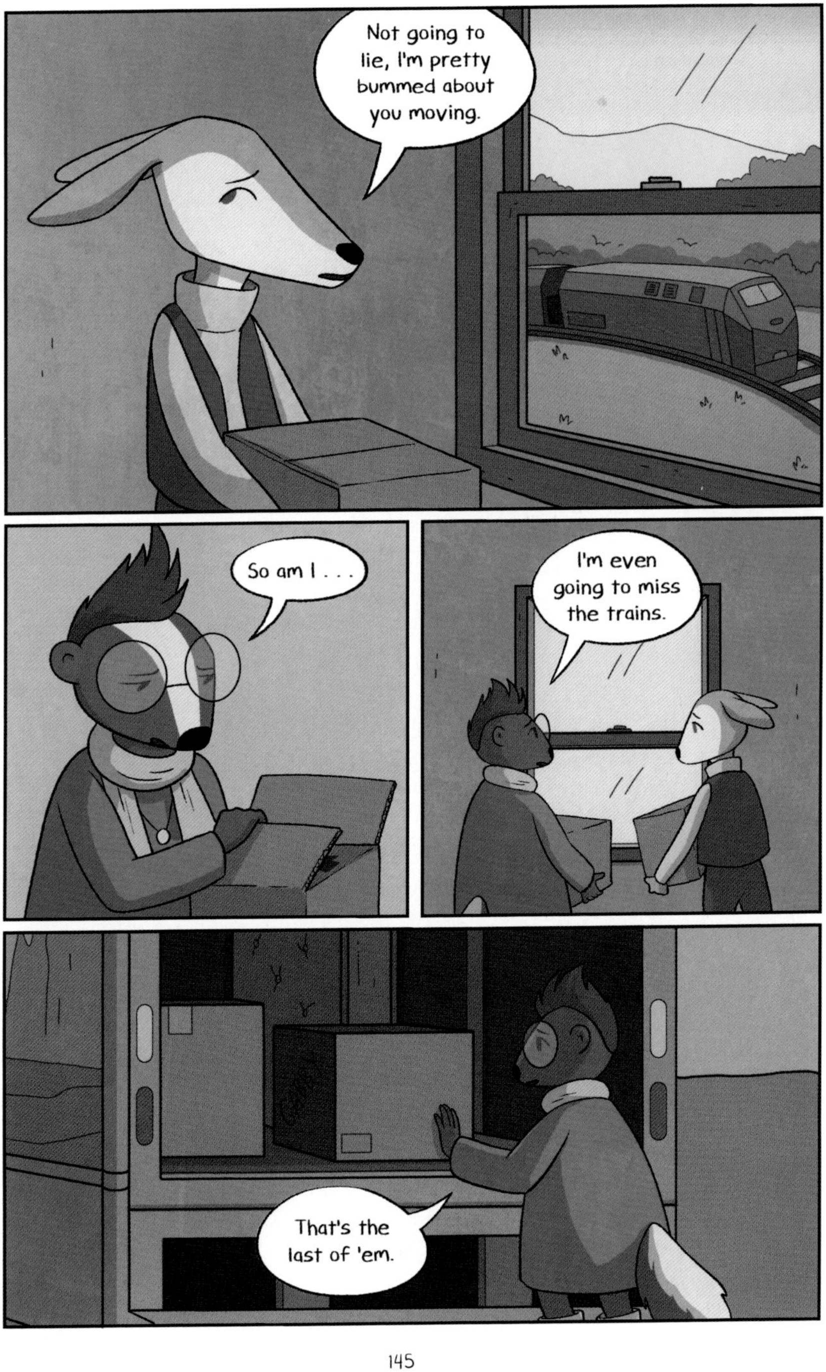
Not going to lie, I'm pretty bummed about you moving.
So am I . . .
I'm even going to miss the trains.
That's the last of 'em.

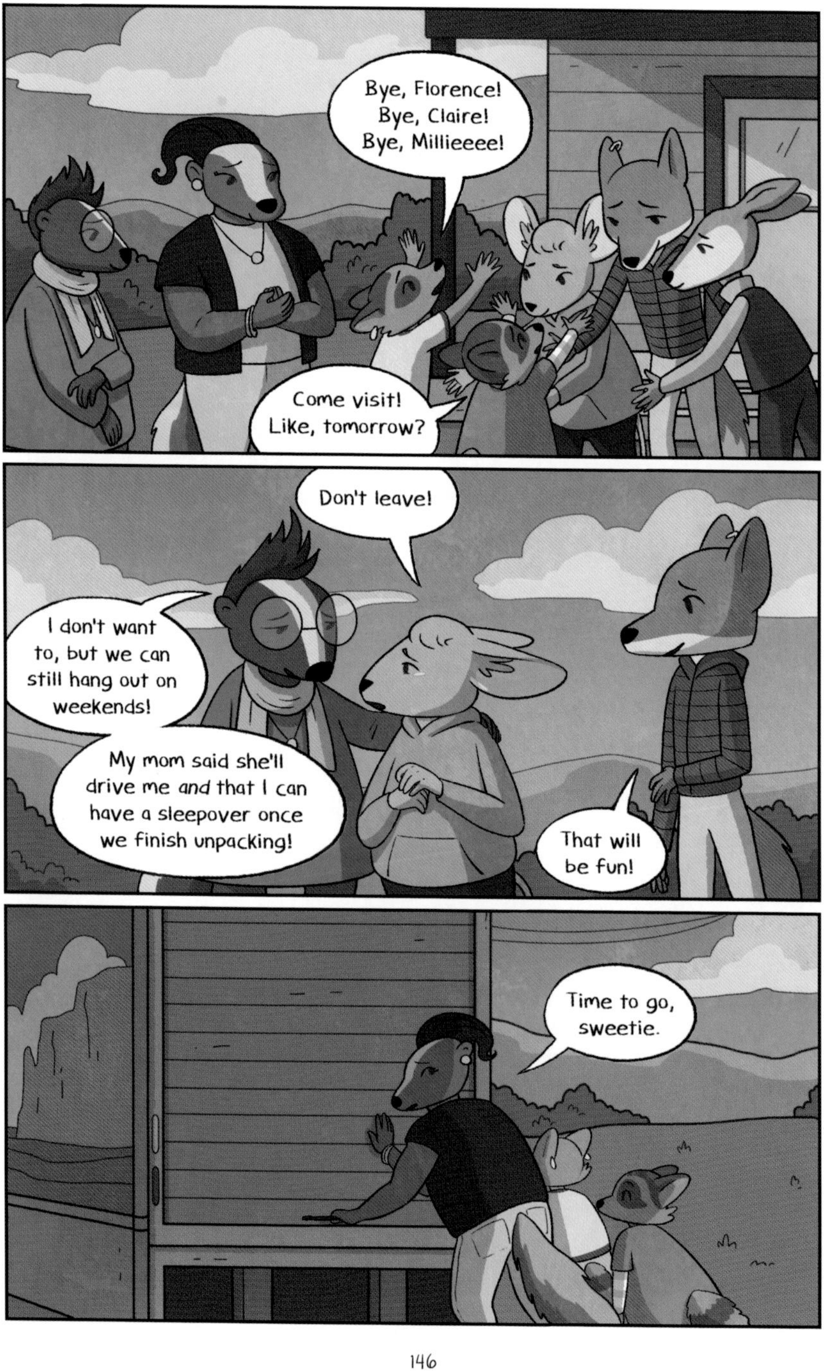
Bye, Florence!
Bye, Claire!
Bye, Millieeee!
Come visit!
Like, tomorrow?
Don't leave!
I don't want to, but we can still hang out on weekends!
My mom said she'll drive me *and* that I can have a sleepover once we finish unpacking!
That will be fun!
Time to go, sweetie.

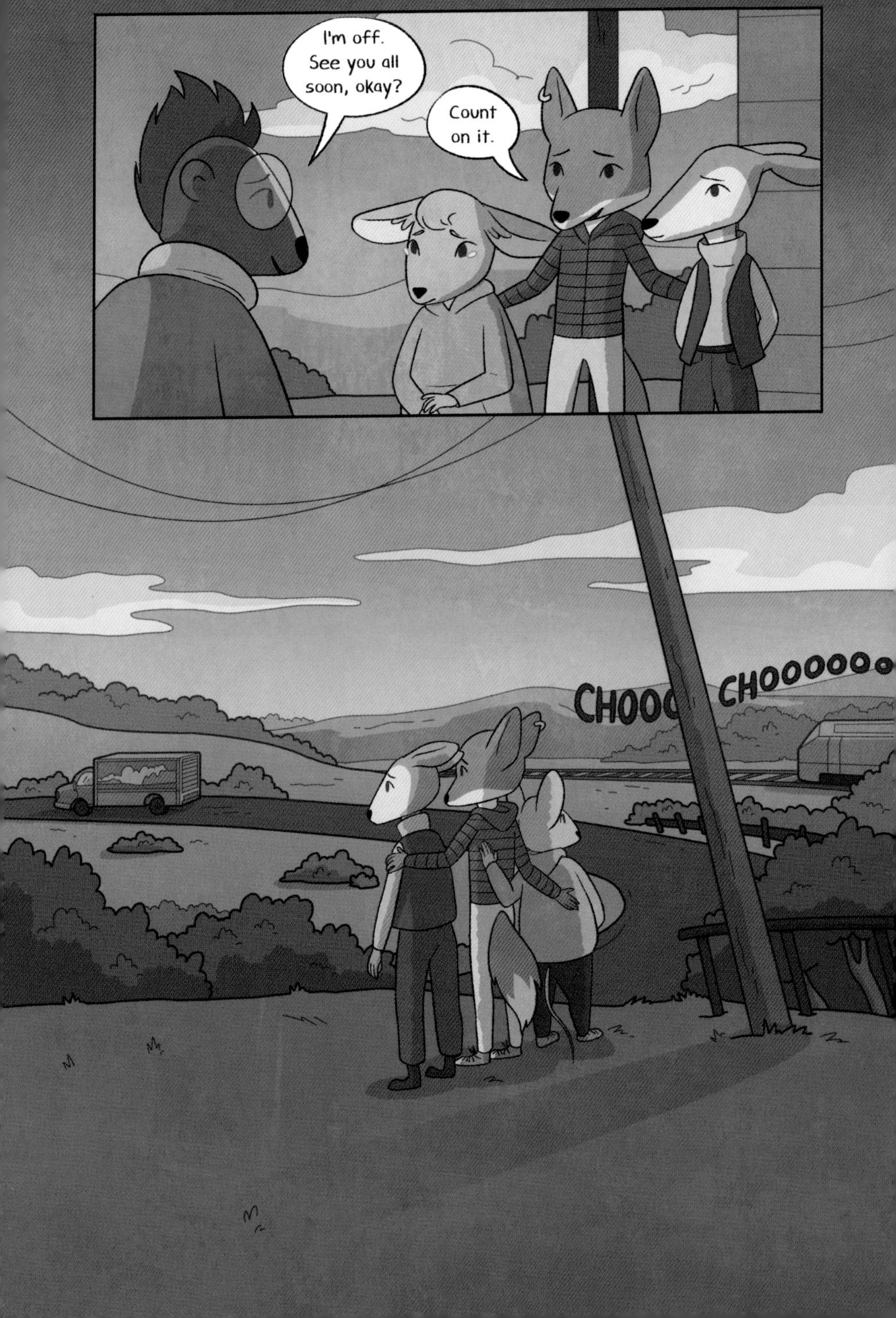
I'm off.
See you all
soon, okay?
Count
on it.
CHOOO
CHOOOOOo

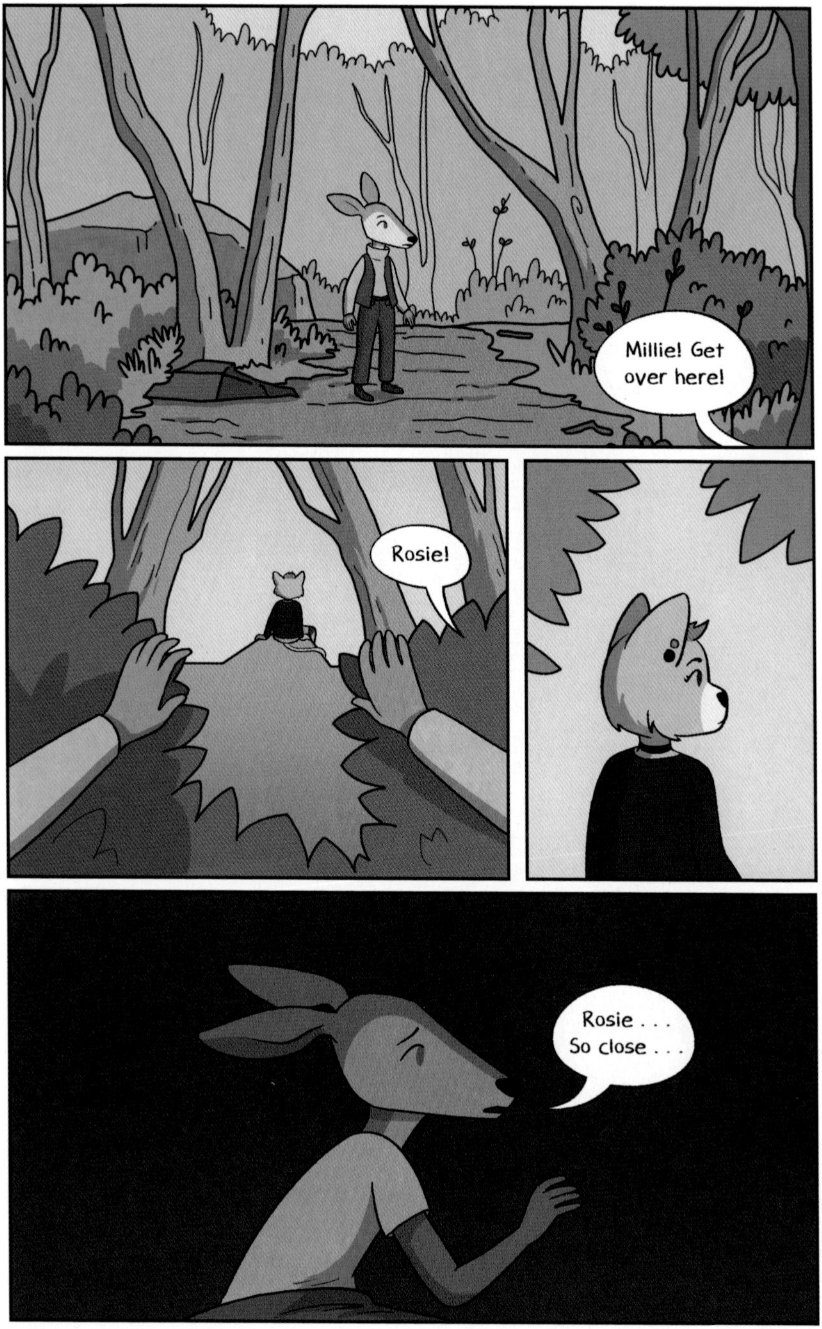
Millie! Get over here!
Rosie!
Rosie . . .
So close . . .

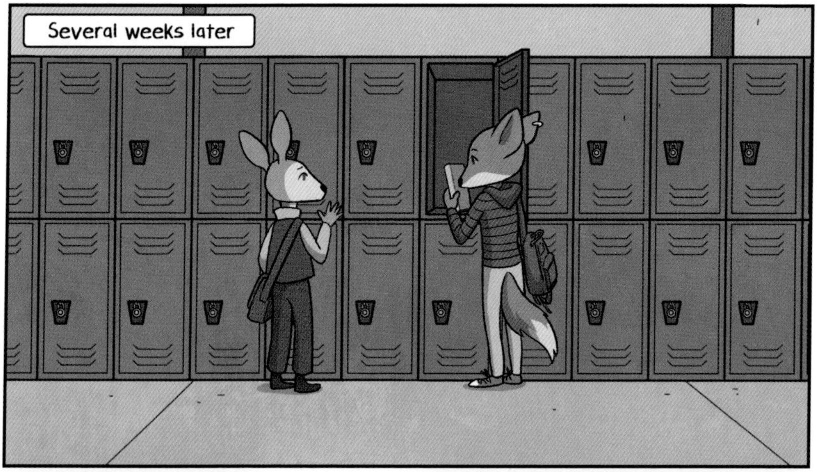
Several weeks later

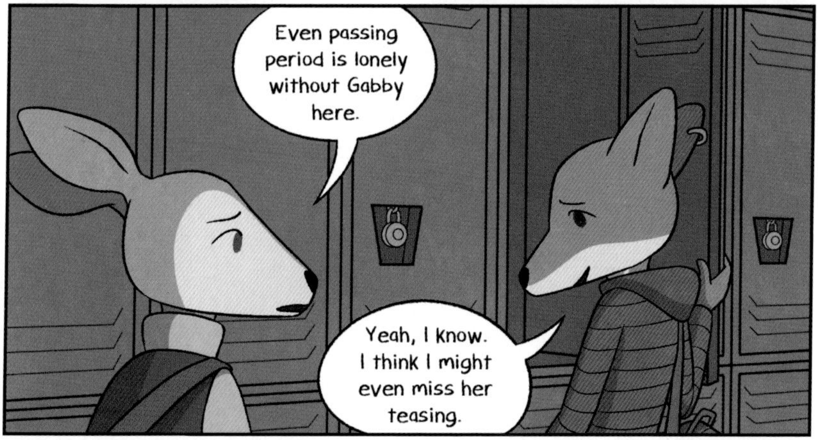
Even passing period is lonely without Gabby here.
Yeah, I know. I think I might even miss her teasing.

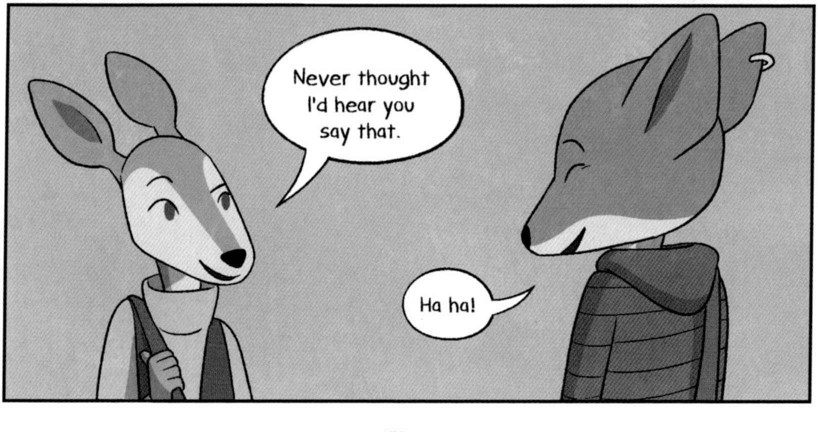
Never thought I'd hear you say that.
Ha ha!

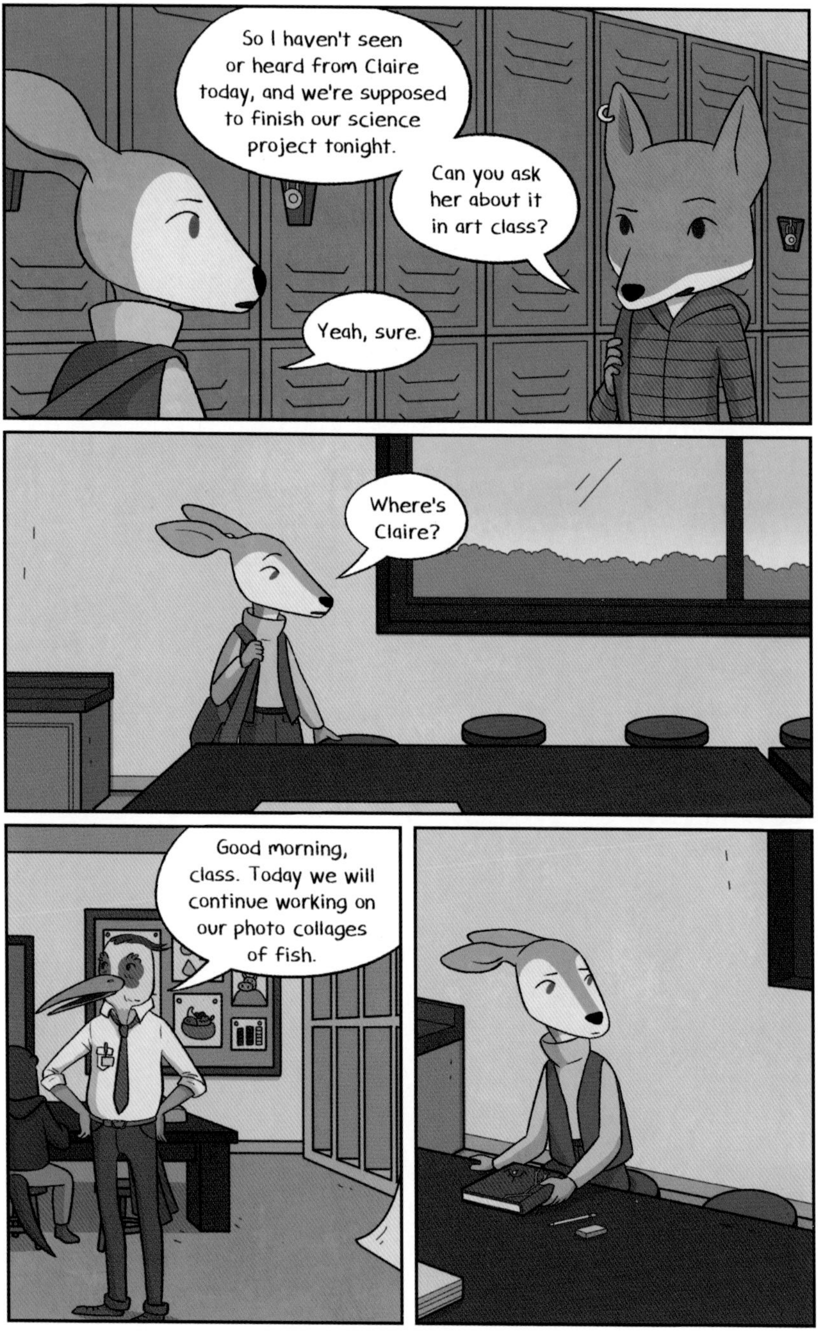
So I haven't seen or heard from Claire today, and we're supposed to finish our science project tonight.
Can you ask her about it in art class?
Yeah, sure.
Where's Claire?
Good morning, class. Today we will continue working on our photo collages of fish.

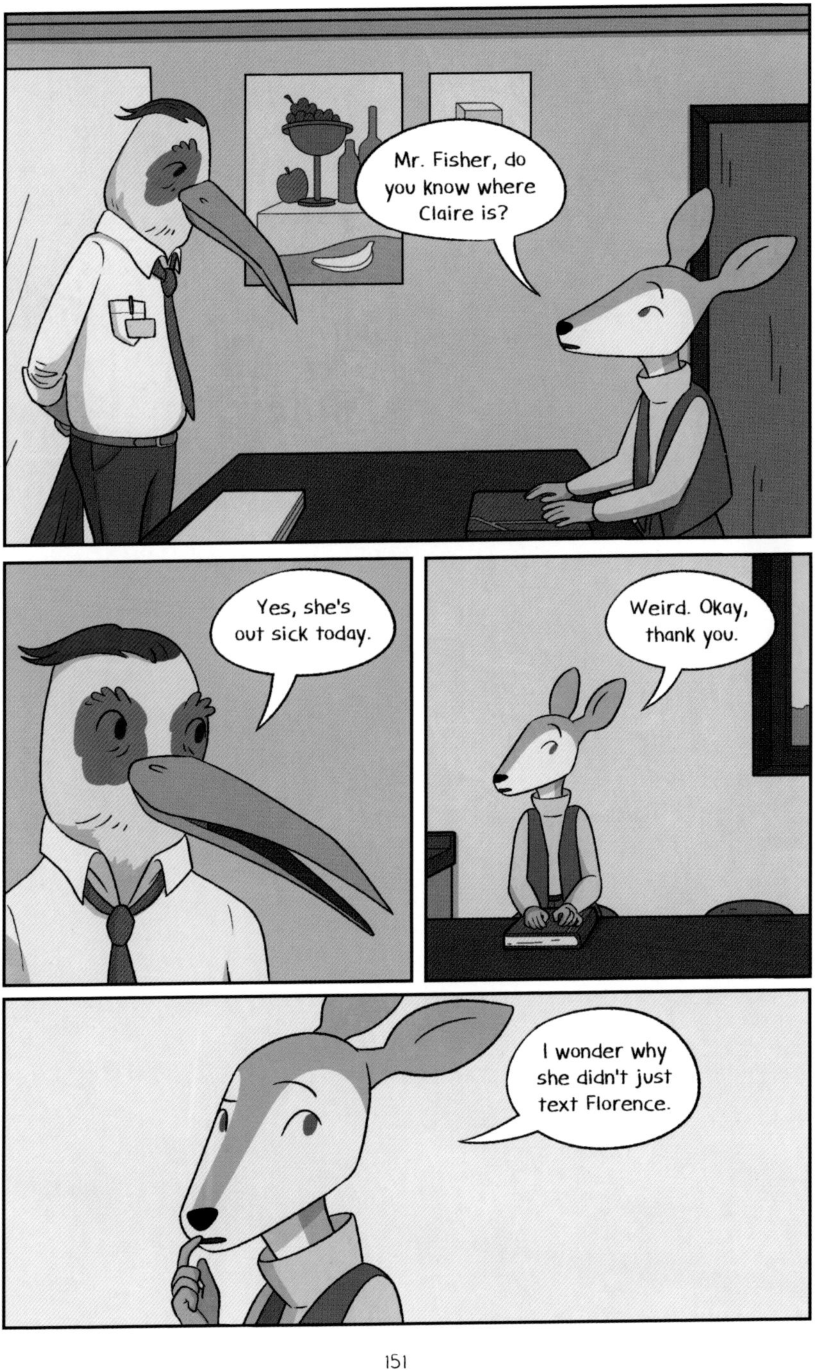
Mr. Fisher, do you know where Claire is?
Yes, she's out sick today.
Weird. Okay, thank you.
I wonder why she didn't just text Florence.

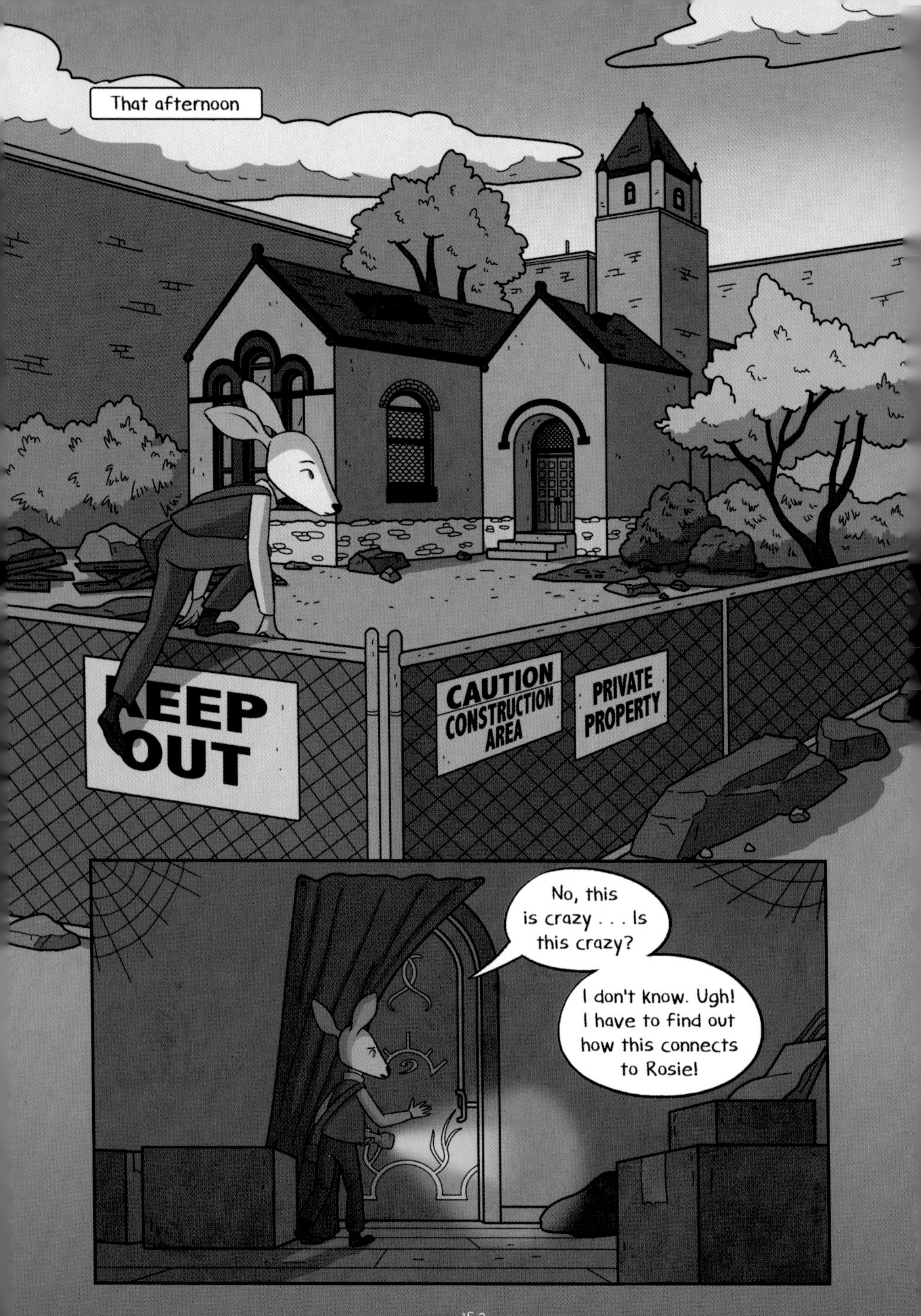
That afternoon
KEEP OUT
CAUTION CONSTRUCTION AREA
PRIVATE PROPERTY
No, this is crazy . . . Is this crazy?
I don't know. Ugh! I have to find out how this connects to Rosie!

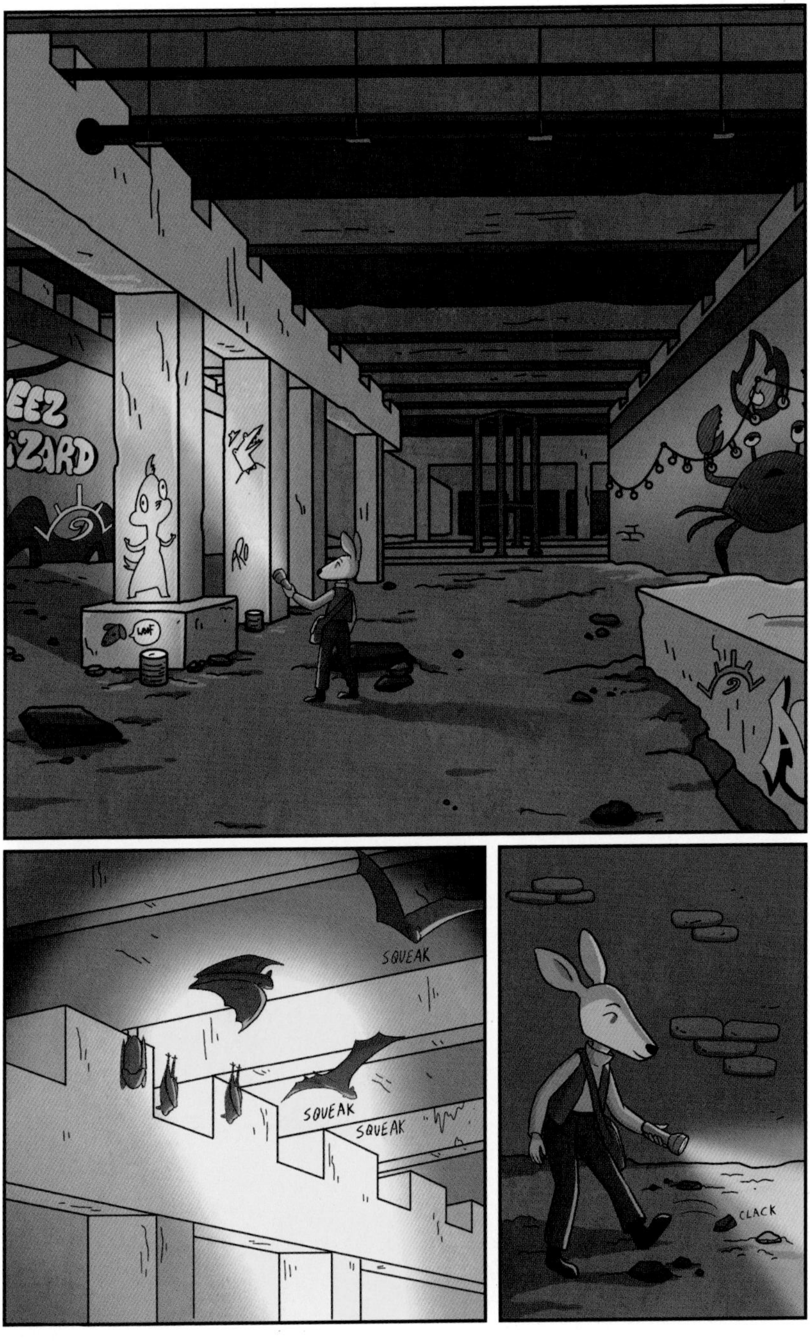
WOOF
SQUEAK
SQUEAK
SQUEAK
CLACK

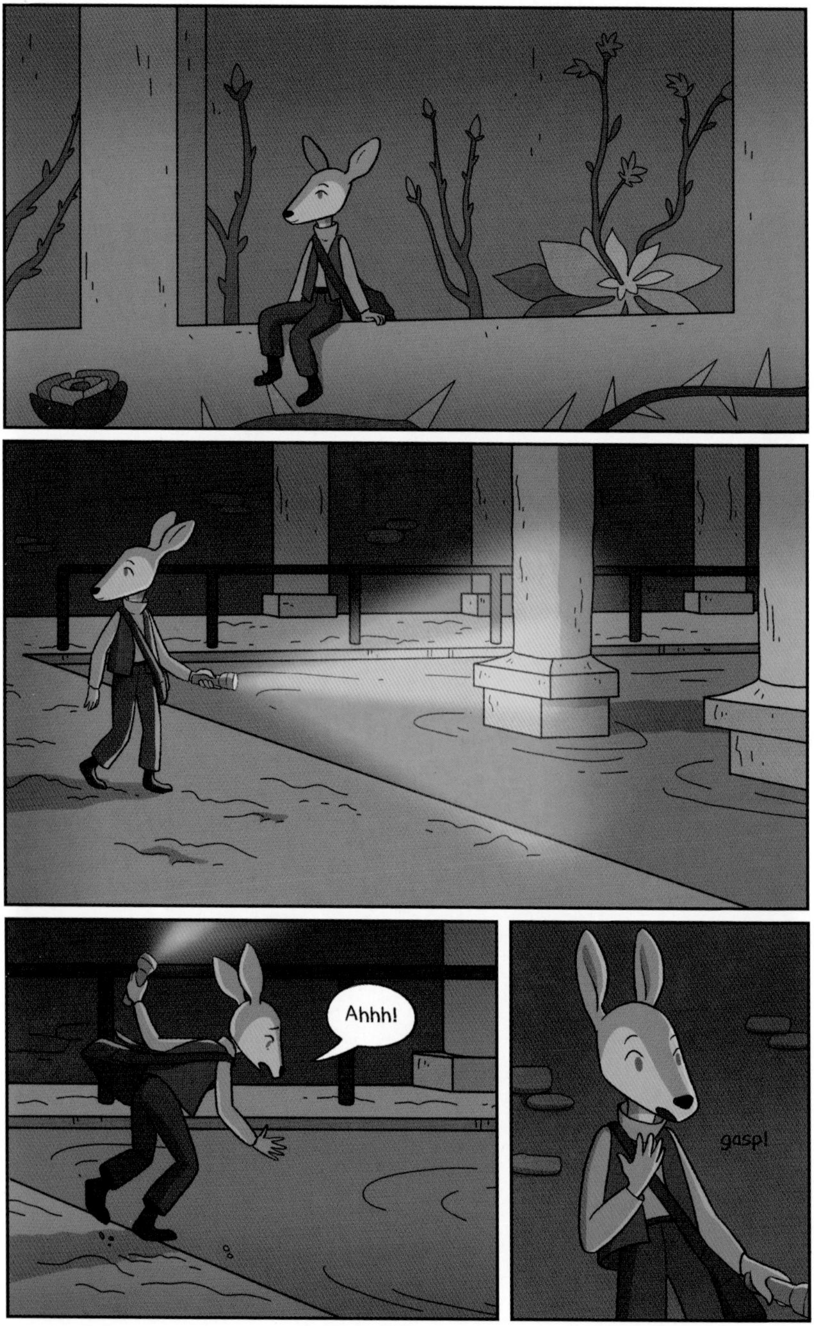
Ahhh!
gasp!

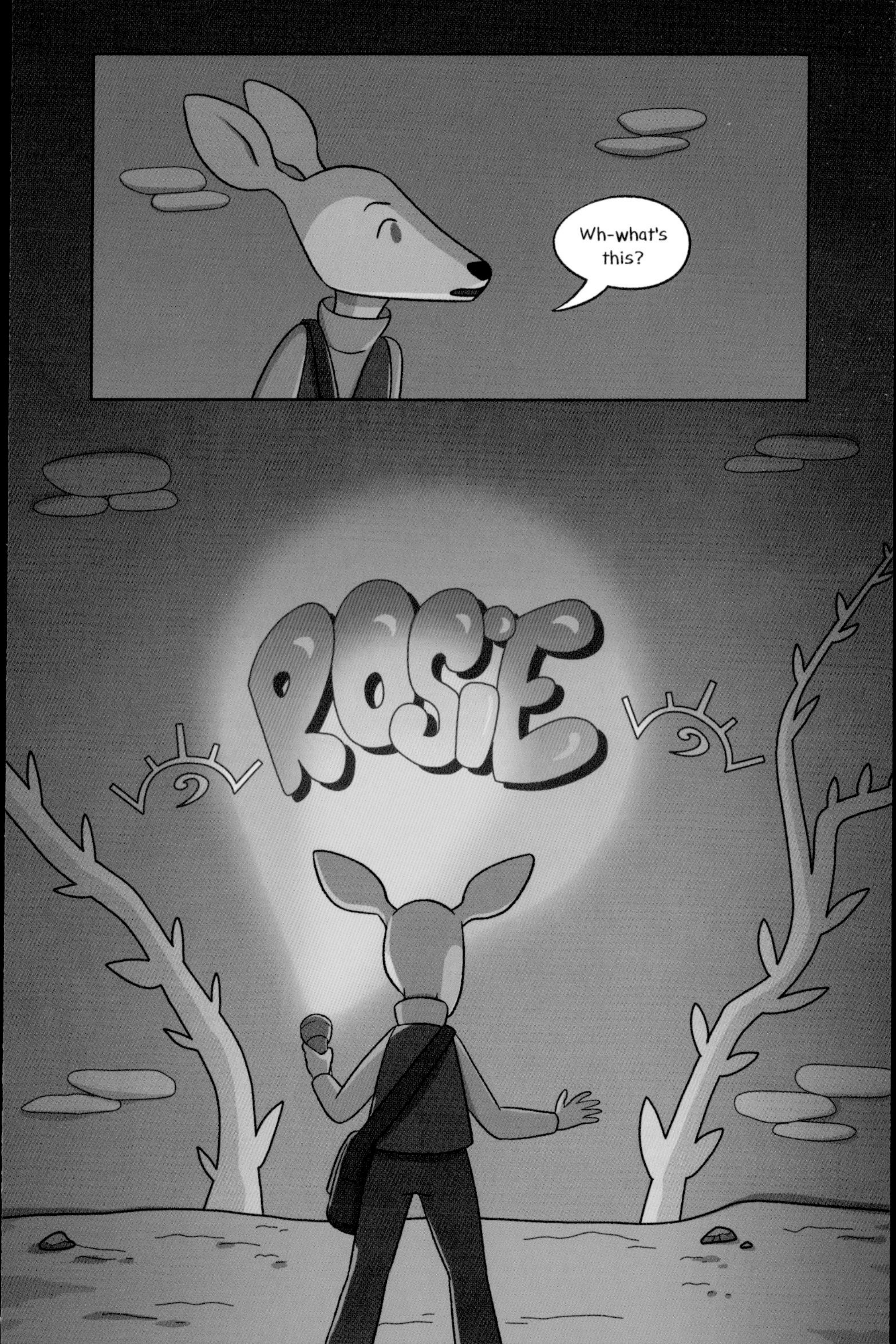
Wh-what's this?
ROSIE

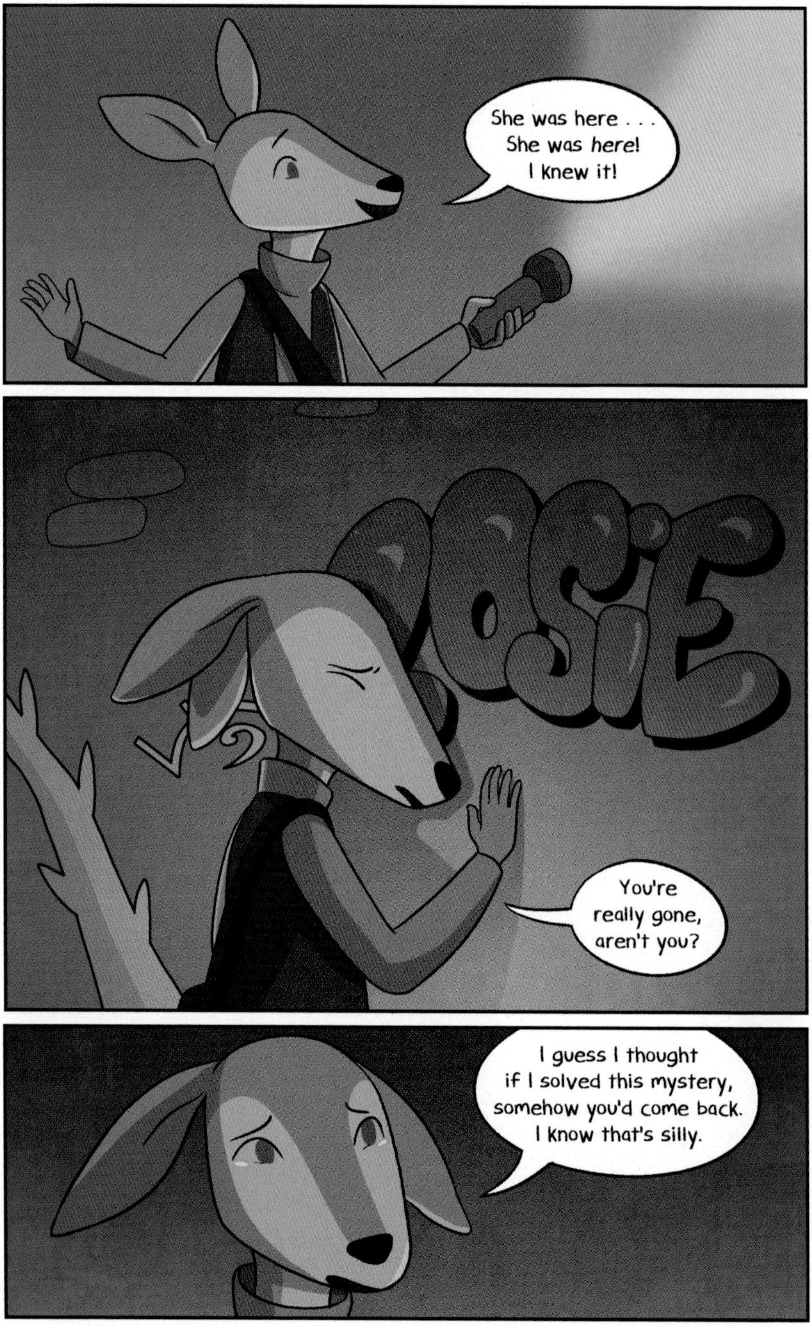
She was here . . . She was *here*! I knew it!
You're really gone, aren't you?
I guess I thought if I solved this mystery, somehow you'd come back. I know that's silly.

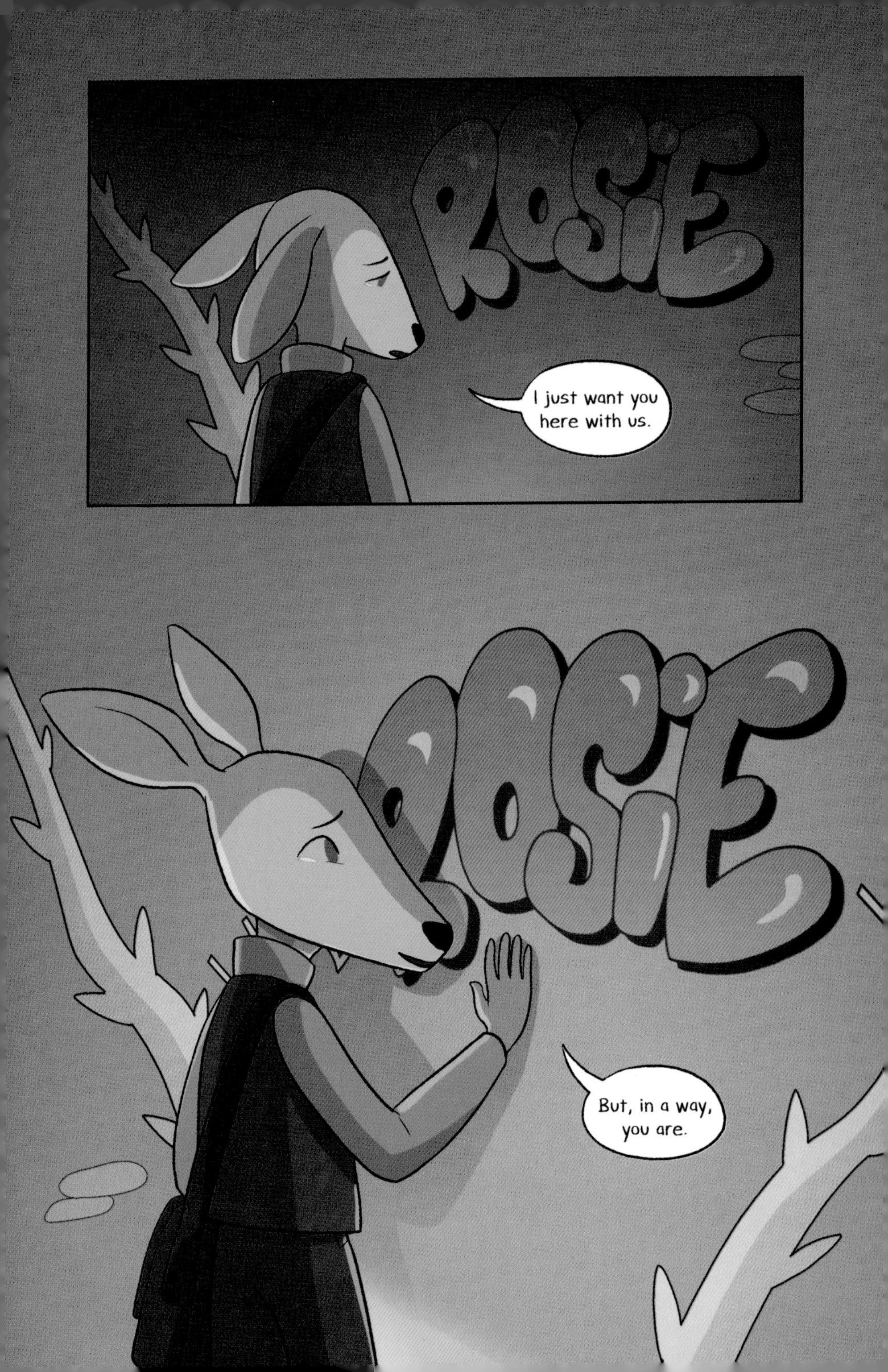
ROSIE
I just want you here with us.
ROSIE
But, in a way, you are.

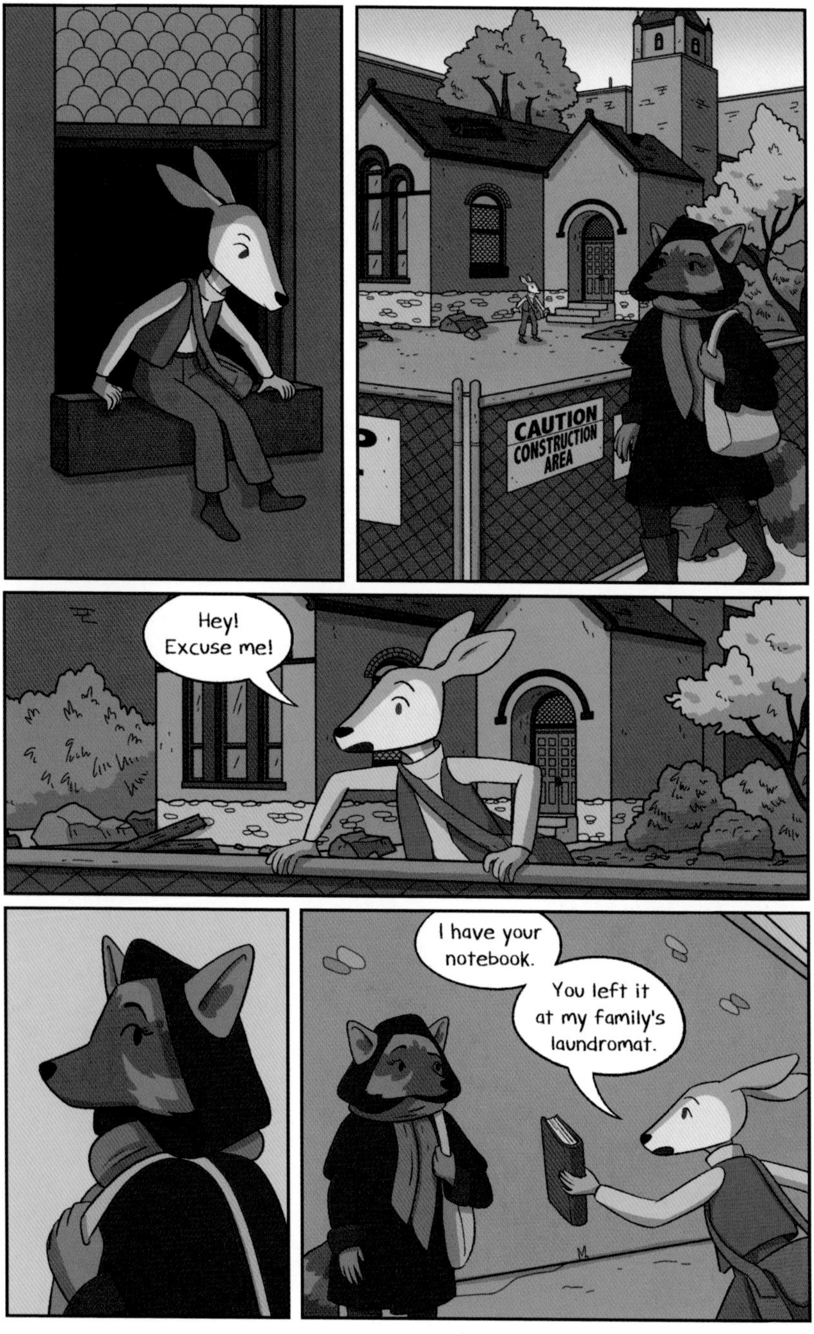

CAUTION CONSTRUCTION AREA
Hey! Excuse me!
I have your notebook.
You left it at my family's laundromat.

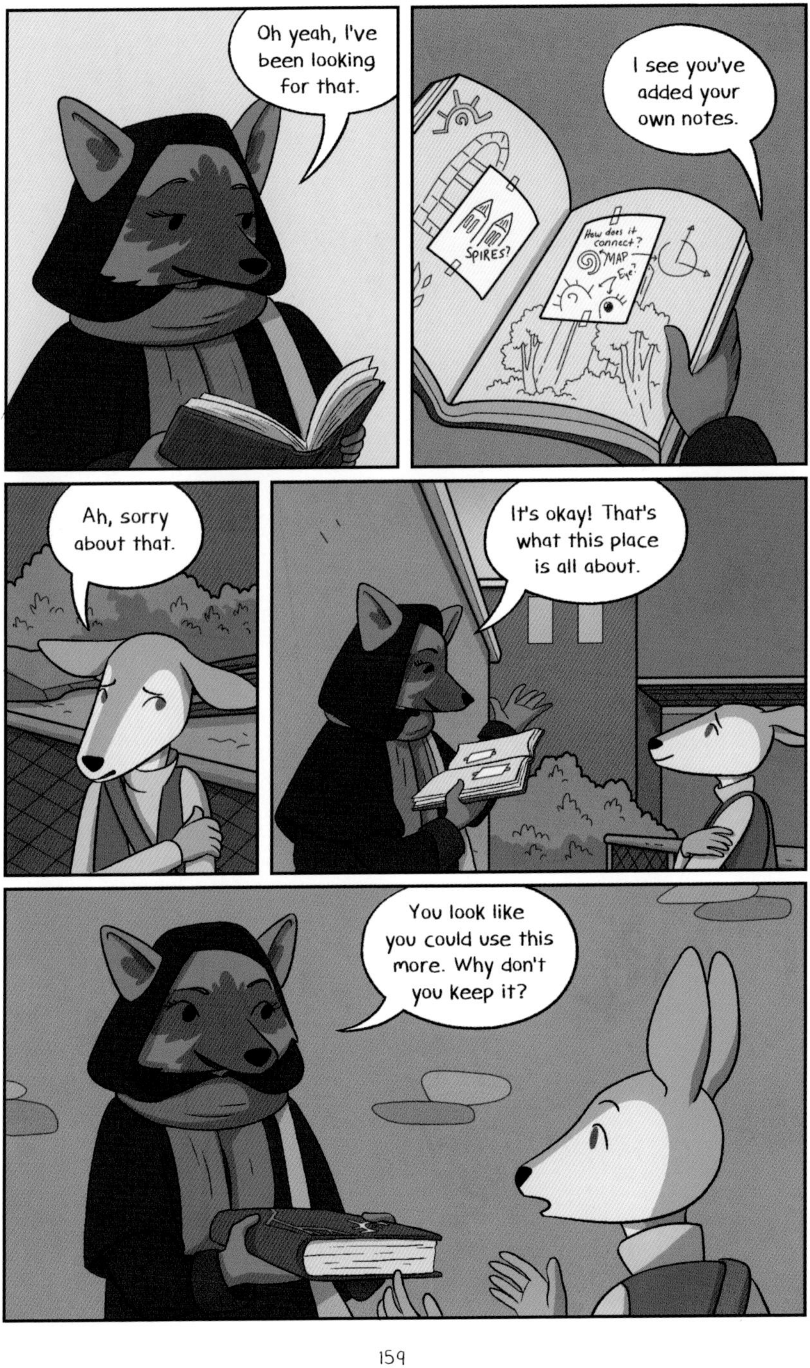
Oh yeah, I've been looking for that.
I see you've added your own notes.
SPIRES?
How does it connect?
MAP
Eye?
Ah, sorry about that.
It's okay! That's what this place is all about.
You look like you could use this more. Why don't you keep it?

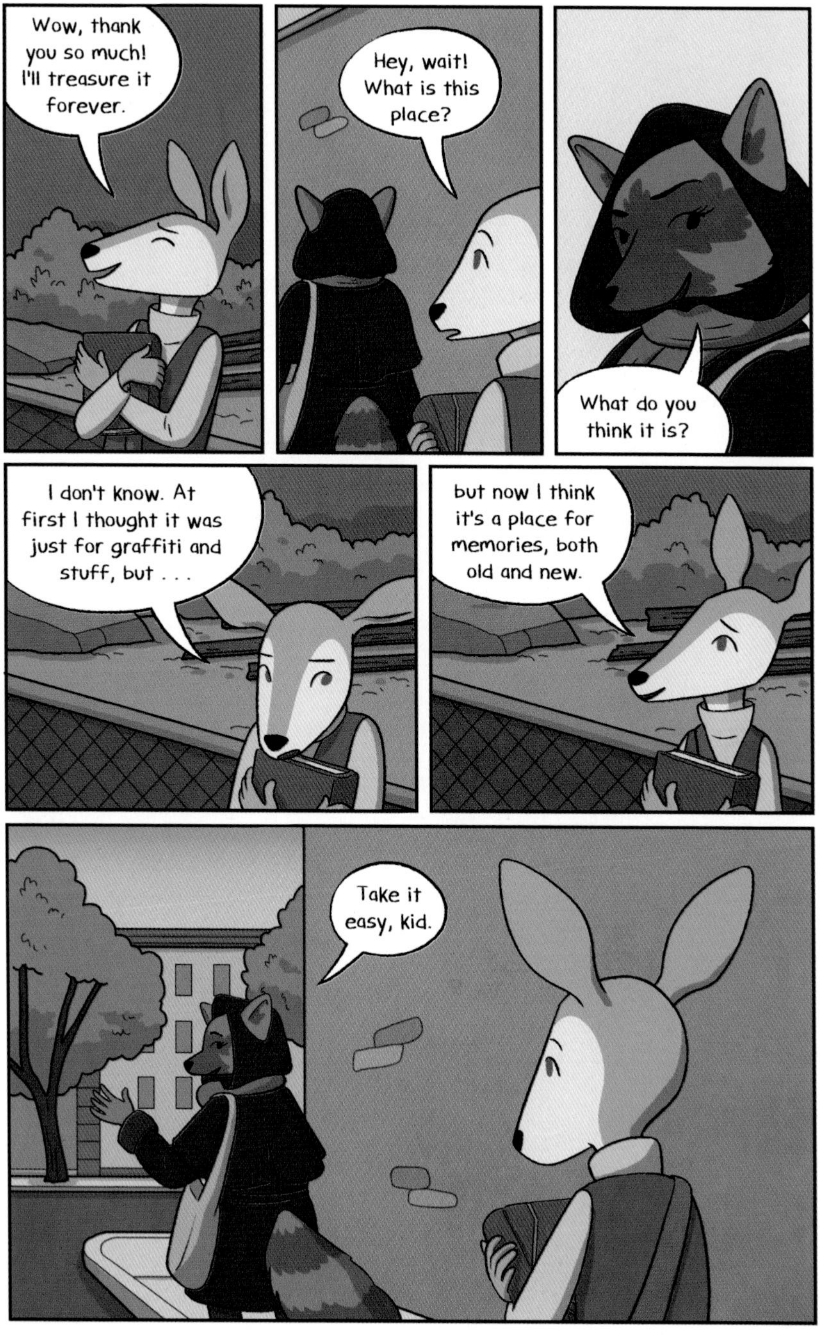
Wow, thank you so much! I'll treasure it forever.
Hey, wait! What is this place?
What do you think it is?
I don't know. At first I thought it was just for graffiti and stuff, but . . .
but now I think it's a place for memories, both old and new.
Take it easy, kid.

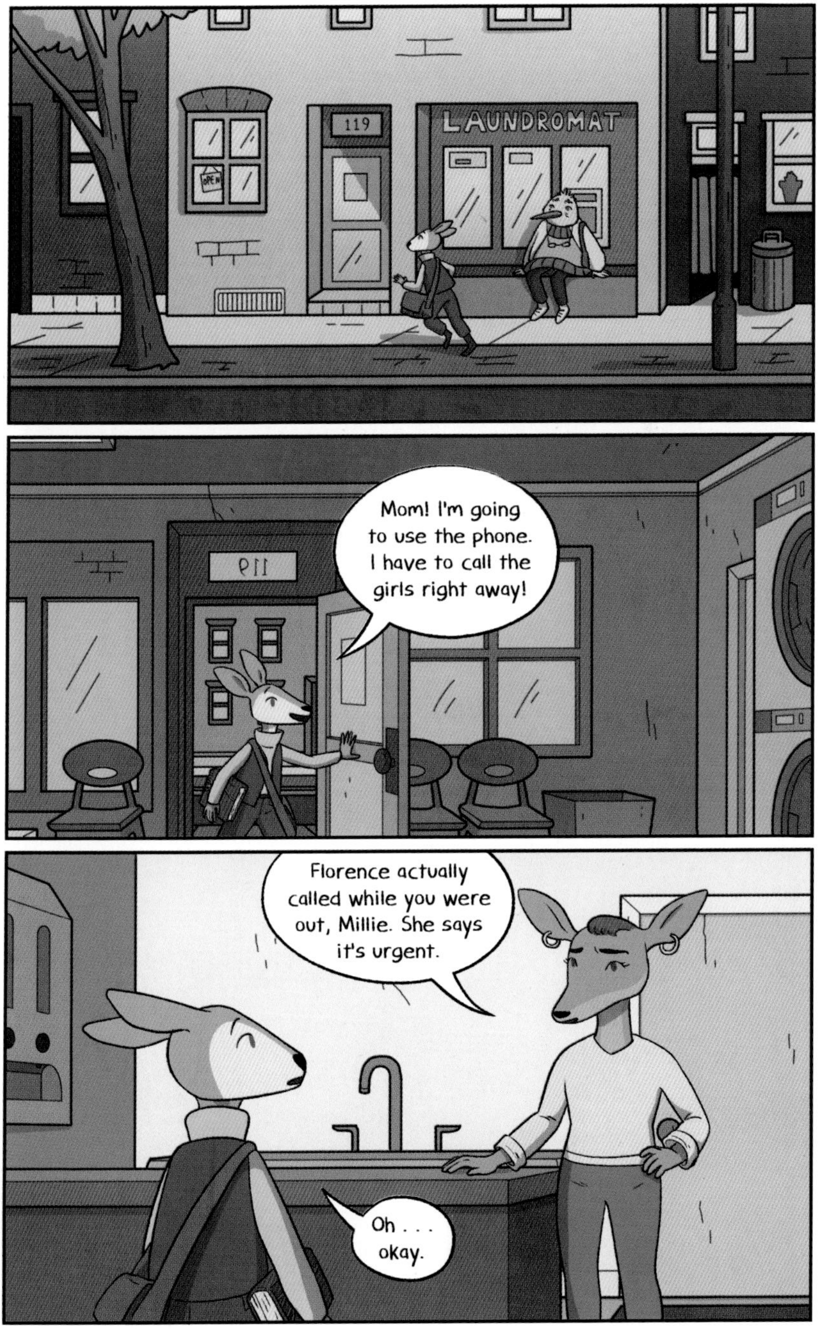

119
LAUNDROMAT
OPEN
119
Mom! I'm going to use the phone. I have to call the girls right away!
Florence actually called while you were out, Millie. She says it's urgent.
Oh . . . okay.

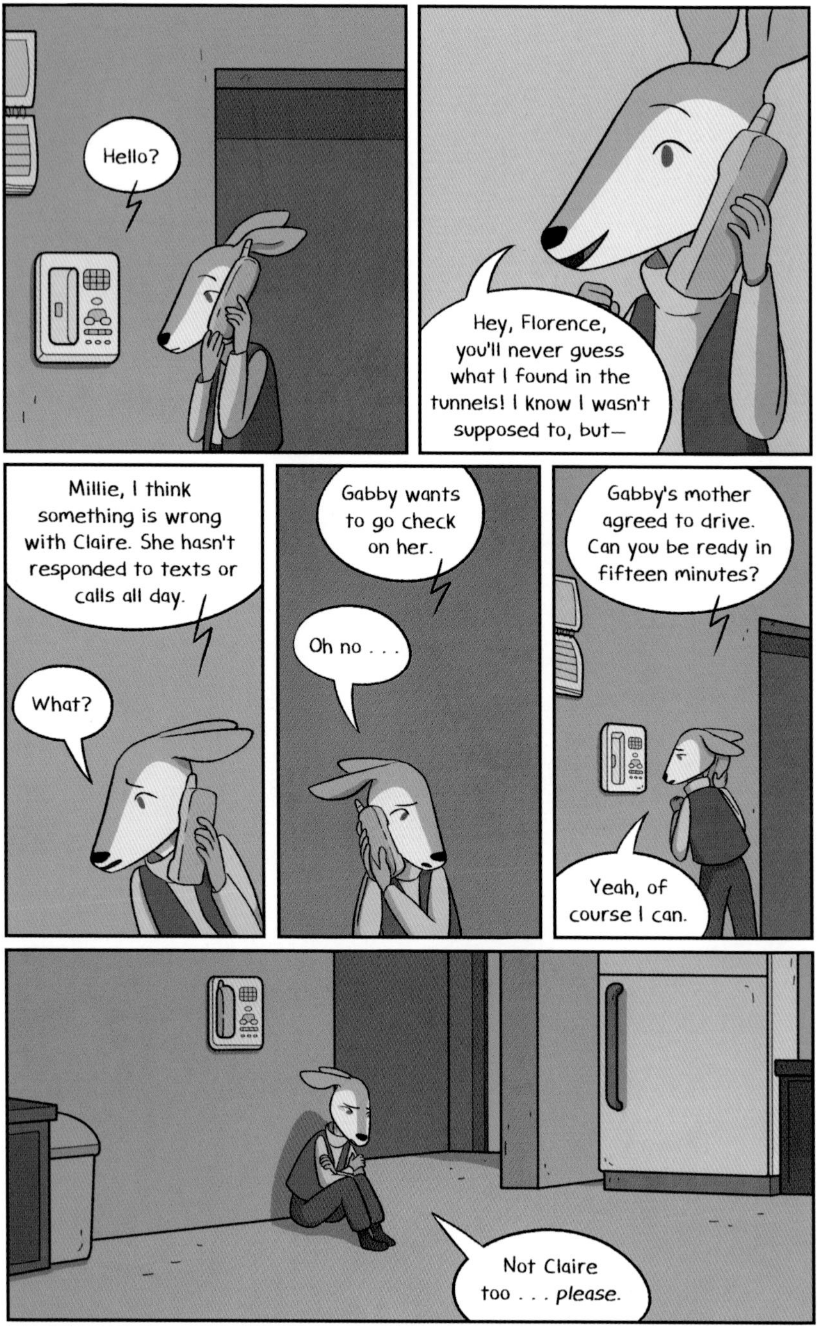
Hello?
Hey, Florence, you'll never guess what I found in the tunnels! I know I wasn't supposed to, but—
Millie, I think something is wrong with Claire. She hasn't responded to texts or calls all day.
What?
Gabby wants to go check on her.
Oh no . . .
Gabby's mother agreed to drive. Can you be ready in fifteen minutes?
Yeah, of course I can.
Not Claire too . . . *please*.

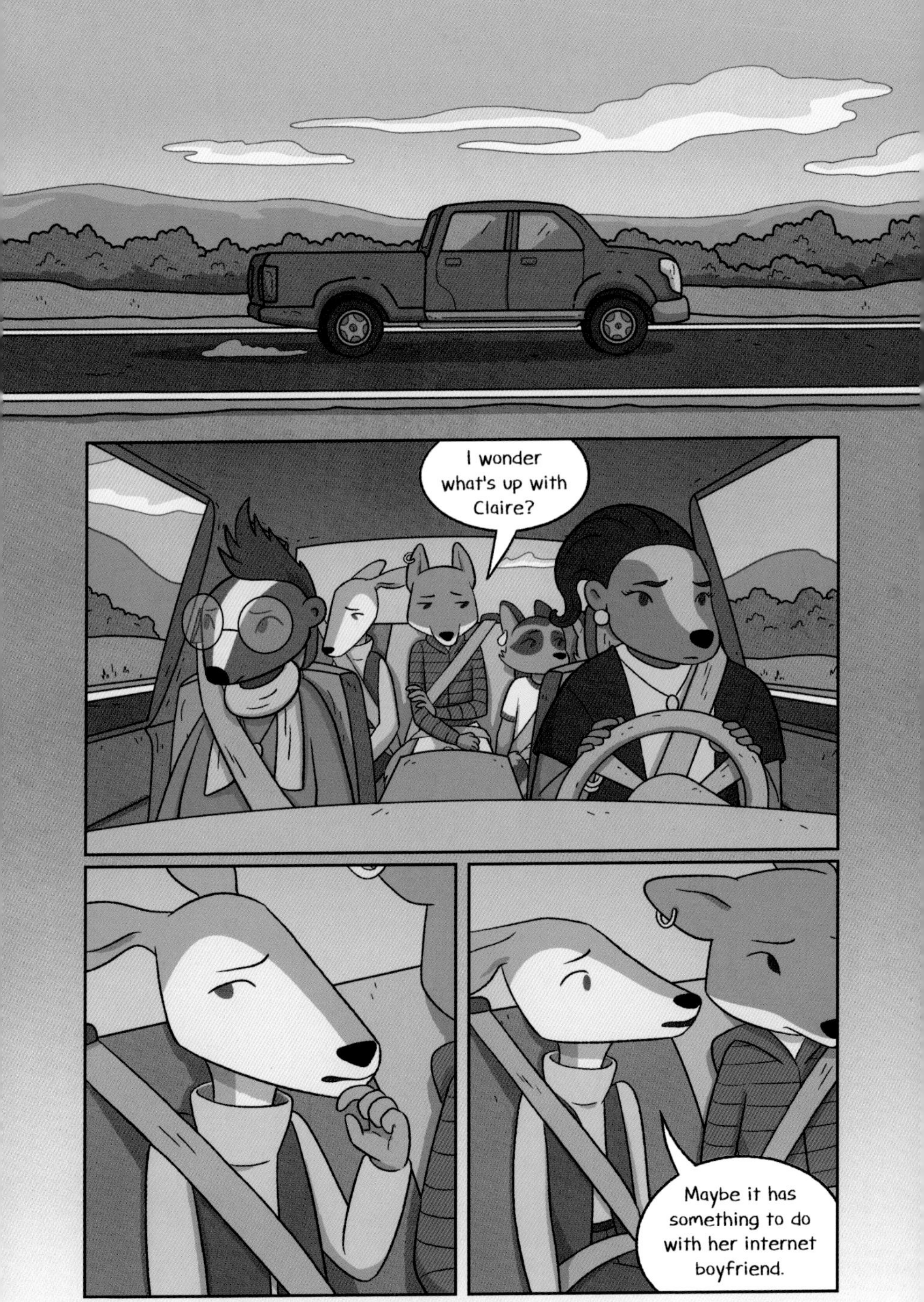
I wonder what's up with Claire?
Maybe it has something to do with her internet boyfriend.

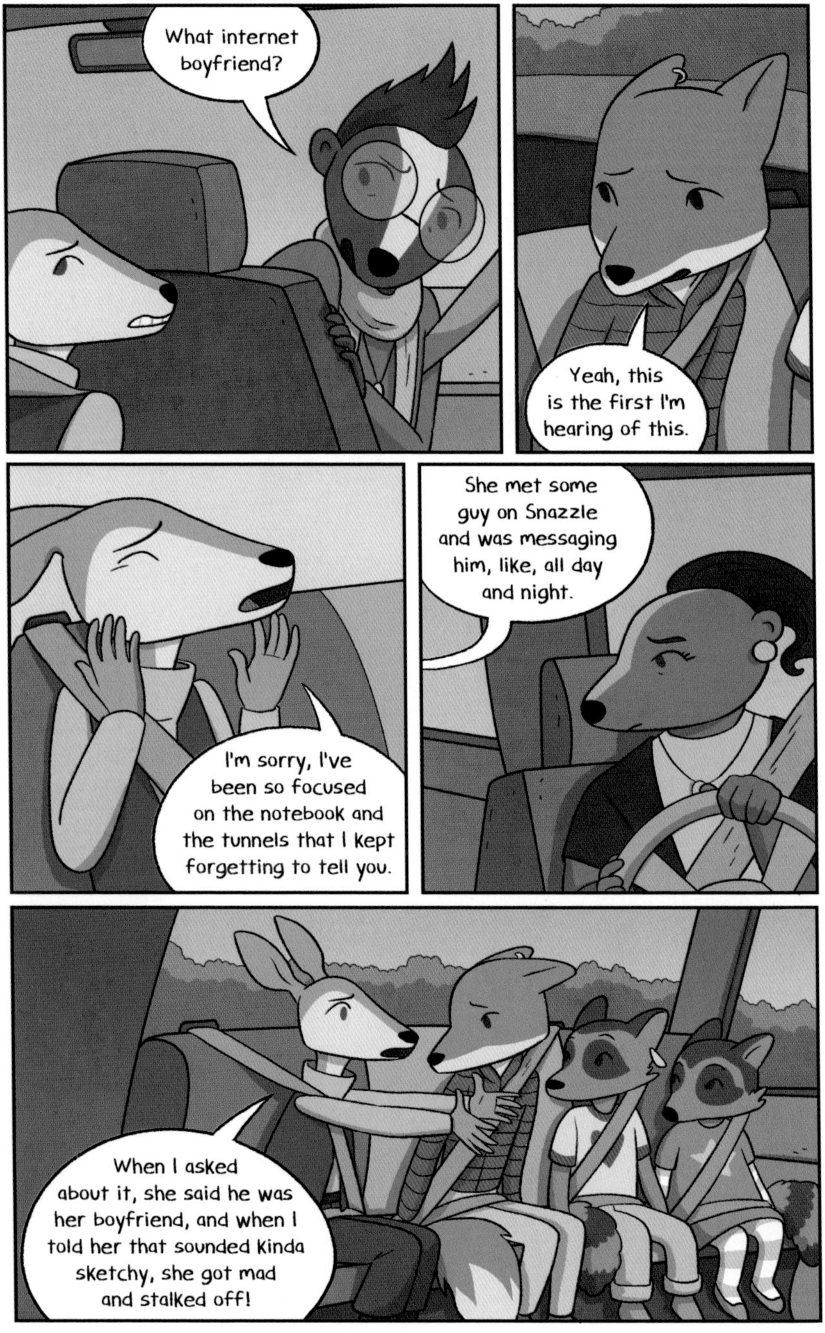
What internet boyfriend?
Yeah, this is the first I'm hearing of this.
I'm sorry, I've been so focused on the notebook and the tunnels that I kept forgetting to tell you.
She met some guy on Snazzle and was messaging him, like, all day and night.
When I asked about it, she said he was her boyfriend, and when I told her that sounded kinda sketchy, she got mad and stalked off!

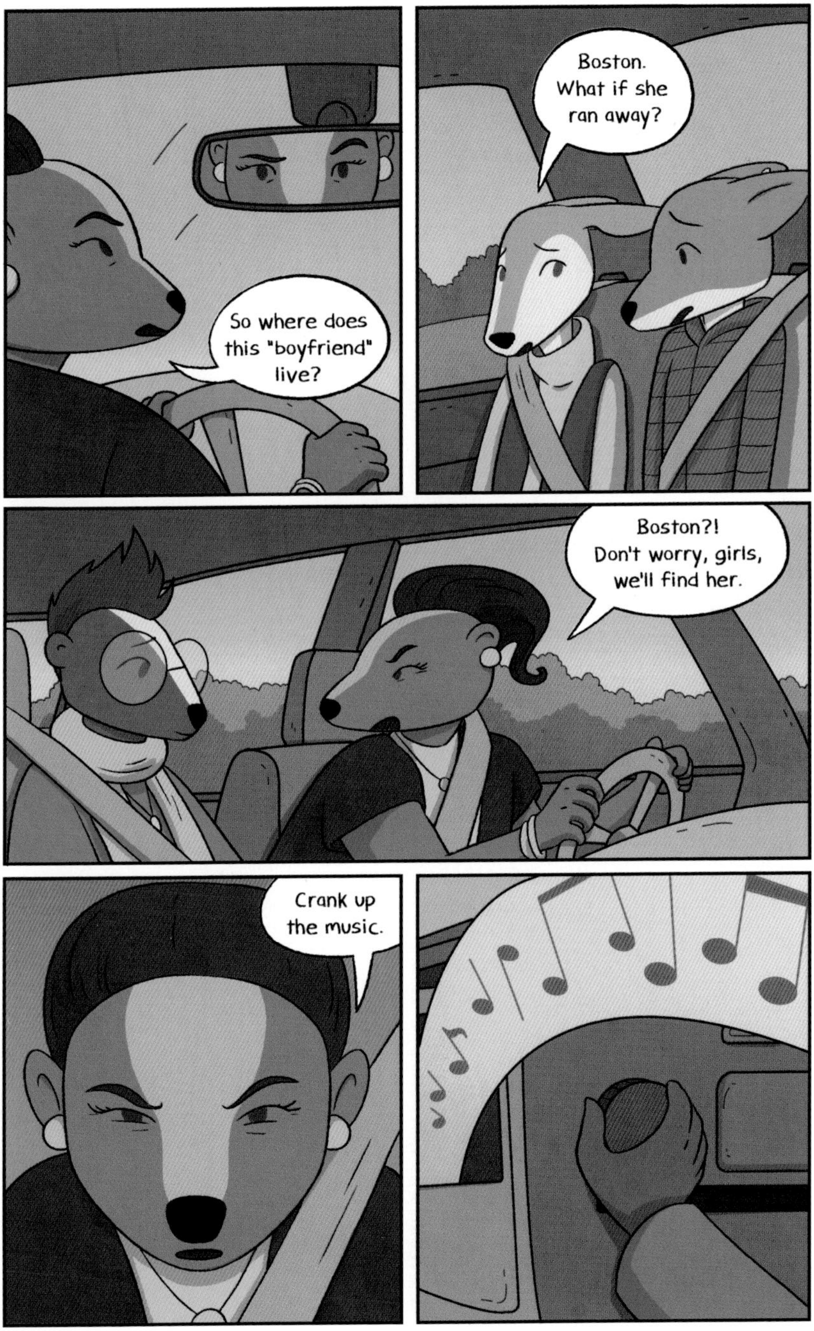
So where does this "boyfriend" live?
Boston. What if she ran away?
Boston?! Don't worry, girls, we'll find her.
Crank up the music.

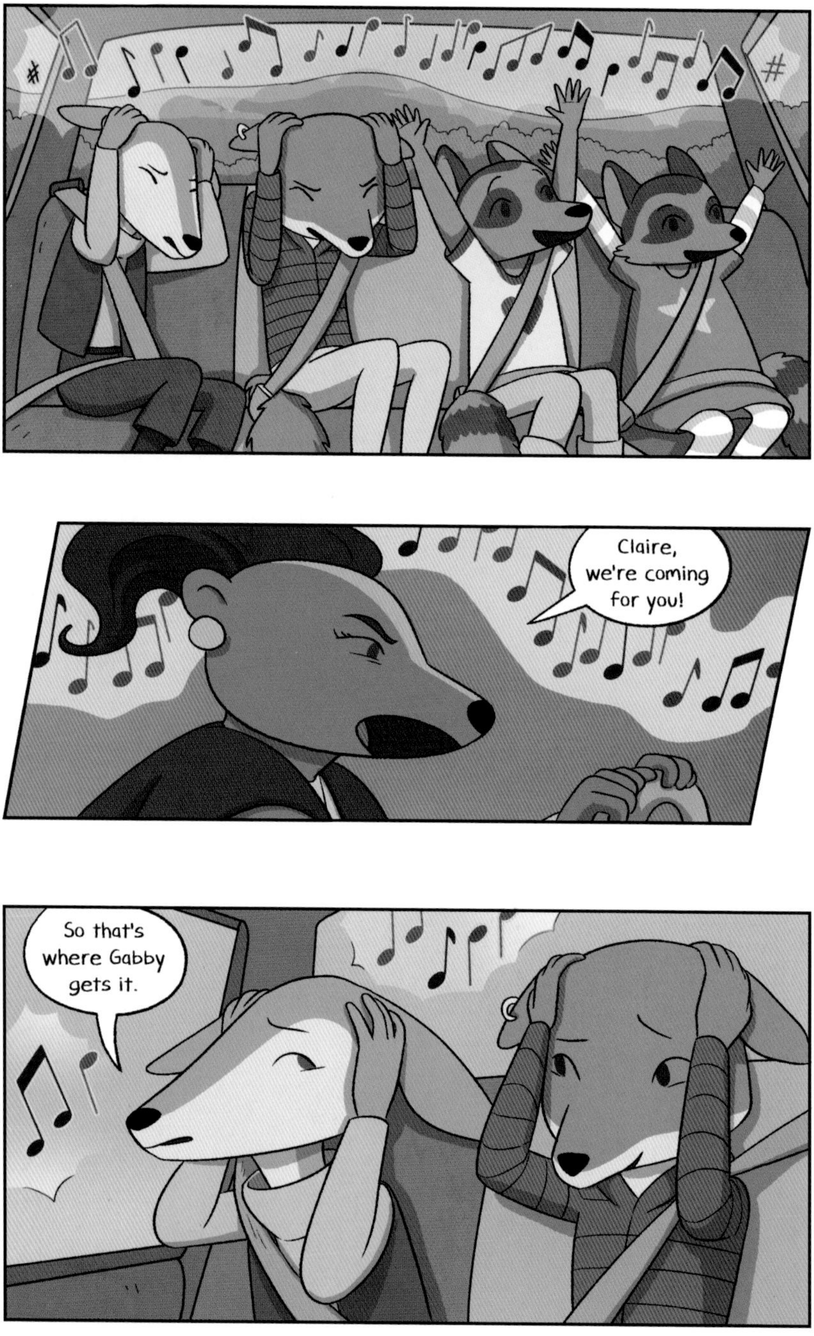
Claire, we're coming for you!
So that's where Gabby gets it.

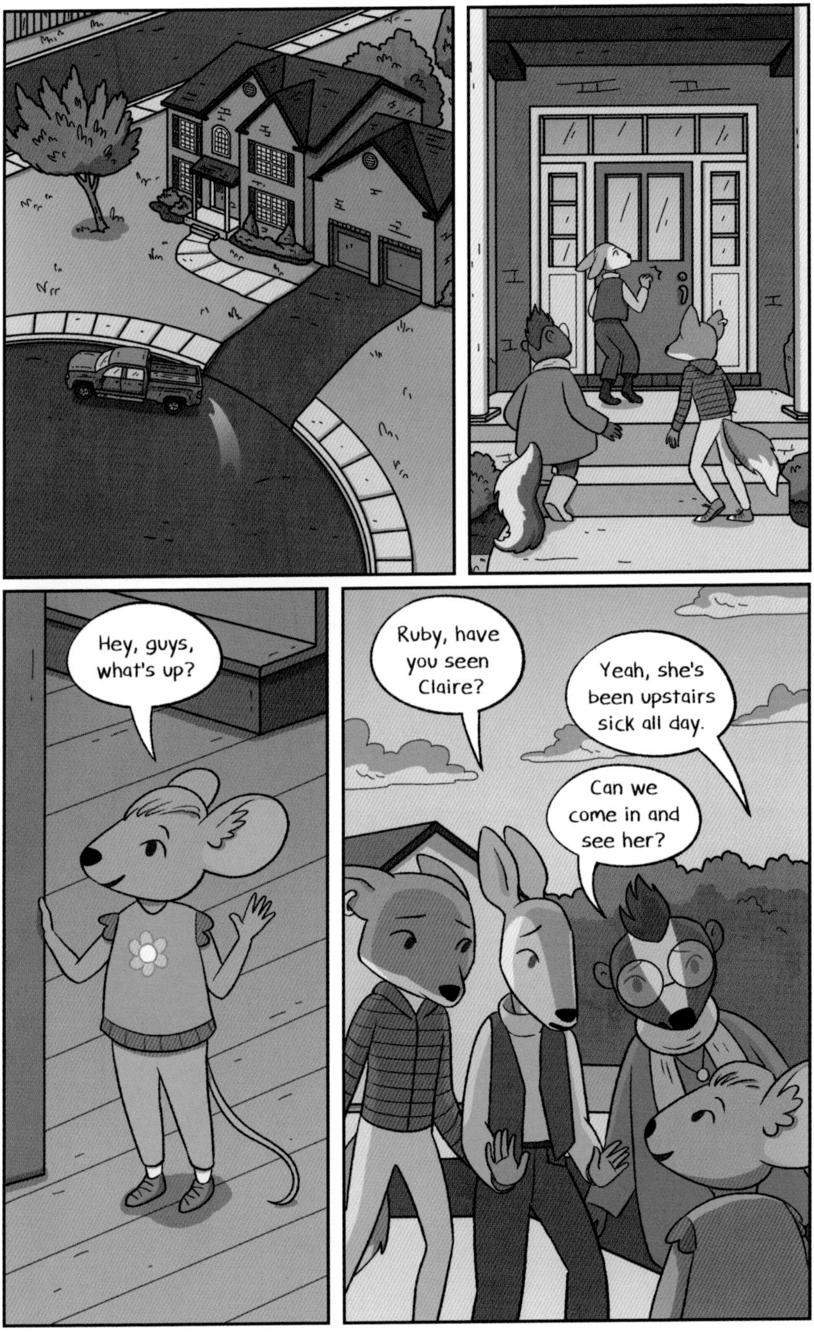
Hey, guys, what's up?
Ruby, have you seen Claire?
Yeah, she's been upstairs sick all day.
Can we come in and see her?

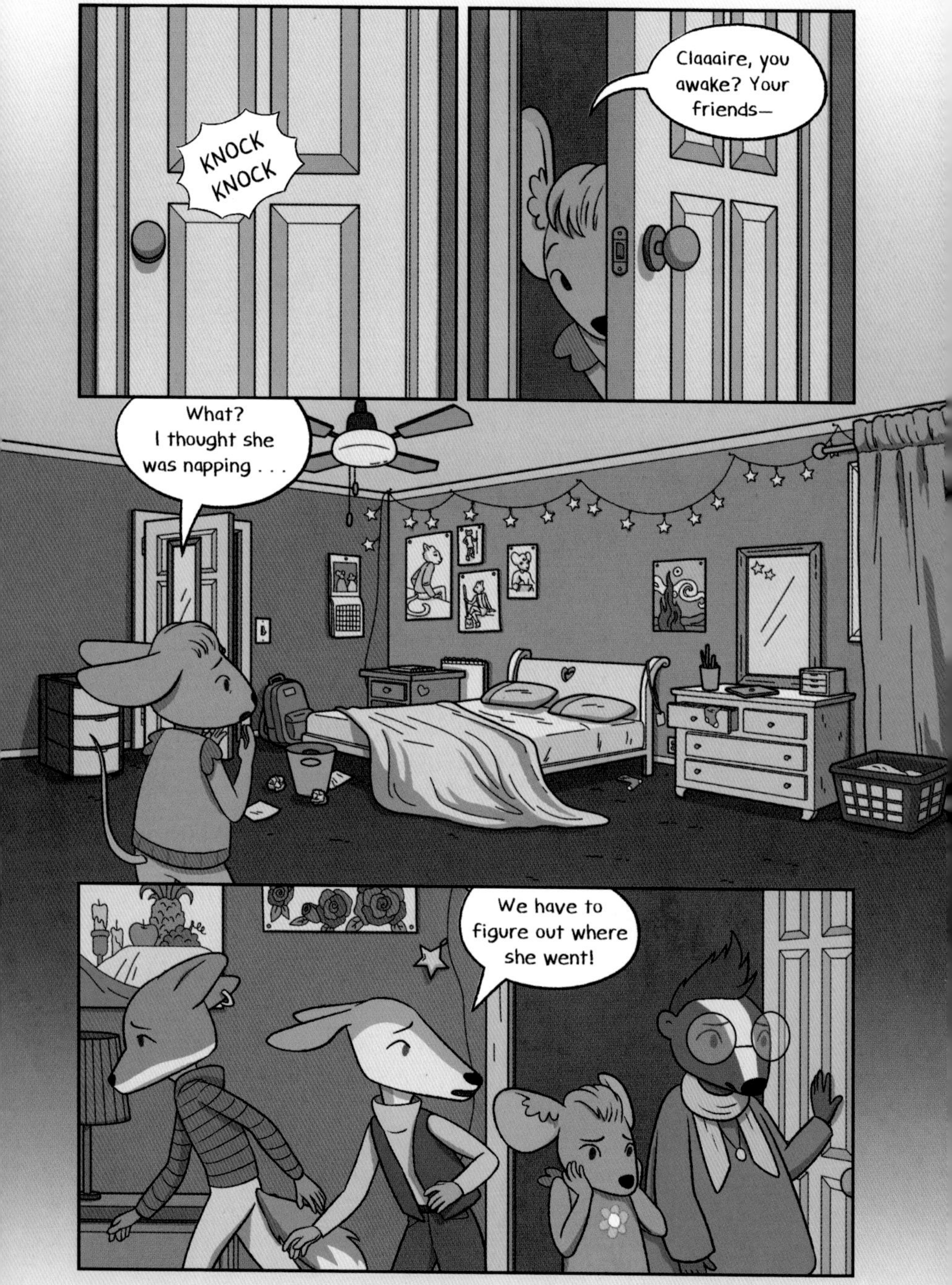
KNOCK KNOCK
Claaaire, you awake? Your friends—
What? I thought she was napping . . .
We have to figure out where she went!

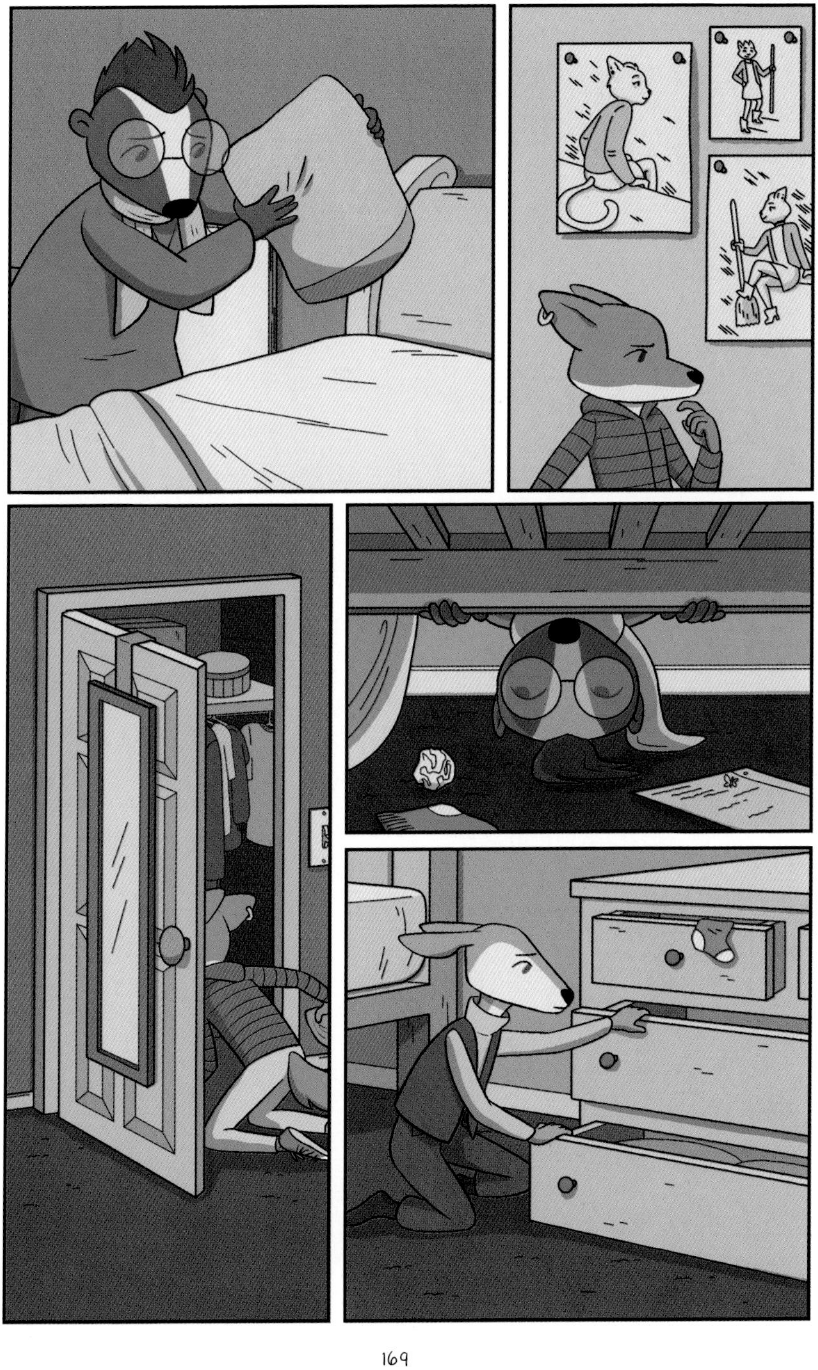

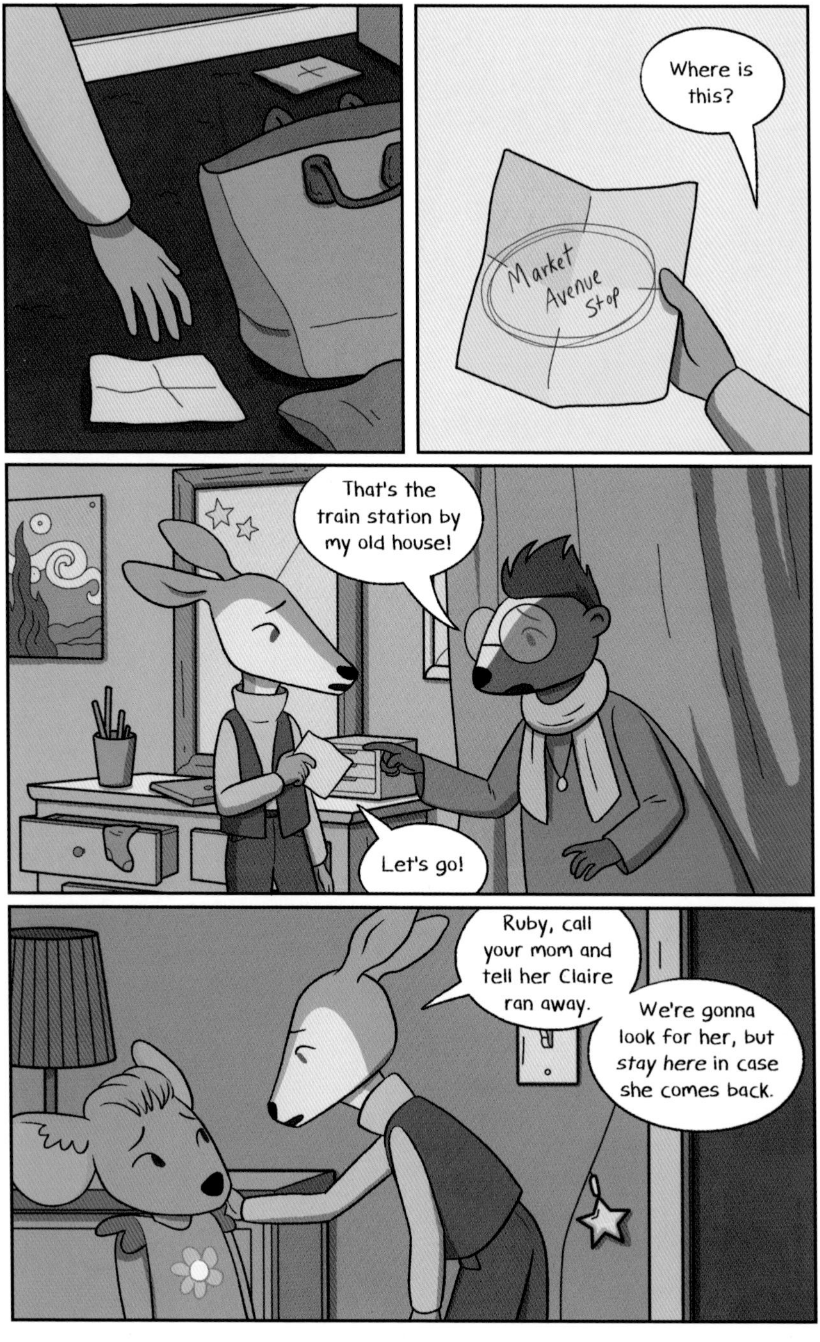
Where is this?
Market Avenue Stop
That's the train station by my old house!
Let's go!
Ruby, call your mom and tell her Claire ran away.
We're gonna look for her, but *stay here* in case she comes back.

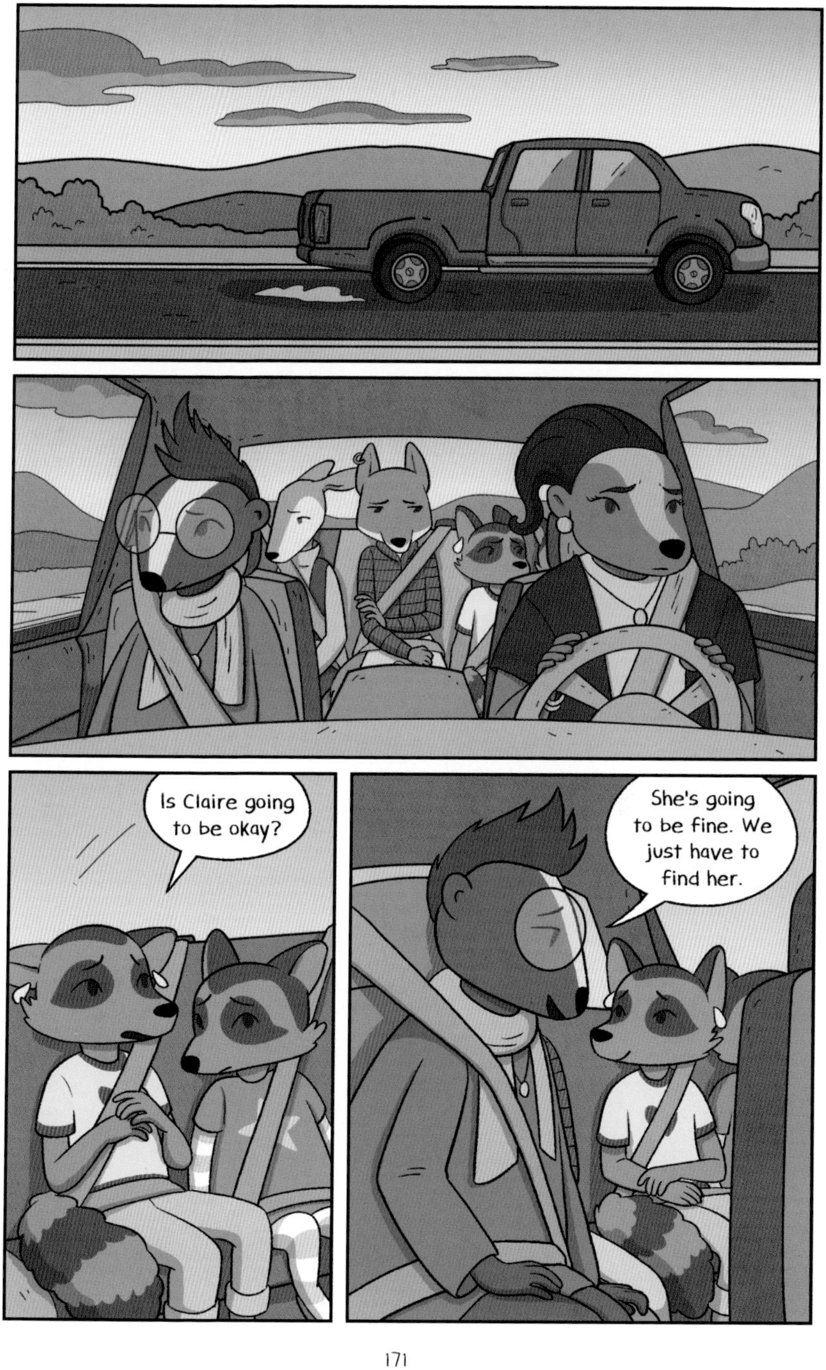

Is Claire going to be okay?
She's going to be fine. We just have to find her.

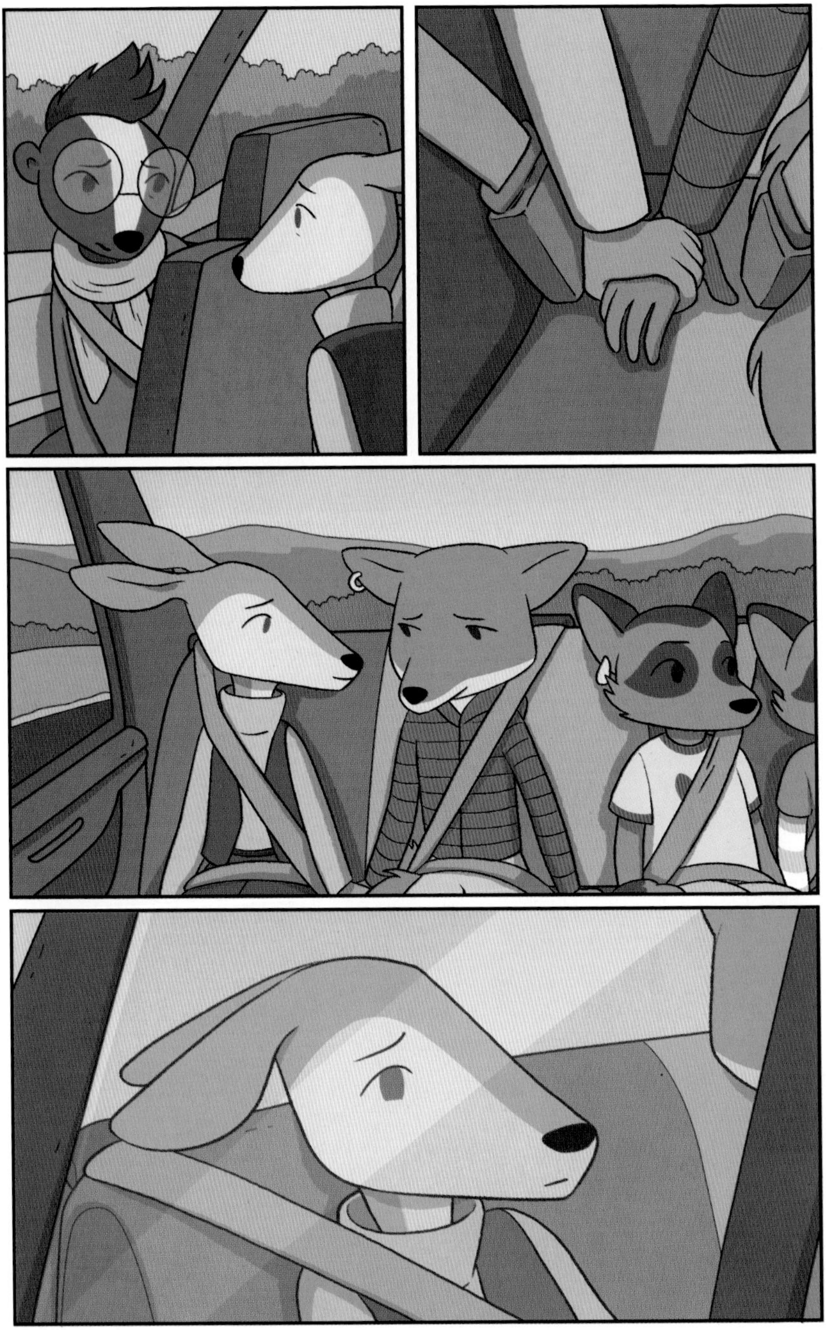

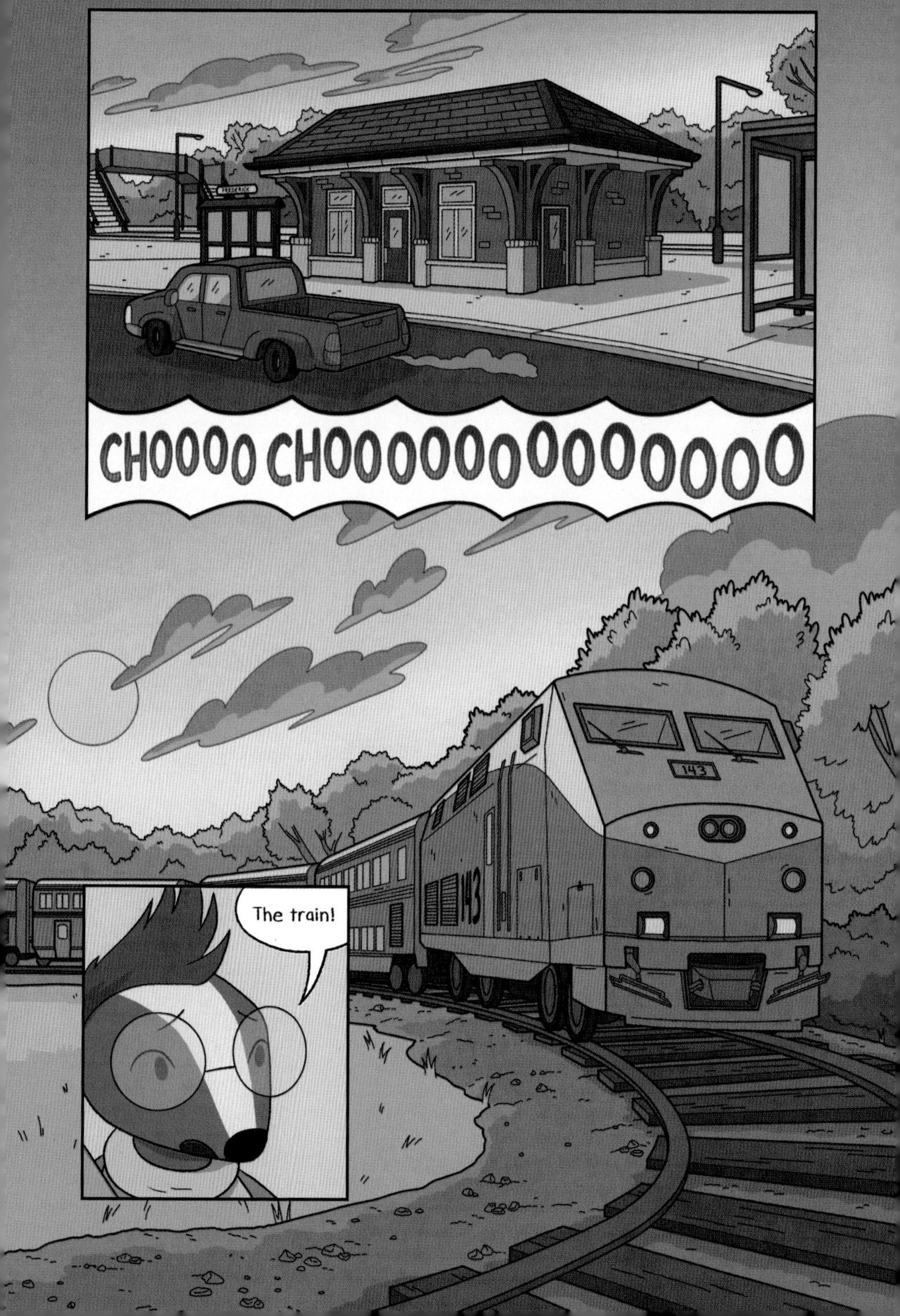
FREDERICK
CHOOOO CHOOOOOOOOOOOOO
The train!

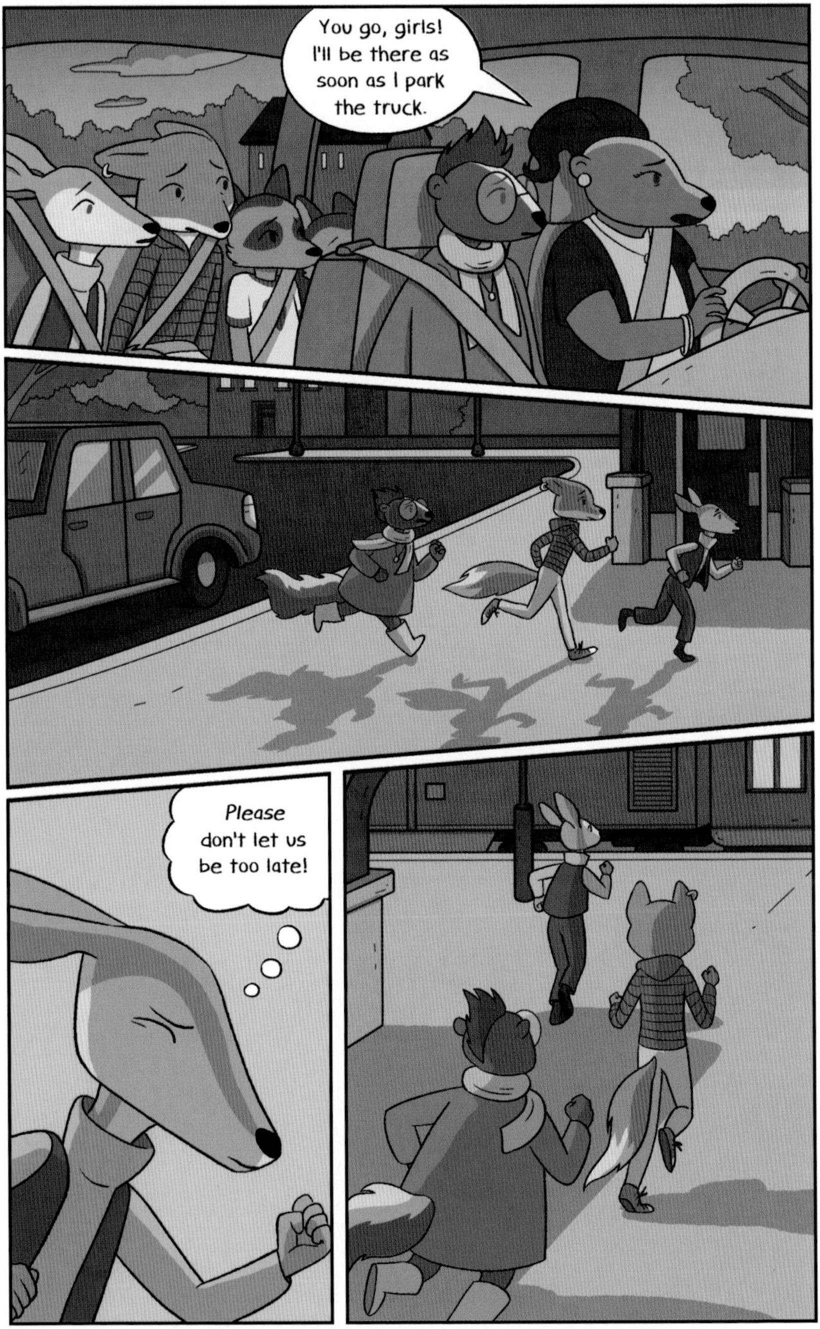
You go, girls! I'll be there as soon as I park the truck.
Please don't let us be too late!

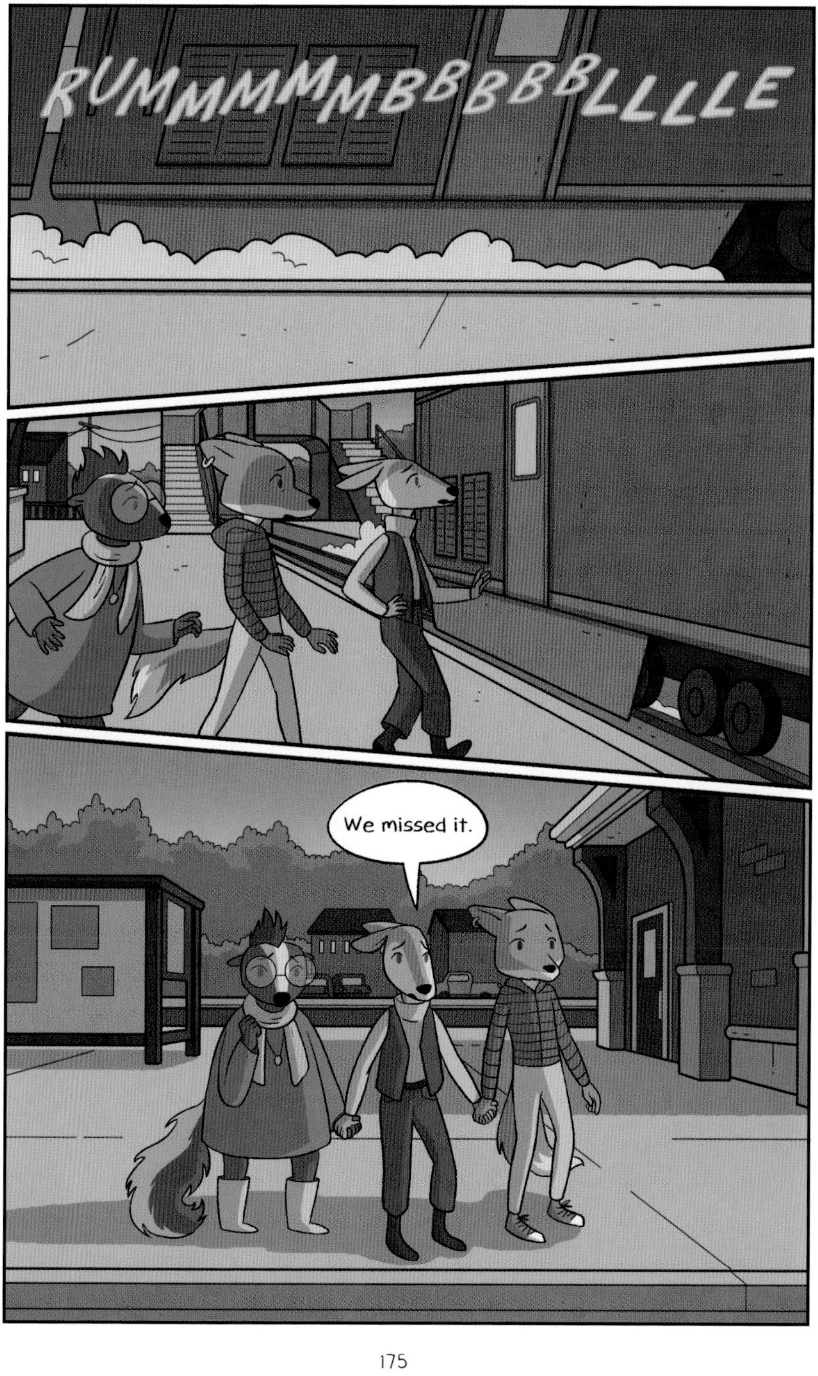
RUMMMMMMBBBBBBLLLLLE
We missed it.

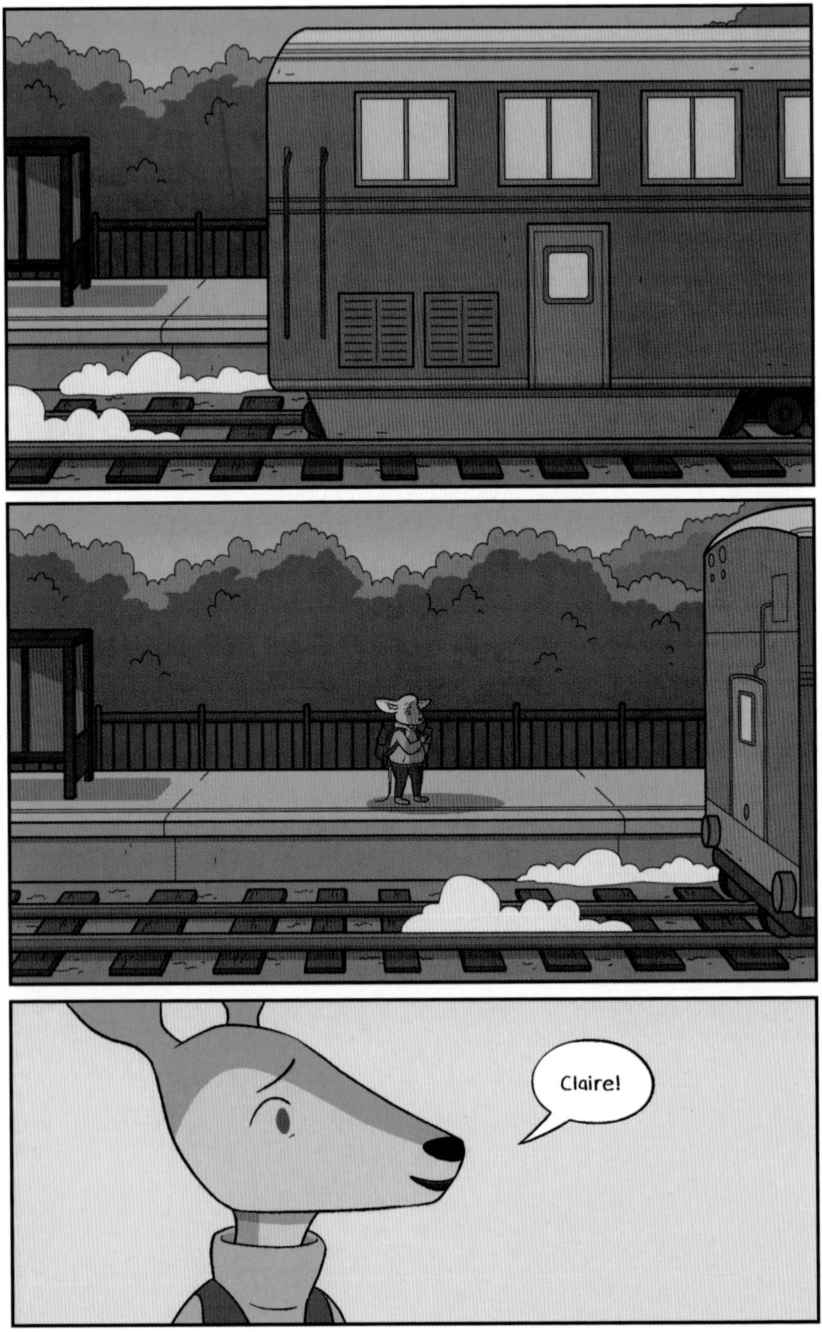
Claire!

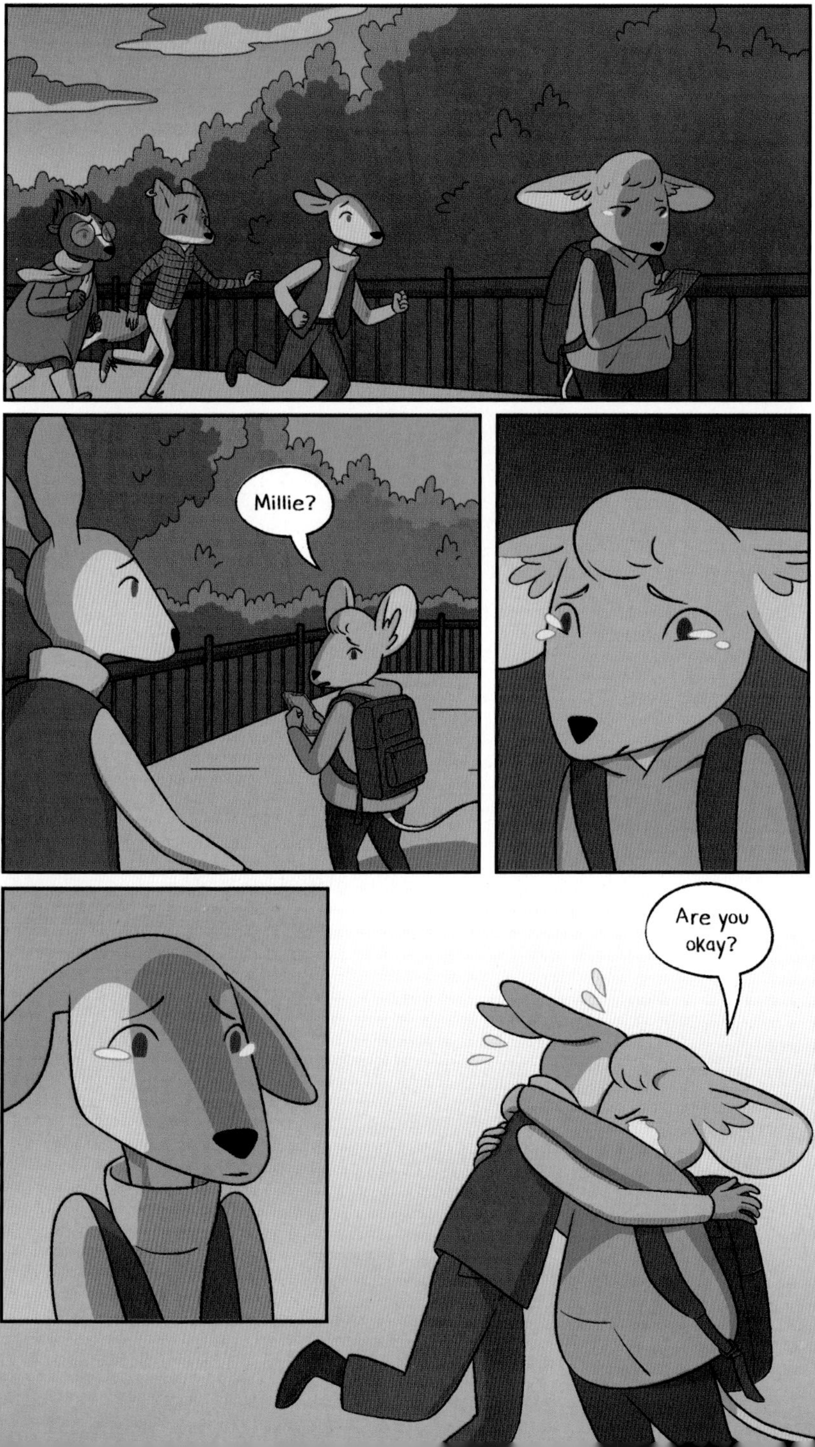
Millie?
Are you okay?

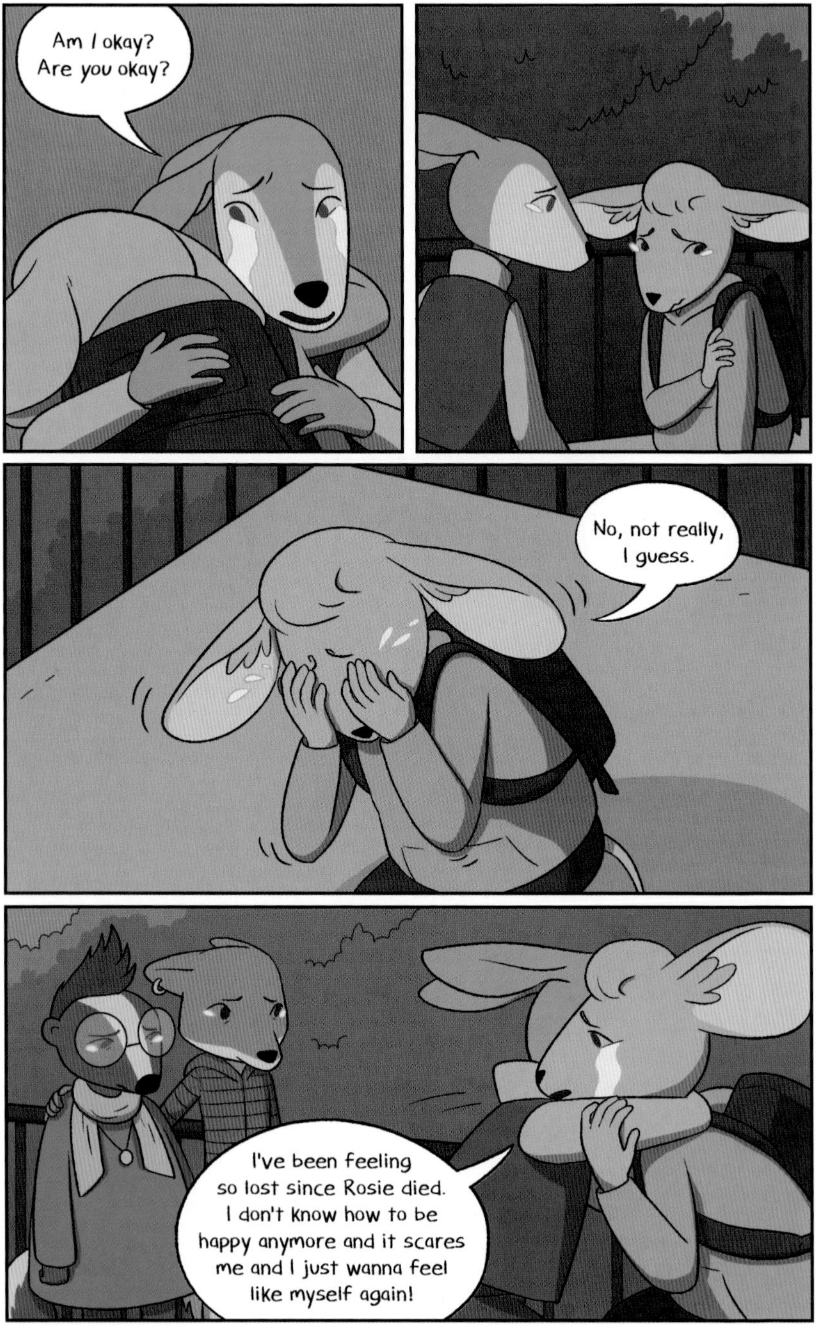
Am I okay?
Are you okay?
No, not really,
I guess.
I've been feeling
so lost since Rosie died.
I don't know how to be
happy anymore and it scares
me and I just wanna feel
like myself again!

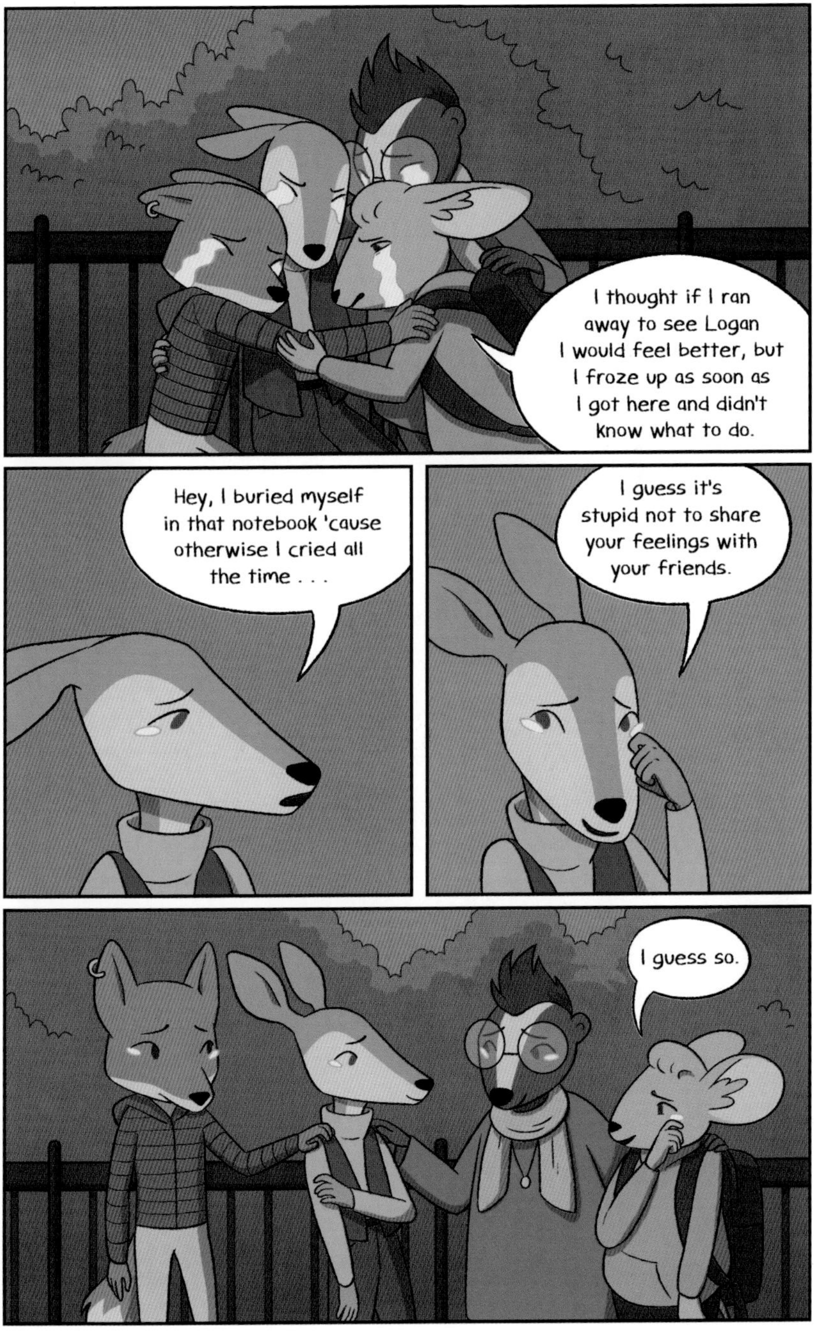
I thought if I ran away to see Logan I would feel better, but I froze up as soon as I got here and didn't know what to do.
Hey, I buried myself in that notebook 'cause otherwise I cried all the time . . .
I guess it's stupid not to share your feelings with your friends.
I guess so.

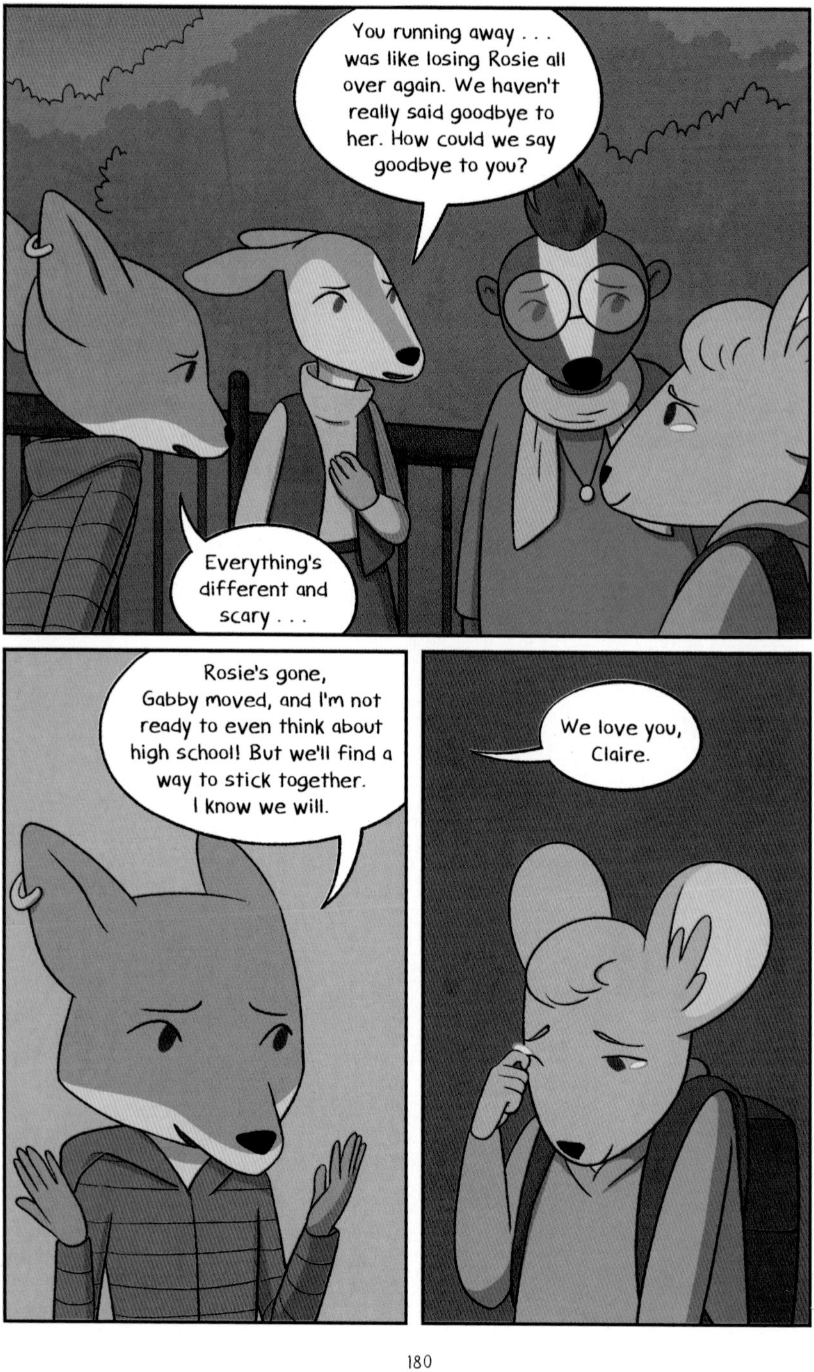
You running away . . . was like losing Rosie all over again. We haven't really said goodbye to her. How could we say goodbye to you?
Everything's different and scary . . .
Rosie's gone, Gabby moved, and I'm not ready to even think about high school! But we'll find a way to stick together. I know we will.
We love you, Claire.

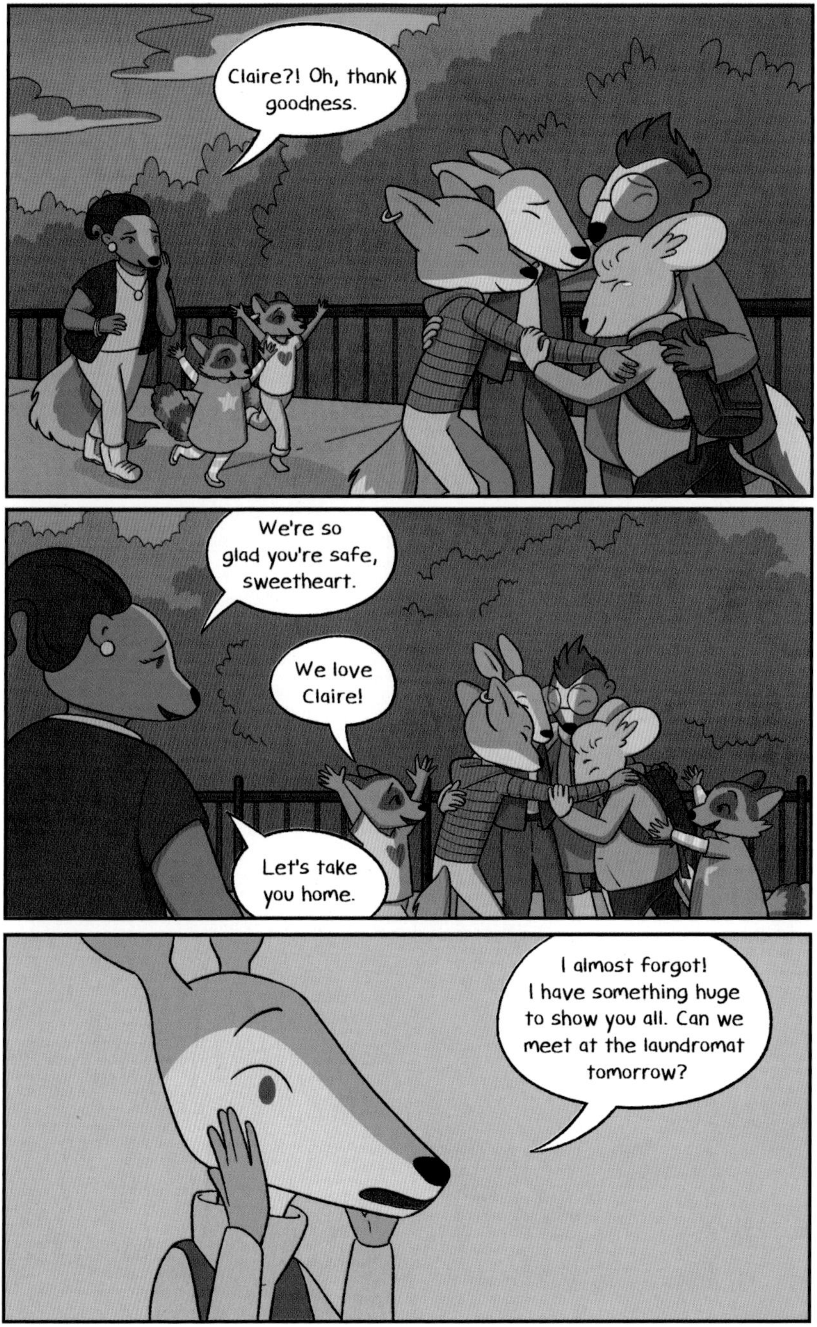
Claire?! Oh, thank goodness.
We're so glad you're safe, sweetheart.
We love Claire!
Let's take you home.
I almost forgot! I have something huge to show you all. Can we meet at the laundromat tomorrow?

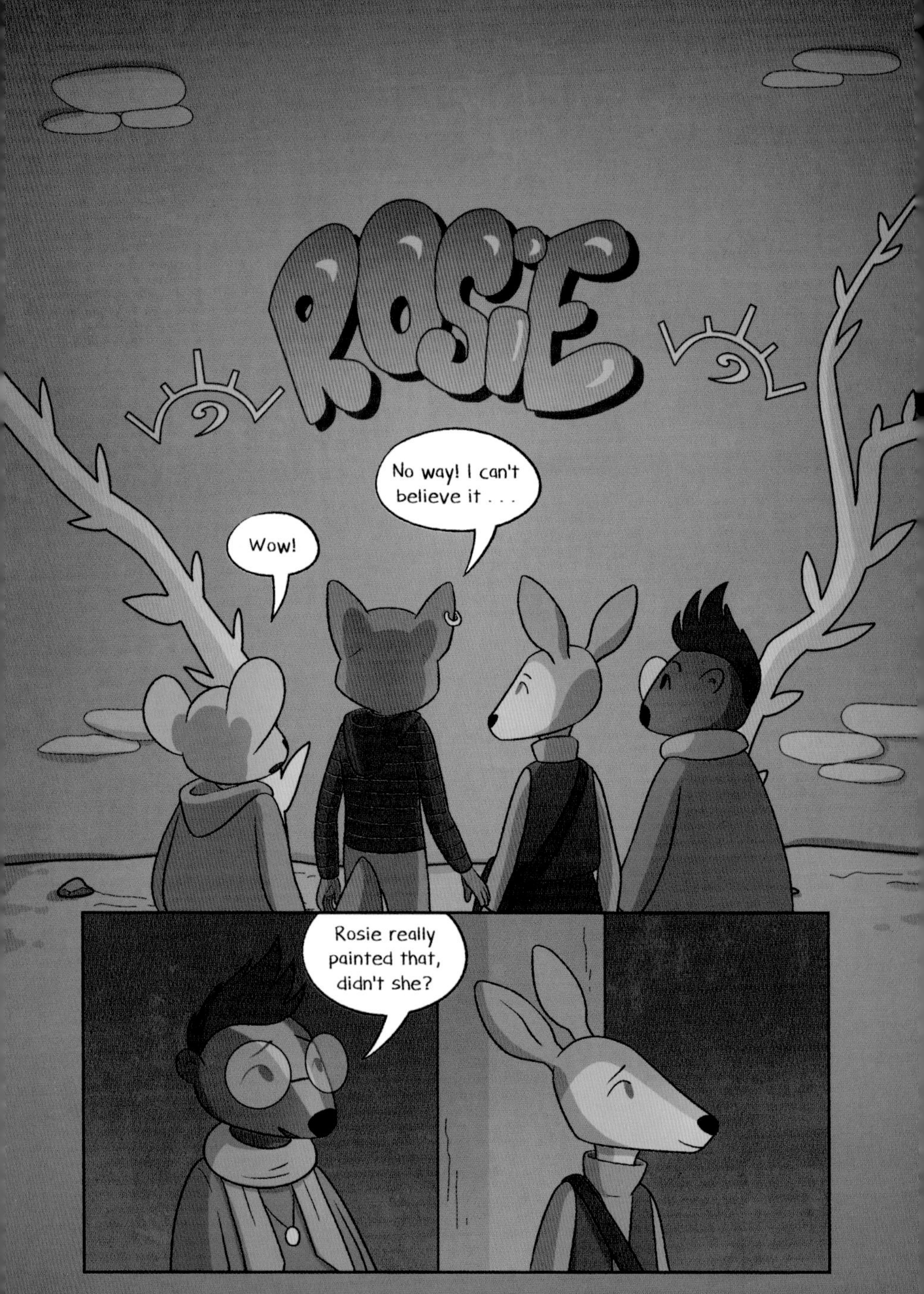
ROSIE
Wow!
No way! I can't believe it . . .
Rosie really painted that, didn't she?

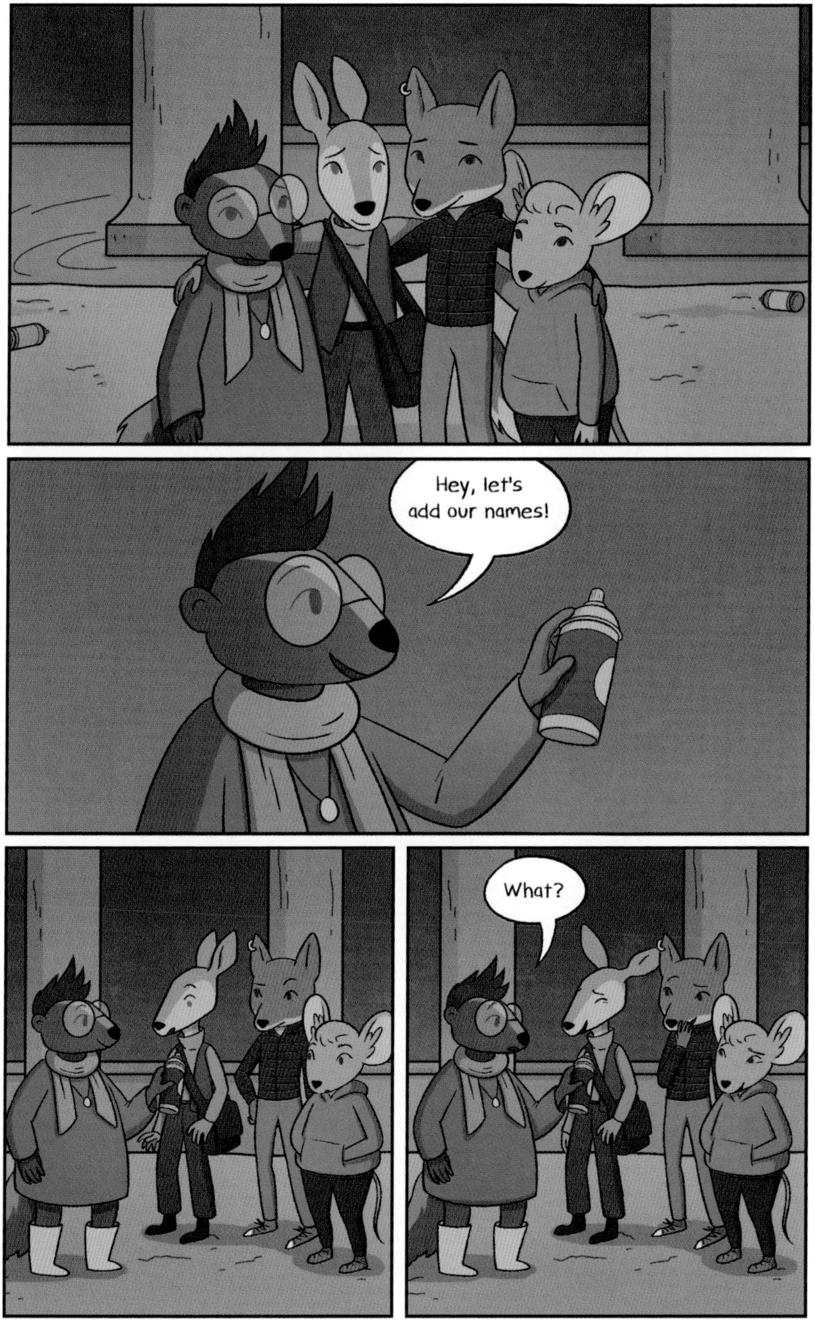
Hey, let's add our names!
What?

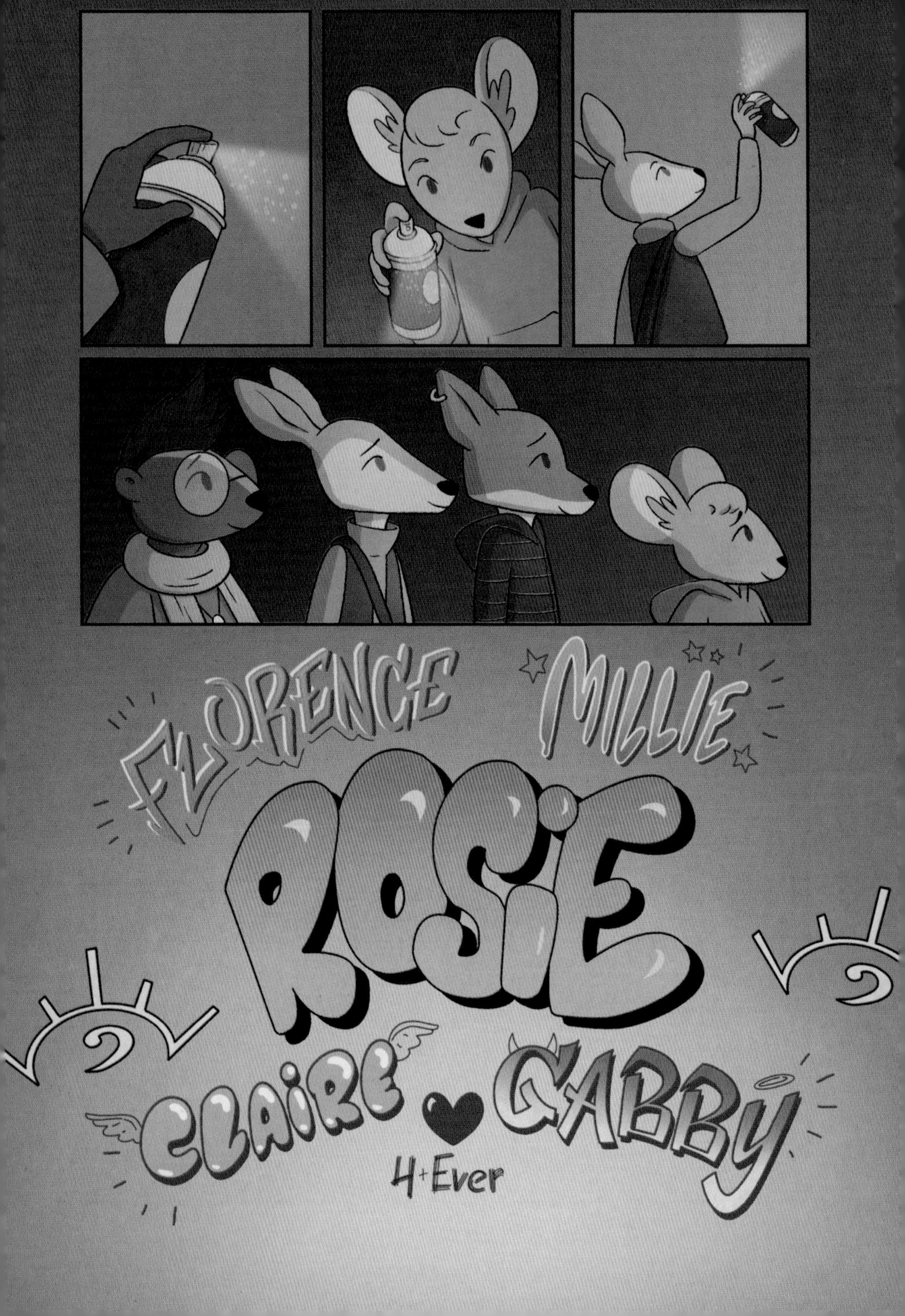
FLORENCE
MILLIE
ROSIE
CLAIRE
GABBY
4+Ever

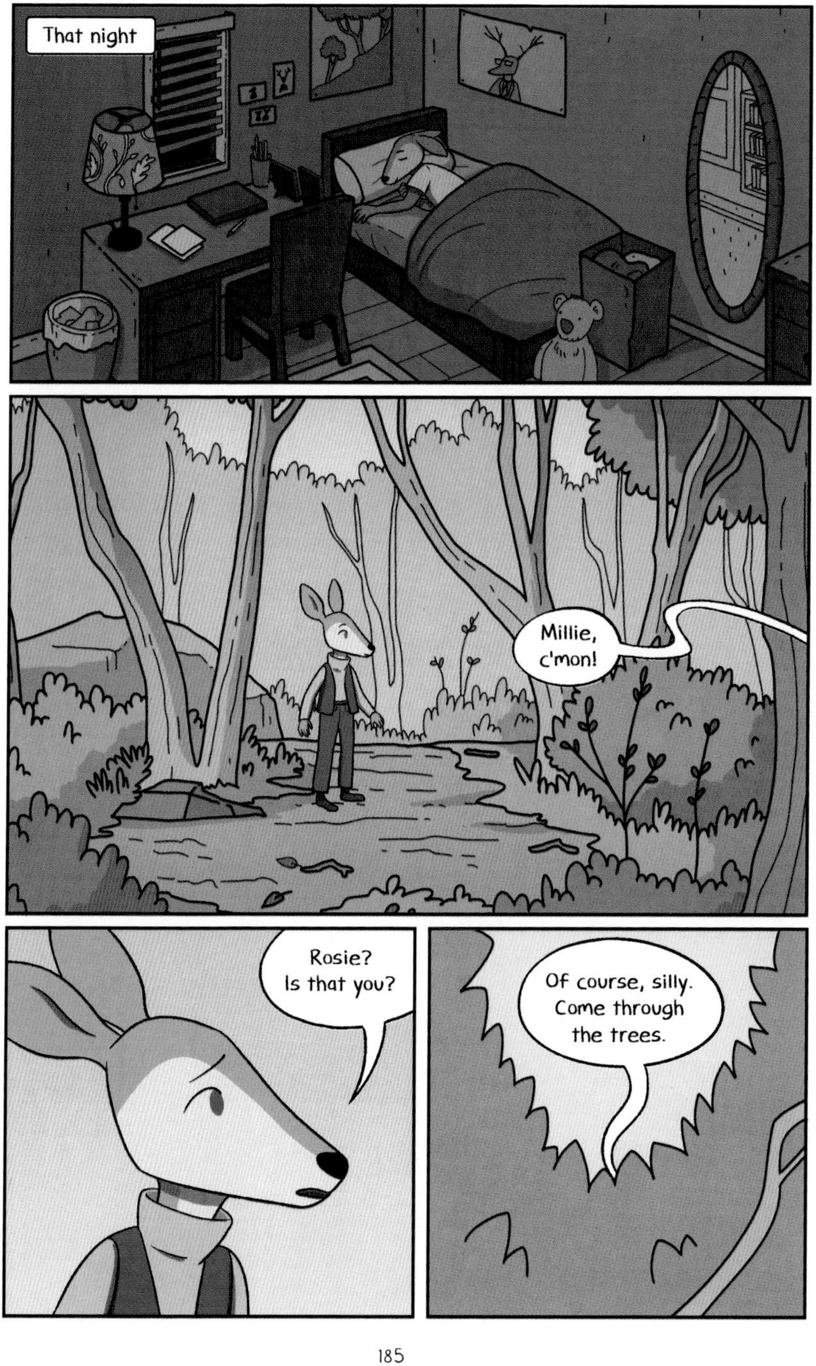
That night
Millie, c'mon!
Rosie? Is that you?
Of course, silly. Come through the trees.

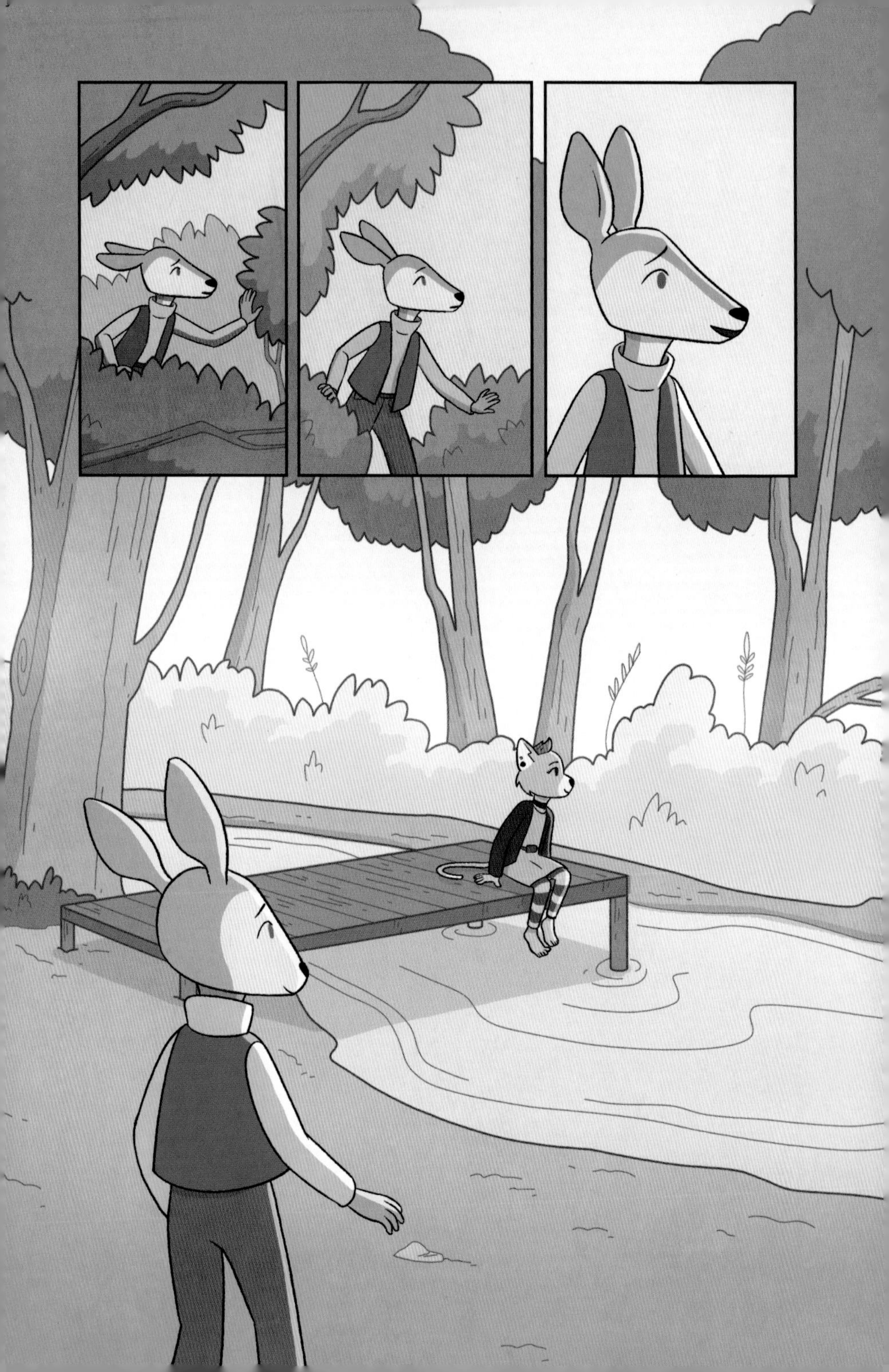

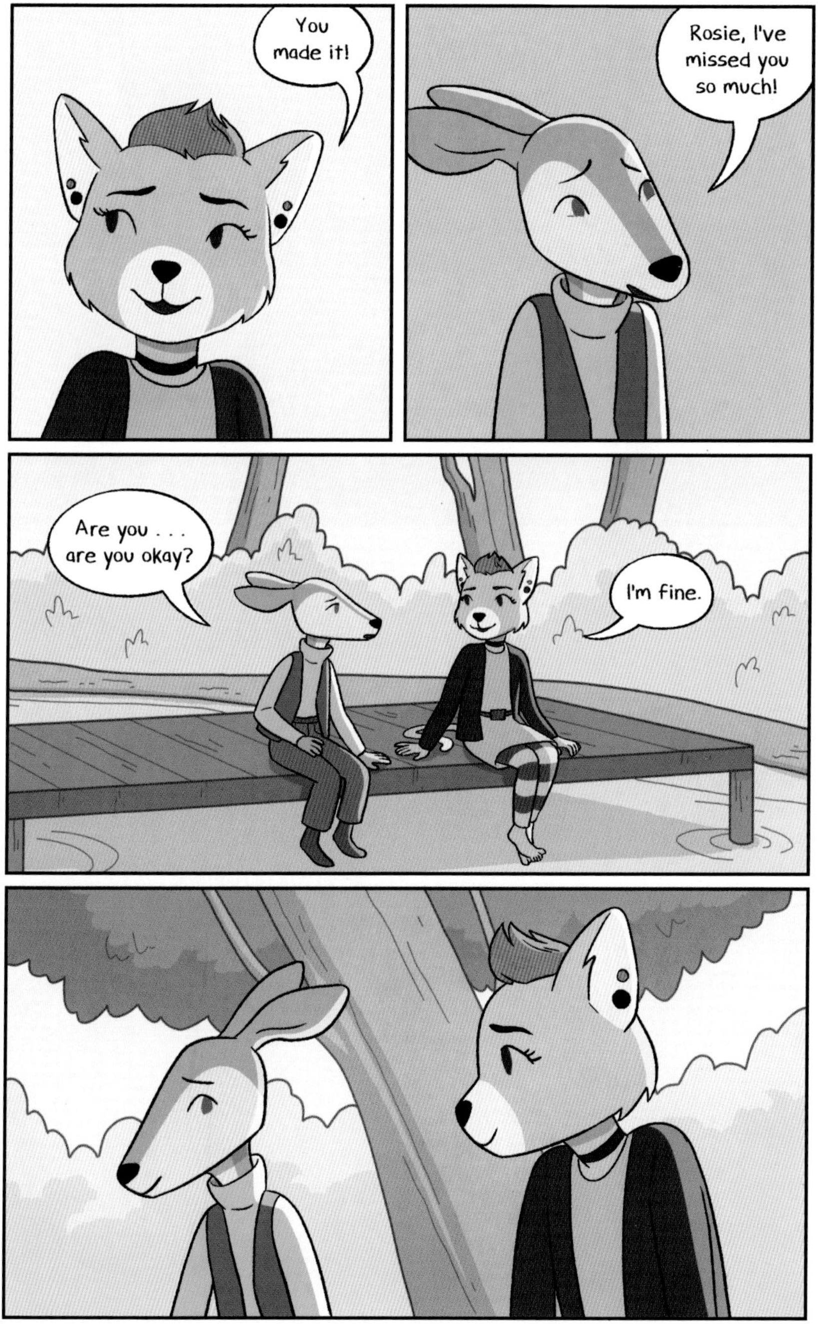
You made it!
Rosie, I've missed you so much!
Are you . . . are you okay?
I'm fine.

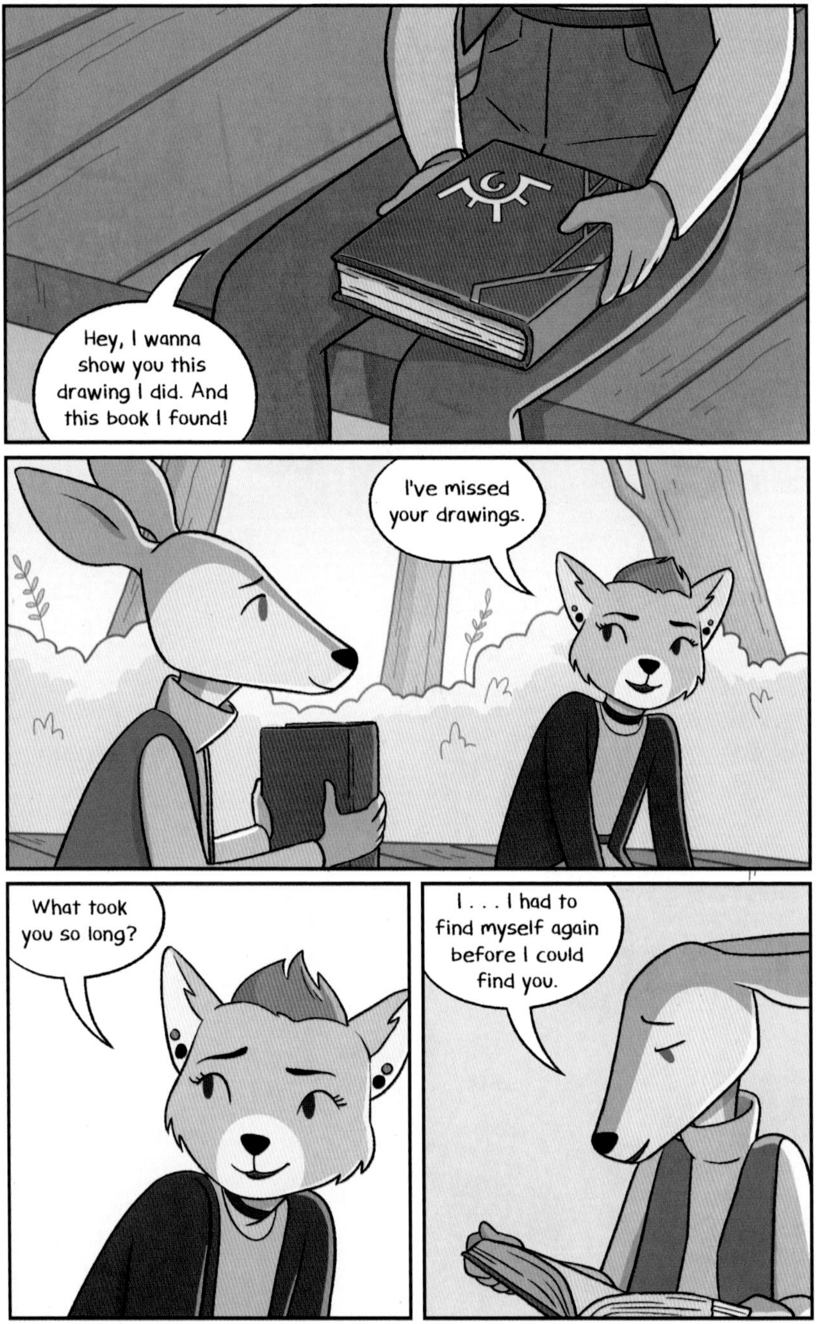
Hey, I wanna show you this drawing I did. And this book I found!
I've missed your drawings.
What took you so long?
I . . . I had to find myself again before I could find you.

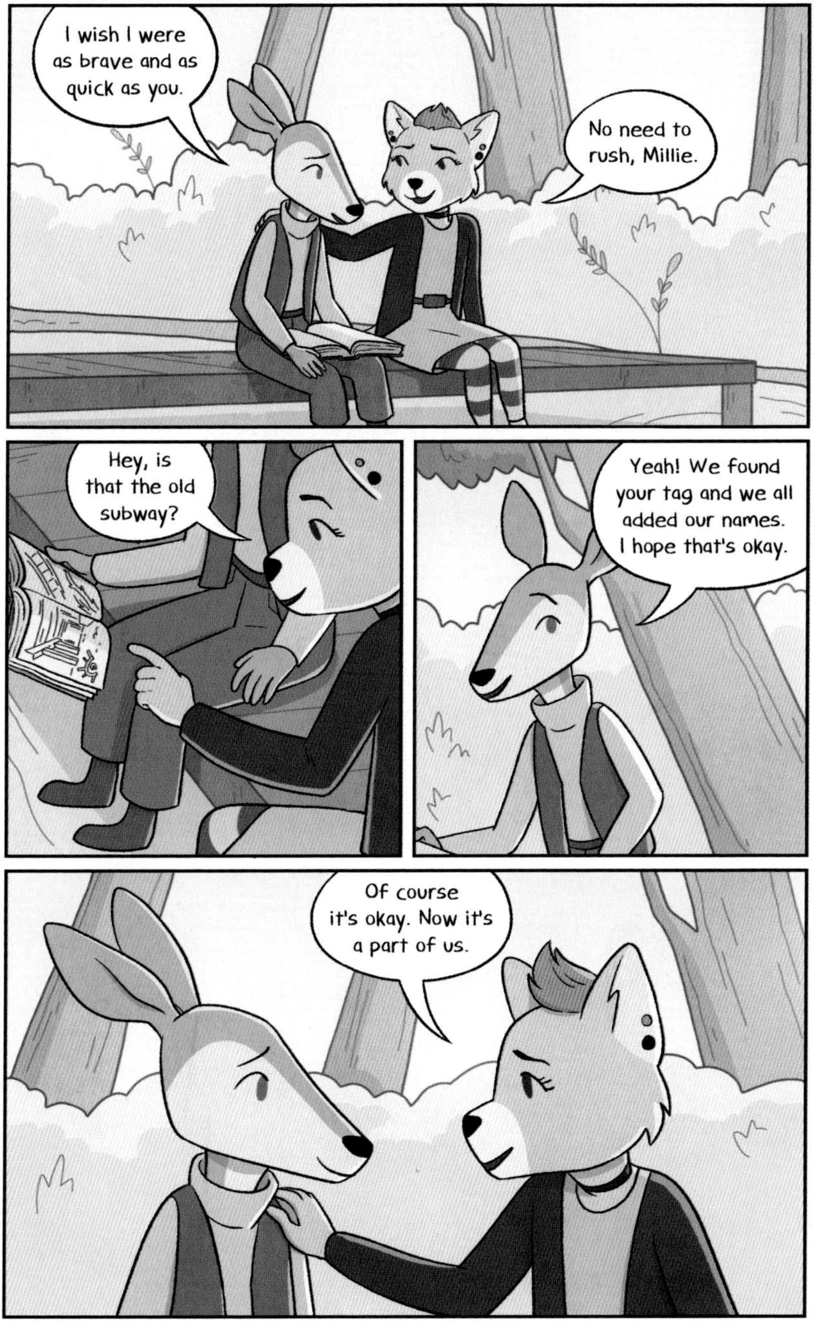
I wish I were as brave and as quick as you.
No need to rush, Millie.
Hey, is that the old subway?
Yeah! We found your tag and we all added our names. I hope that's okay.
Of course it's okay. Now it's a part of us.

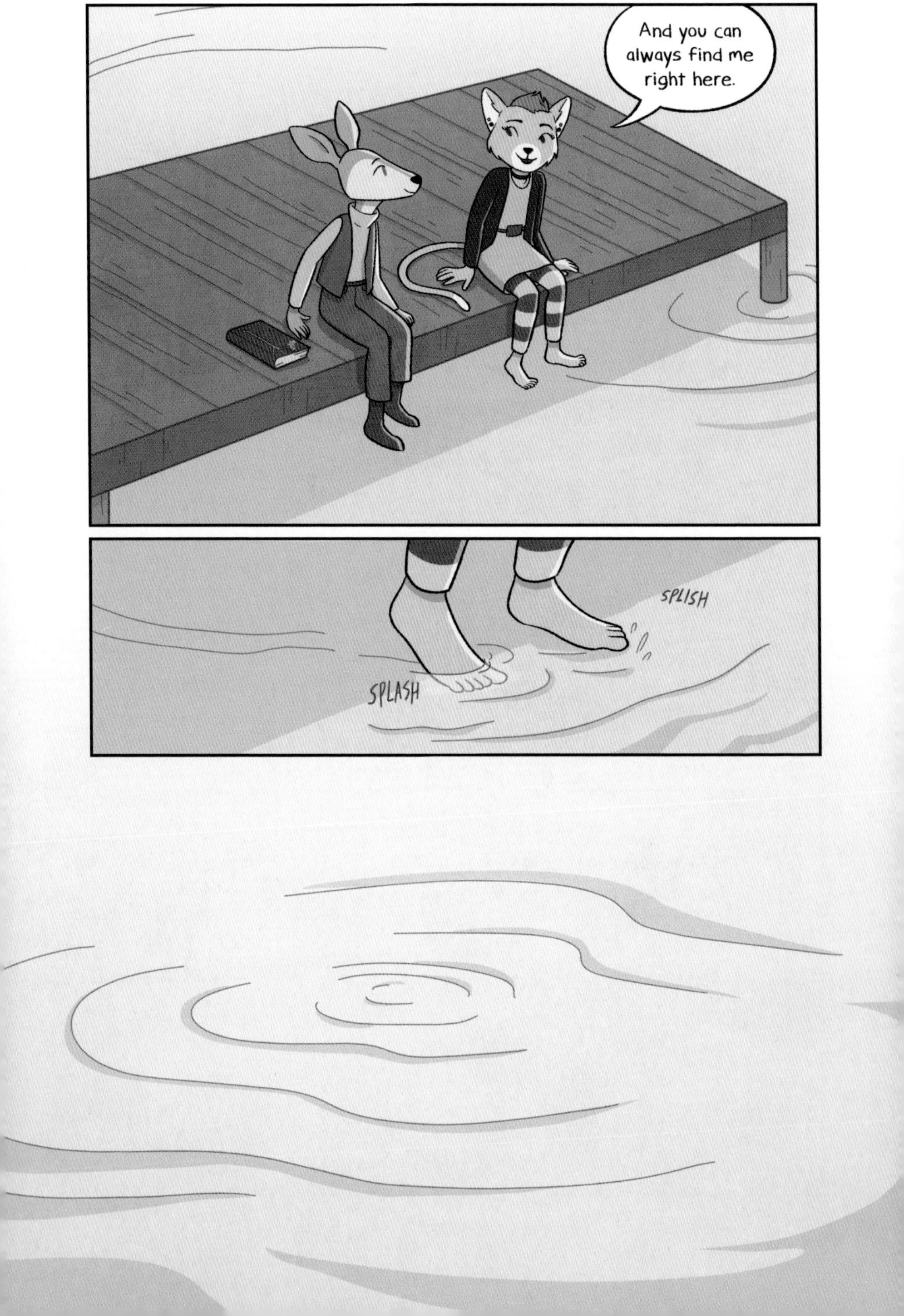

And you can always find me right here.
SPLISH
SPLASH

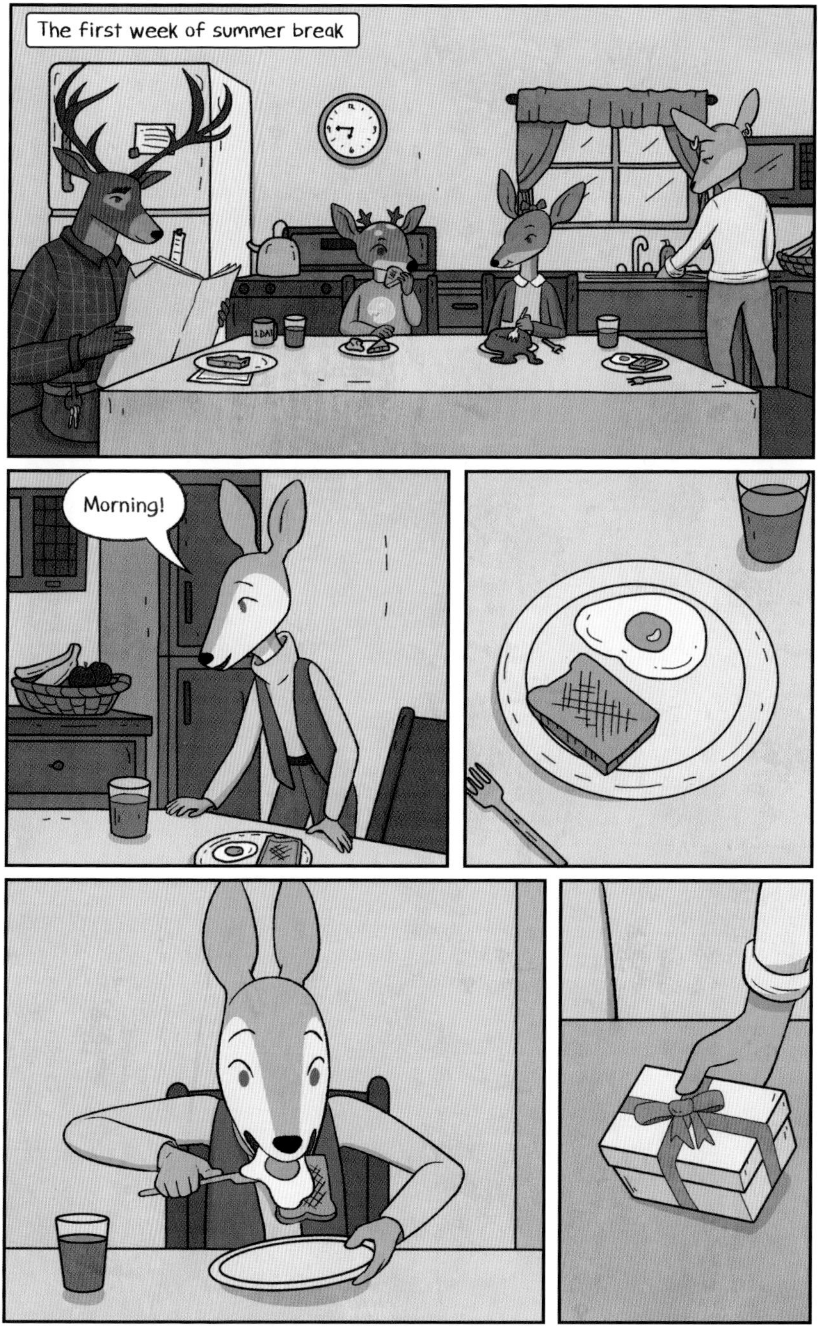
The first week of summer break
Morning!

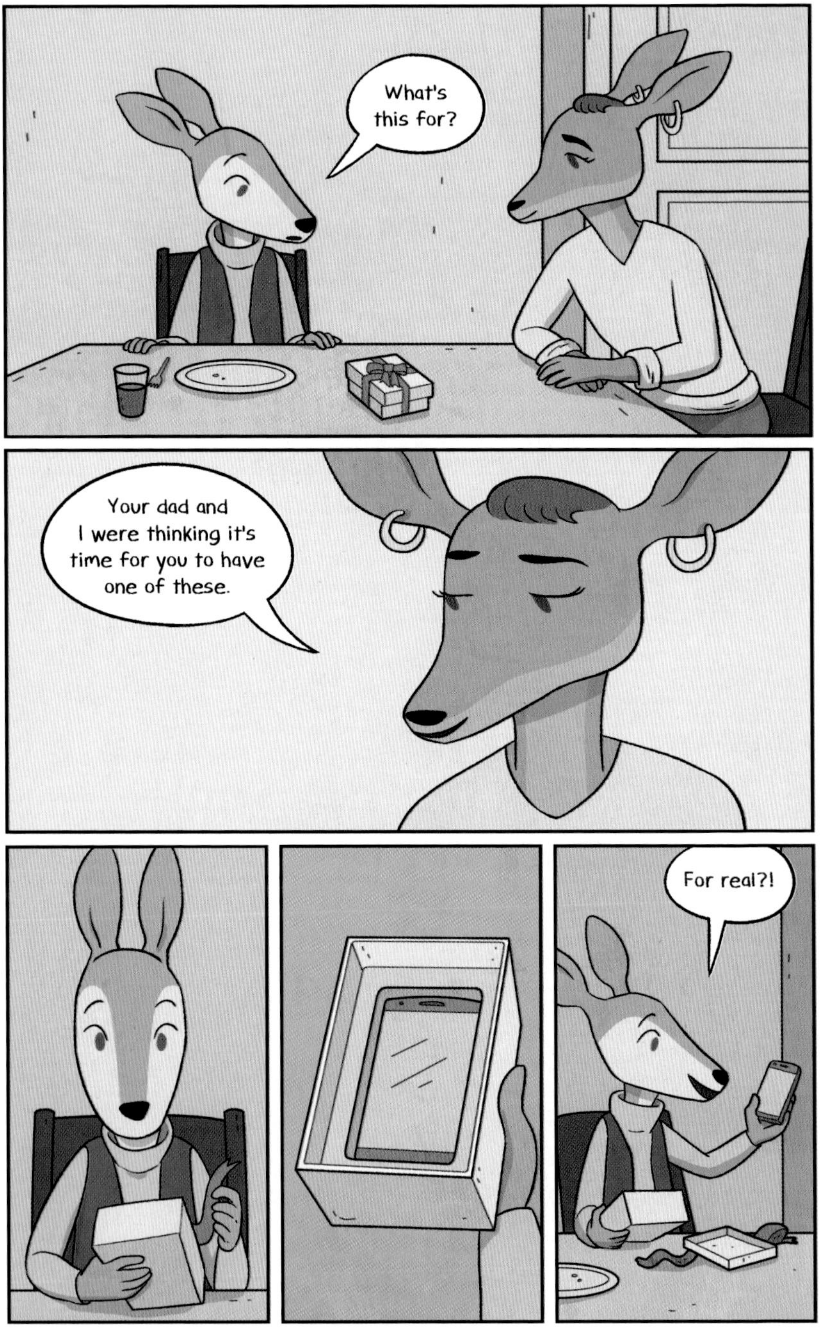
What's this for?
Your dad and I were thinking it's time for you to have one of these.
For real?!

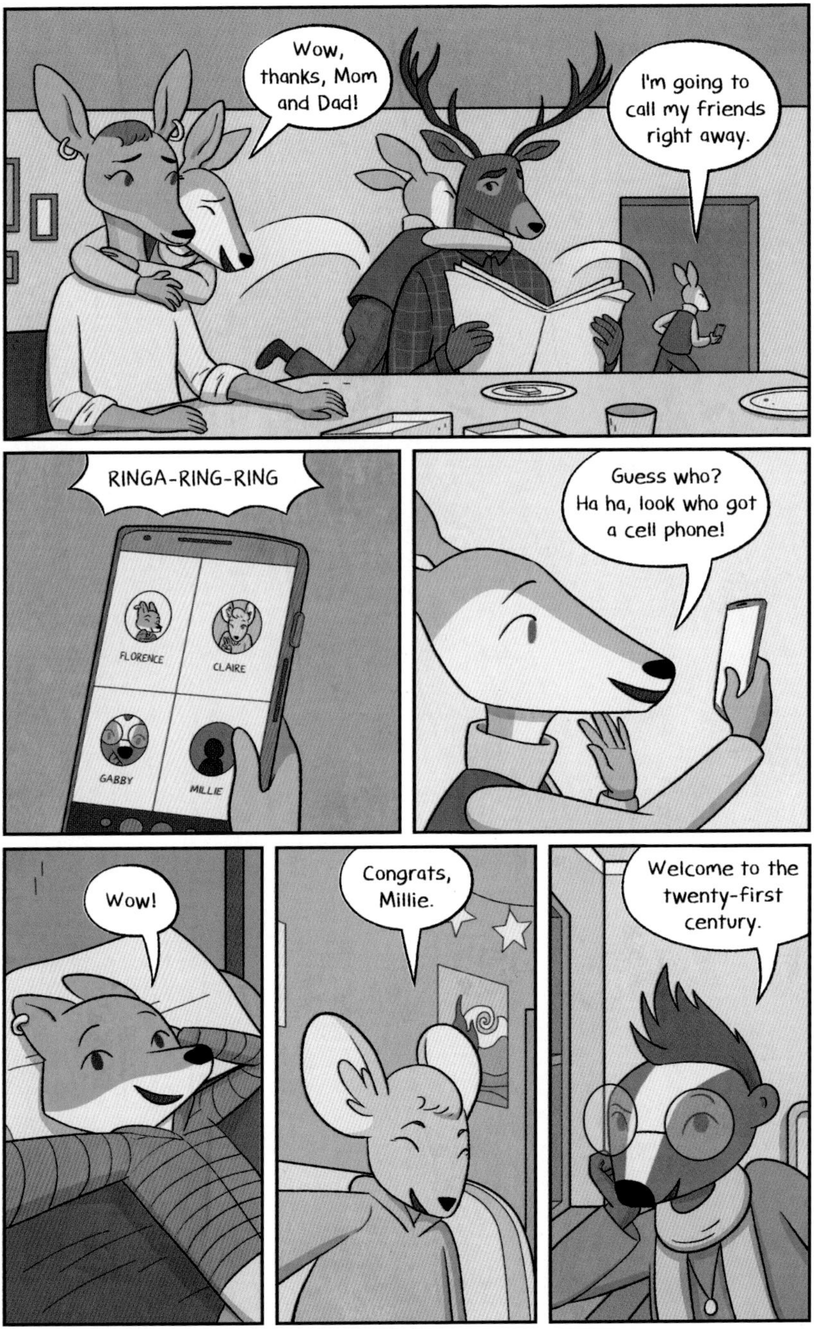
Wow, thanks, Mom and Dad!
I'm going to call my friends right away.
RINGA-RING-RING
FLORENCE
CLAIRE
GABBY
MILLIE
Guess who? Ha ha, look who got a cell phone!
Wow!
Congrats, Millie.
Welcome to the twenty-first century.

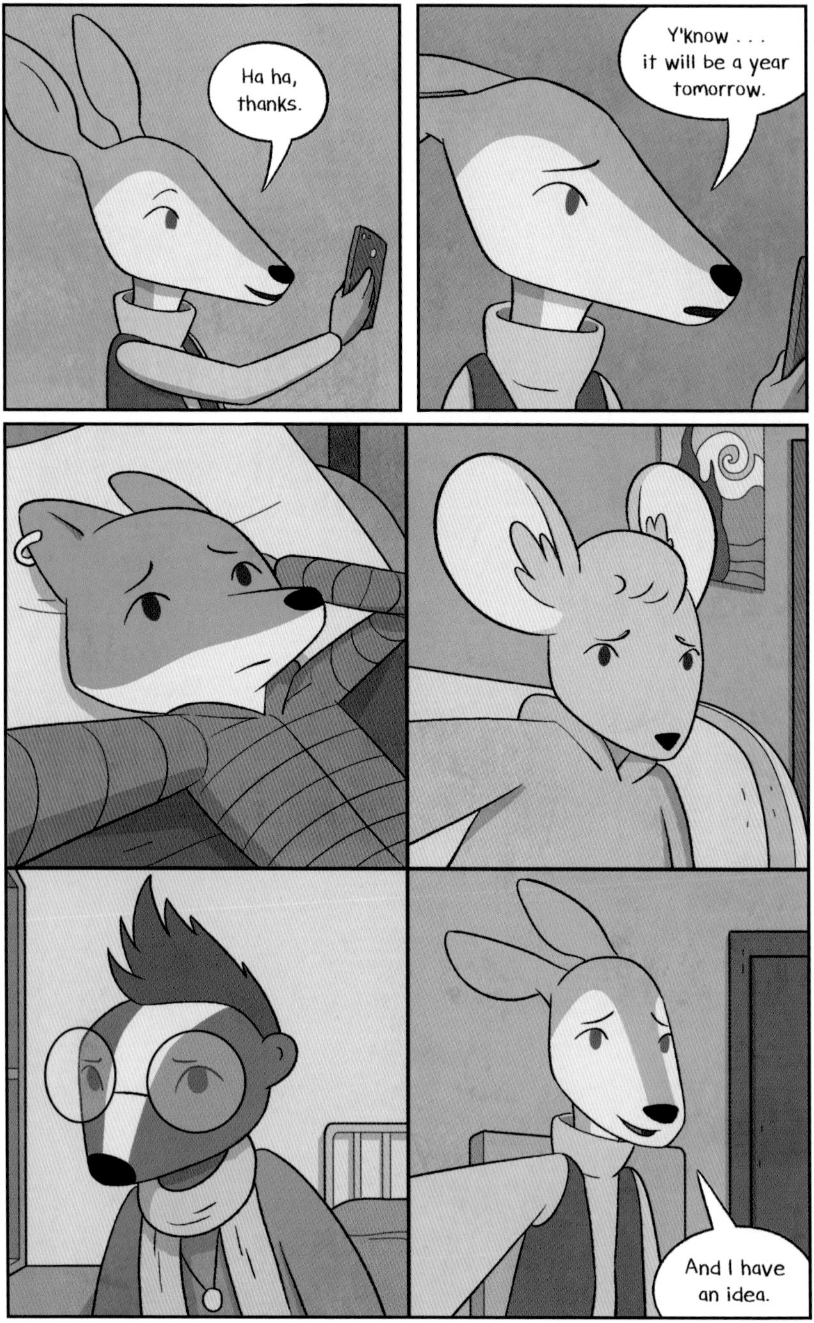
Ha ha,
thanks.
Y'know . . .
it will be a year
tomorrow.
And I have
an idea.

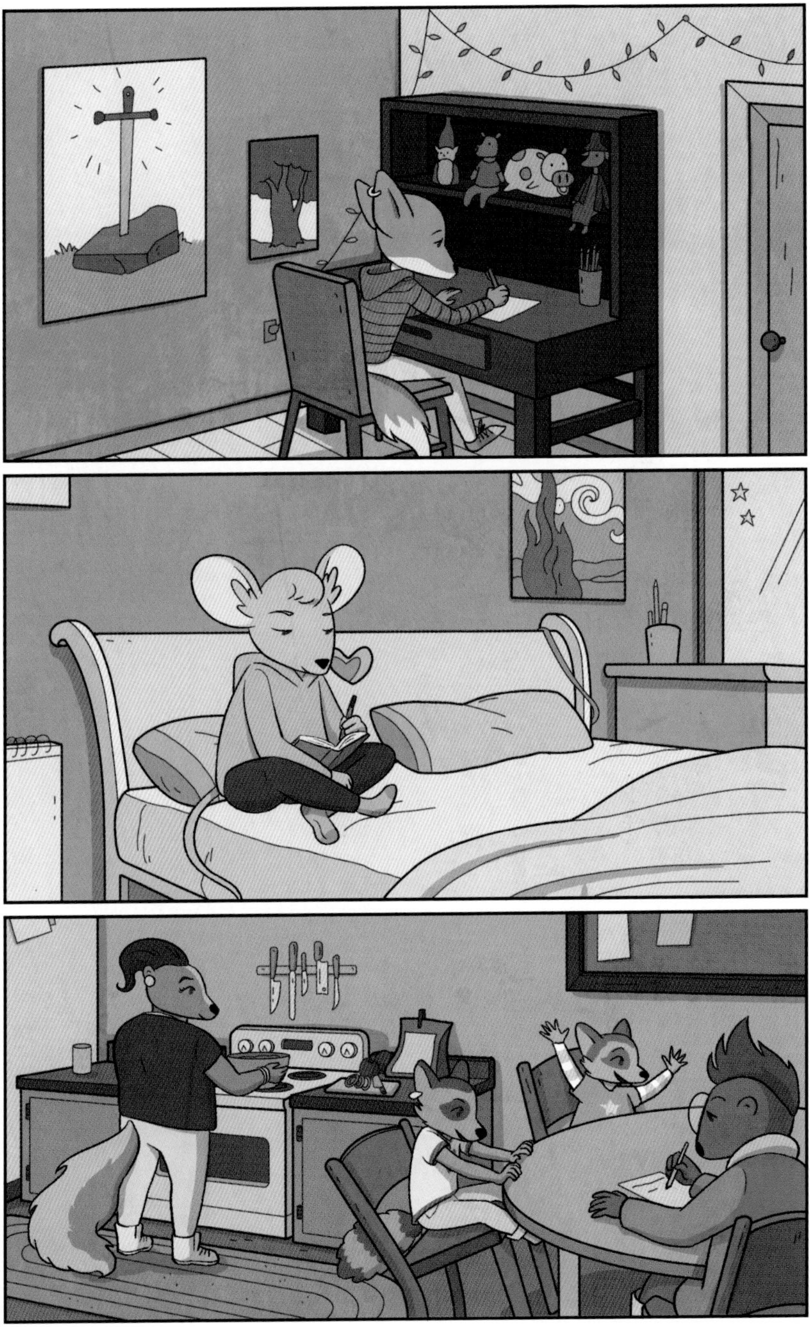

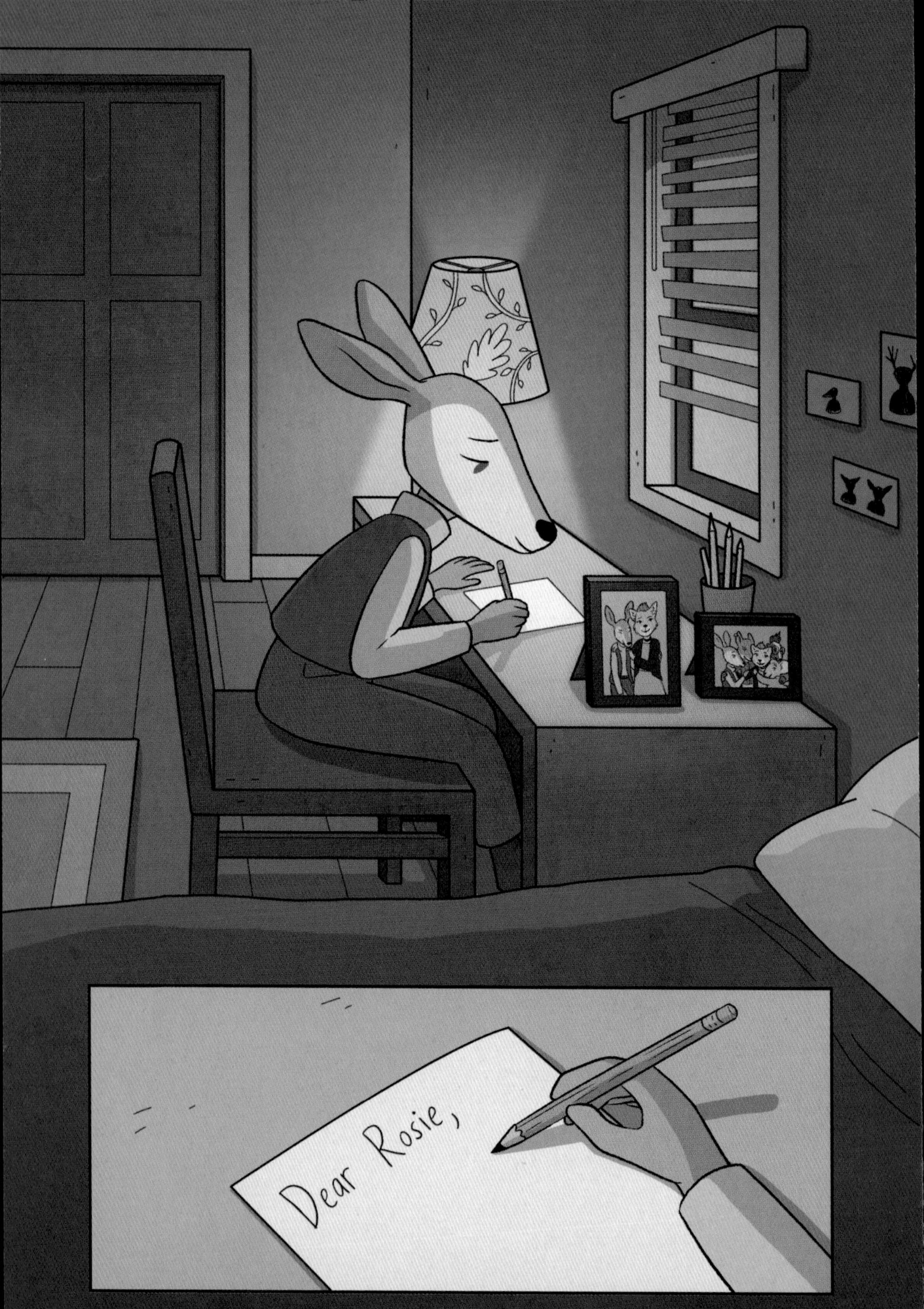
Dear Rosie,

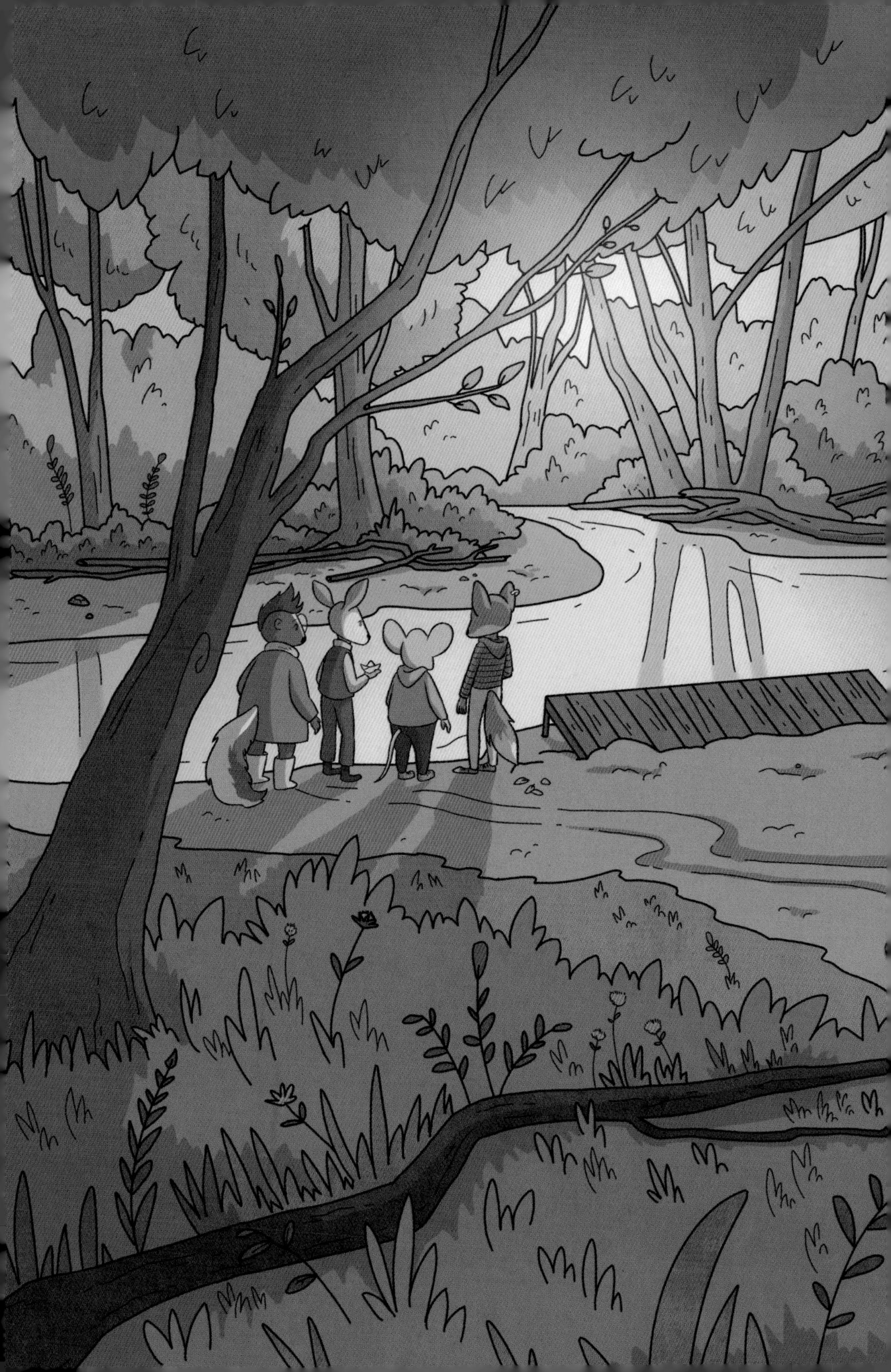

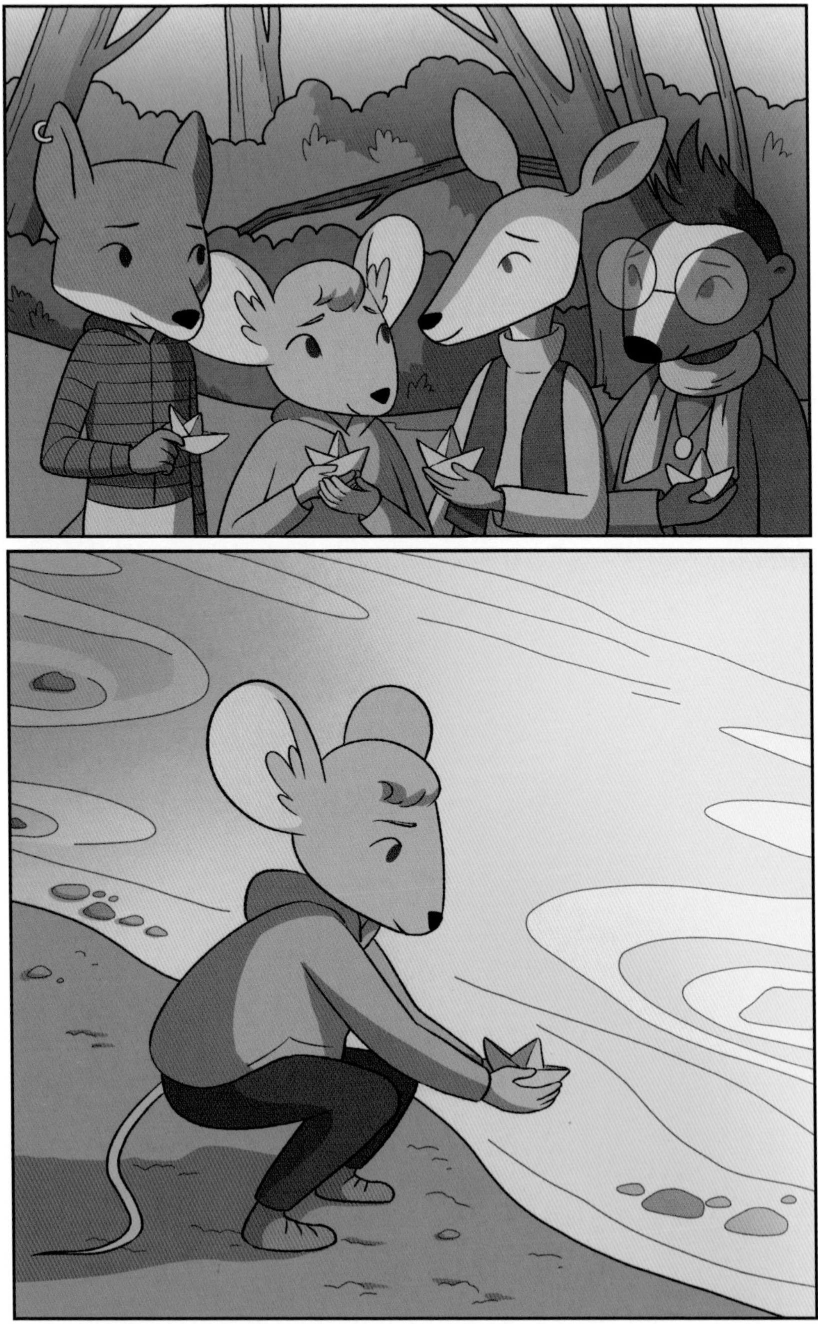

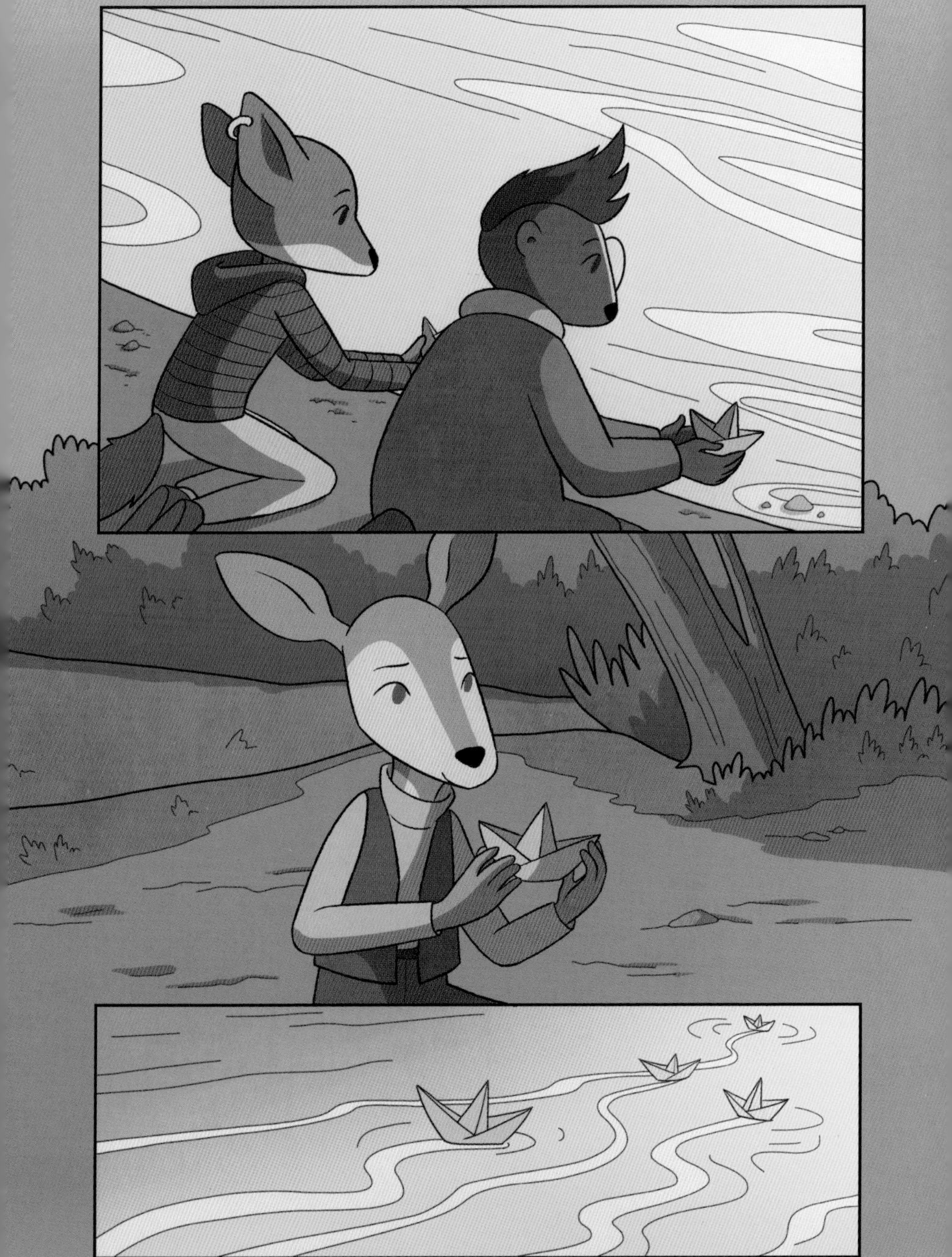

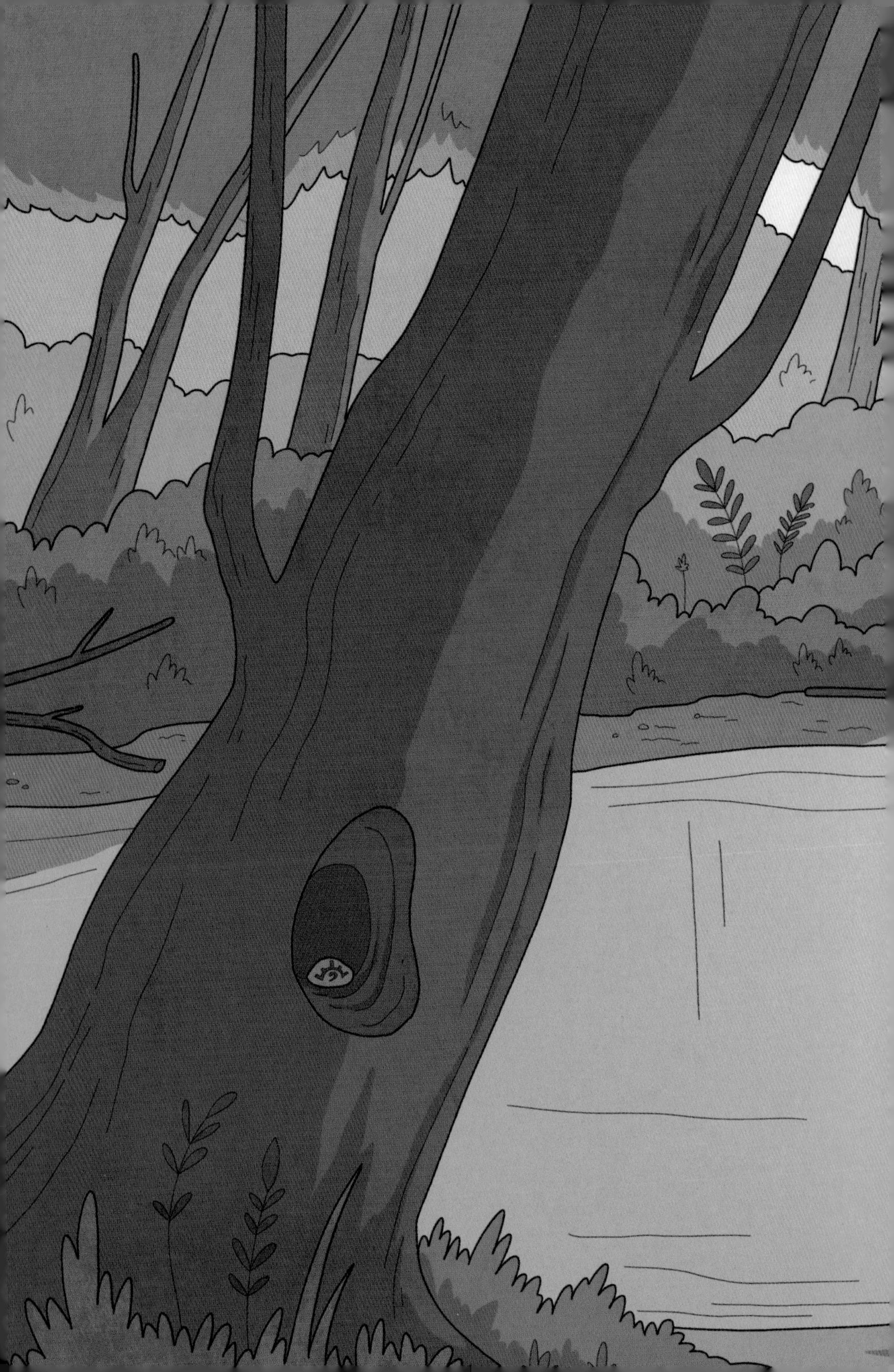

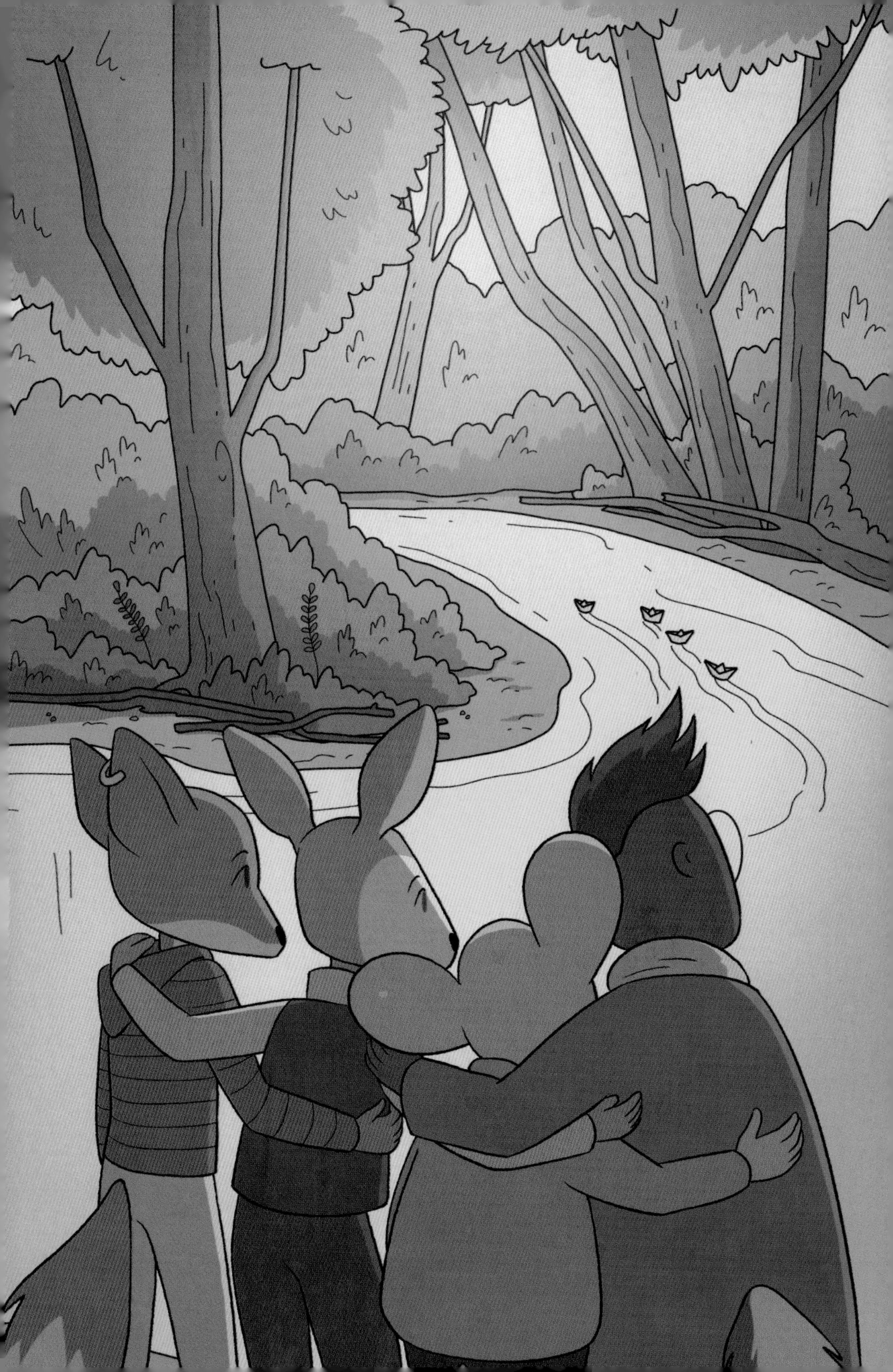

Annalee

In middle school, from left: Beattie, Emily, Annalee, Ingrid

AUTHOR'S NOTE

Dear Rosie is a work of fiction, heavily inspired by real-life events. Millie and her best friends are based on my friend group from middle school: Annalee, Beattie, Emily, and Ingrid. I remember middle school being an exceptionally difficult time, but my friends were always there to offer laughter and a helping hand. We were true friends right from the start, and I will always be grateful for that.

Annalee passed away suddenly when I was in college. After she died, I found myself adrift and drowning in grief. I wished I had my old middle school friends around me, but we had all moved to different states and could not easily come together.

It's been more than ten years since Annalee's death, but I clearly remember her laugh and her jubilant smile. Grief still sneaks up on me when I hear a certain song or go to a certain place where memories of her are strongest, but I am thankful to have healed enough to have crafted this story. *Dear Rosie* allowed me to inhabit our shared memories during all those working months—I relived the sleepovers, art classes, bonfires, and, most of all, the love.

I hope this story helps others working their way through a loss. It can be an isolating experience, and I encourage anyone struggling to talk to a friend, relative, or trusted teacher. Personally, I found putting my feelings down on paper extremely cathartic, and I still do. On the anniversary of Annalee's death, I go to the creek where we all laughed and played, and send a letter to her downstream. I like to think that she still reads them.

Meghan

ABOUT THE BOOK

Dear Rosie is set in our hometown of Frederick, Maryland, a beautiful area packed with history, alive with culture, and bearing a distinctive skyline. Our story is just as much about Frederick as it is about its inhabitants.

Downtown is known for its clustered church spires, as immortalized by the poet John Greenleaf Whittier. The footpath along Carroll Creek is a bustling thoroughfare, populated by restaurants, art galleries, and quaint, inviting shops. The laundromat that served as inspiration for Millie's home and family business is no longer open, but its charm as a local gathering place lives on in our book.

All of our characters are wildlife local to Maryland and were given unique looks and silhouettes so as to be immediately recognizable, even from far away.

ACKNOWLEDGMENTS

Thank you to my husband and collaborator, Tom Pickwood, for his tireless hours spent writing and rewriting dialogue, helping to make this the best version of our story, and for all the delicious dinners that kept me going through each late night. Thank you to my family for supporting my journey as an artist, from childhood all the way to this moment. Thank you to Emily Foose for giving valuable feedback when this story was in its infancy. And thank you to Rachael for embarking on this wild adventure with me! I couldn't have done it without you. —M.B.

Thank you to my entire family for always encouraging my interest in art. You are the reason I pursued my career, and I will forever be grateful. Love you all! Special thanks to my husband, Van, for being so loving, patient, and supportive while I worked nonstop for many months. Thank you for holding our lives together. And a huge thank-you to Meghan for inviting me to work on such a special project and for always roping me into her wild schemes. It's a dream come true to be published, and I wouldn't have made it this far without you. —R.B.

Thank you to the entire publishing team at Knopf: Erin, Juliet, April, Gianna, and all our copy editors. Erin, your astute observations made this story grow into its own. Thank you for taking a chance on us. Thank you to our agents, Uwe and Brent at Triada US Literary, for believing in us from the start.

Thank you to our hometown, Frederick, Maryland, a spirited and vibrant community full of public art and hidden treasures.

And last but not least, thank you to our dear, loving friends for life: Annalee, Beattie, Emily, and Ingrid. You filled middle school with camaraderie and laughter and made a shy girl feel at home. The time we spent together will always be in our hearts. —M.B. and R.B.